PEADER THOMAS

GUSTAV HENRI

VOL.2

Or as I like to call it ...
THE ISLAND OF TINY AUNTS!

D1505132

GUARANTEE:
ALL THE WORDS IN THIS BOOK HAVE BEEN
CONSTRUCTED FROM HIGH QUALITY, PREMIUM LETTERS,
SUPPLIED FROM THE WORLD'S GREATEST ALPHABETS,
AND ARE COMPATIBLE WITH MOST STANDARD EYEBALLS.

RED COMET PRESS
BROOKLYN

INTRODUCING

WALKING SHOES

RUNNING SHOES

STANDING STILL SHOES

NUT-AND-FRUIT-FREE TRAIL MIX (ALL RIGHT, IT'S JUST CHOCOLATE)

INFLATABLE TRAVEL PILLOW

LIKES

- Having a midnight snack
- Adjusting watch
- Having another midnight snack

DISLIKES

- Waiting
- Blue cheese
- Early mornings
- Waiting for blue cheese early in the morning

GUSTAV

INFLATABLE FOUR-POSTER BED

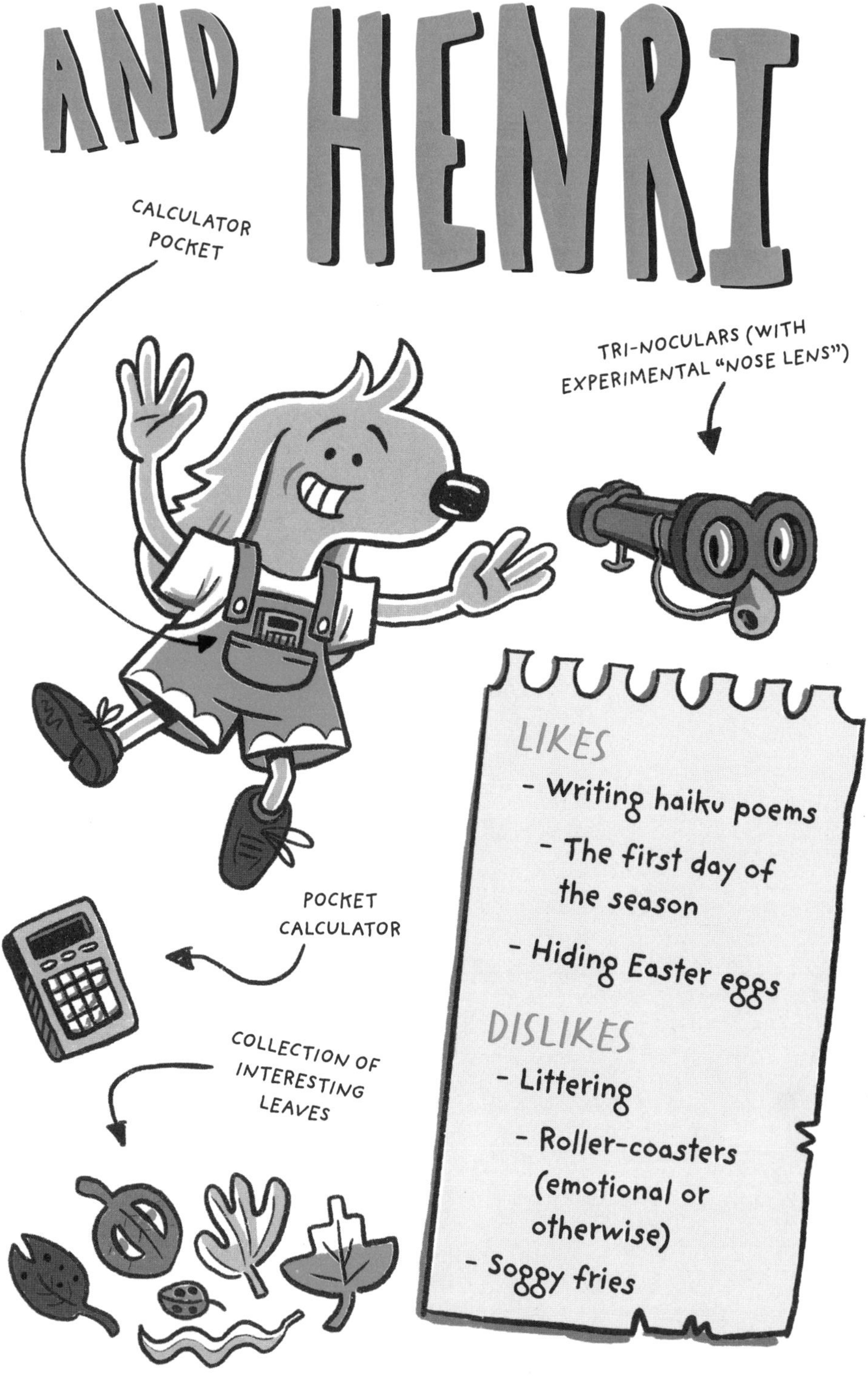
AND HENRI
CALCULATOR POCKET
TRI-NOCULARS (WITH EXPERIMENTAL "NOSE LENS")
POCKET CALCULATOR
COLLECTION OF INTERESTING LEAVES
LIKES
- Writing haiku poems
- The first day of the season
- Hiding Easter eggs
DISLIKES
- Littering
- Roller-coasters (emotional or otherwise)
- Soggy fries

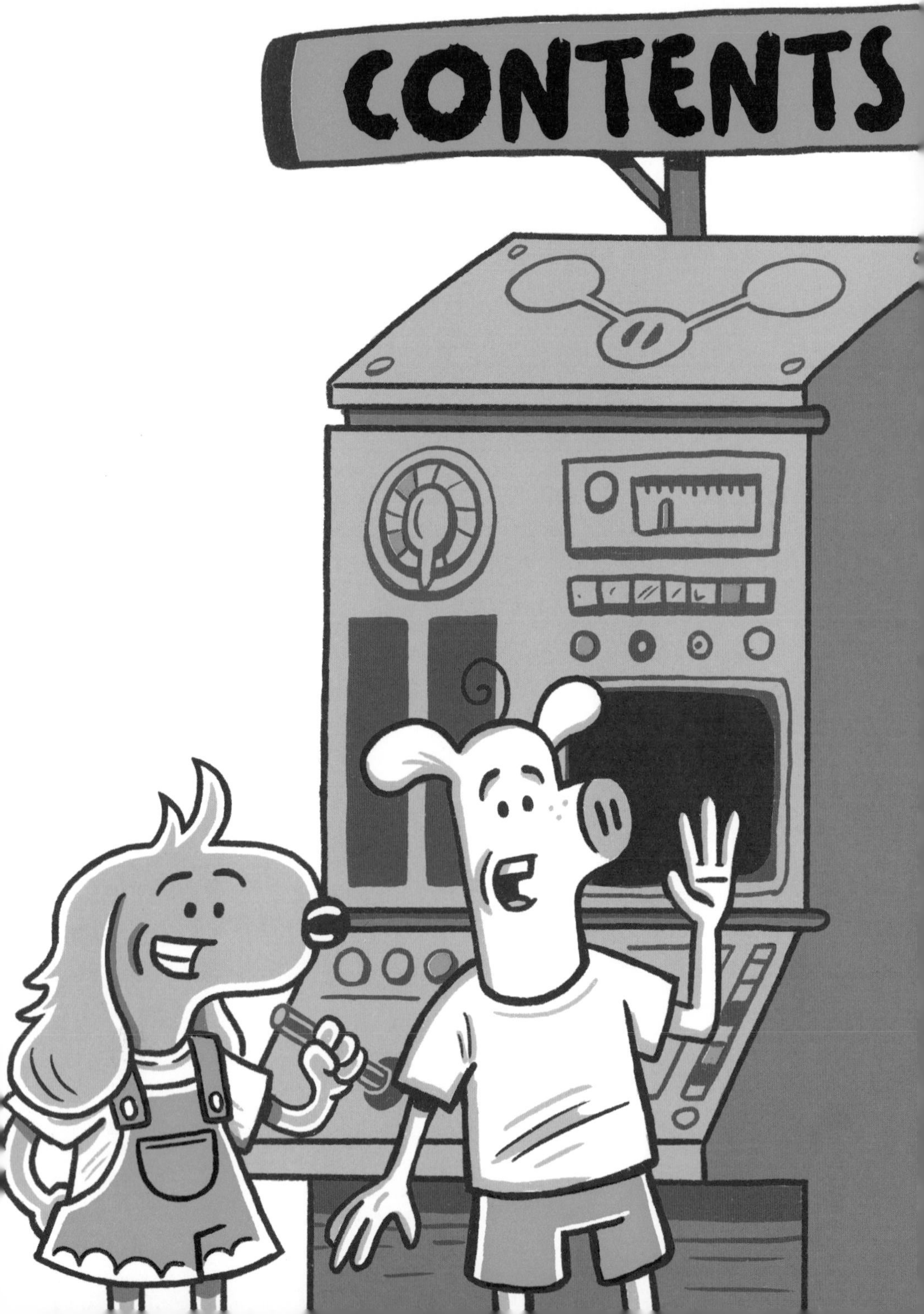
CONTENTS

-O-MATIC

GUSTAV, LOST PIG

3

GUSTAV, MICRO-PIG

43

DETECTIVE GUSTAV AND THE GREAT-AUNT HUNT

81

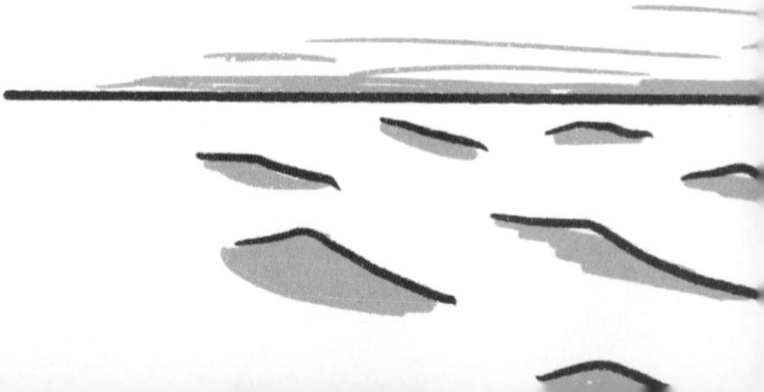

GUSTAV,
LOST
PIG
FULL BOAR POWER PADDLE
MAP OF THE UNKNOWN
GUSTAV'S JOURNAL
KEEP OUT!

IT WAS THE BEST DAY OF THE WEEKEND,* AND HENRI NORMAL AND HER BEST FRIEND, GUSTAV, ONLY WANTED TO DO ONE THING.

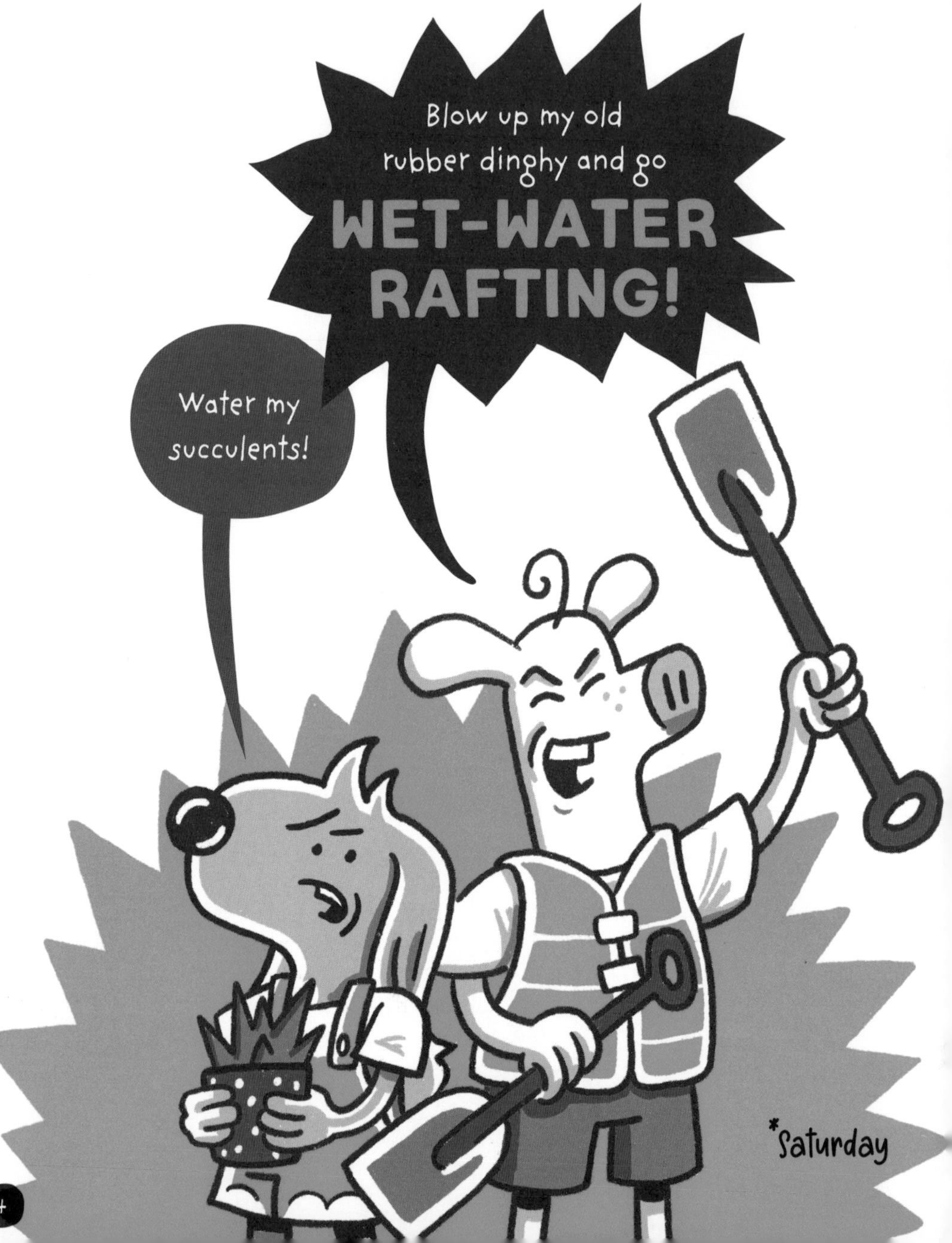

Blow up my old rubber dinghy and go WET-WATER RAFTING!
Water my succulents!

*Saturday

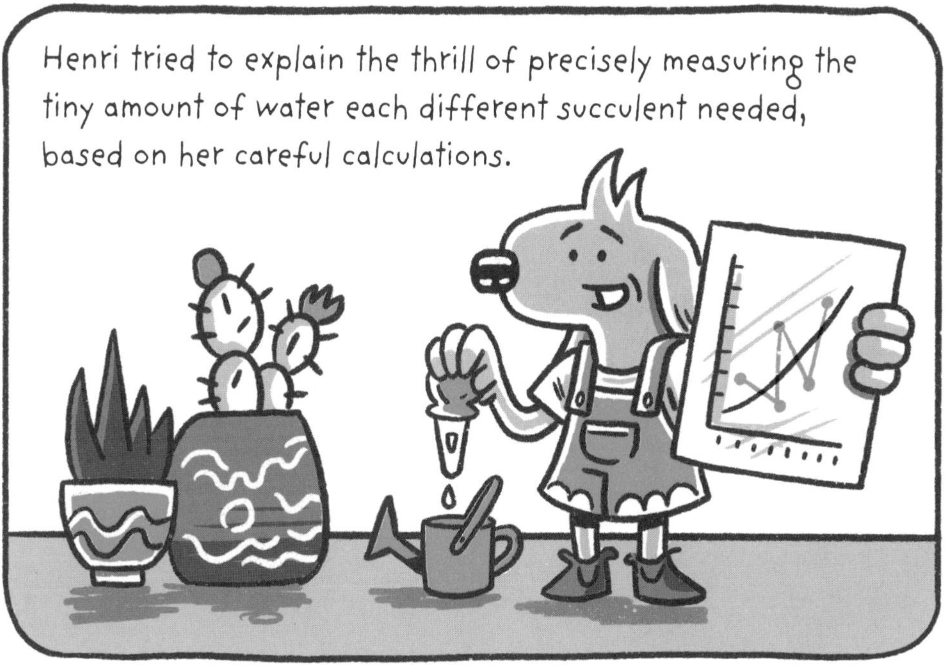
Henri tried to explain the thrill of precisely measuring the tiny amount of water each different succulent needed, based on her careful calculations.

But Gustav insisted.

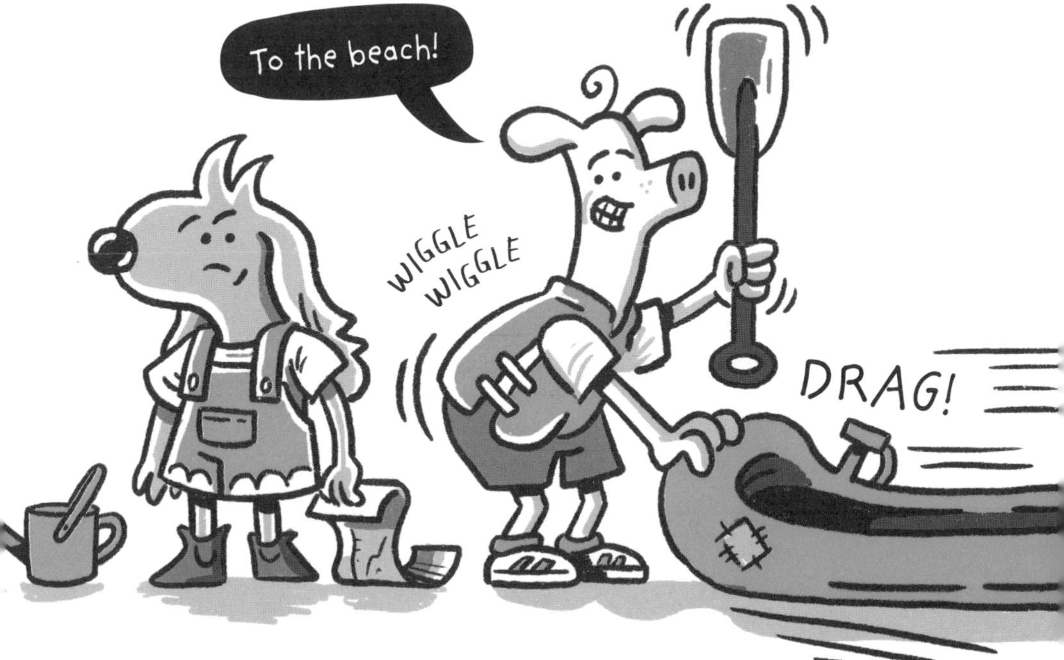
To the beach!
WIGGLE WIGGLE
DRAG!

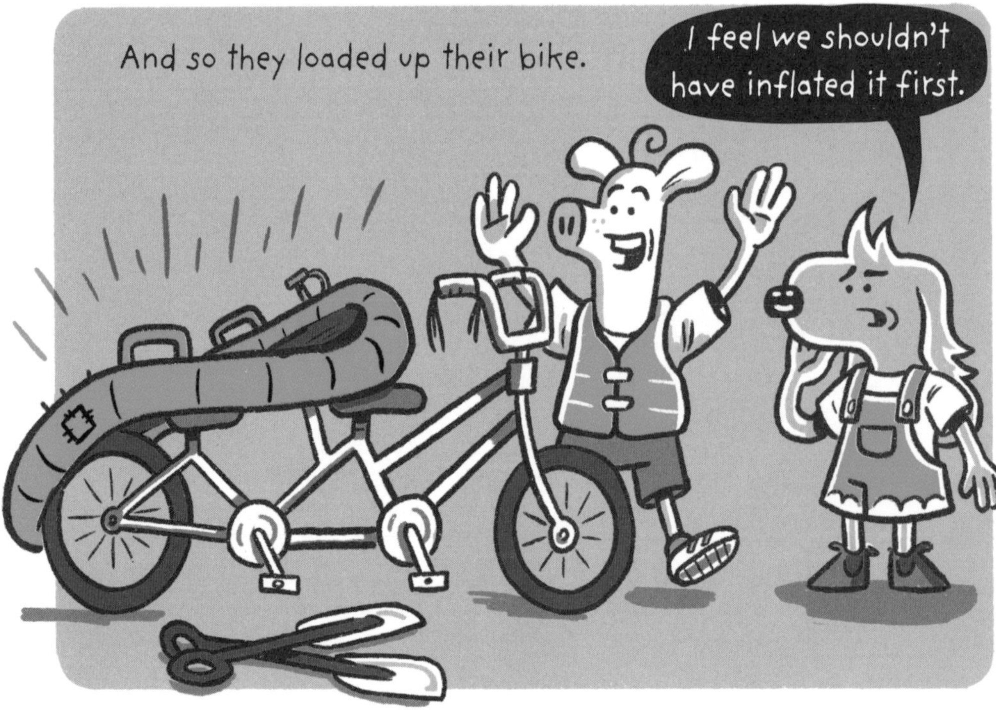
And so they loaded up their bike.
I feel we shouldn't have inflated it first.

When they arrived at the beach,
it was a beautiful, calm day.

"How peaceful,"
said Henri.

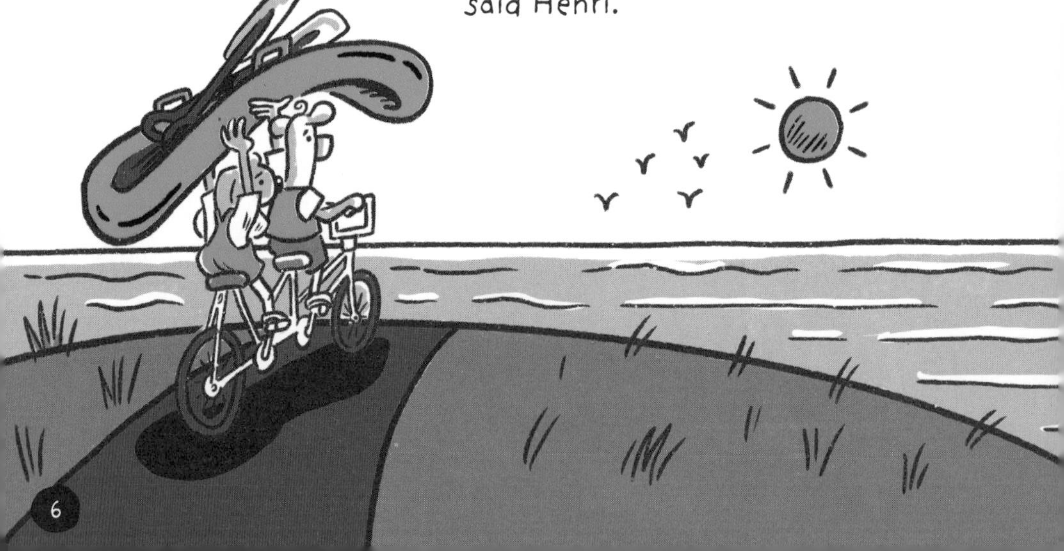

"Oh, buttersnacks," sighed Gustav as they cast off.

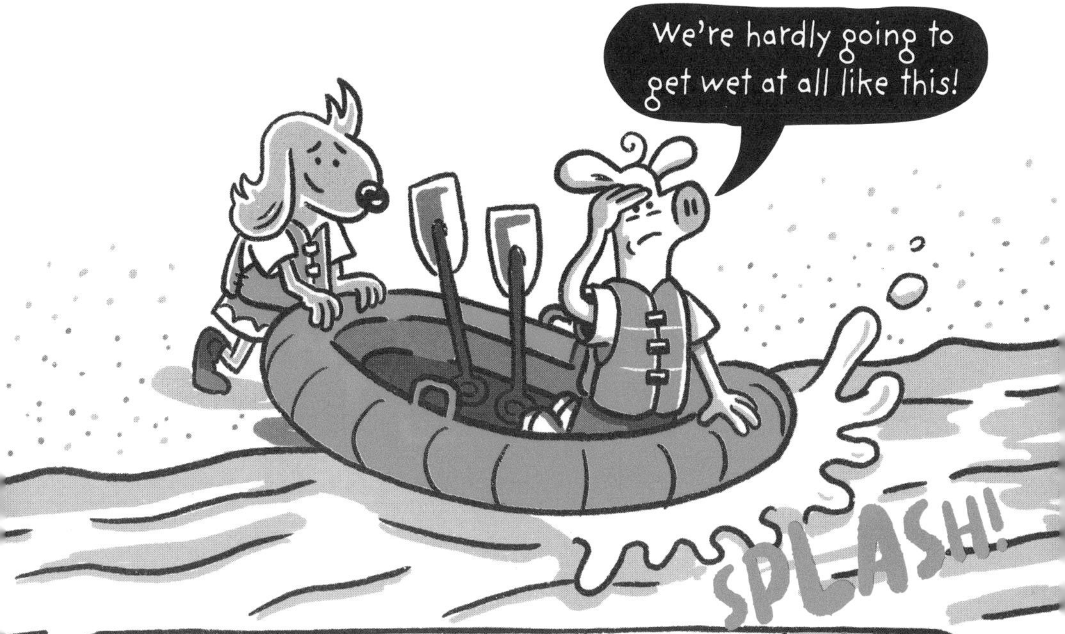
We're hardly going to get wet at all like this!
SPLASH!

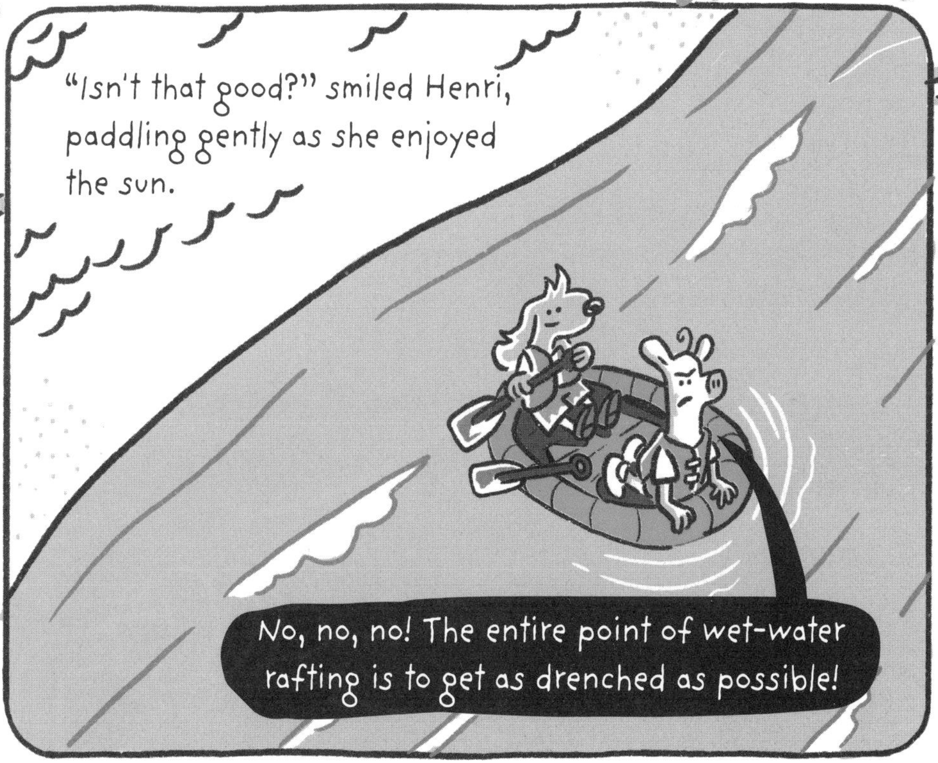
"Isn't that good?" smiled Henri, paddling gently as she enjoyed the sun.
No, no, no! The entire point of wet-water rafting is to get as drenched as possible!

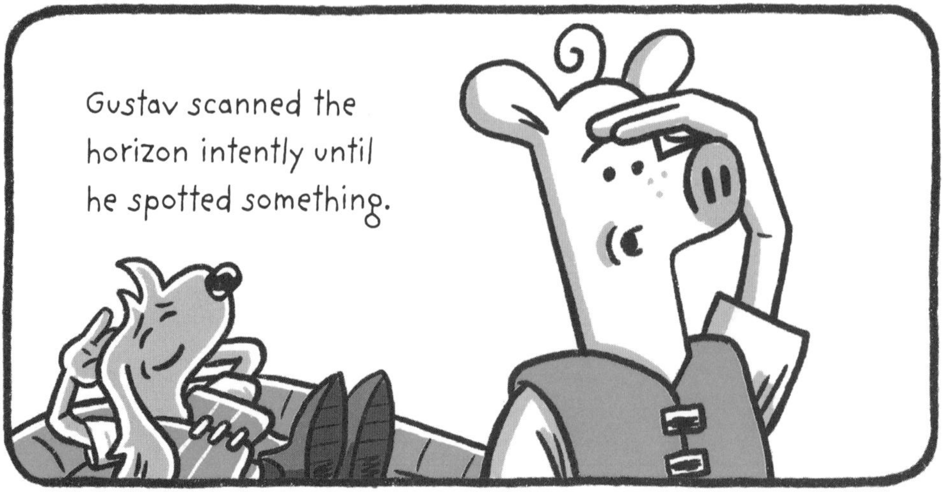
Gustav scanned the horizon intently until he spotted something.

"There! A cloud!" he shouted, steering the raft toward it.

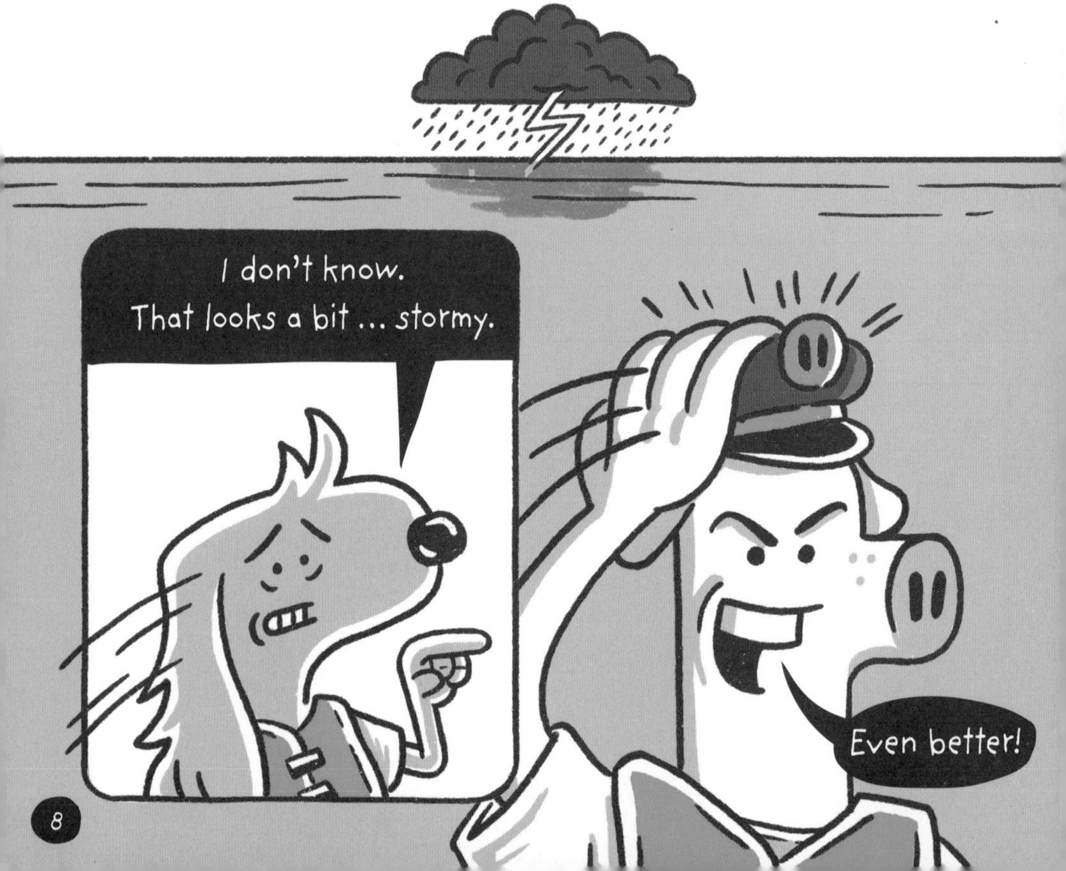
I don't know. That looks a bit ... stormy.
Even better!

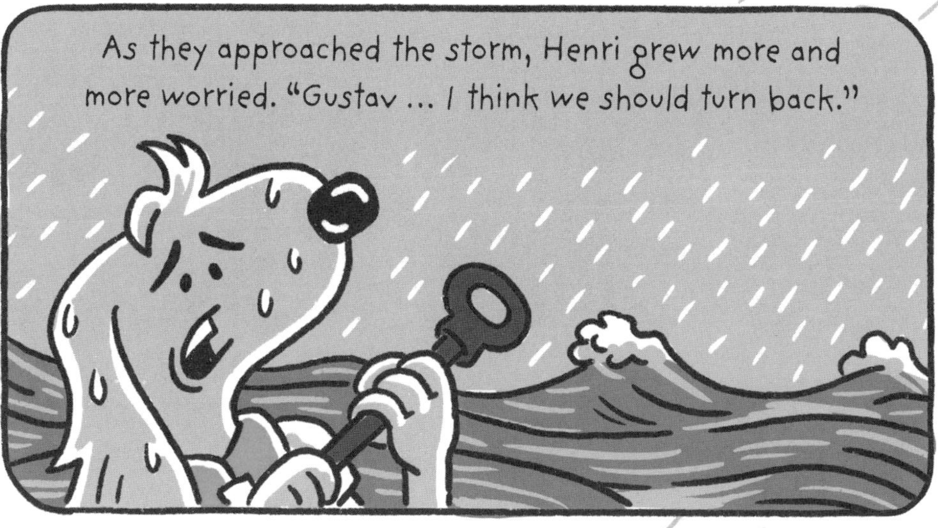
As they approached the storm, Henri grew more and more worried. "Gustav ... I think we should turn back."

But Gustav plowed on. The waves rose up, and rain began to pour down. It was hard to tell where the ocean ended and the air began.

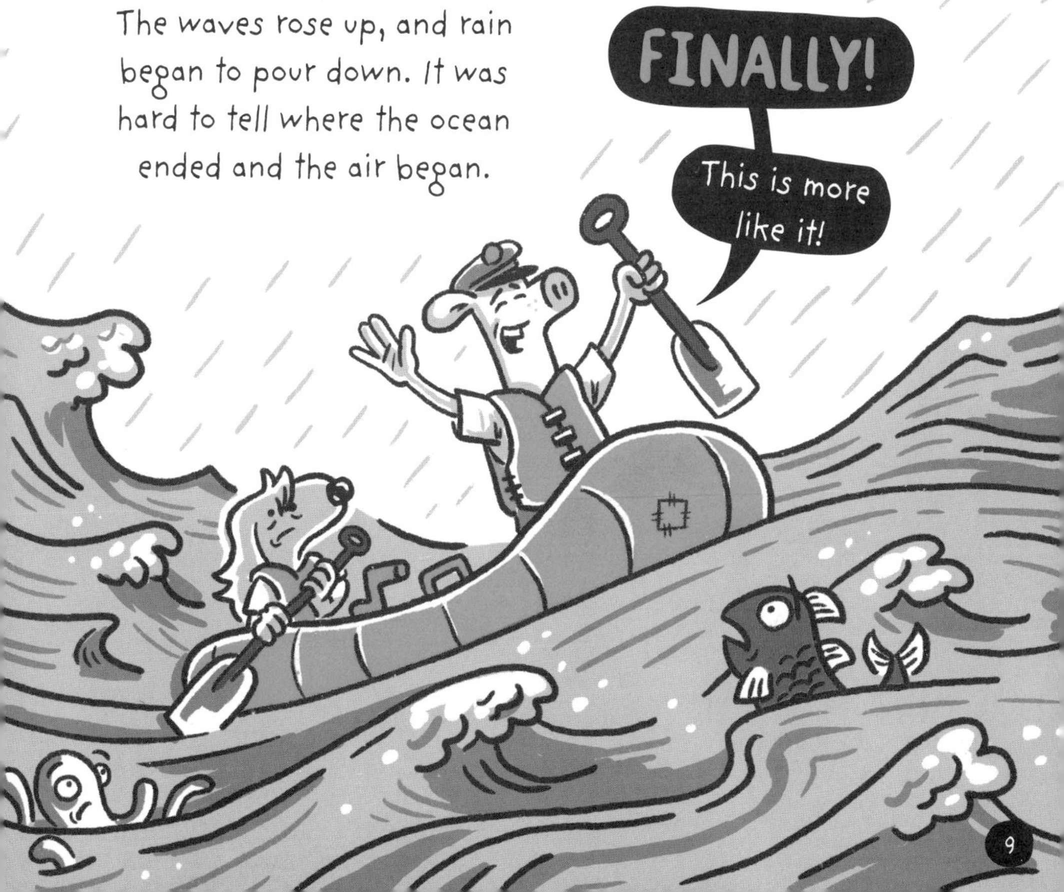
FINALLY!
This is more like it!

"We have to head to shore!" gargled Henri through a mouthful of spray.

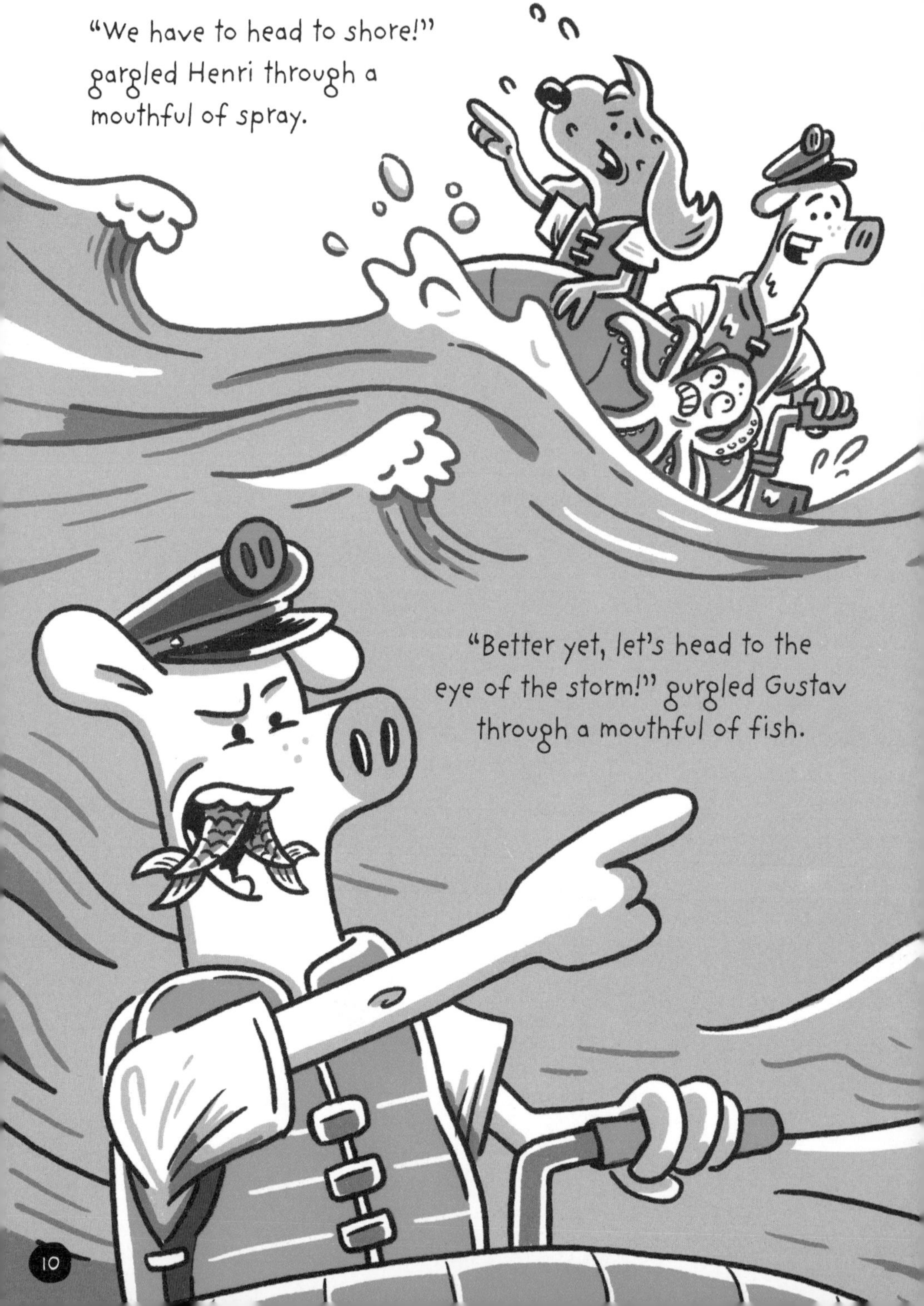

"Better yet, let's head to the eye of the storm!" gurgled Gustav through a mouthful of fish.

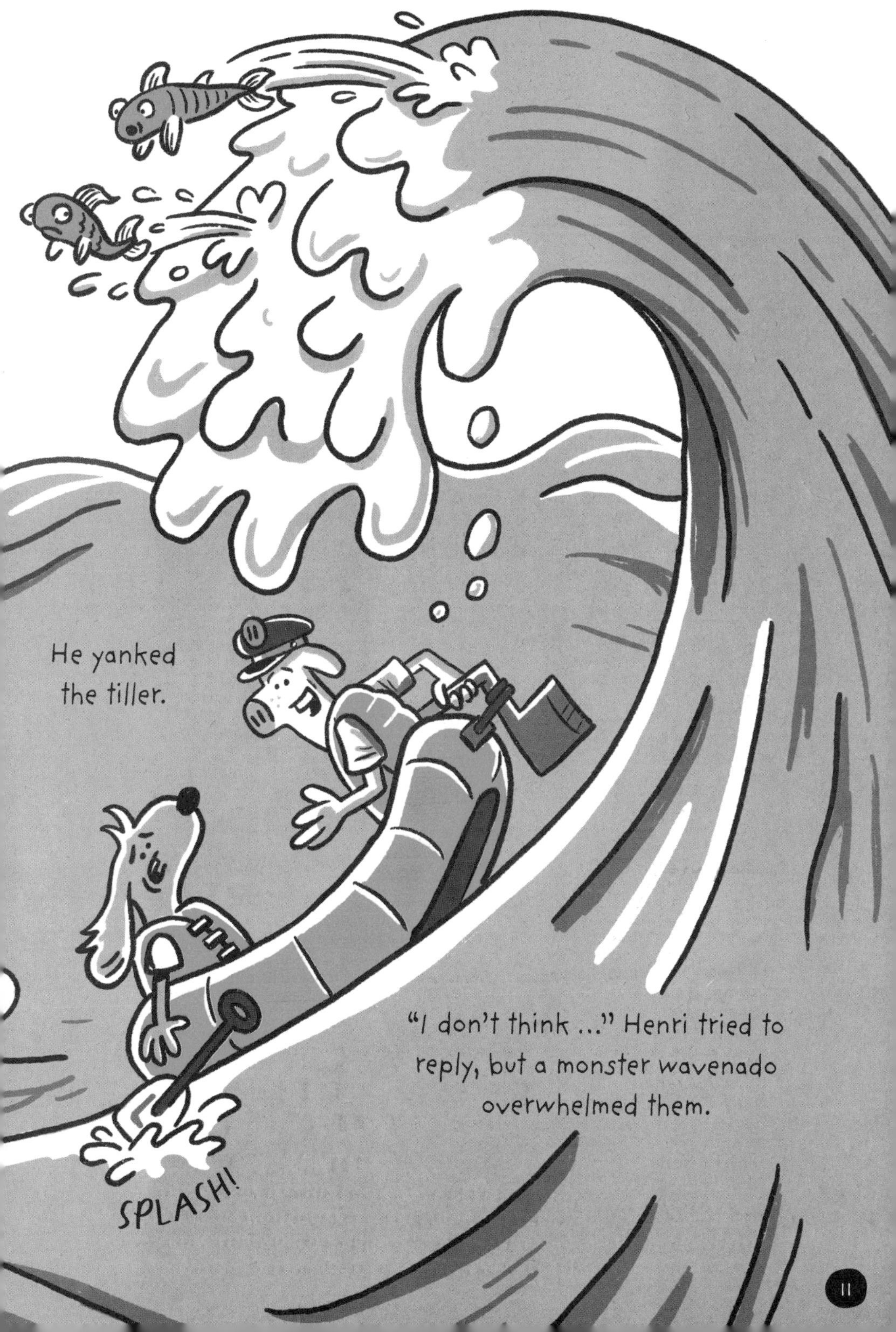
SPLASH!

He yanked the tiller.

"I don't think ..." Henri tried to reply, but a monster wavenado overwhelmed them.

Gustav and Henri clung to the wreck of the dinghy until the storm finally cleared. When they looked around, they were in the shallows of a desert island.

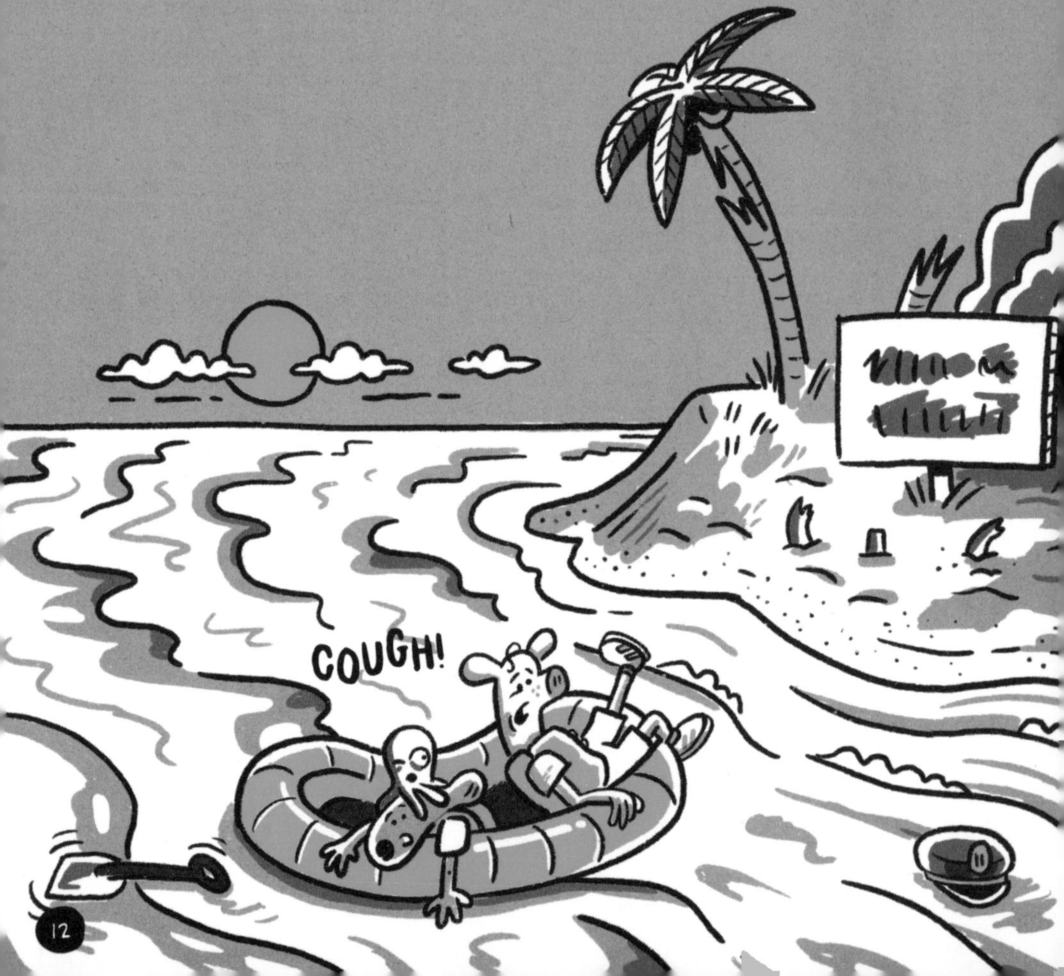
COUGH!

They dragged themselves up the shore
and collapsed on the sand.

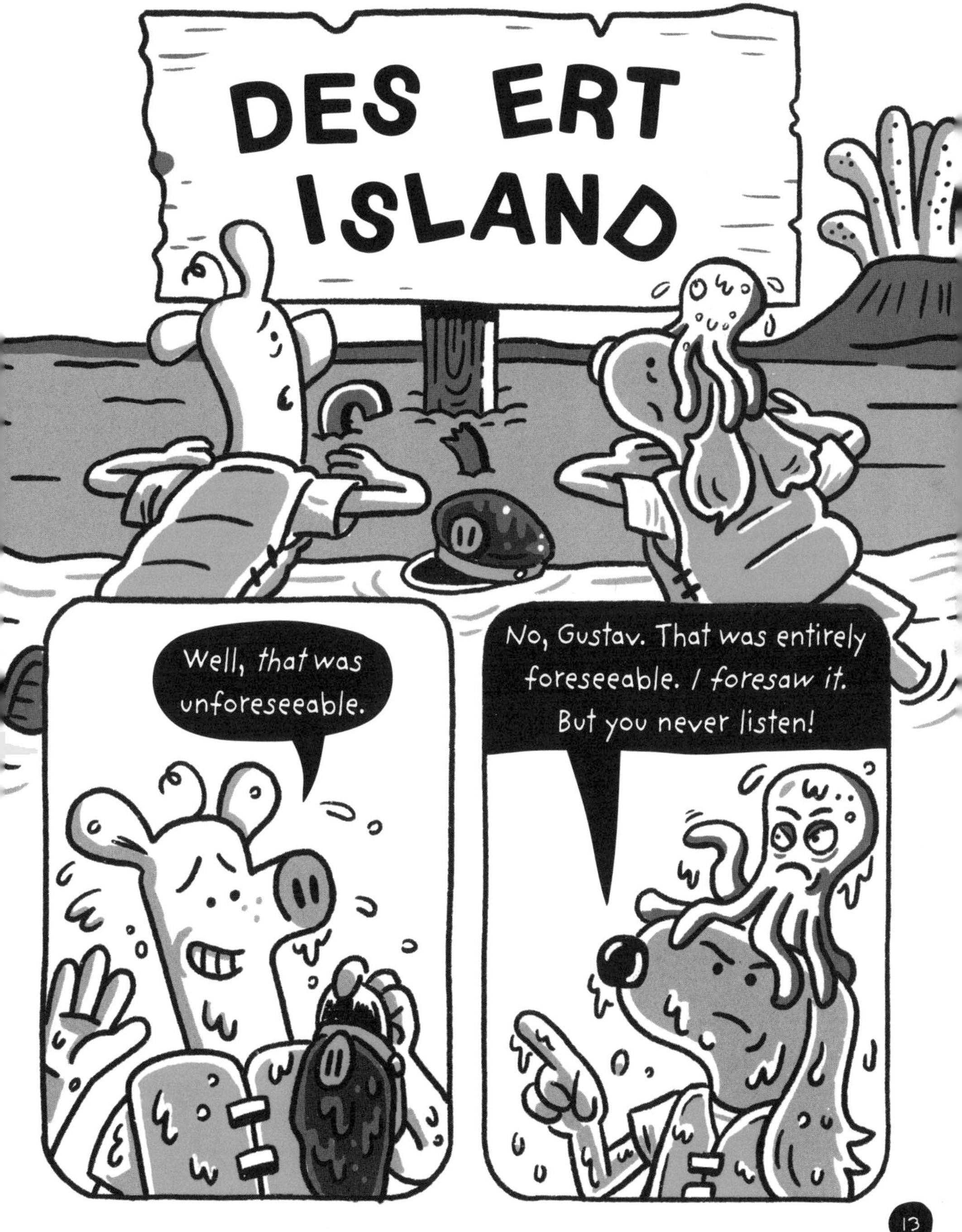
DES ERT
ISLAND
Well, *that* was unforeseeable.
No, Gustav. That was entirely foreseeable. *I foresaw it.* But you never listen!

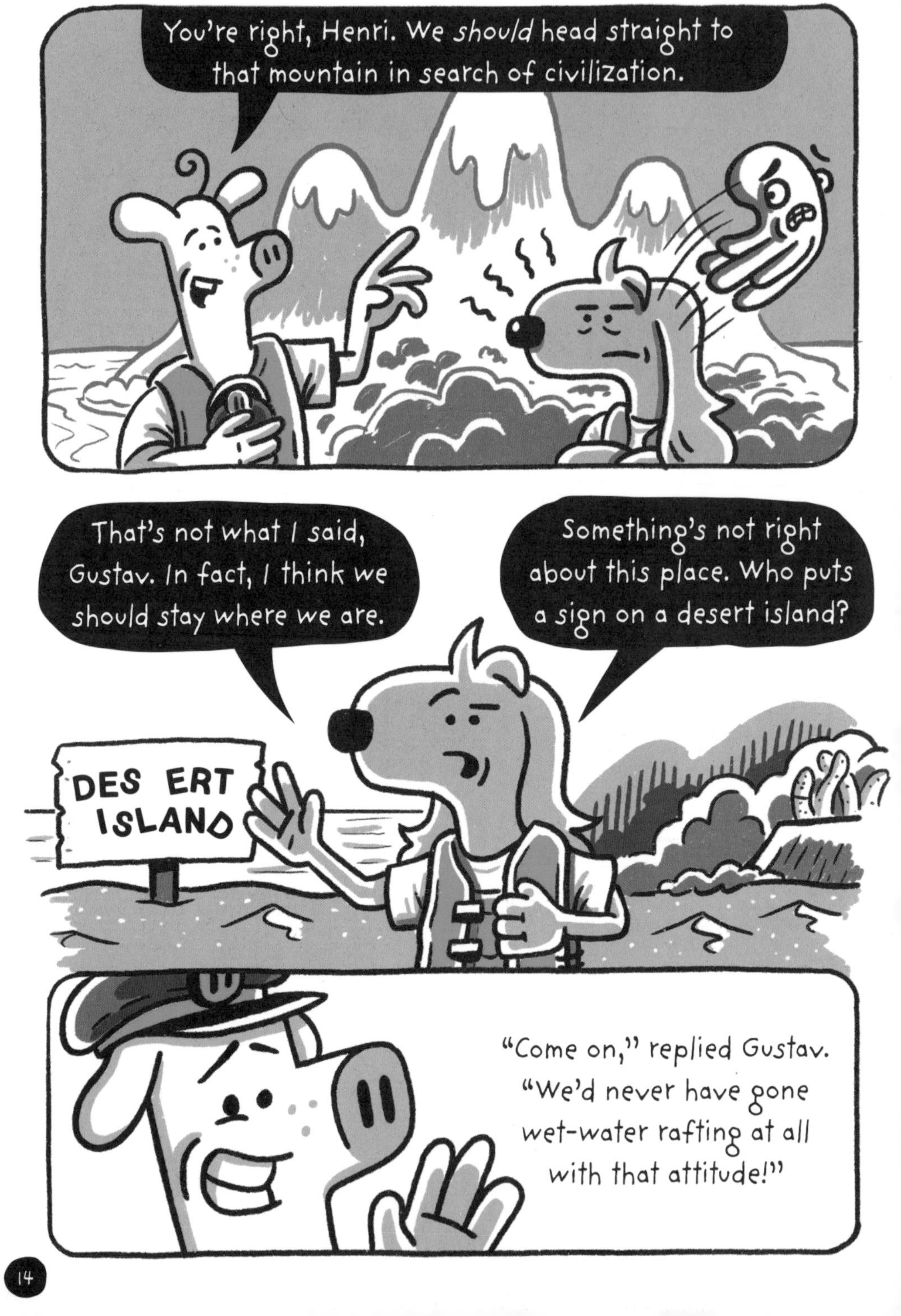
You're right, Henri. We *should* head straight to that mountain in search of civilization.
That's not what I said, Gustav. In fact, I think we should stay where we are.
Something's not right about this place. Who puts a sign on a desert island?
DES ERT ISLAND
"Come on," replied Gustav. "We'd never have gone wet-water rafting at all with that attitude!"

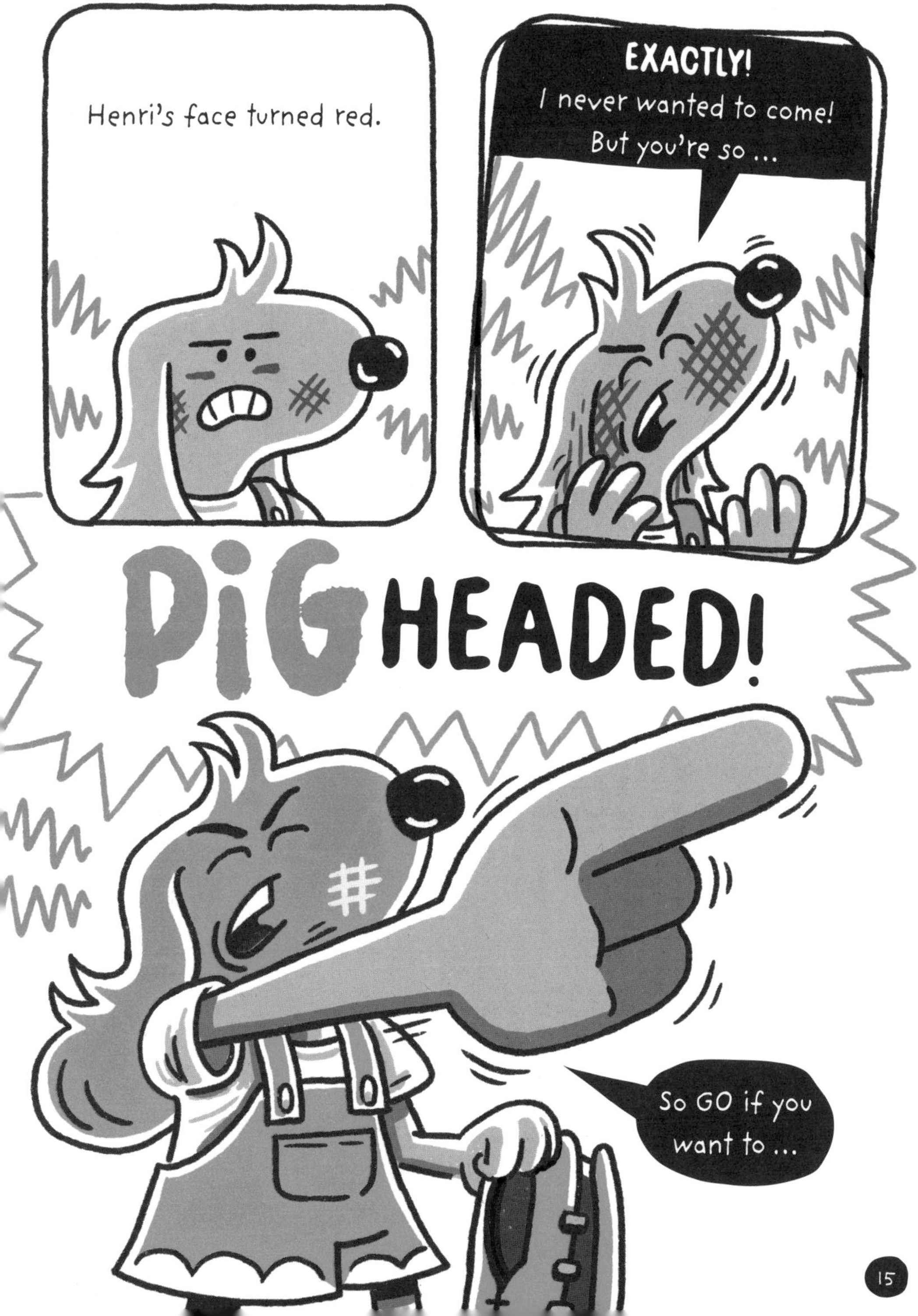

Henri's face turned red.
EXACTLY!
I never wanted to come!
But you're so ...
PIG HEADED!
So GO if you want to ...

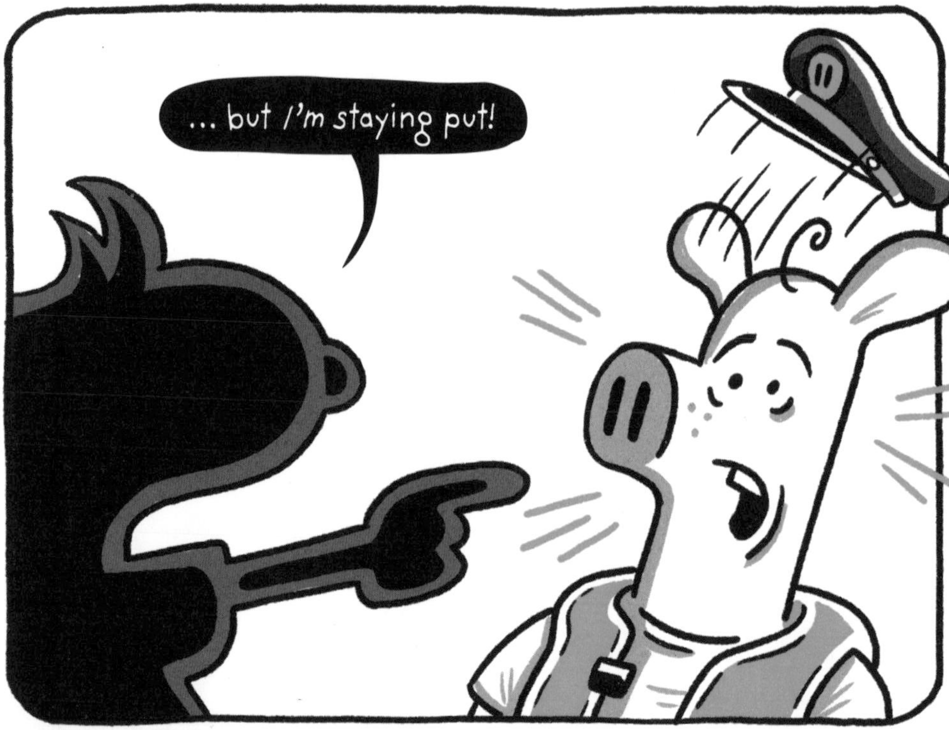
... but I'm staying put!

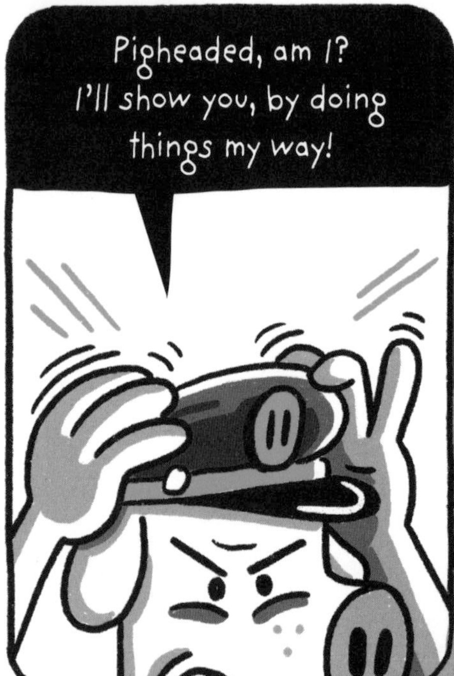
Pigheaded, am I? I'll show you, by doing things my way!

Gustav adjusted his captain's hat and stomped off into the jungle.

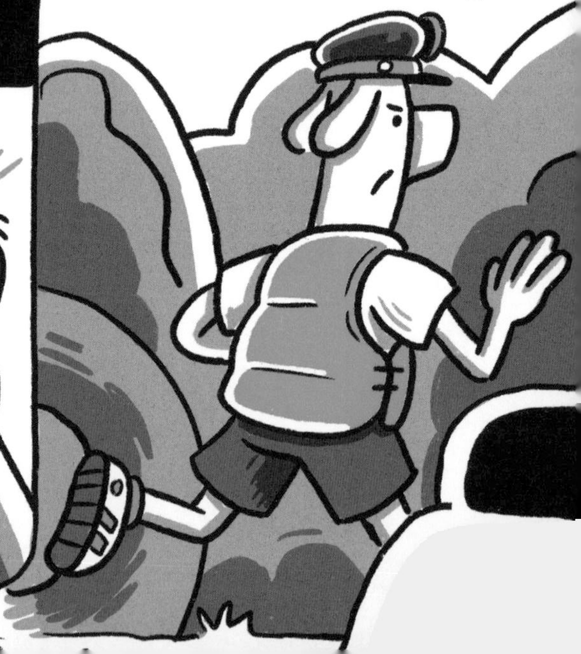

Henri was upset. This was the first time she and Gustav had had a real fight.

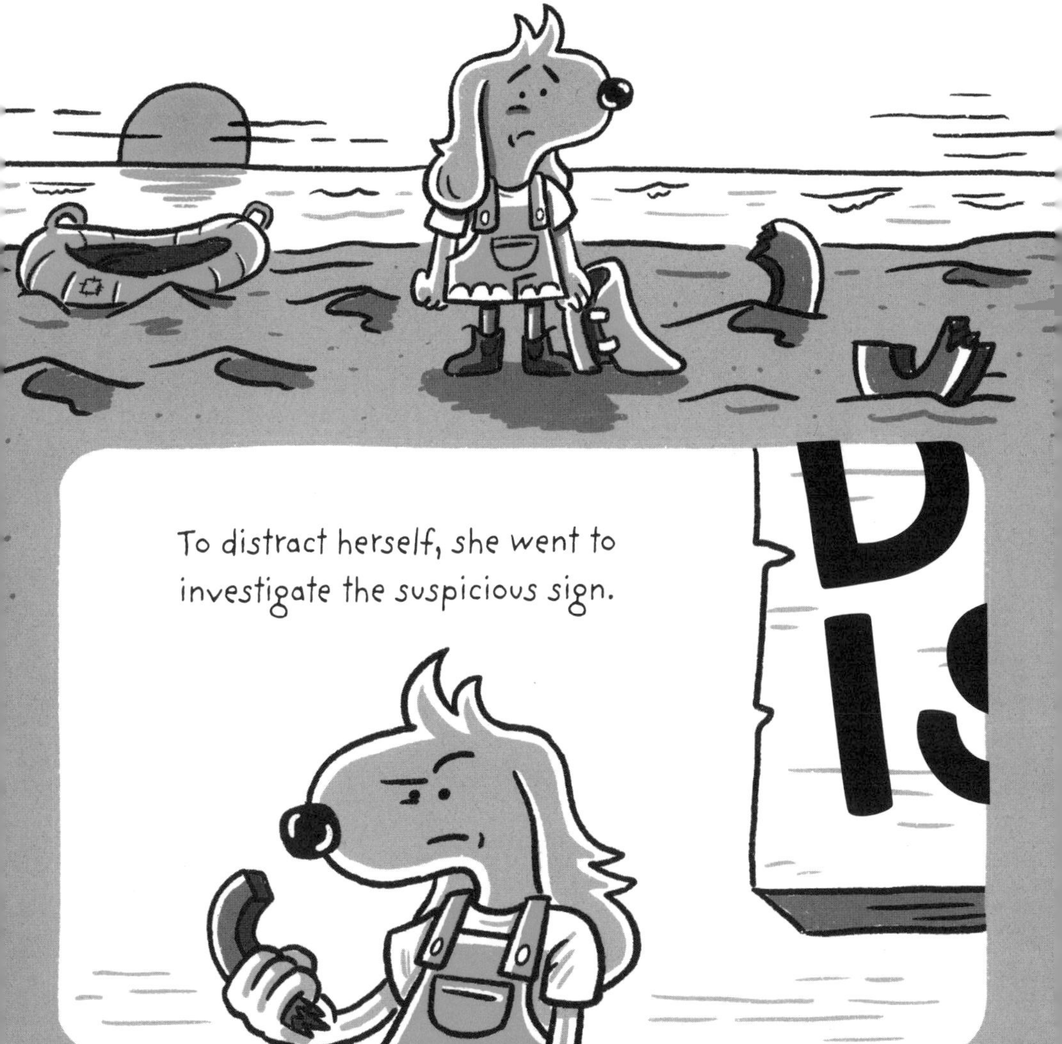
To distract herself, she went to investigate the suspicious sign.

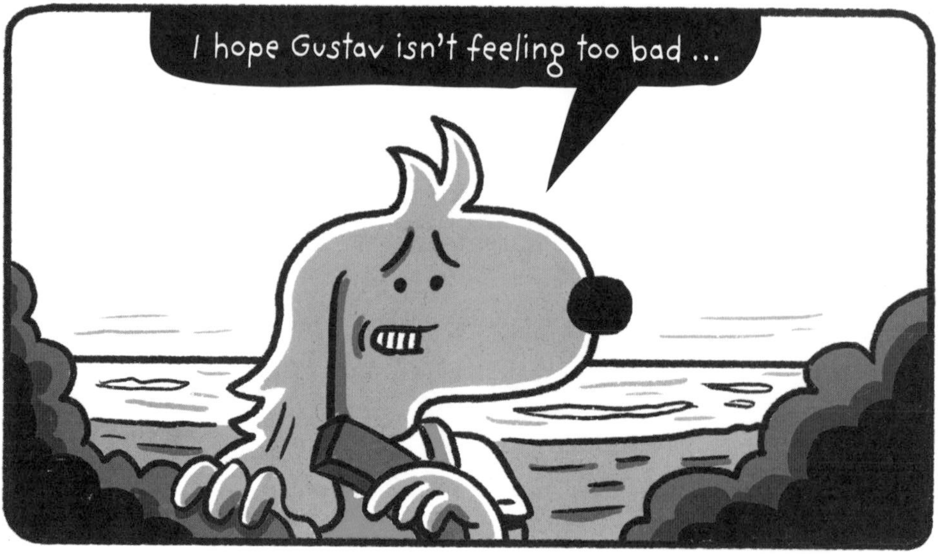
I hope Gustav isn't feeling too bad ...

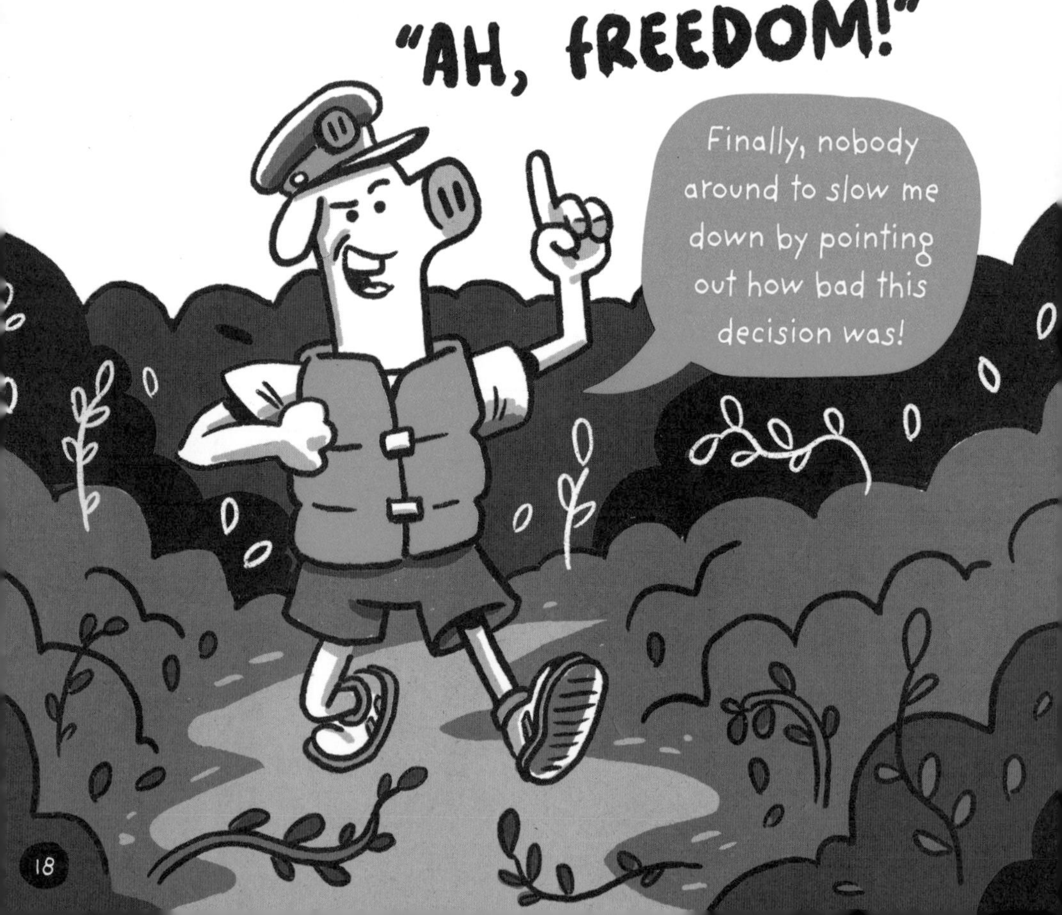
"AH, FREEDOM!"
Finally, nobody around to slow me down by pointing out how bad this decision was!

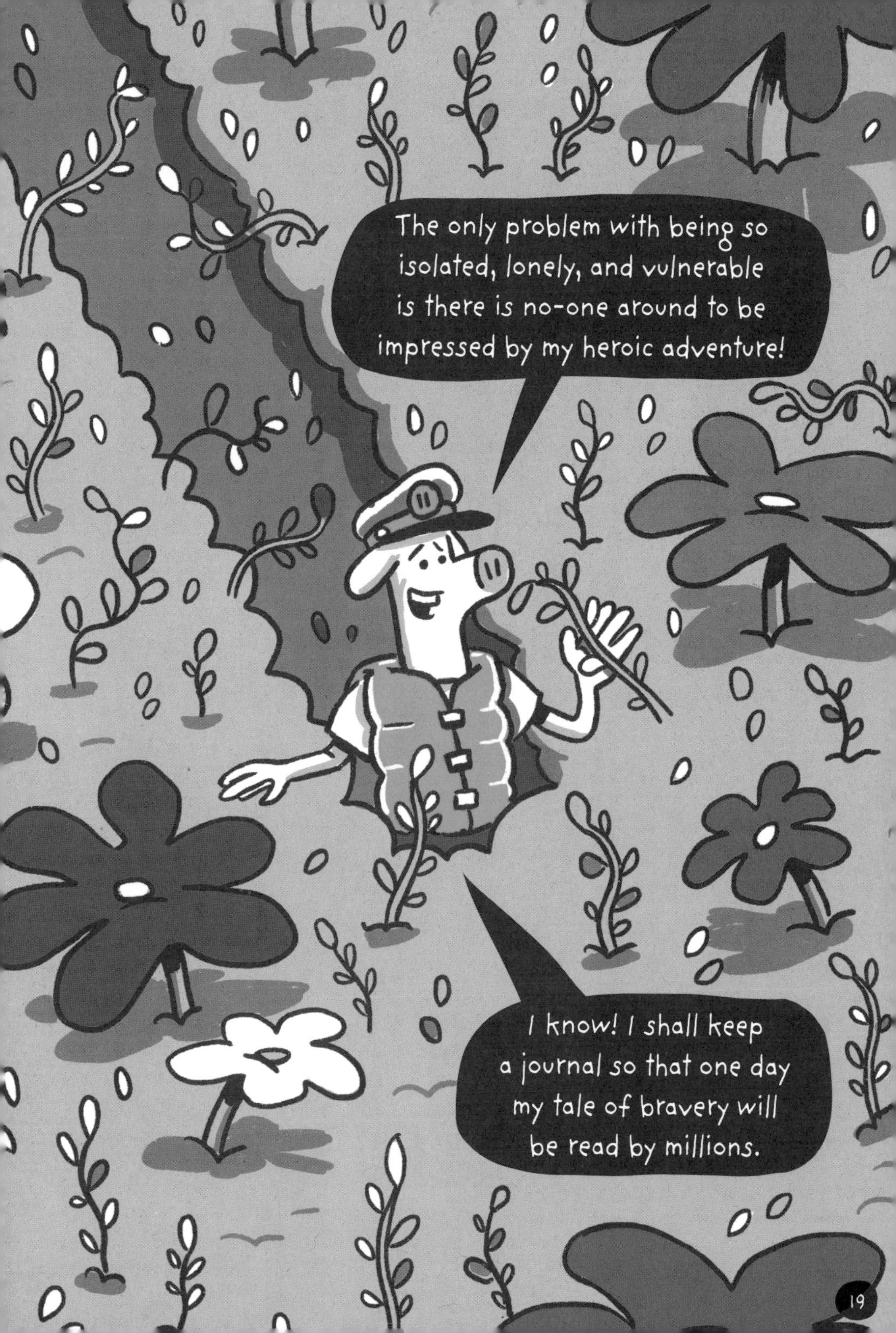
The only problem with being so isolated, lonely, and vulnerable is there is no-one around to be impressed by my heroic adventure!
I know! I shall keep a journal so that one day my tale of bravery will be read by millions.

The Journal of
GUSTAV –
<u>LONE</u> Adventurer

Sticky vines dragged at my clothes and strange
mushrooms squashed under my feet as I began

my noble quest to ~~prove Henri wrong about~~
~~everything~~ seek help for my landing party.

Noble

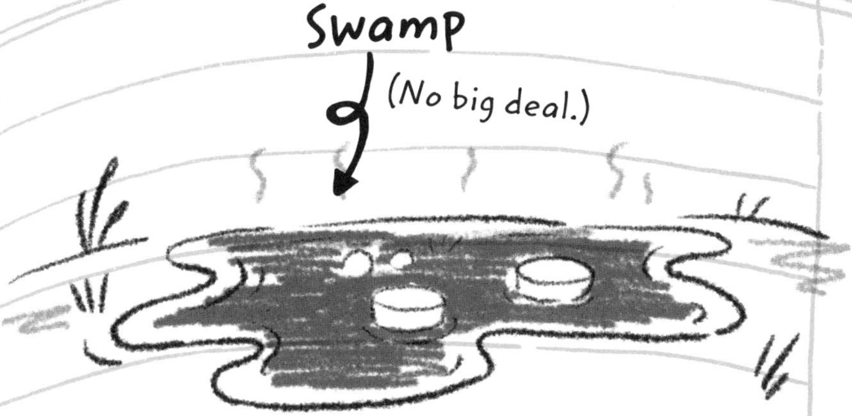
Swamp
(No big deal.)

Eventually, the path led me to a wide swamp. A certain dog I know would have considered going around it, but I had made up my mind.

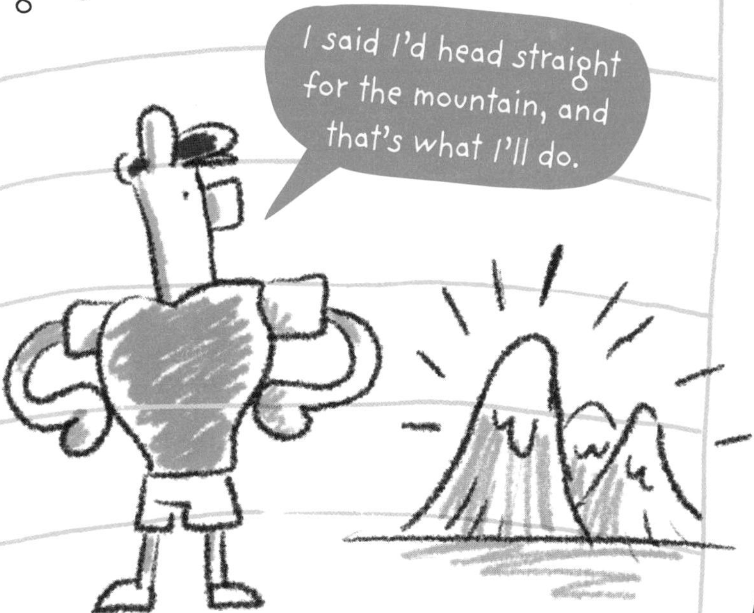
I said I'd head straight for the mountain, and that's what I'll do.

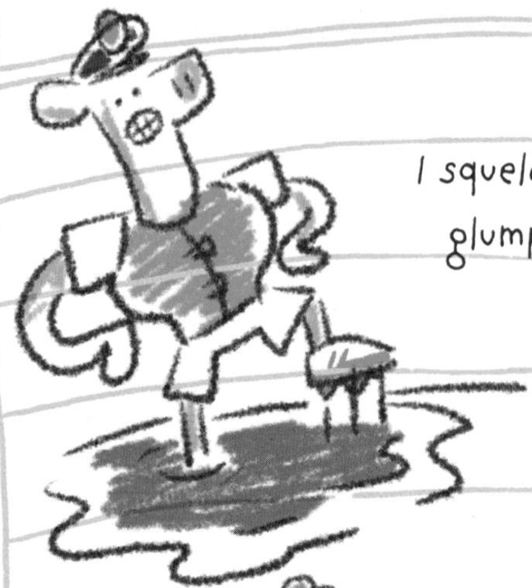

I squelched gallantly into the glumphing, slurping mire.

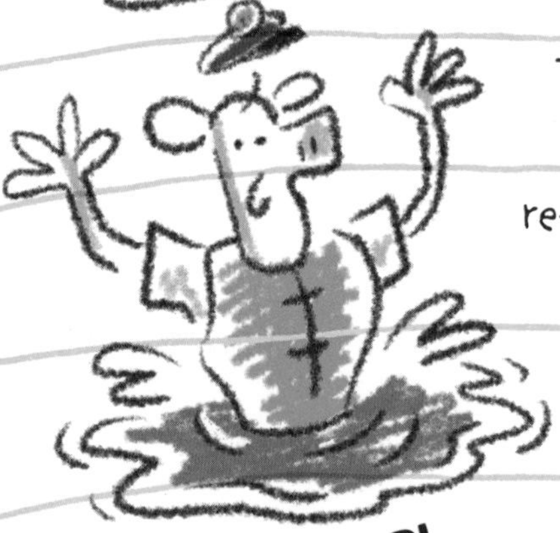

The gloop got deeper and deeper, but I refused to panic.

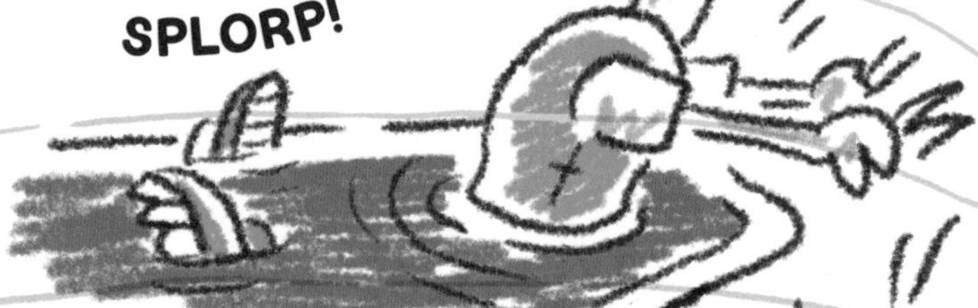
SPLORP!

I pushed on, losing my shoes and socks as I dragged myself out the other side.

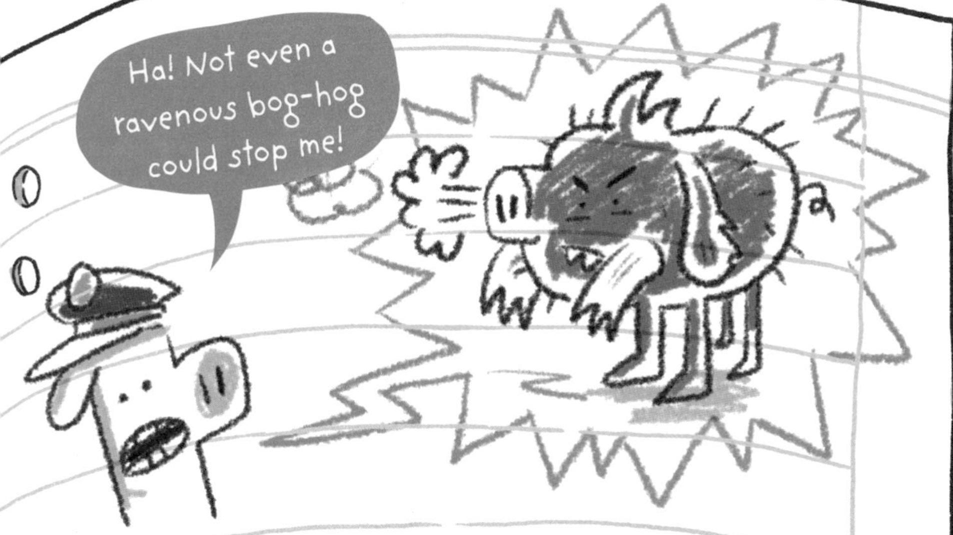
Ha! Not even a ravenous bog-hog could stop me!

I limped victoriously onward, bravely ignoring the strange sounds that seemed to follow me.

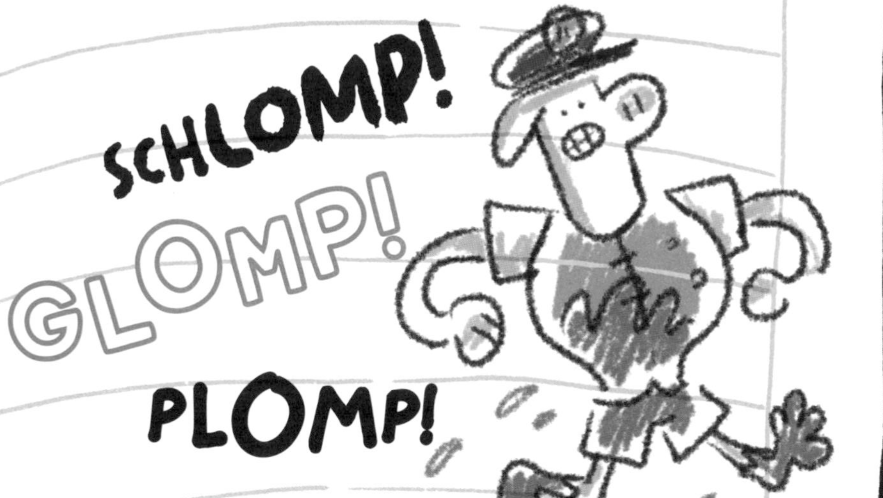
SCHLOMP!
GLOMP!
PLOMP!

Next I came upon a
deep gully, but instead of
bypassing it, I carried
straight on—

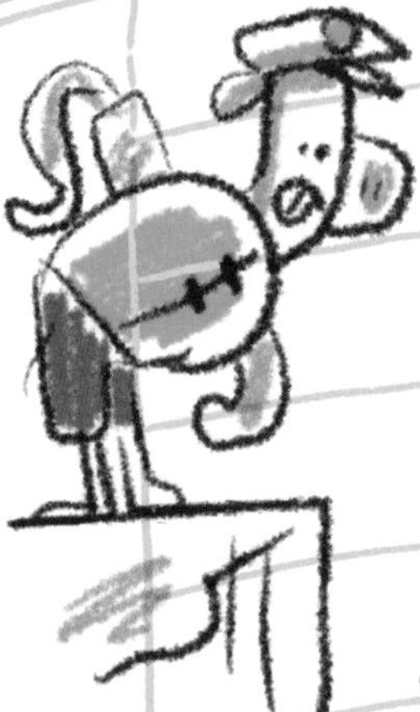

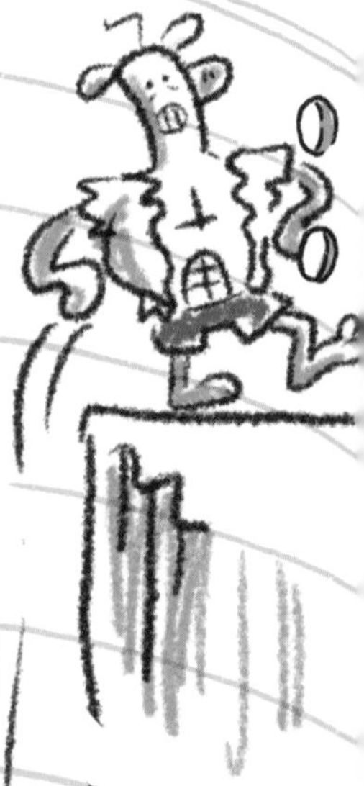

sliding down the
bank and finding
myself tangled in
a pit of writhing
pythons.

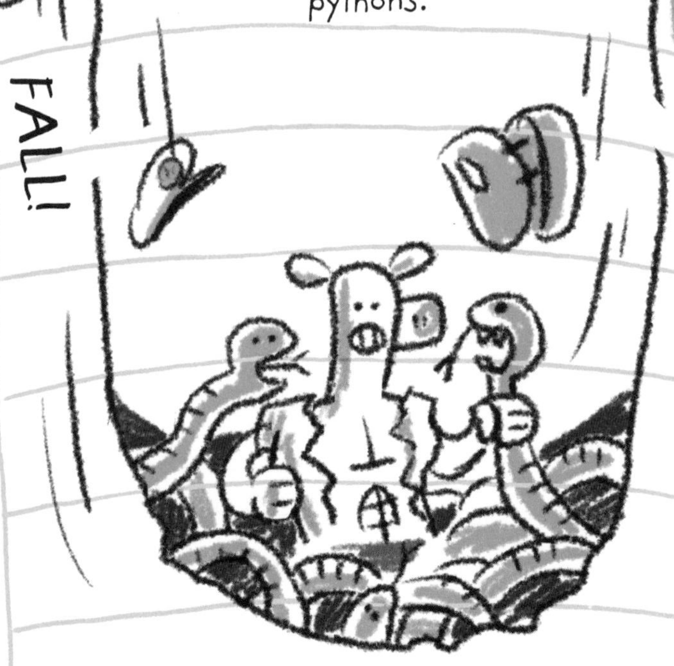
FALL!

I lost my life jacket and hat, but wriggled
to freedom as night fell.

Taking shelter in a cave filled with unusual stalactites, I began to have very slight doubts about some of my choices.

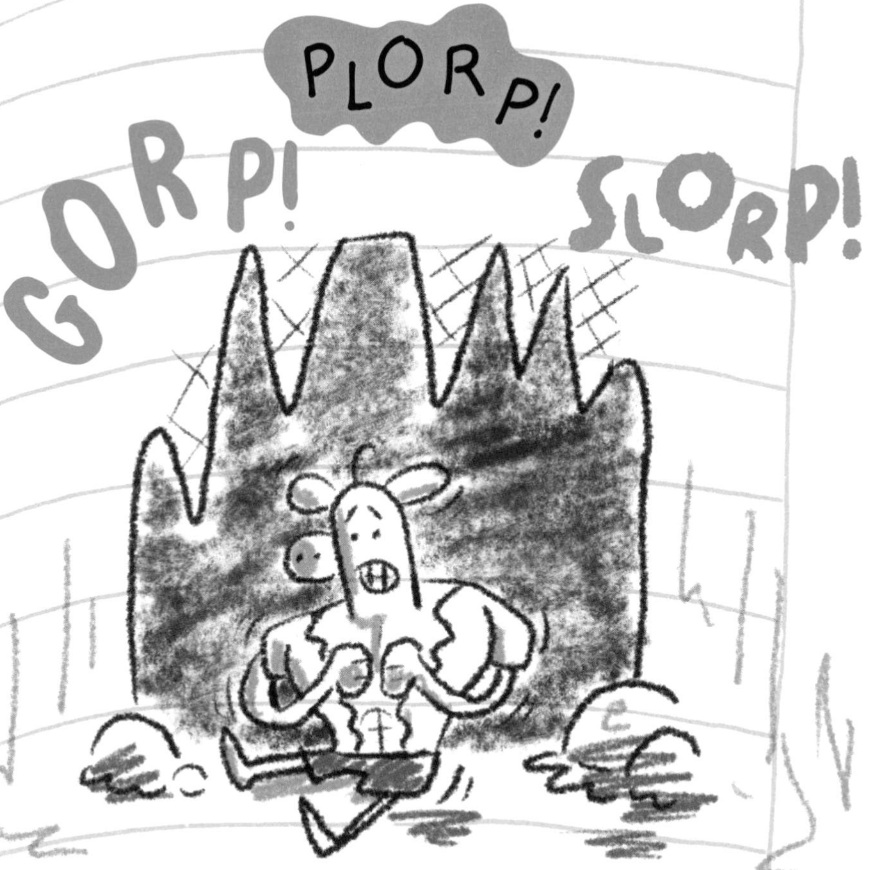
PLORP!
GORP!
SLORP!

The cave was cold and slimy, and the terrifying noises (that I wasn't scared of at all) seemed to be getting closer.

In a final act of courage,
I fled into the night.

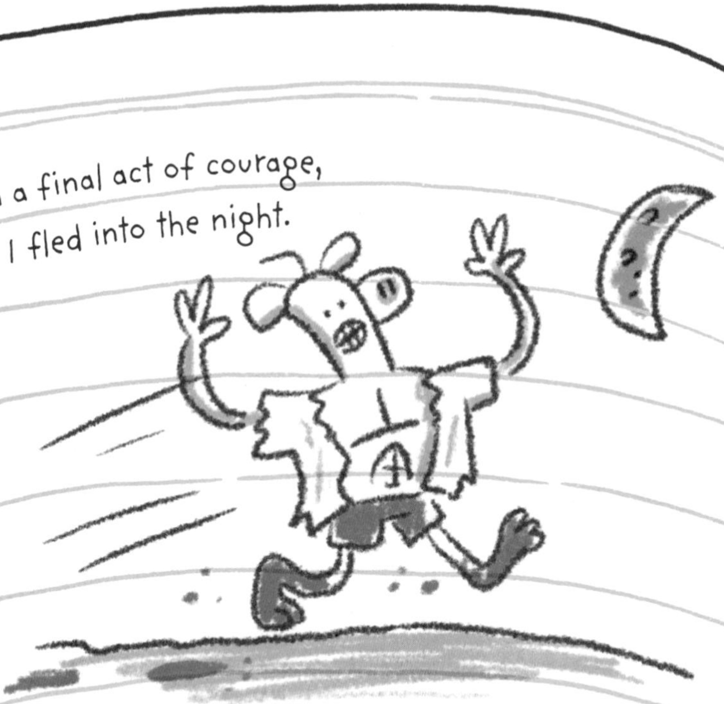

I was now sure that slithering through the
darkness behind me was the ravenous bog-hog.

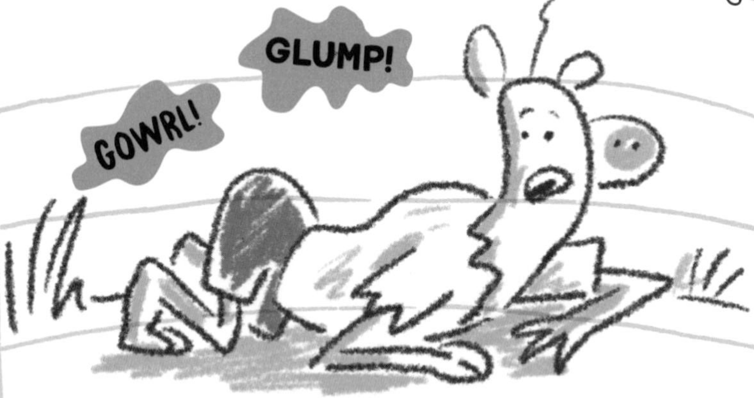
GOWRL!
GLUMP!

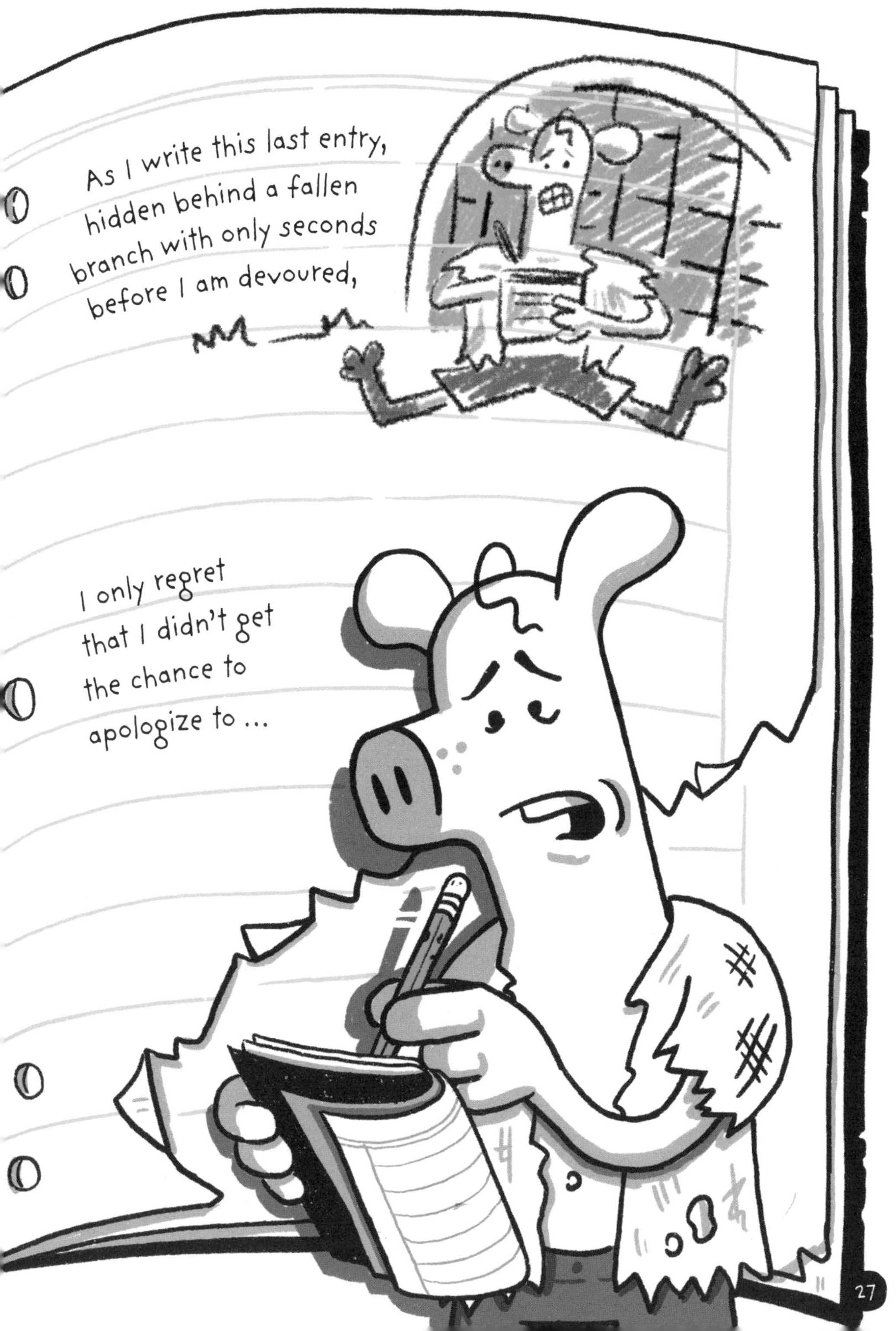
As I write this last entry,
hidden behind a fallen
branch with only seconds
before I am devoured,
I only regret
that I didn't get
the chance to
apologize to ...

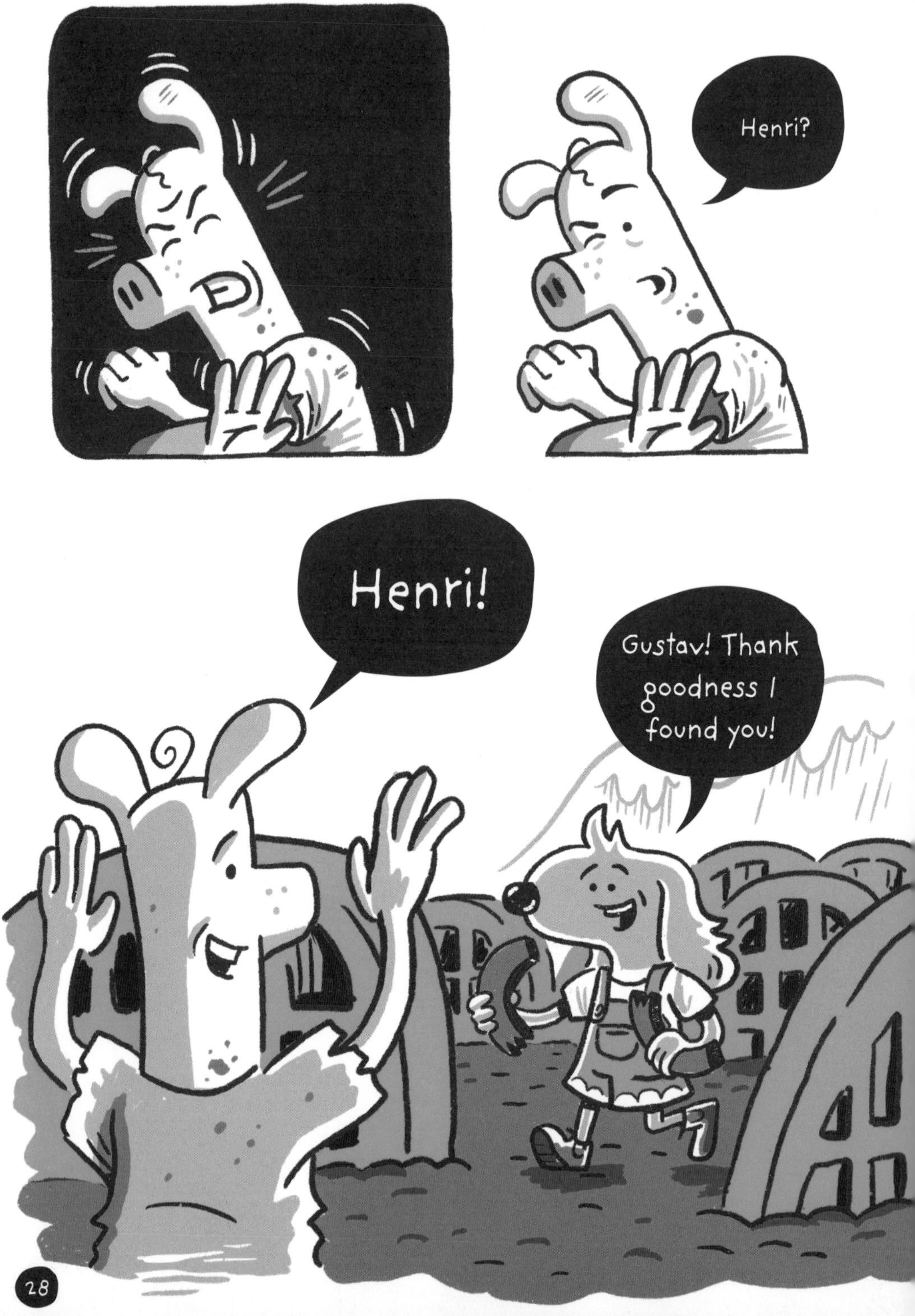
Henri?
Henri!
Gustav! Thank goodness I found you!

"Henri, I'm so sorry. I should have listened to you," blurted Gustav. "But I wish you had never followed me. Now we're both lost on this forsaken island—surrounded by mud and snakes, with nowhere to shelter but freezing caves."

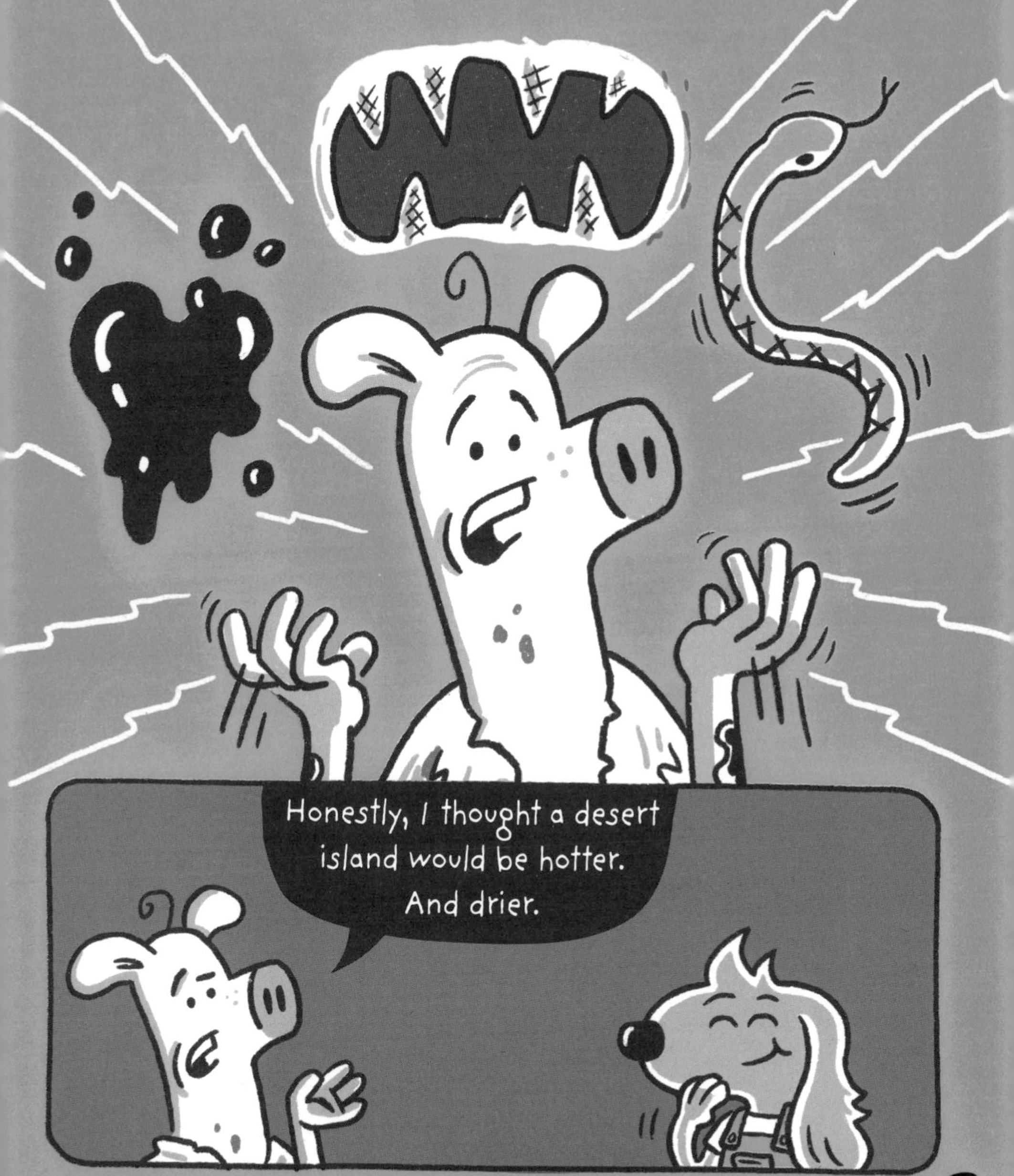
Honestly, I thought a desert island would be hotter. And drier.

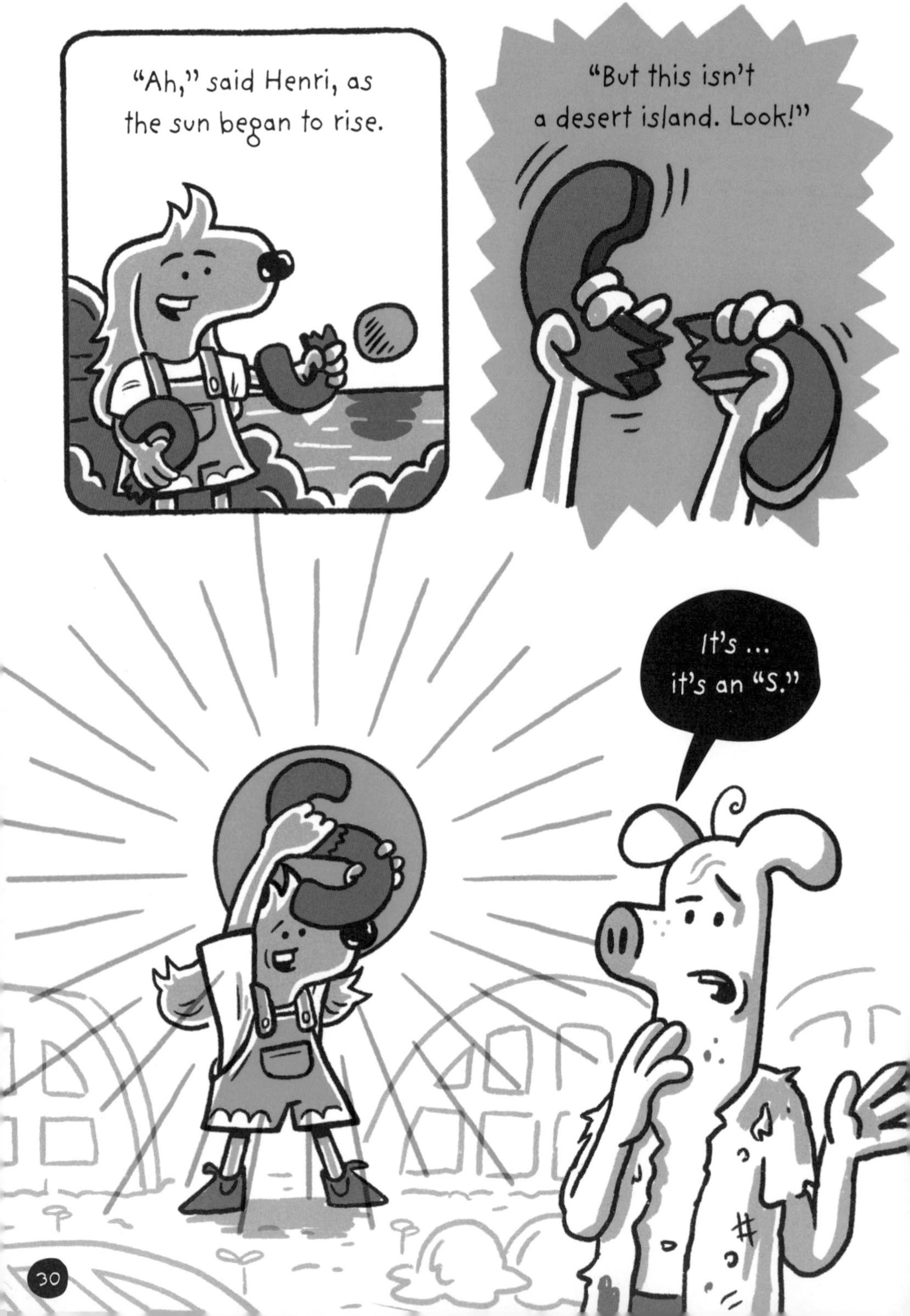
"Ah," said Henri, as the sun began to rise.
"But this isn't a desert island. Look!"
It's ... it's an "S."

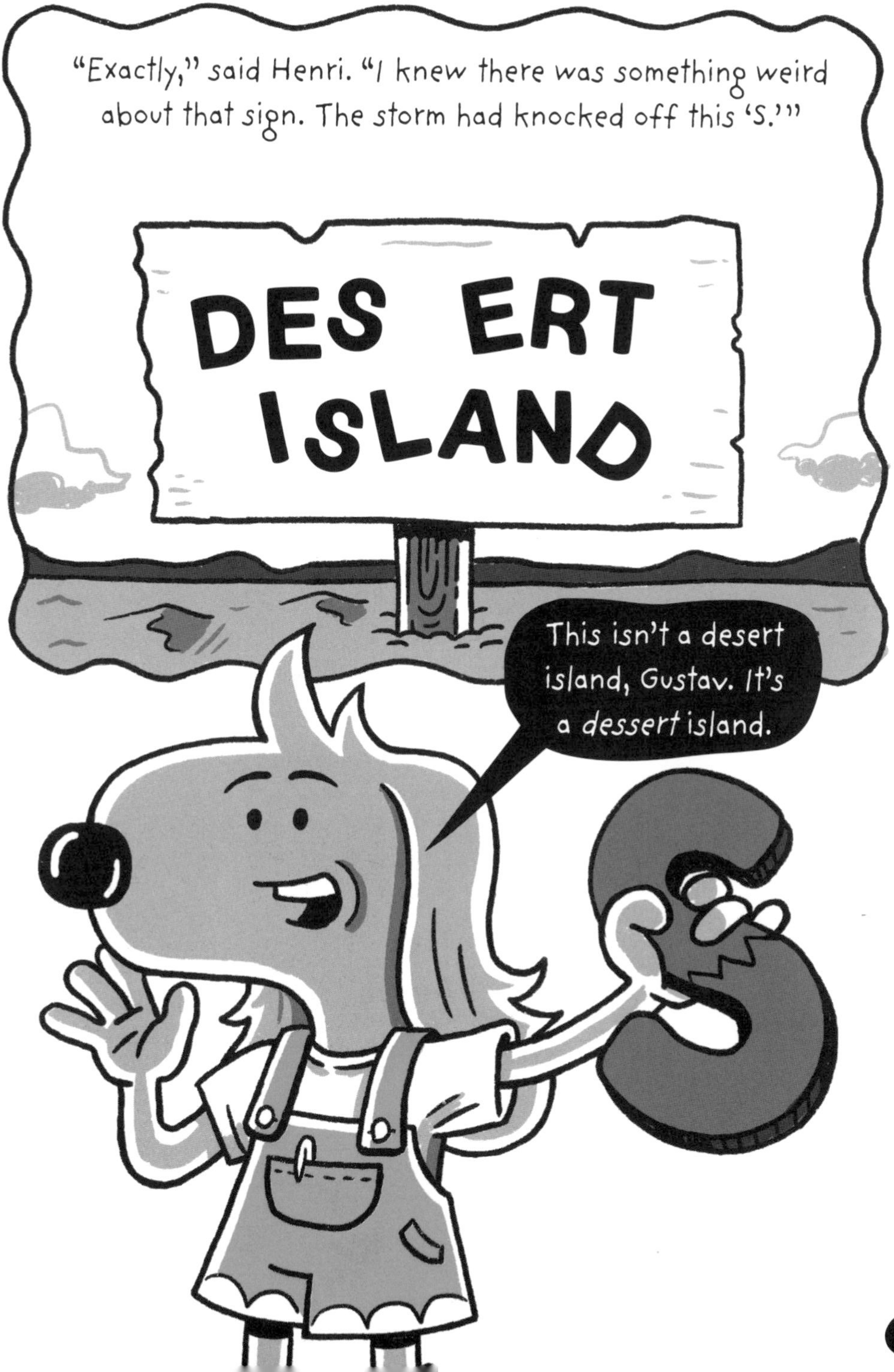
"Exactly," said Henri. "I knew there was something weird about that sign. The storm had knocked off this 'S.'"
DES ERT
ISLAND
This isn't a desert island, Gustav. It's a *dessert* island.

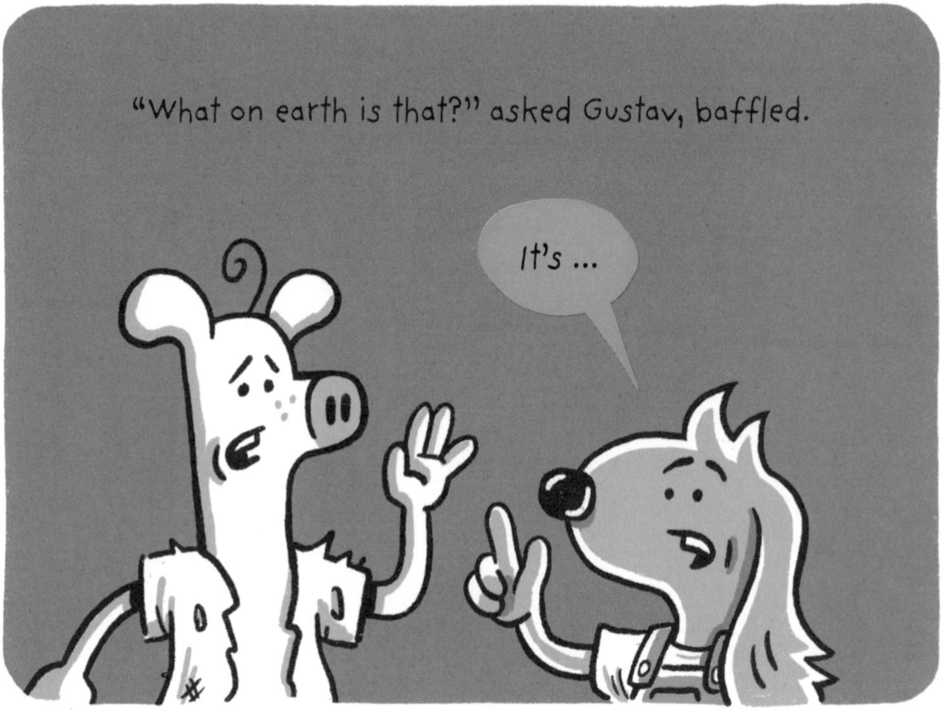
"What on earth is that?" asked Gustav, baffled.
It's ...

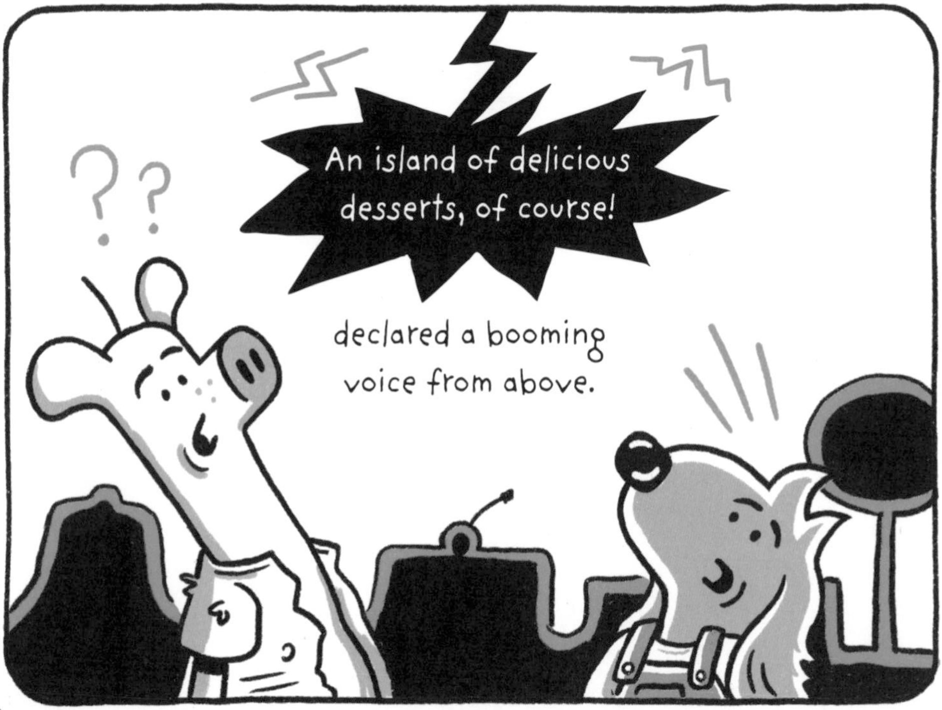
An island of delicious desserts, of course!
declared a booming voice from above.

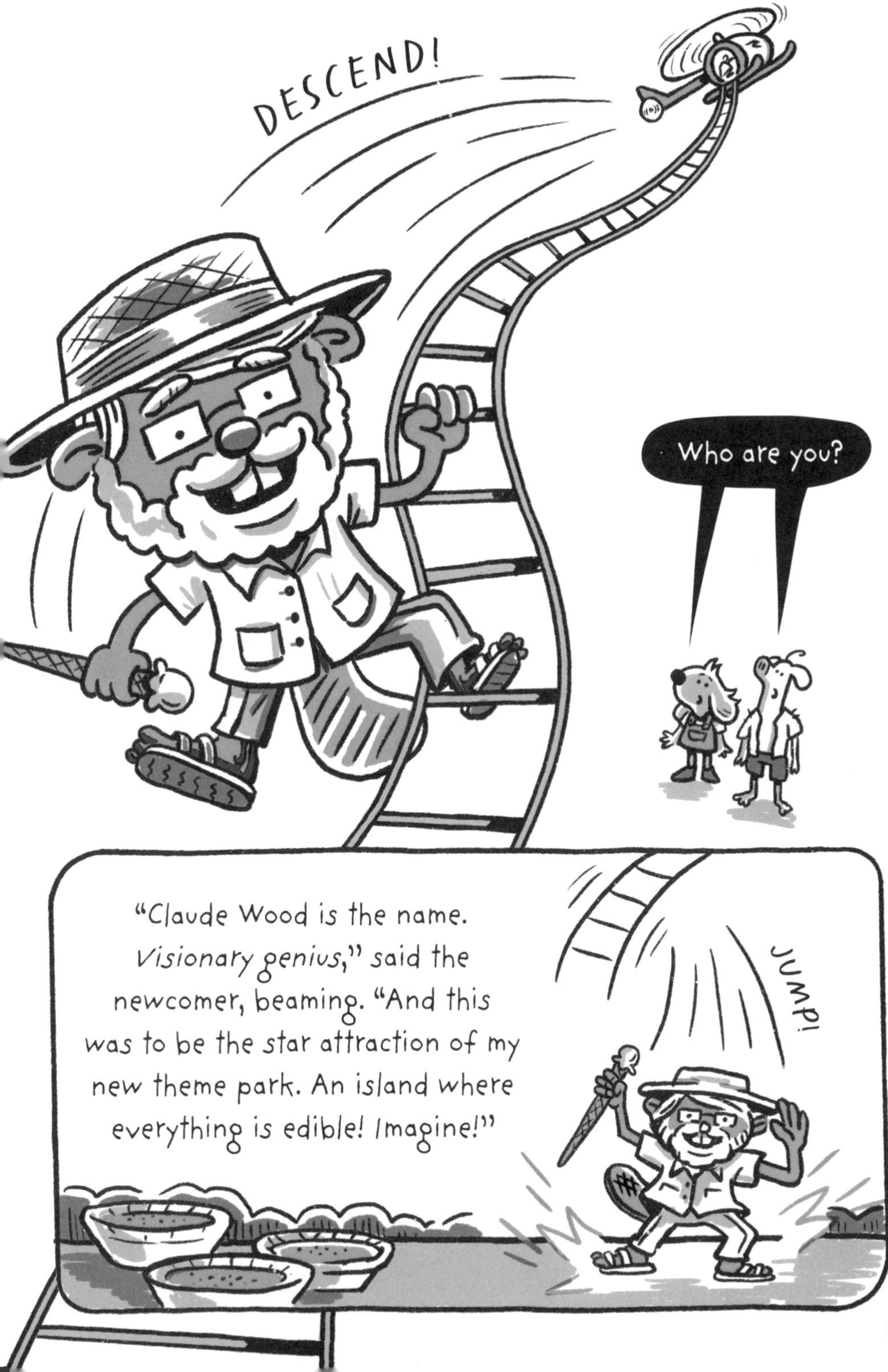
DESCEND!
Who are you?
"Claude Wood is the name. *Visionary genius*," said the newcomer, beaming. "And this was to be the star attraction of my new theme park. An island where everything is edible! Imagine!"
JUMP!

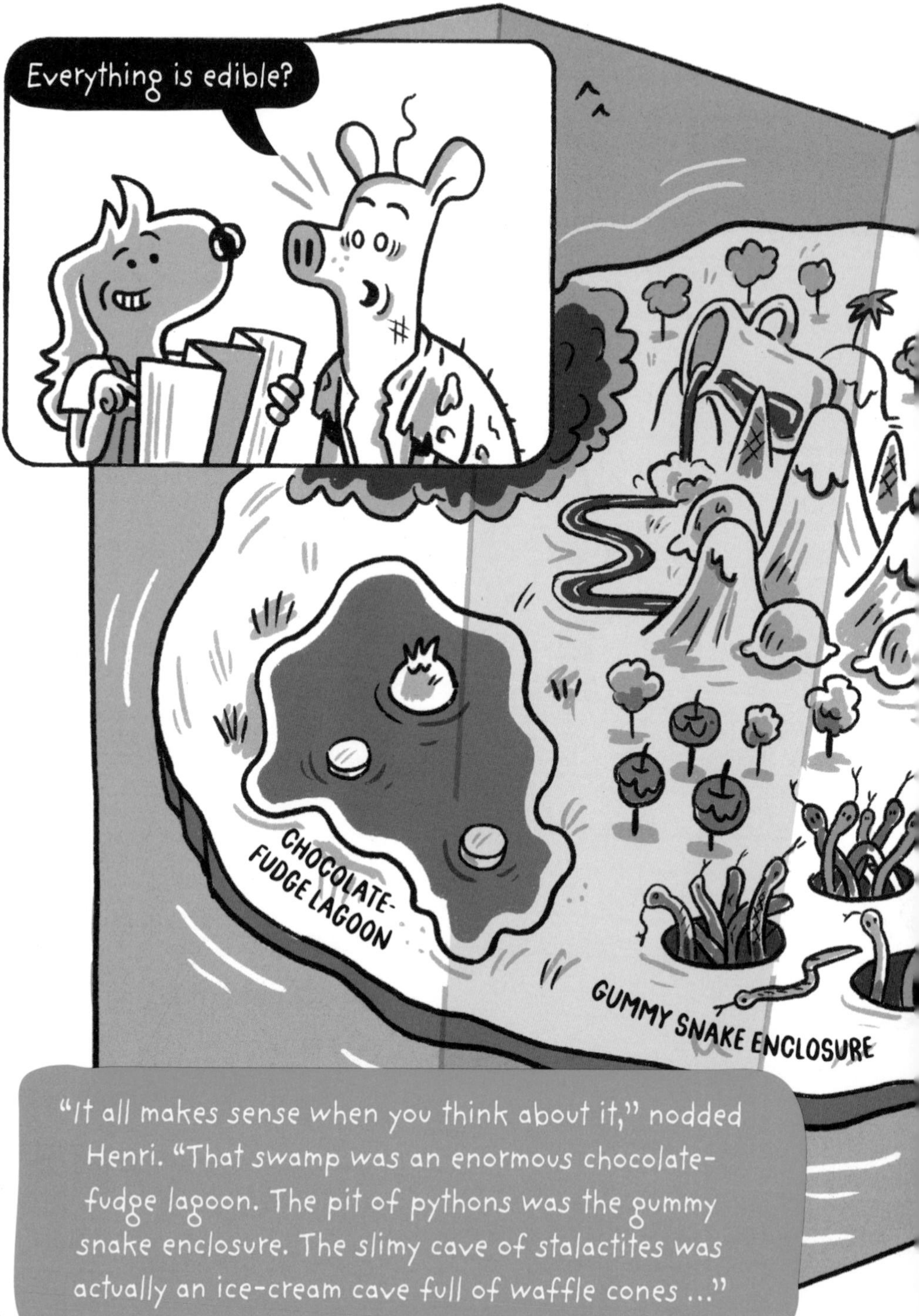
Everything is edible?
CHOCOLATE-FUDGE LAGOON
GUMMY SNAKE ENCLOSURE
"It all makes sense when you think about it," nodded Henri. "That swamp was an enormous chocolate-fudge lagoon. The pit of pythons was the gummy snake enclosure. The slimy cave of stalactites was actually an ice-cream cave full of waffle cones ..."

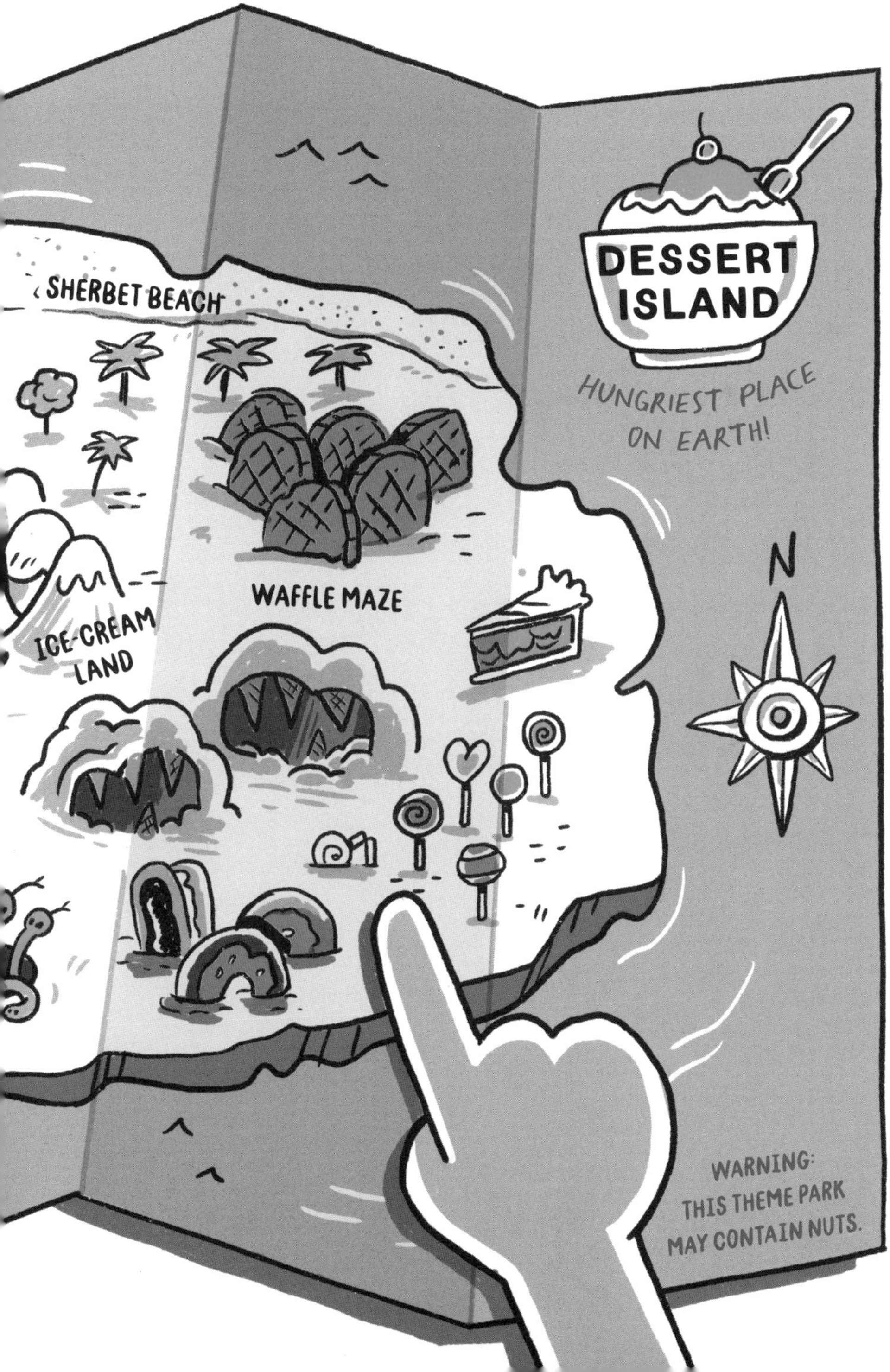
SHERBET BEACH
DESSERT ISLAND
HUNGRIEST PLACE ON EARTH!
WAFFLE MAZE
ICE-CREAM LAND
N
WARNING: THIS THEME PARK MAY CONTAIN NUTS.

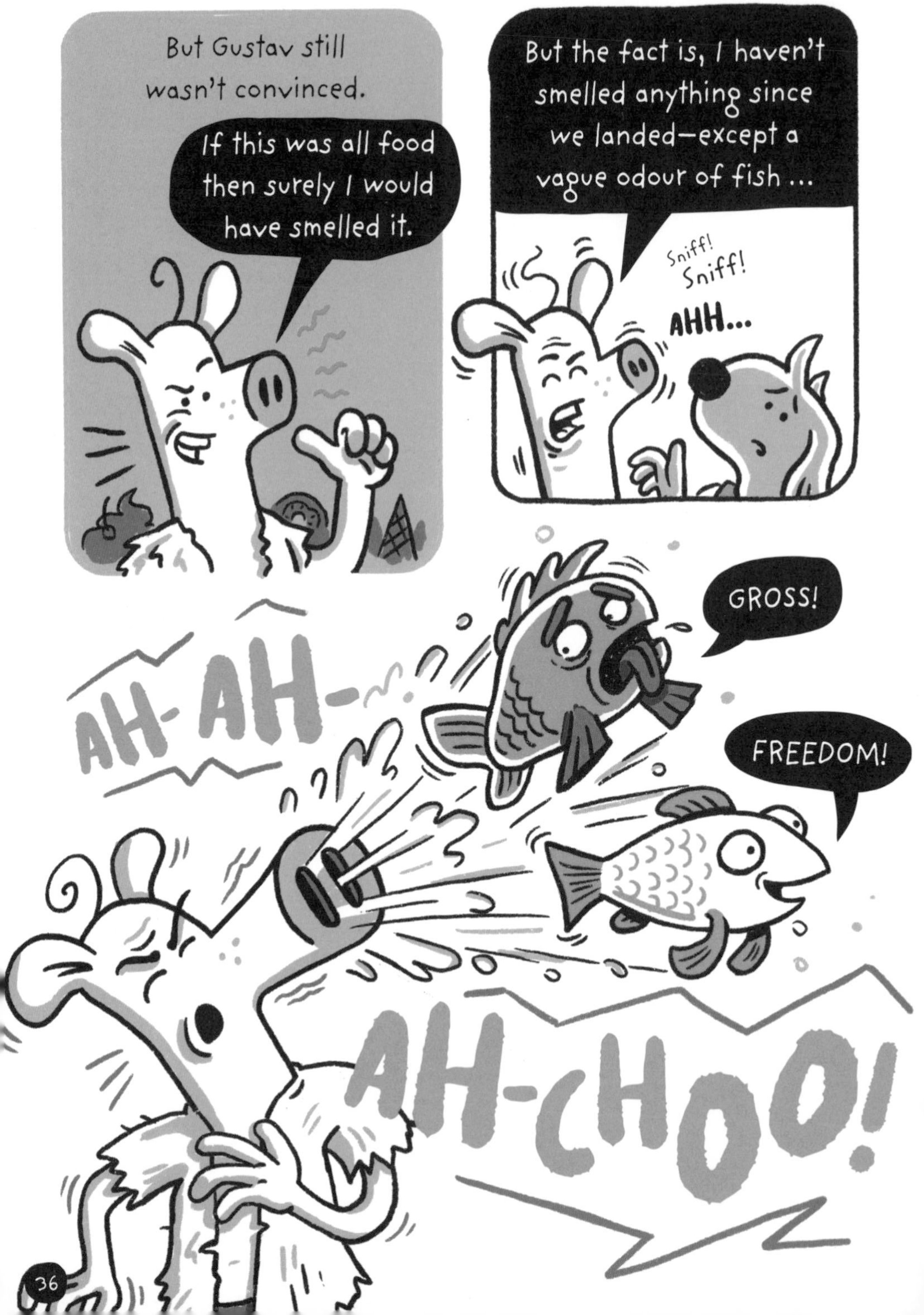
But Gustav still wasn't convinced.
If this was all food then surely I would have smelled it.
But the fact is, I haven't smelled anything since we landed—except a vague odour of fish ...
Sniff! Sniff!
AHH...
AH-AH-
GROSS!
FREEDOM!
AH-CHOO!

Well, I guess that explains that ...

Sniff! Sniff!

Claude frowned. "We were supposed to open tomorrow. That is, until this storm came and knocked out all my electricity."

"Now all this food will go to waste, unless you know of some way to dispose of an entire island's worth of desserts in 24 hours?"

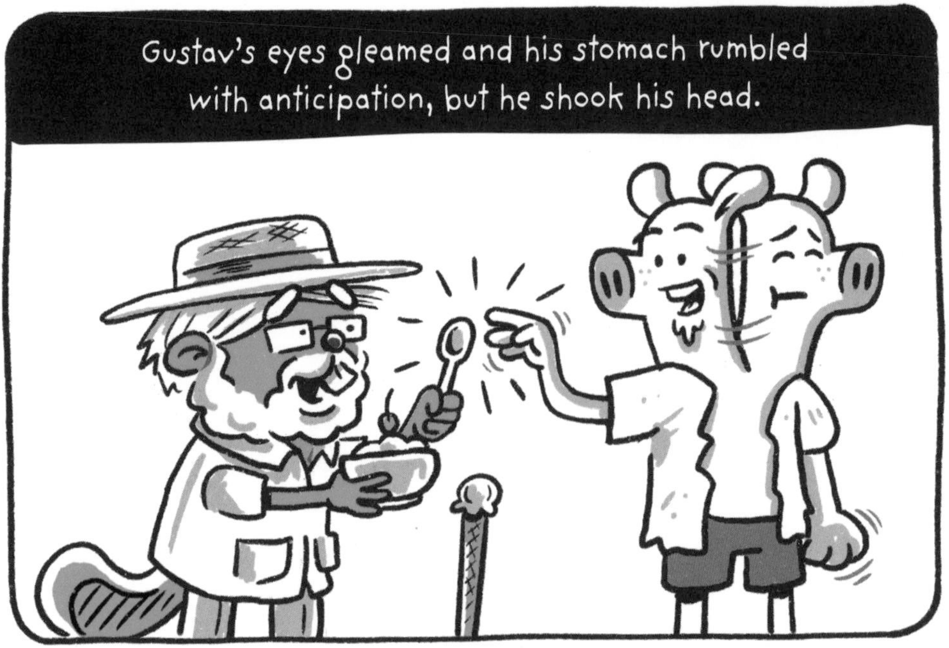
Gustav's eyes gleamed and his stomach rumbled with anticipation, but he shook his head.

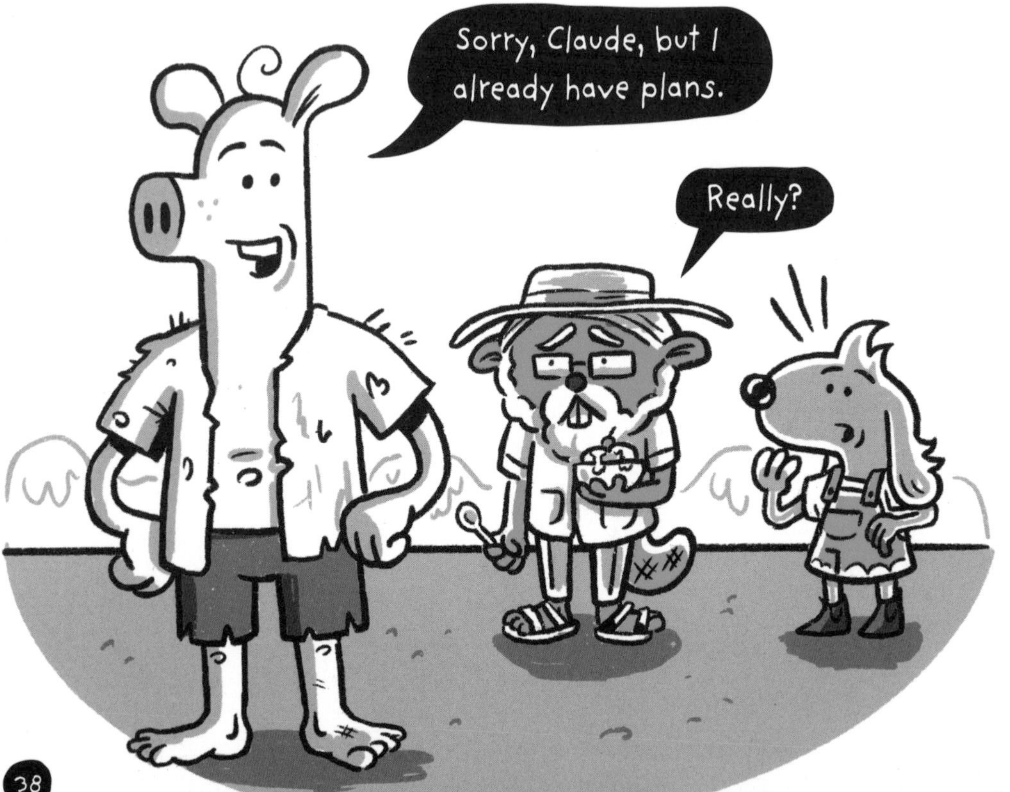
Sorry, Claude, but I already have plans.
Really?

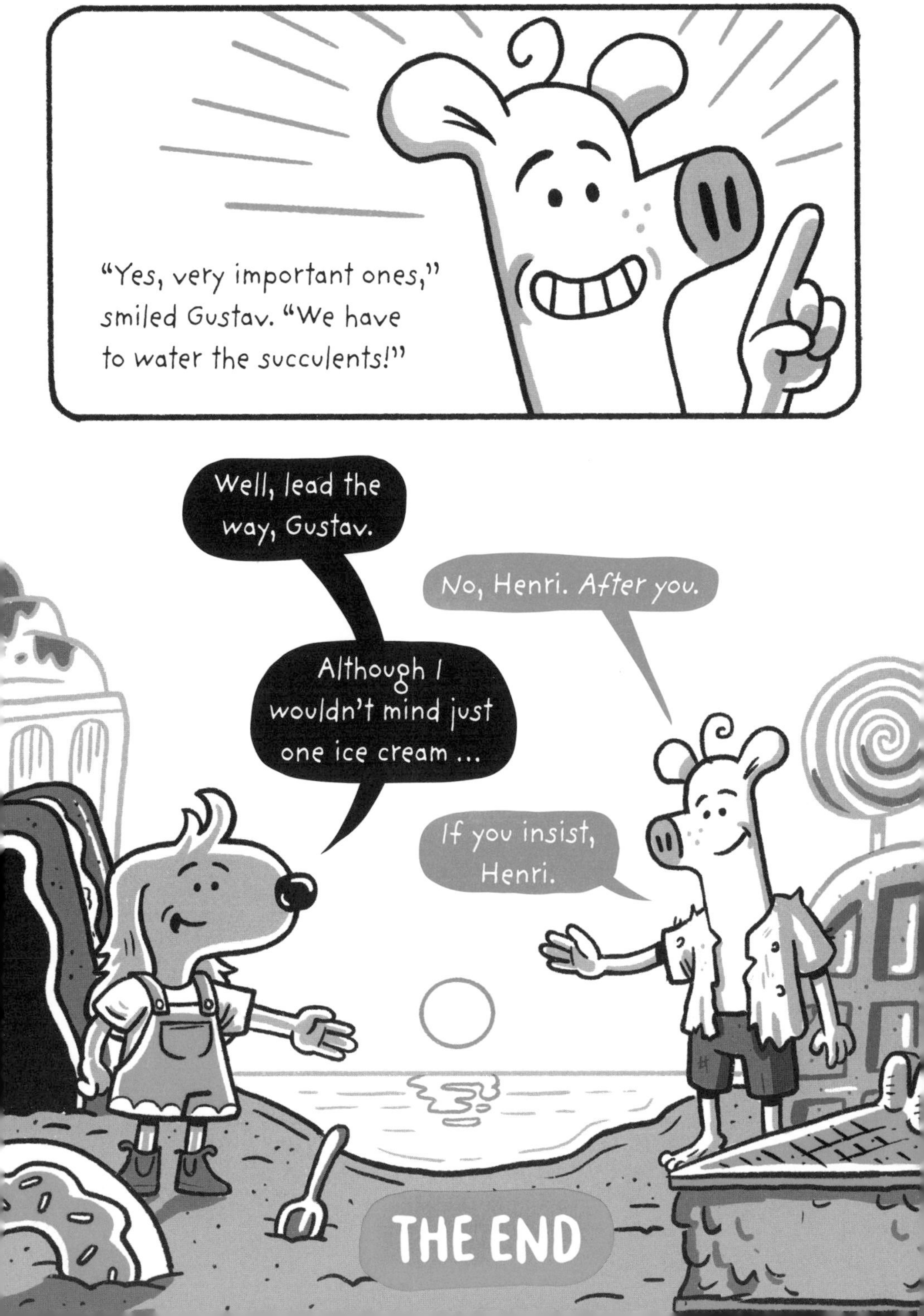
"Yes, very important ones," smiled Gustav. "We have to water the succulents!"
Well, lead the way, Gustav.
Although I wouldn't mind just one ice cream ...
No, Henri. After you.
If you insist, Henri.
THE END

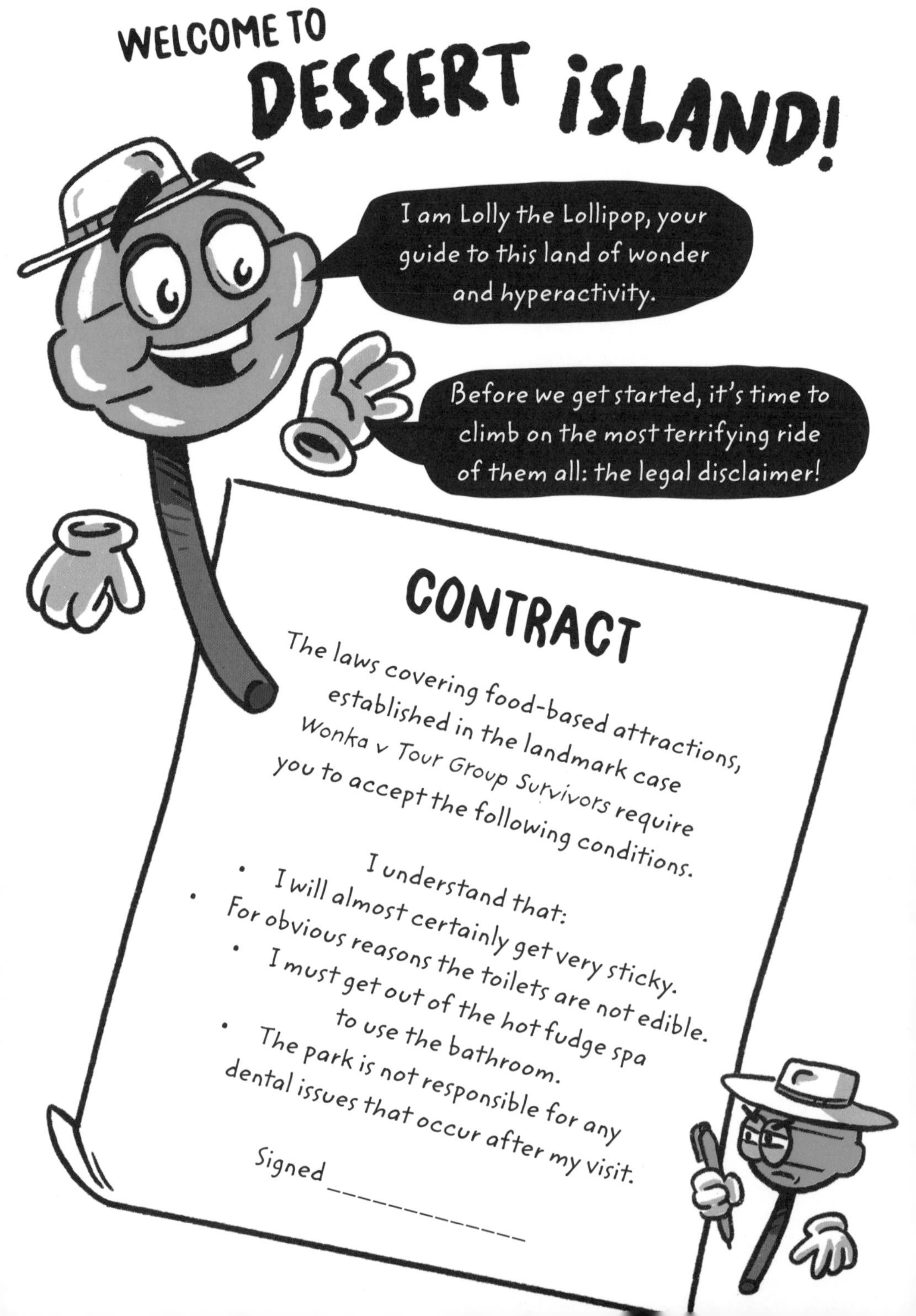
WELCOME TO
DESSERT ISLAND!
I am Lolly the Lollipop, your guide to this land of wonder and hyperactivity.
Before we get started, it's time to climb on the most terrifying ride of them all: the legal disclaimer!
CONTRACT
The laws covering food-based attractions, established in the landmark case Wonka v Tour Group Survivors require you to accept the following conditions.
I understand that:
• I will almost certainly get very sticky.
• For obvious reasons the toilets are not edible.
• I must get out of the hot fudge spa to use the bathroom.
• The park is not responsible for any dental issues that occur after my visit.
Signed ____________

JUST DESSERTS

A team of sugar engineers worked for years to ensure the buildings on Dessert Island are structurally sound while remaining edible. One of our load-bearing caramel beams can support over 50 tons, but will still melt in your mouth!

HISTORY

Dessert Island is just the latest in a long line of confectionary constructions. Witches have used gingerbread to build their houses for hundreds of years. (While our materials may be similar, we wish to point out we are not planning to eat any children.)

CLAUDE WOOD

Our visionary founder, Claude Wood, was inspired by his beaver ancestors, who could eat the very wood from which they built their homes. However, he found most modern wood buildings tasteless—literally! This inspired him to create Dessert Island— the first entirely edible theme park.

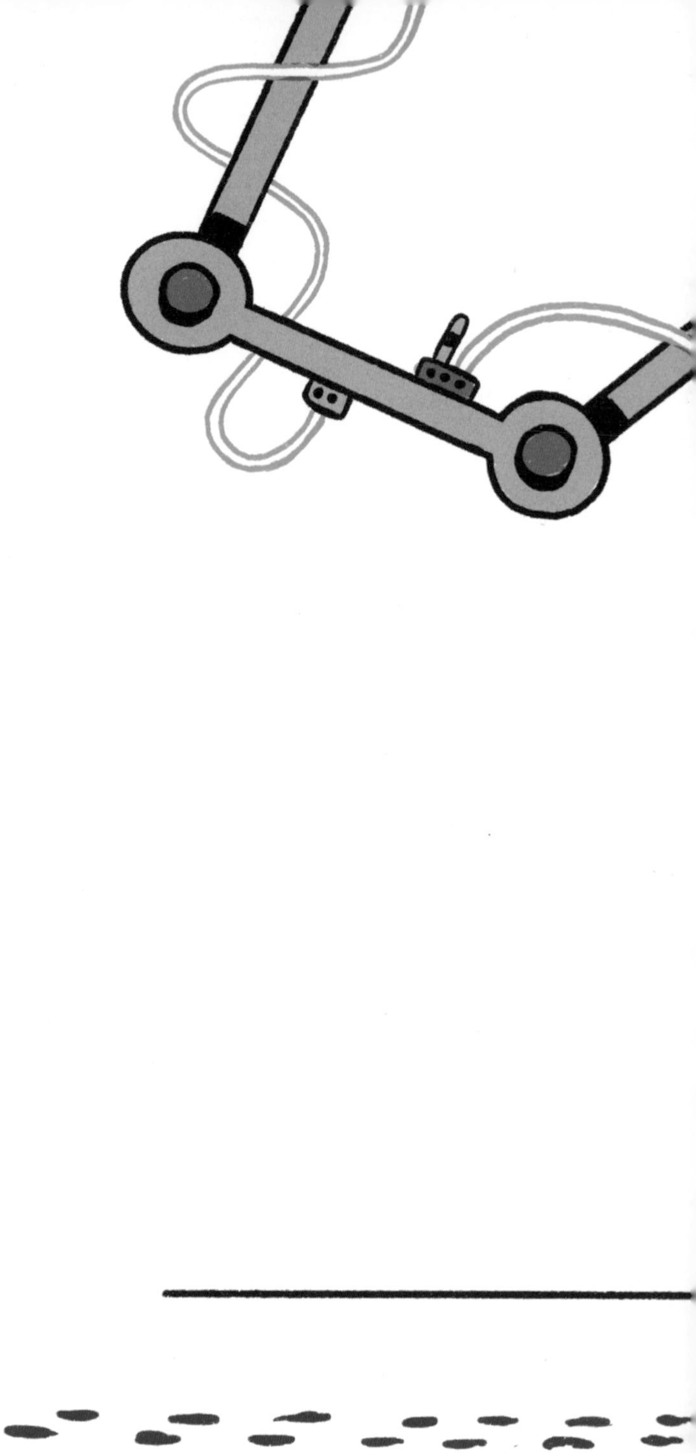

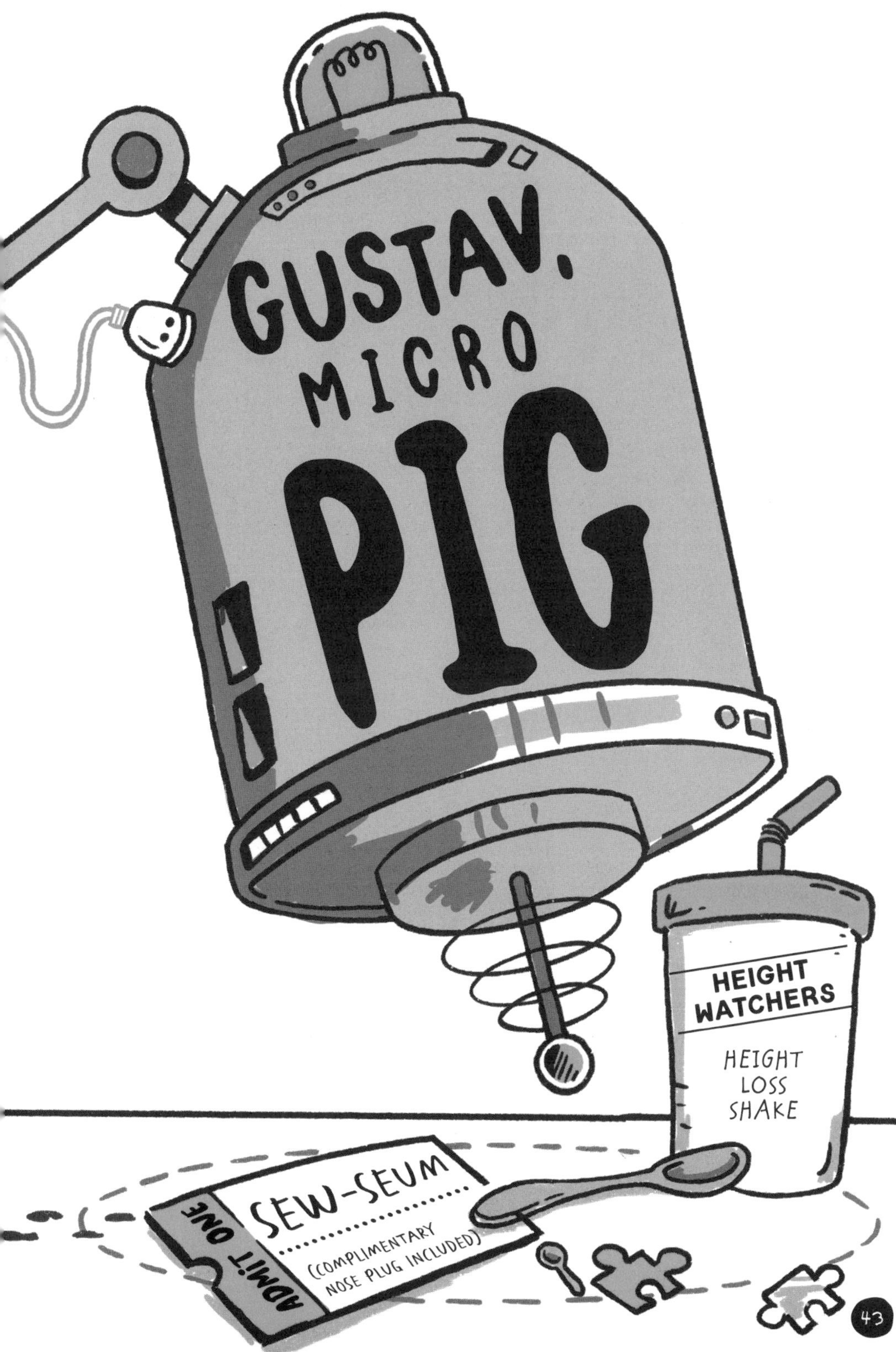
GUSTAV. MICRO PIG
HEIGHT WATCHERS
HEIGHT LOSS SHAKE
ADMIT ONE
SEW-SEUM
(COMPLIMENTARY NOSE PLUG INCLUDED)

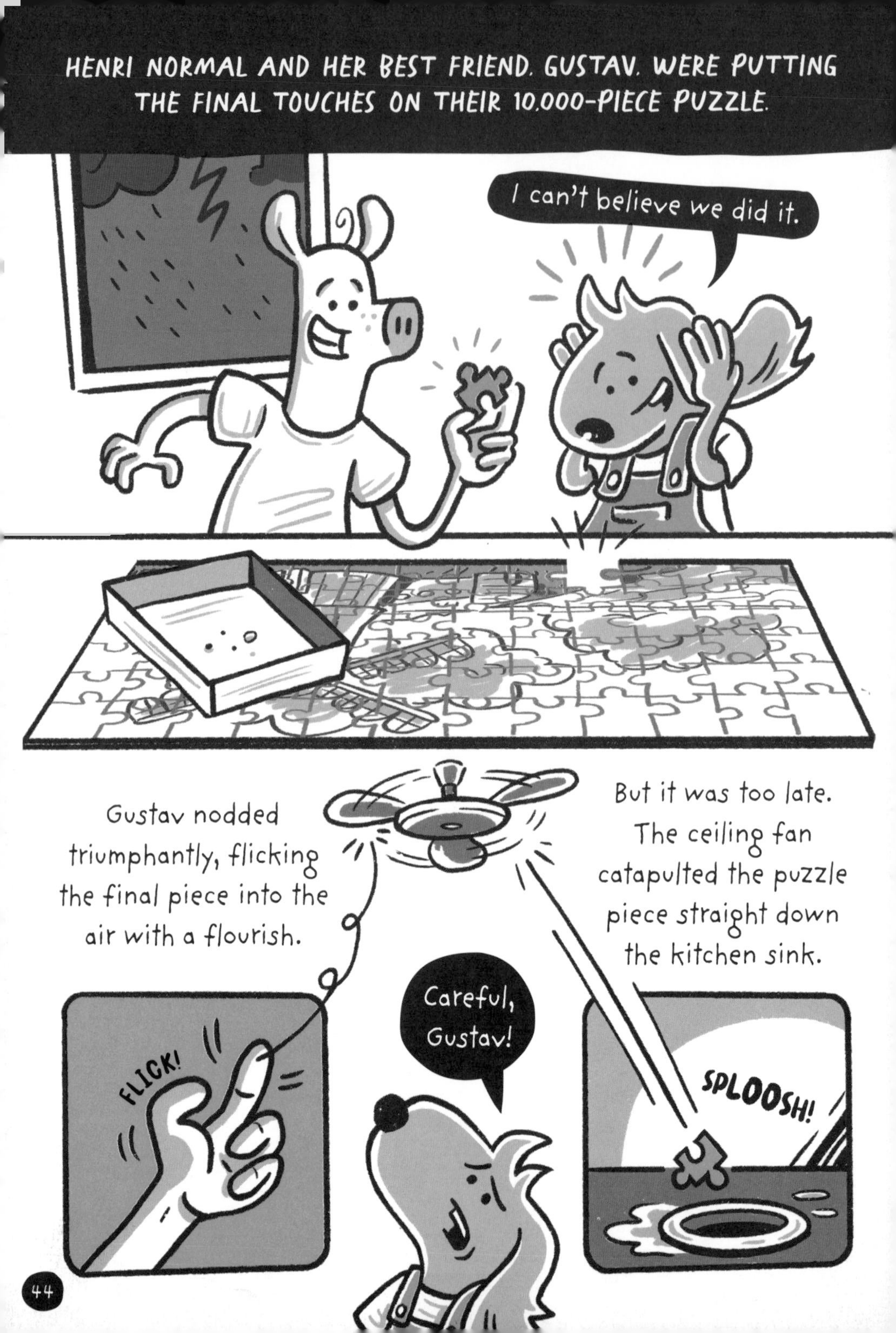
HENRI NORMAL AND HER BEST FRIEND, GUSTAV, WERE PUTTING THE FINAL TOUCHES ON THEIR 10,000-PIECE PUZZLE.
I can't believe we did it.
Gustav nodded triumphantly, flicking the final piece into the air with a flourish.
FLICK!
Careful, Gustav!
But it was too late. The ceiling fan catapulted the puzzle piece straight down the kitchen sink.
SPLOOSH!

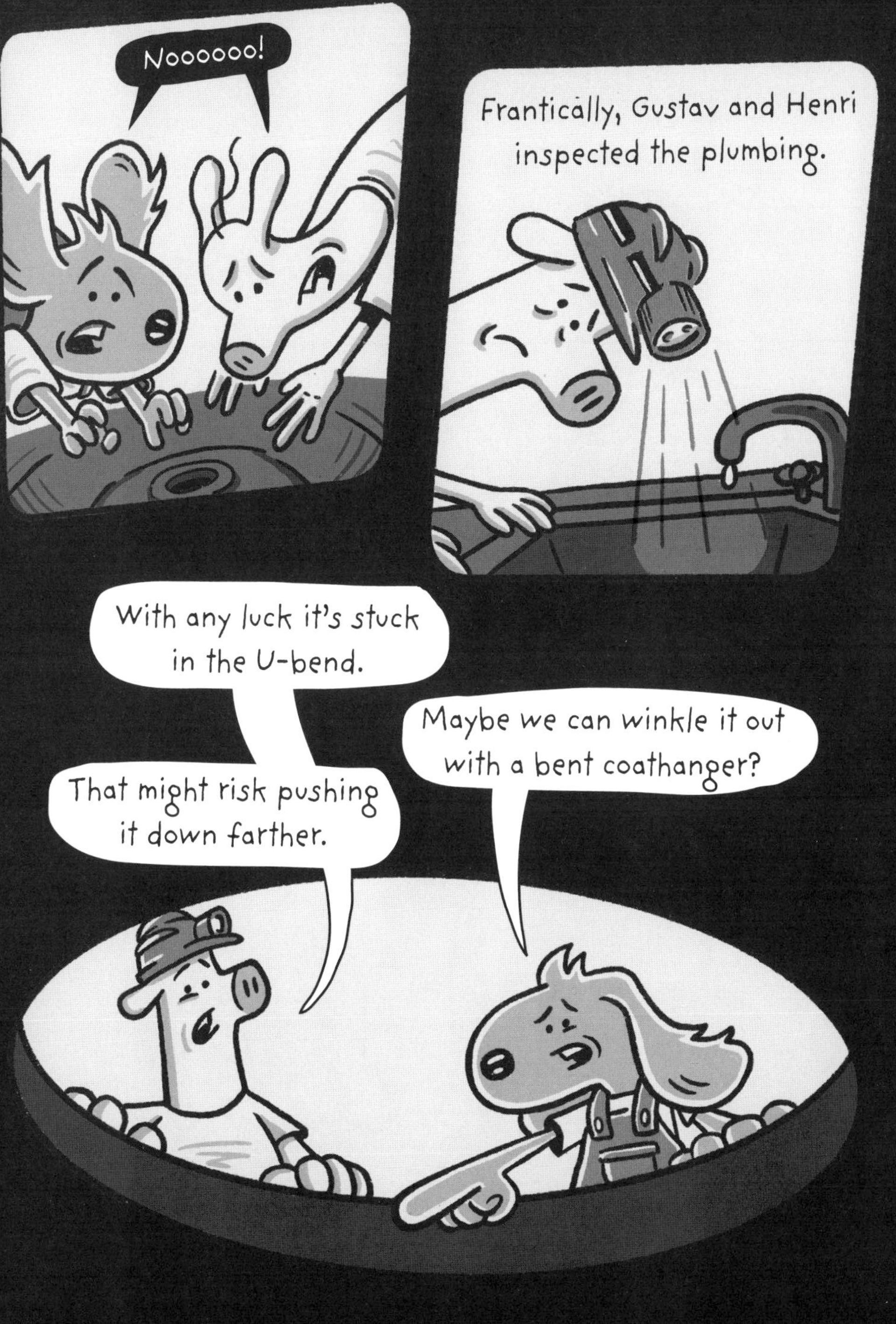
Noooooo!
Frantically, Gustav and Henri inspected the plumbing.
With any luck it's stuck in the U-bend.
Maybe we can winkle it out with a bent coathanger?
That might risk pushing it down farther.

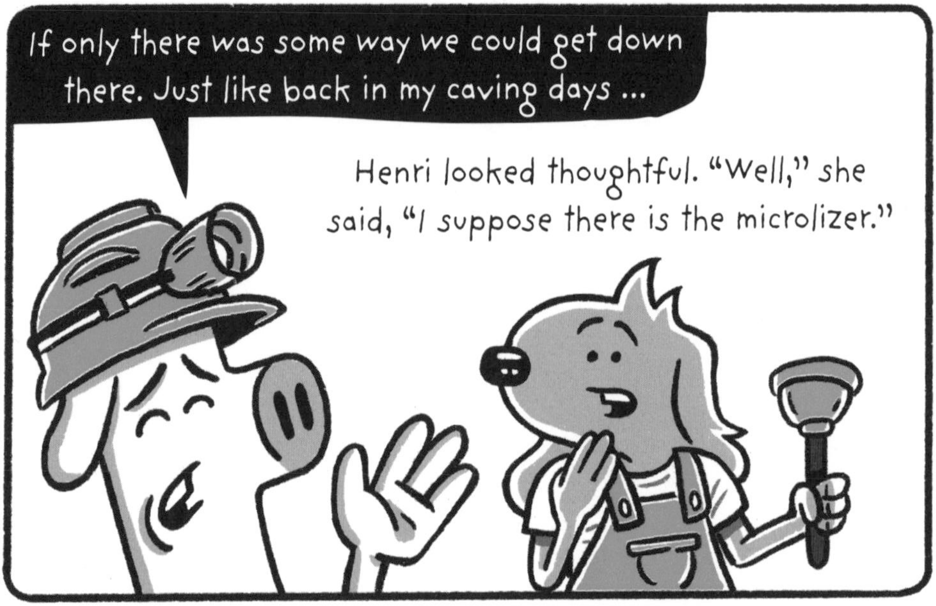
If only there was some way we could get down there. Just like back in my caving days ...
Henri looked thoughtful. "Well," she said, "I suppose there is the microlizer."

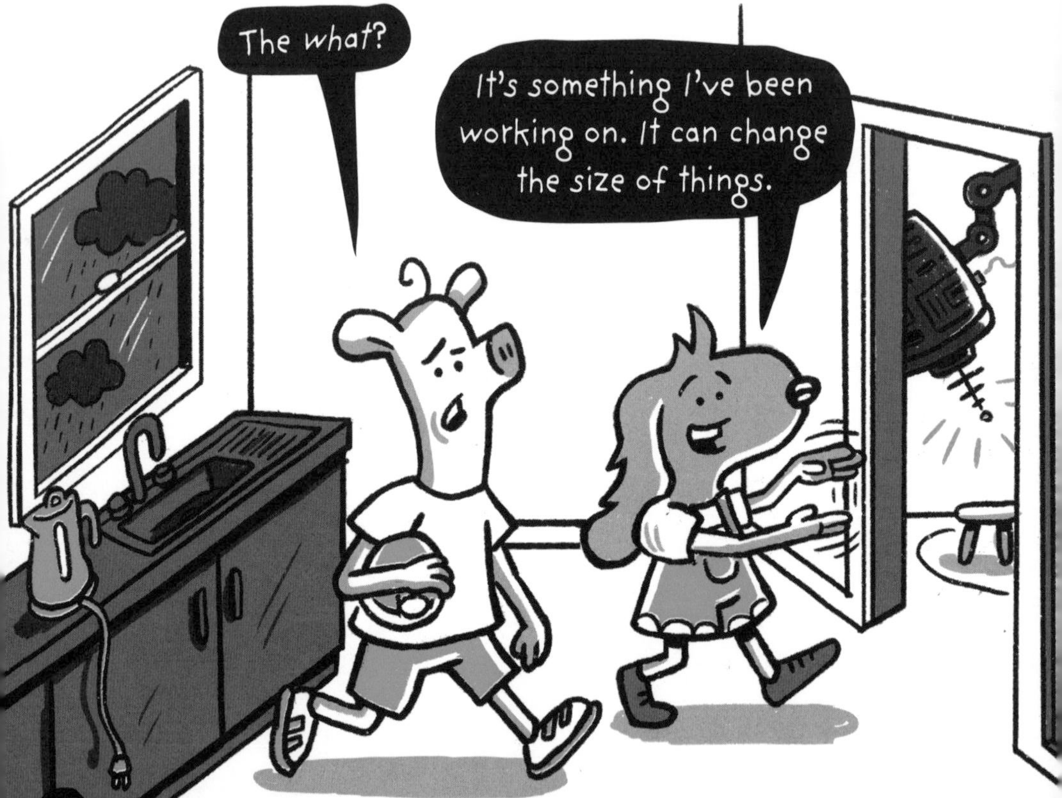
The *what*?
It's something I've been working on. It can change the size of things.

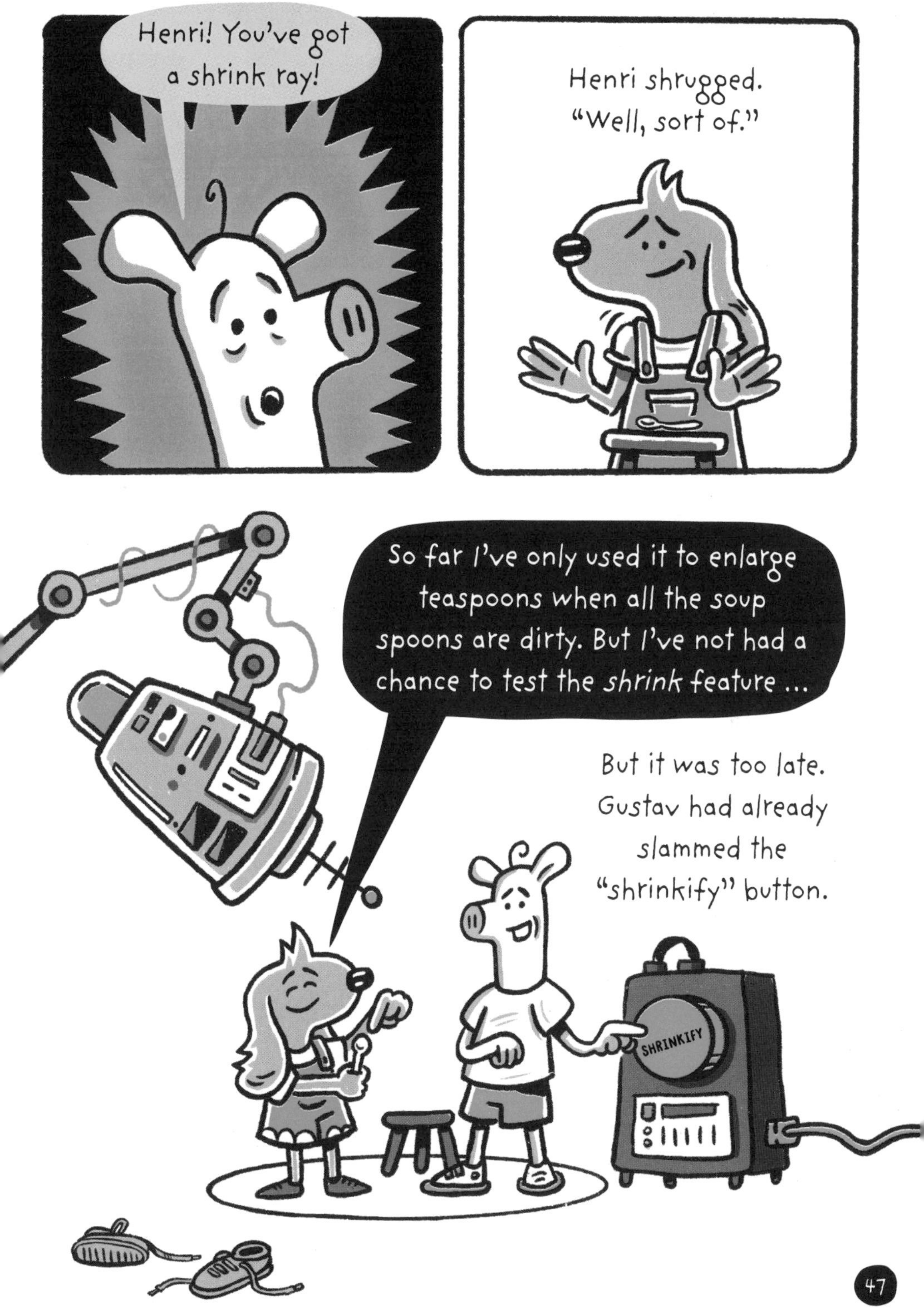
Henri! You've got a shrink ray!
Henri shrugged. "Well, sort of."
So far I've only used it to enlarge teaspoons when all the soup spoons are dirty. But I've not had a chance to test the *shrink* feature ...
But it was too late. Gustav had already slammed the "shrinkify" button.
SHRINKIFY

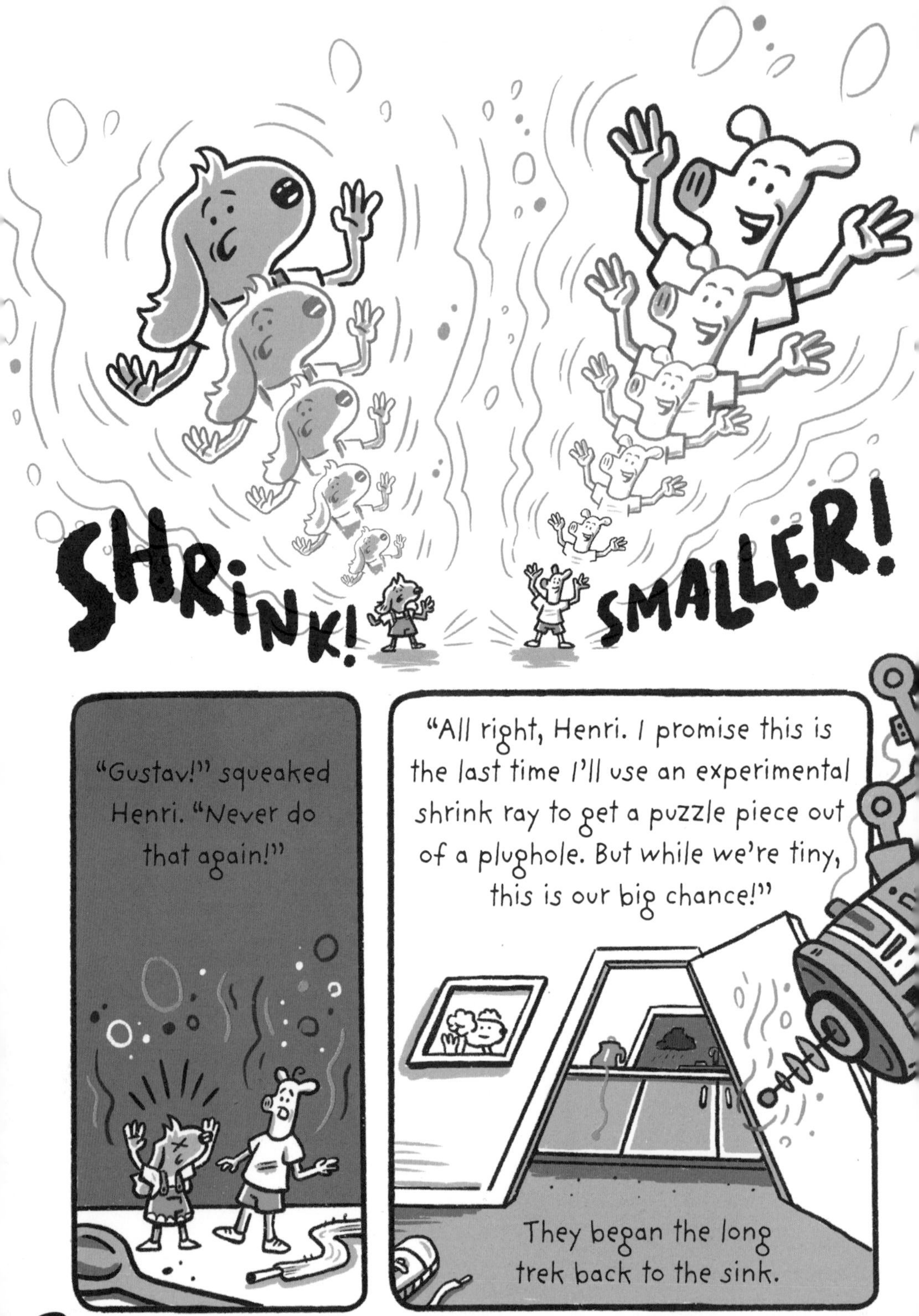
SHRINK!
SMALLER!
"Gustav!" squeaked Henri. "Never do that again!"
"All right, Henri. I promise this is the last time I'll use an experimental shrink ray to get a puzzle piece out of a plughole. But while we're tiny, this is our big chance!"
They began the long trek back to the sink.

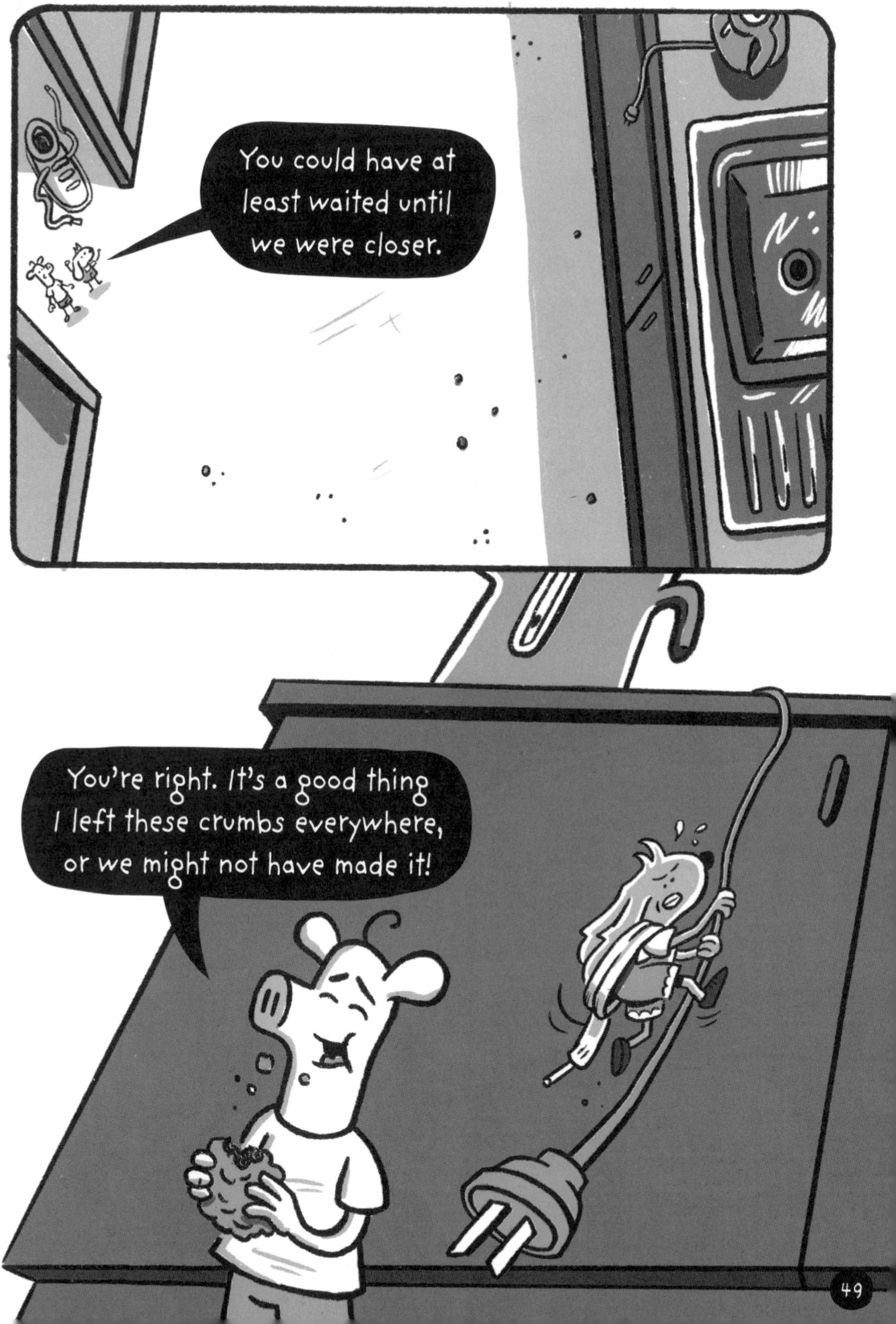
You could have at least waited until we were closer.
You're right. It's a good thing I left these crumbs everywhere, or we might not have made it!

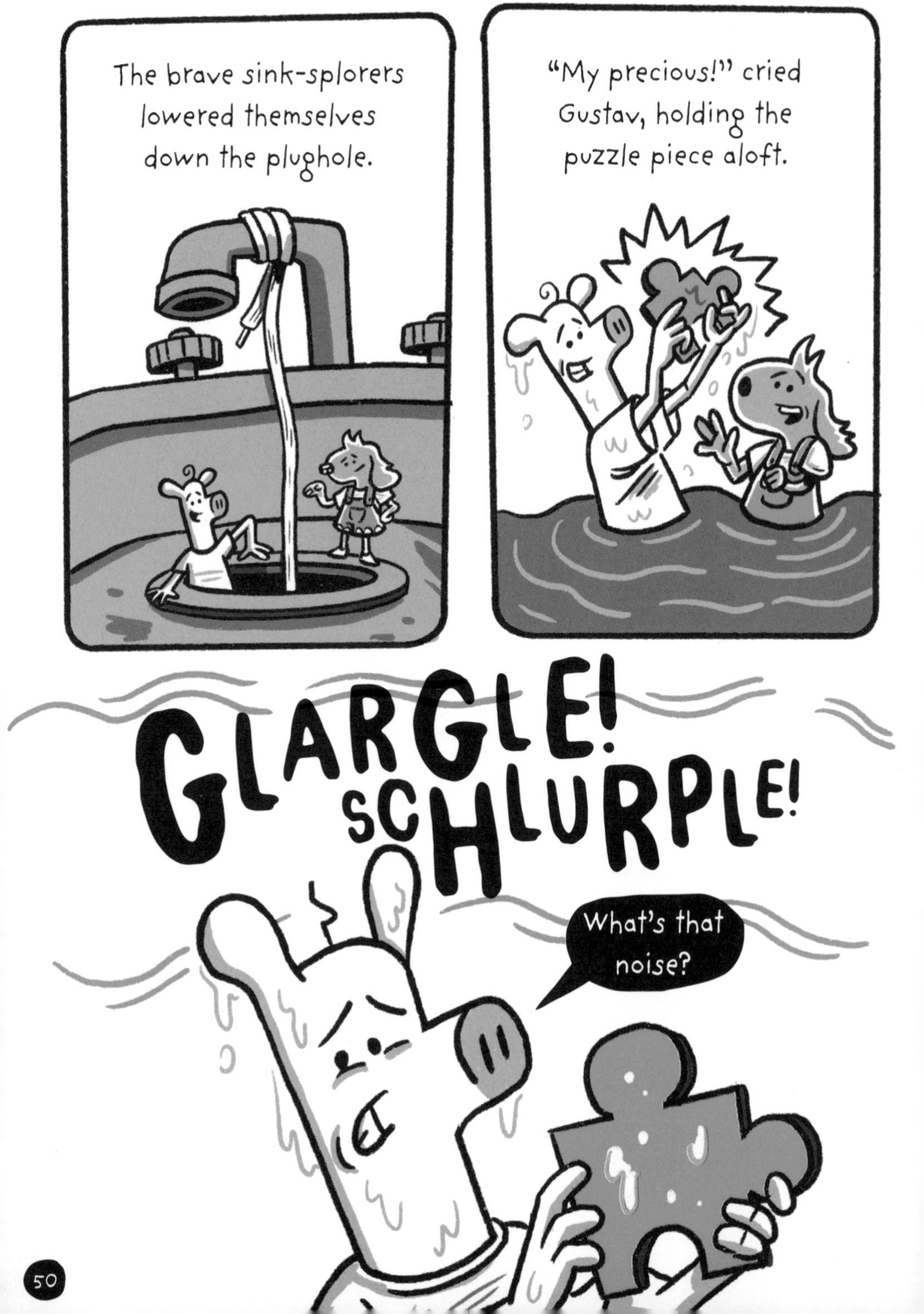
The brave sink-splorers lowered themselves down the plughole.
"My precious!" cried Gustav, holding the puzzle piece aloft.
GLARGLE!
SCHLURPLE!
What's that noise?

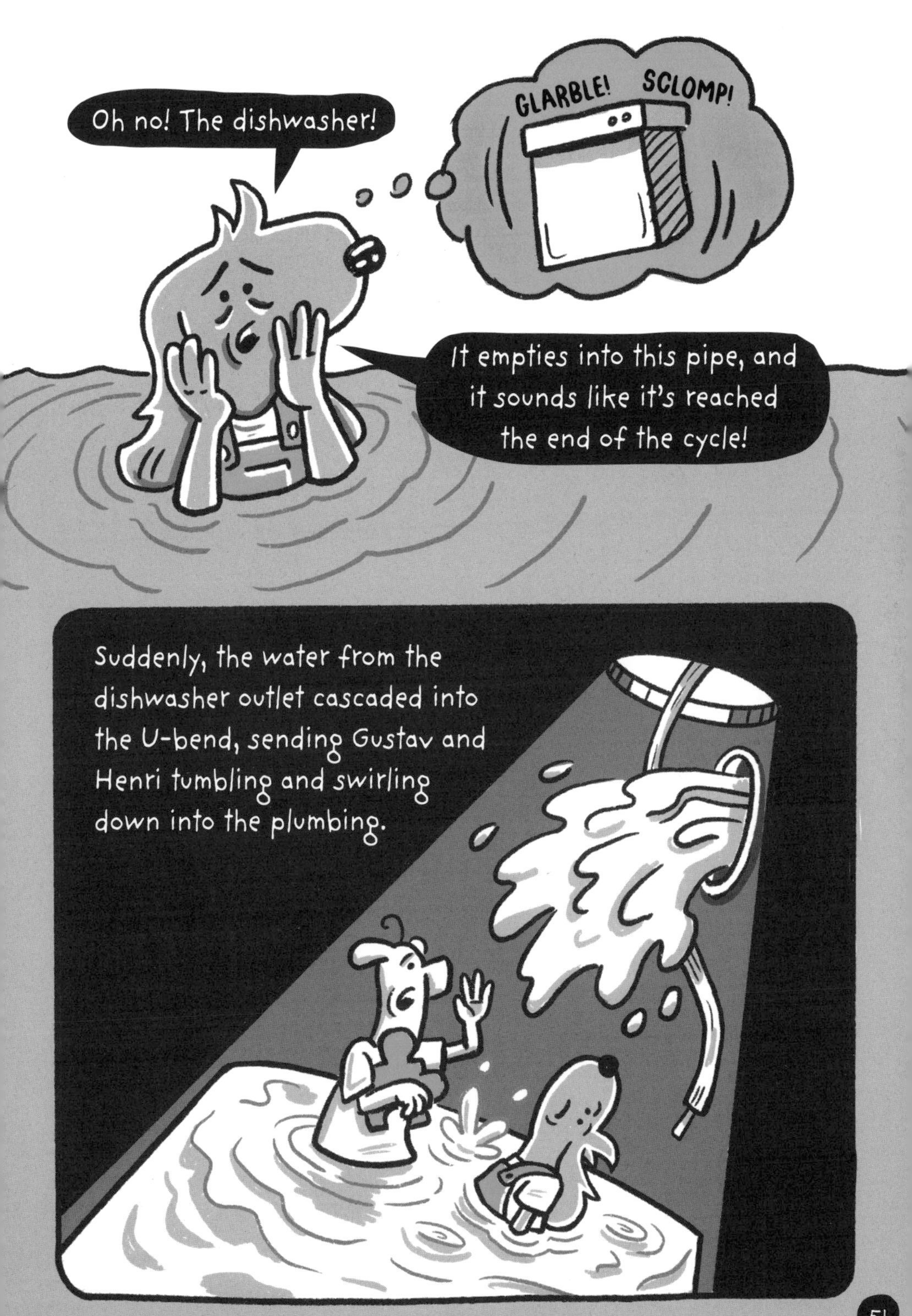
Oh no! The dishwasher!
GLARBLE! SCLOMP!
It empties into this pipe, and it sounds like it's reached the end of the cycle!
Suddenly, the water from the dishwasher outlet cascaded into the U-bend, sending Gustav and Henri tumbling and swirling down into the plumbing.

If this wasn't so terrifying ...
... it would be fun.
But it is terrifying.

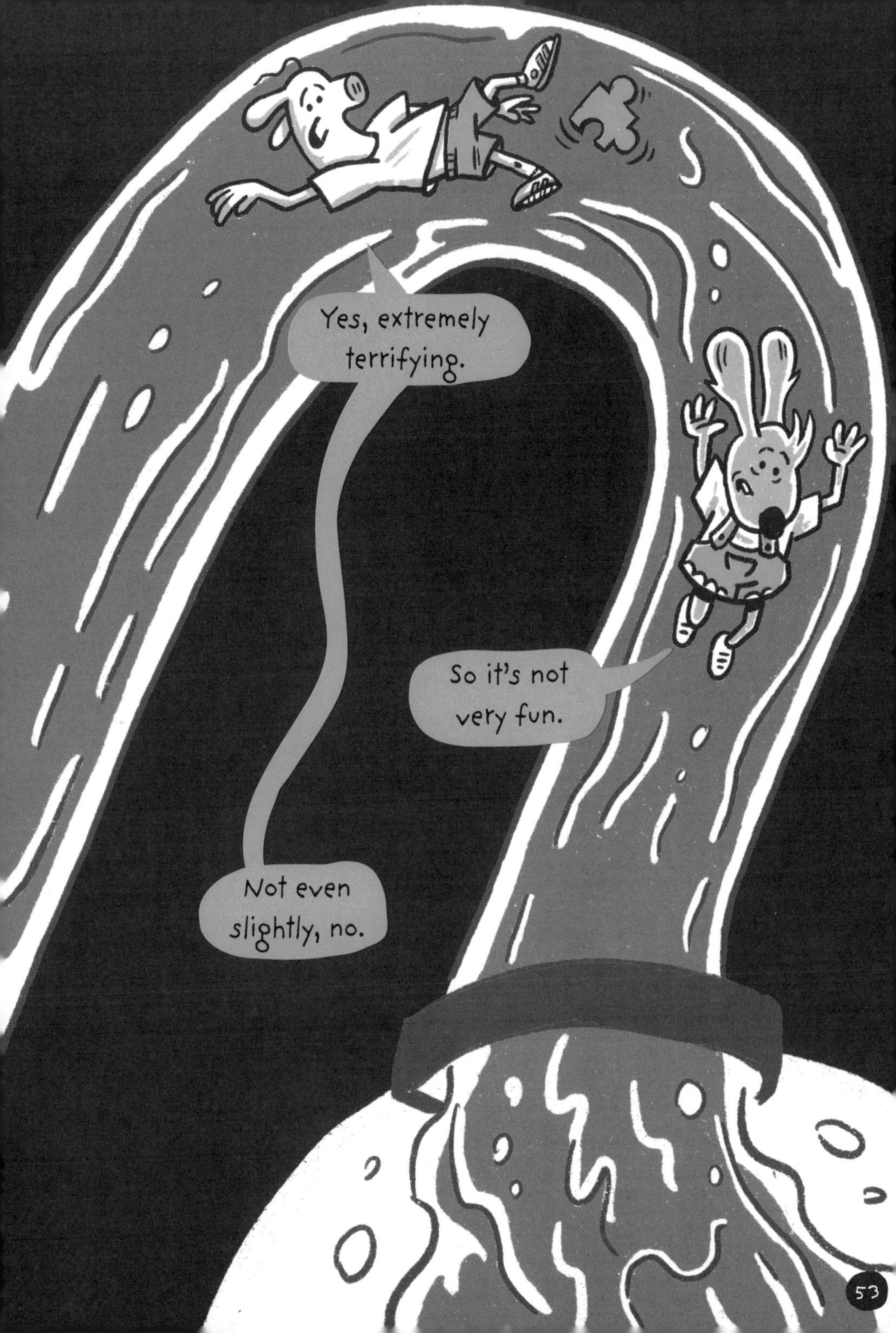
Yes, extremely terrifying.
So it's not very fun.
Not even slightly, no.

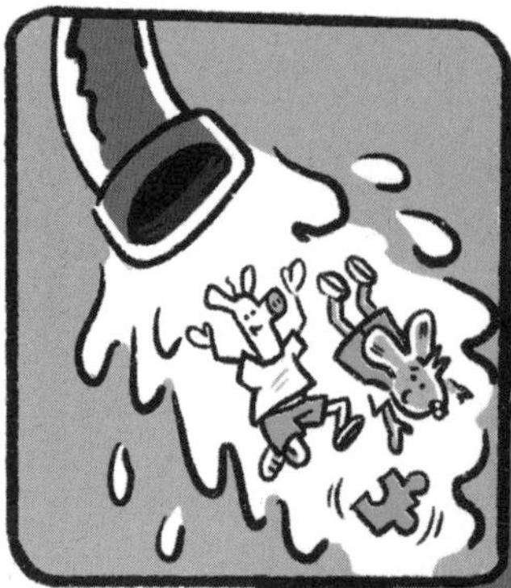

Suddenly, they found themselves caught in a net.

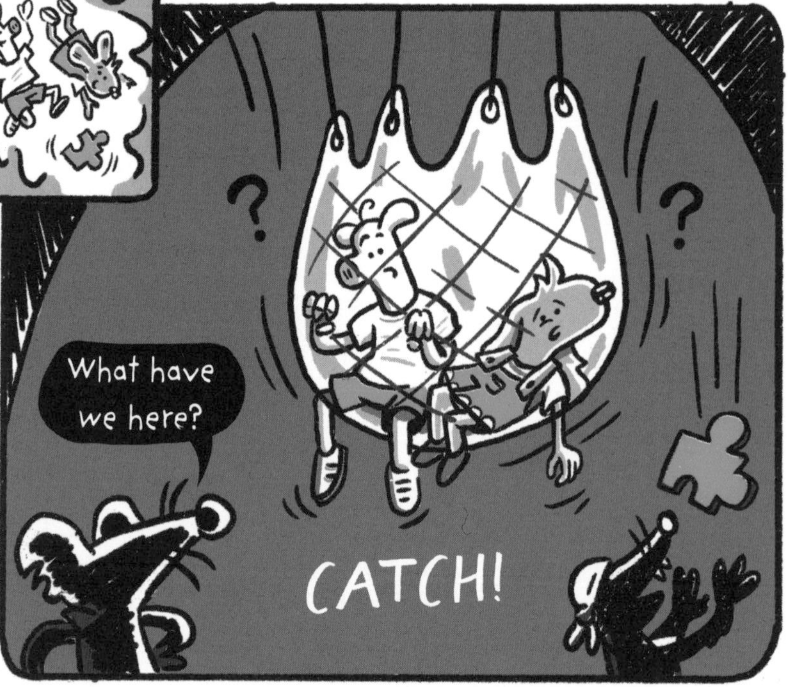

?
?
What have we here?
CATCH!

Then they were dragged aboard a ship.
"Henri!" whispered Gustav. "This is a pie dish!"

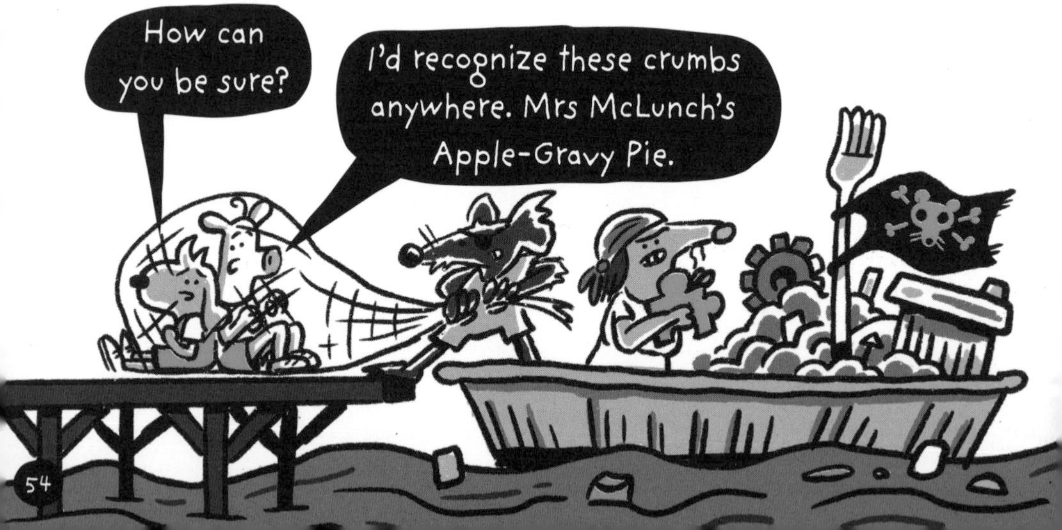

How can you be sure?
I'd recognize these crumbs anywhere. Mrs McLunch's Apple-Gravy Pie.

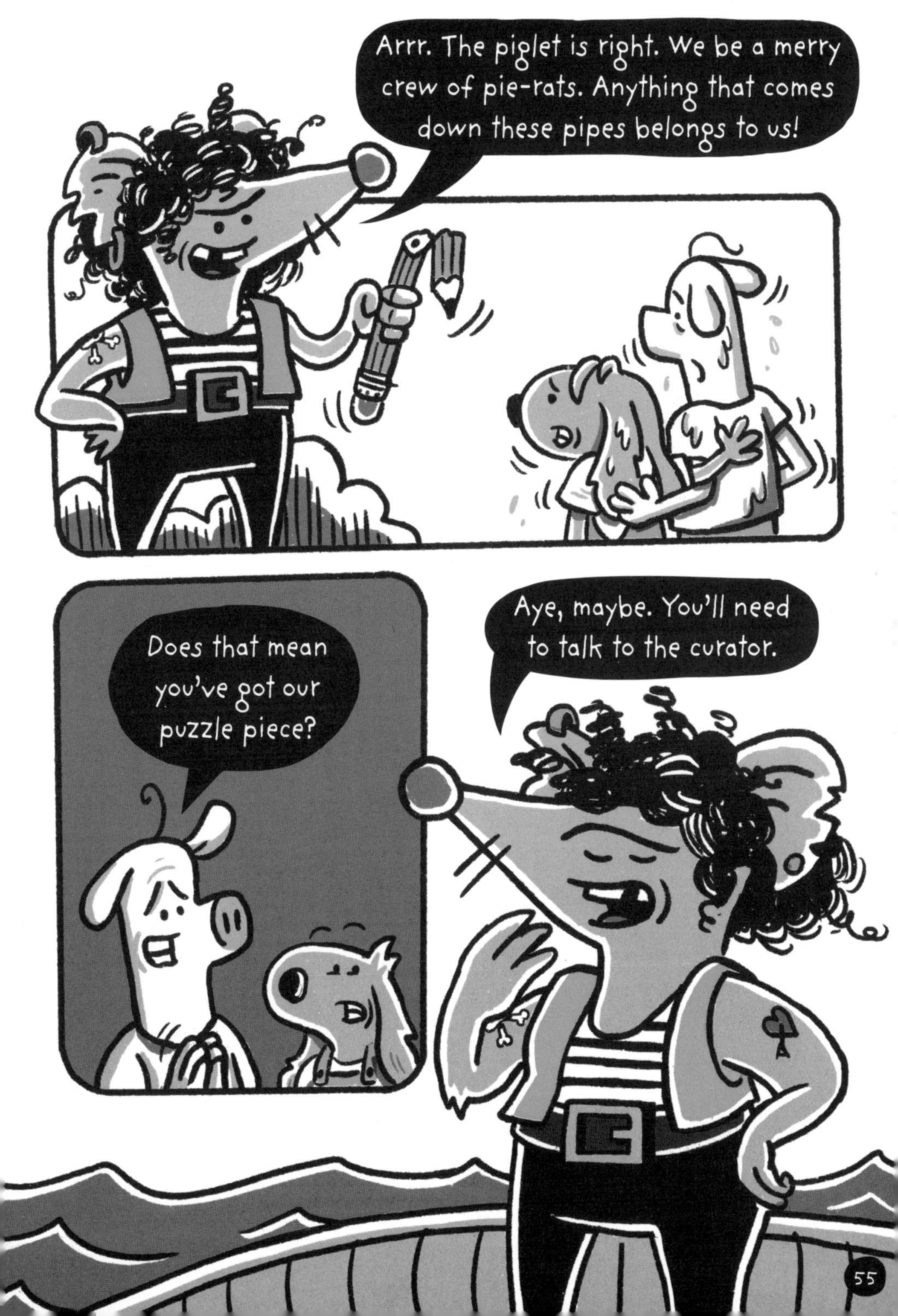
Arrr. The piglet is right. We be a merry crew of pie-rats. Anything that comes down these pipes belongs to us!
Does that mean you've got our puzzle piece?
Aye, maybe. You'll need to talk to the curator.

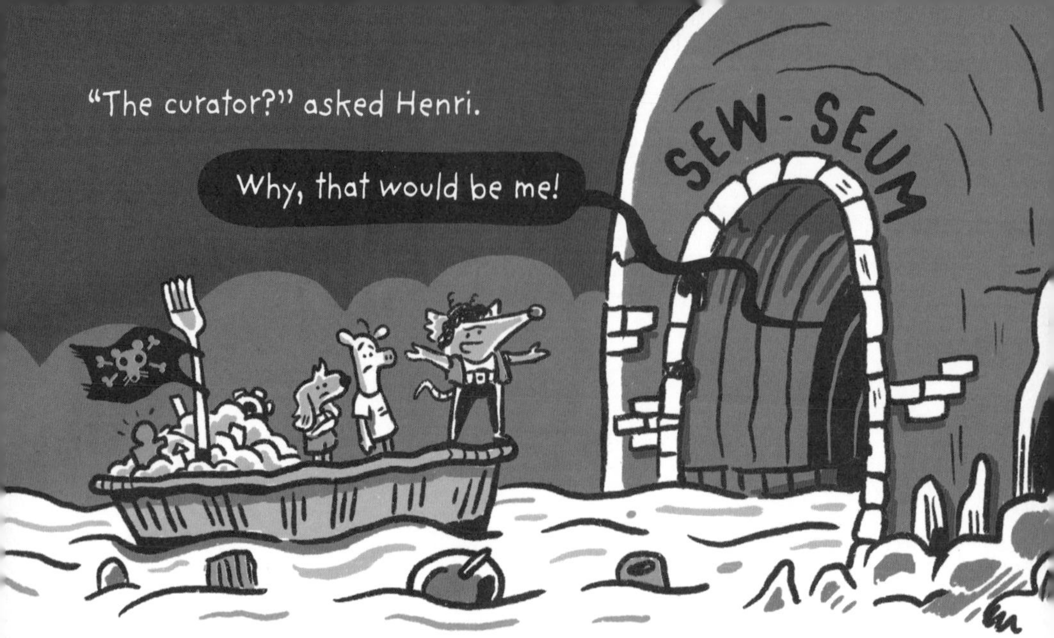
"The curator?" asked Henri.
Why, that would be me!
SEW-SEUM

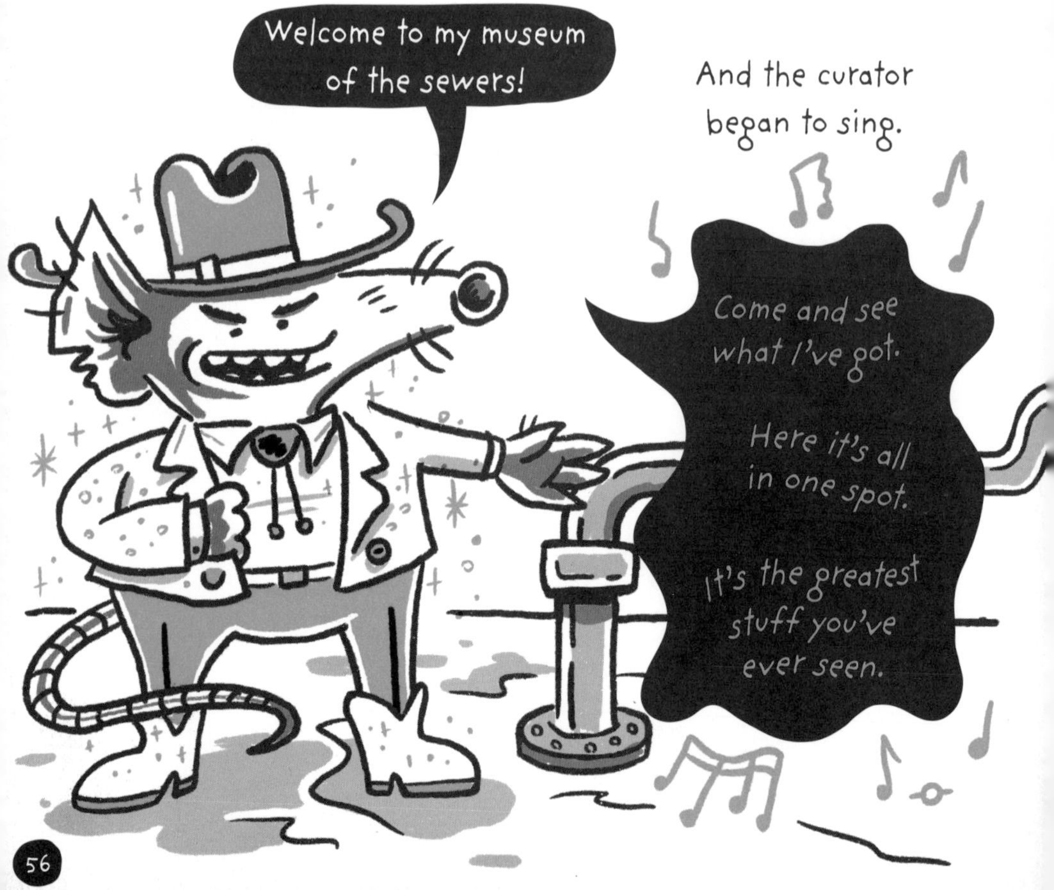
Welcome to my museum of the sewers!
And the curator began to sing.
Come and see what I've got.
Here it's all in one spot.
It's the greatest stuff you've ever seen.

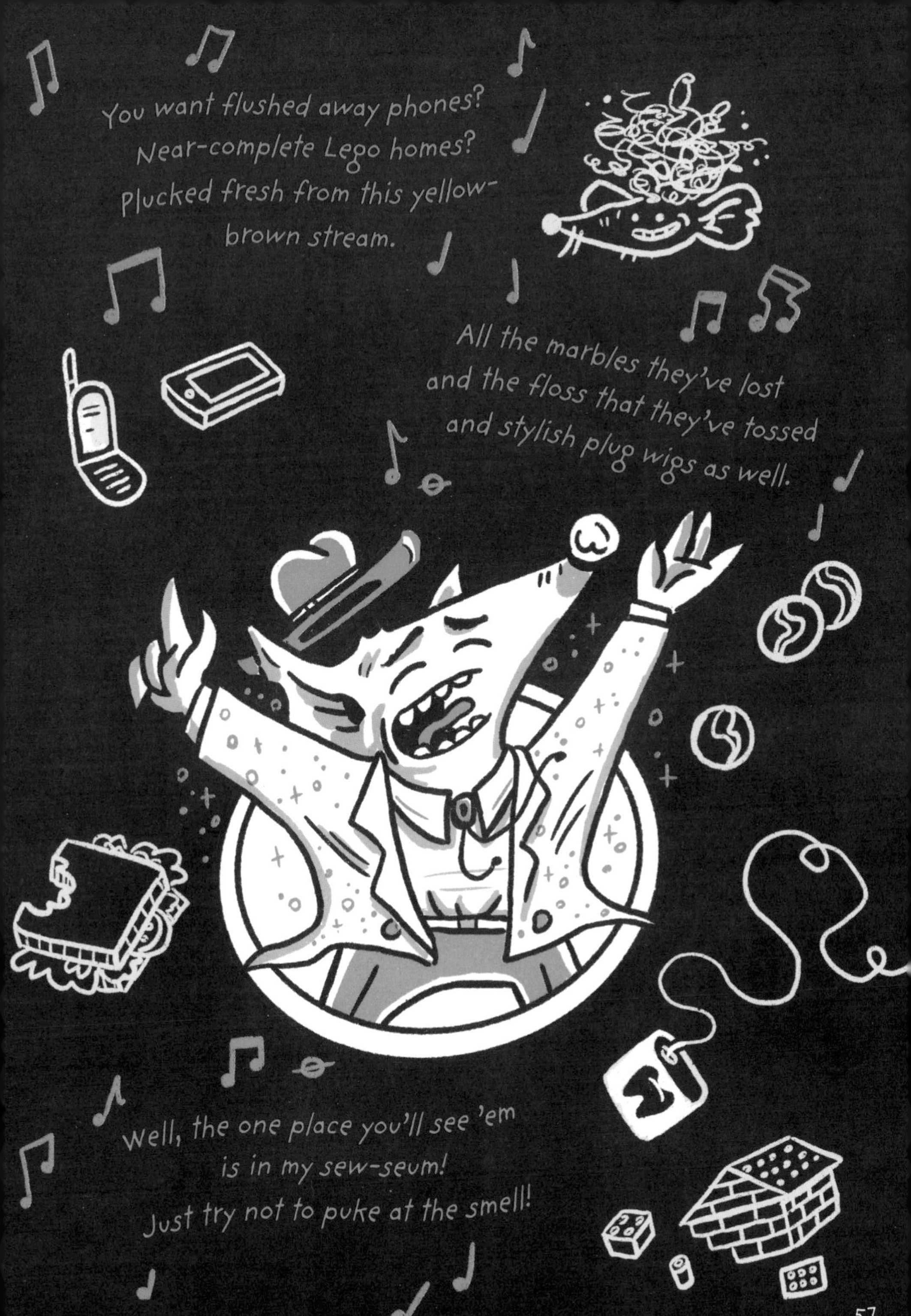
You want flushed away phones?
Near-complete Lego homes?
Plucked fresh from this yellow-
brown stream.
All the marbles they've lost
and the floss that they've tossed
and stylish plug wigs as well.
Well, the one place you'll see 'em
is in my sew-seum!
Just try not to puke at the smell!

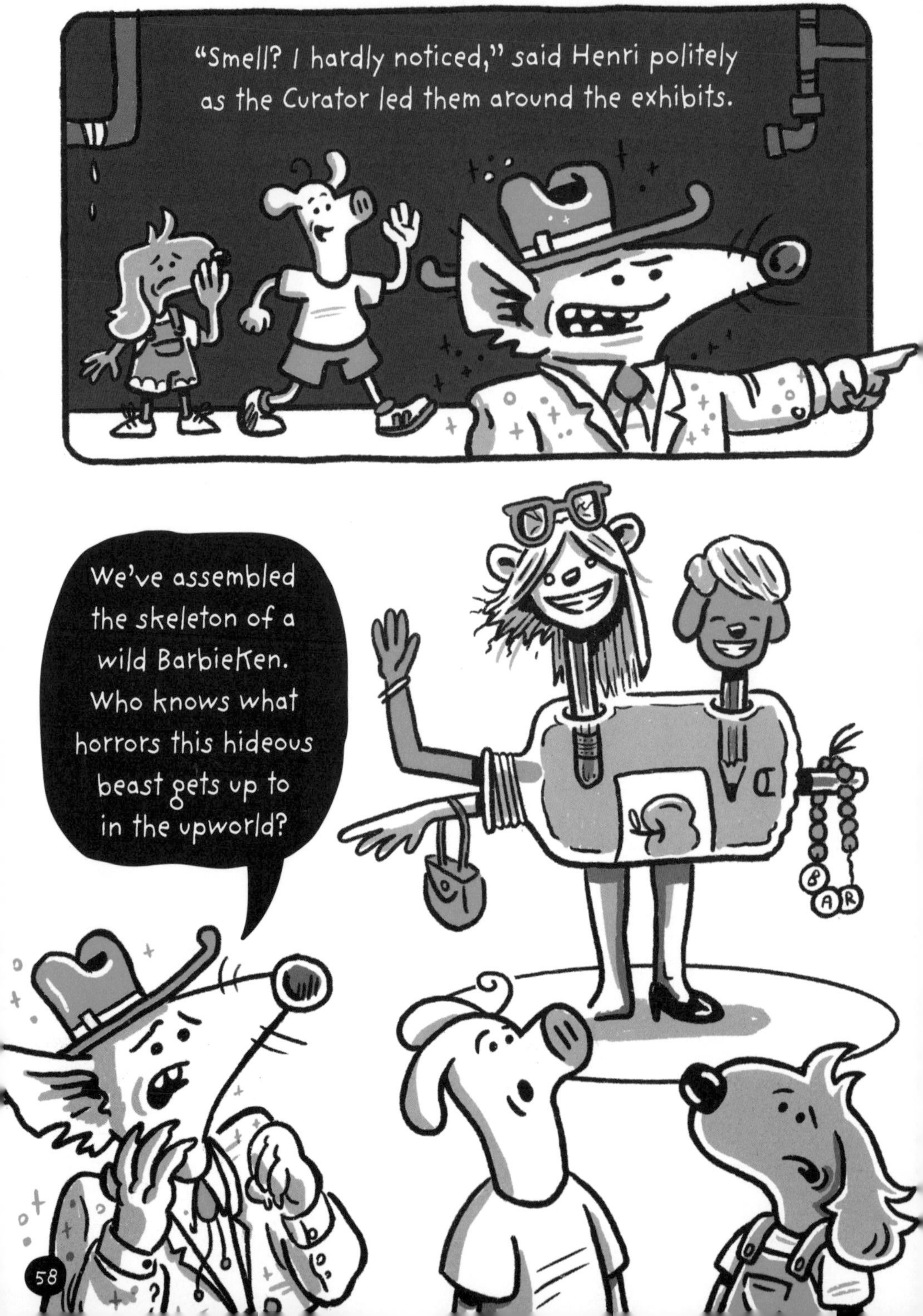
"Smell? I hardly noticed," said Henri politely as the Curator led them around the exhibits.
We've assembled the skeleton of a wild BarbieKen. Who knows what horrors this hideous beast gets up to in the upworld?

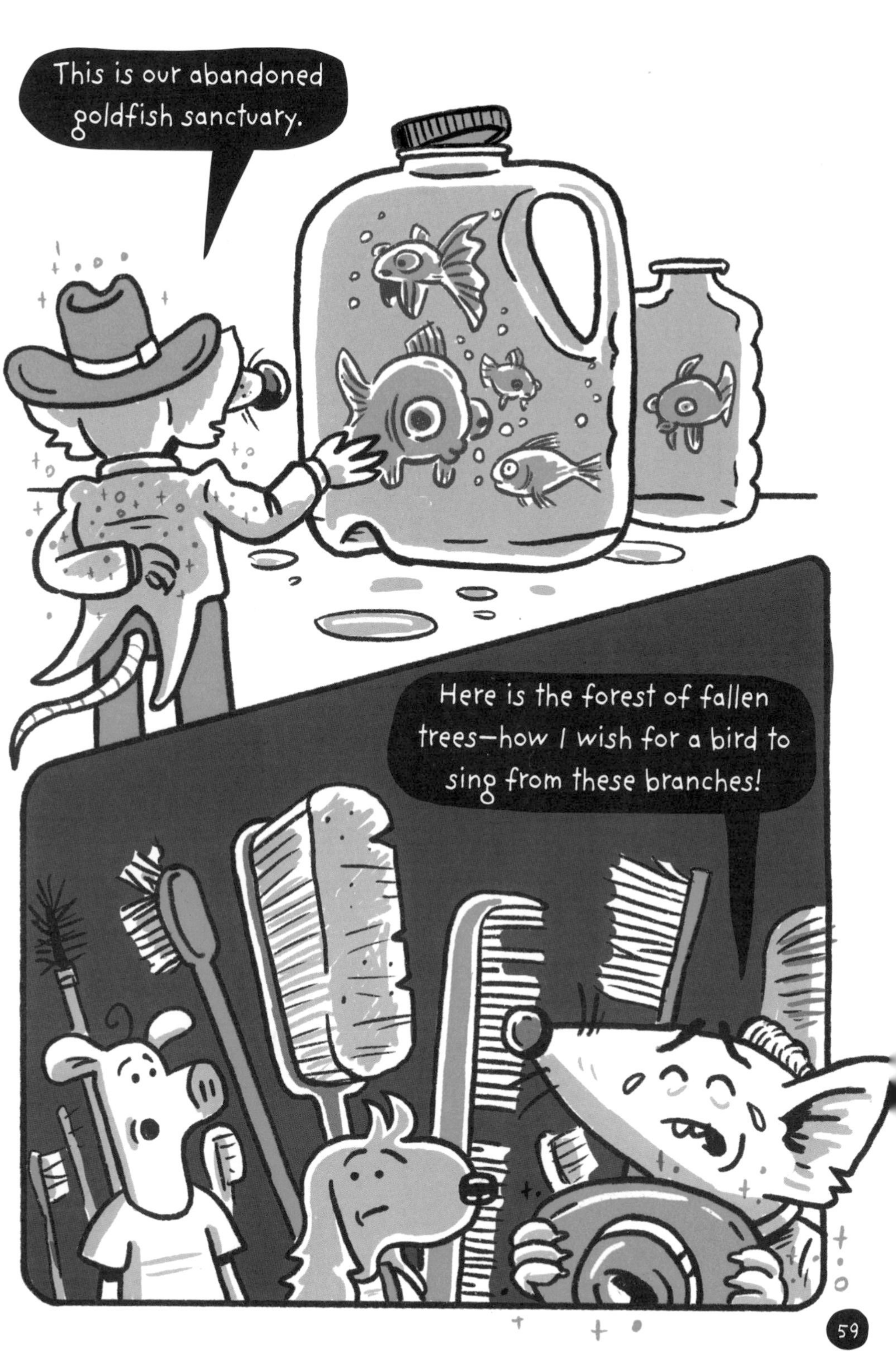
This is our abandoned goldfish sanctuary.
Here is the forest of fallen trees—how I wish for a bird to sing from these branches!

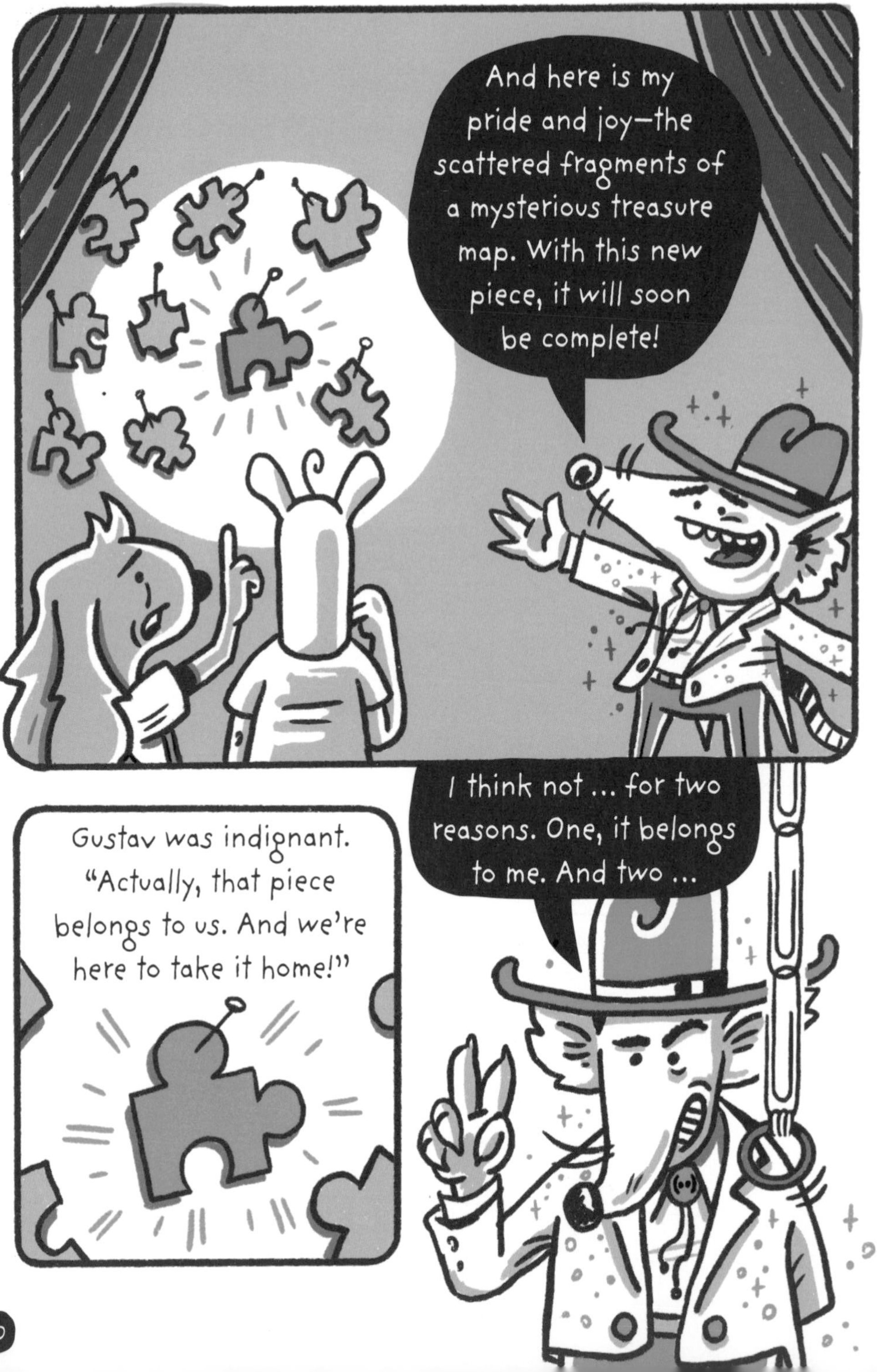
And here is my pride and joy—the scattered fragments of a mysterious treasure map. With this new piece, it will soon be complete!
Gustav was indignant. "Actually, that piece belongs to us. And we're here to take it home!"
I think not ... for two reasons. One, it belongs to me. And two ...

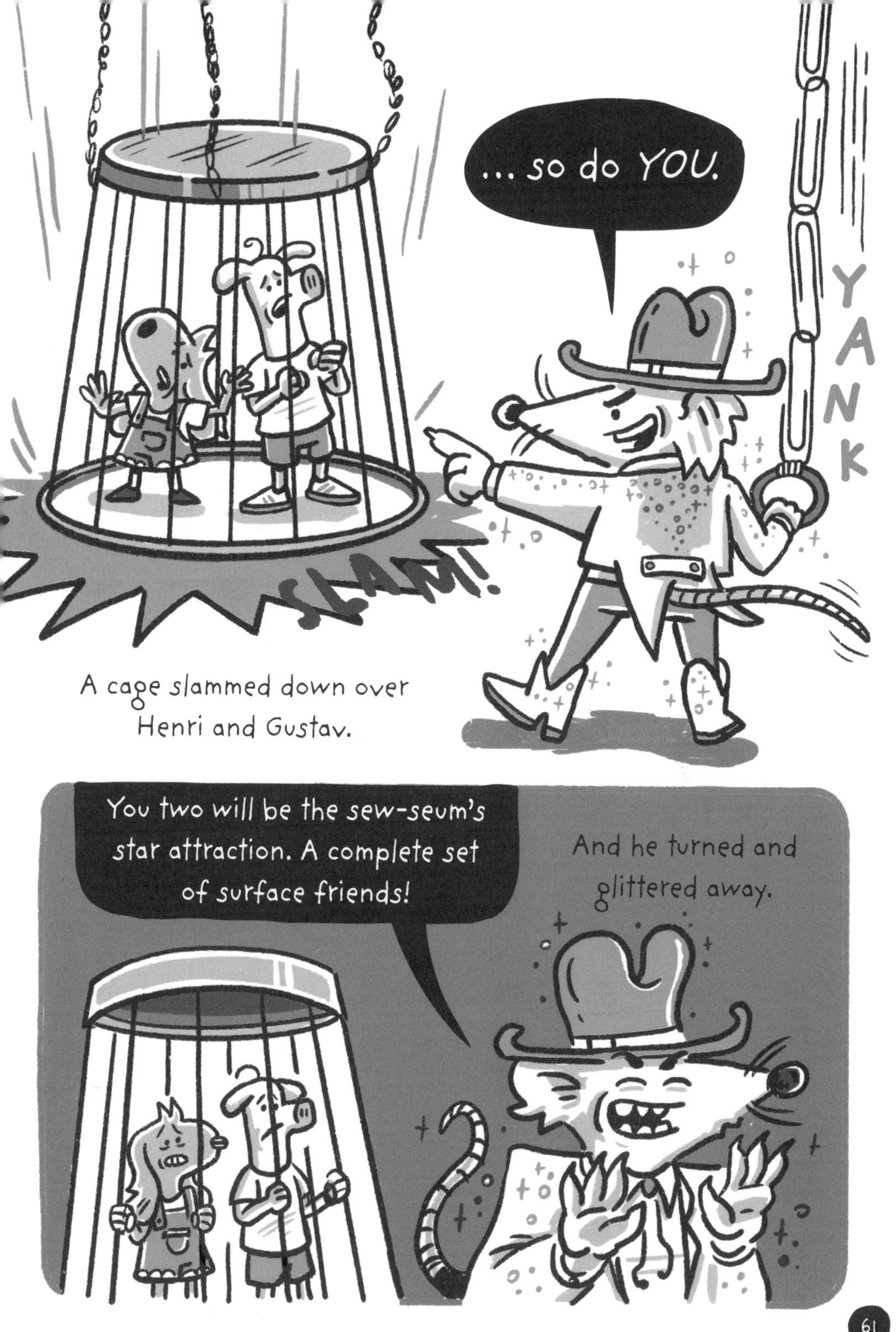
... so do YOU.
YANK
SLAM!
A cage slammed down over Henri and Gustav.
You two will be the sew-seum's star attraction. A complete set of surface friends!
And he turned and glittered away.

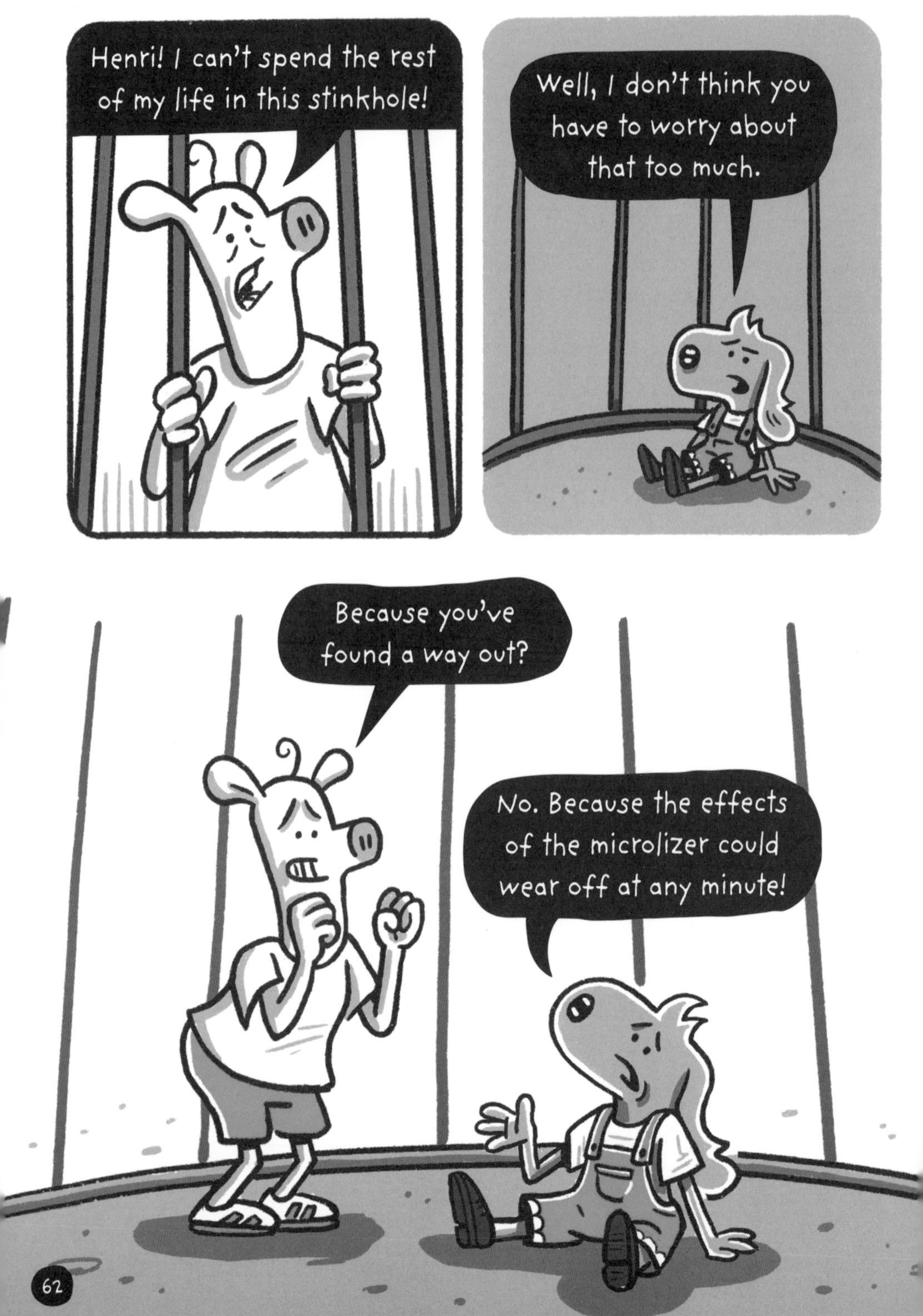
Henri! I can't spend the rest of my life in this stinkhole!
Well, I don't think you have to worry about that too much.
Because you've found a way out?
No. Because the effects of the microlizer could wear off at any minute!

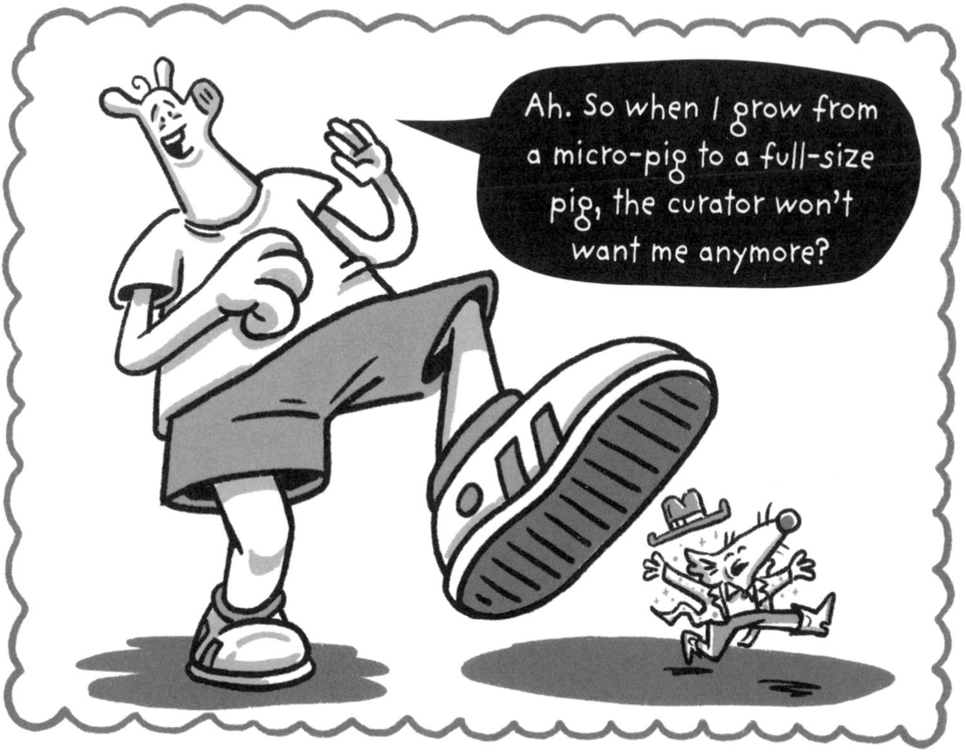
Ah. So when I grow from a micro-pig to a full-size pig, the curator won't want me anymore?

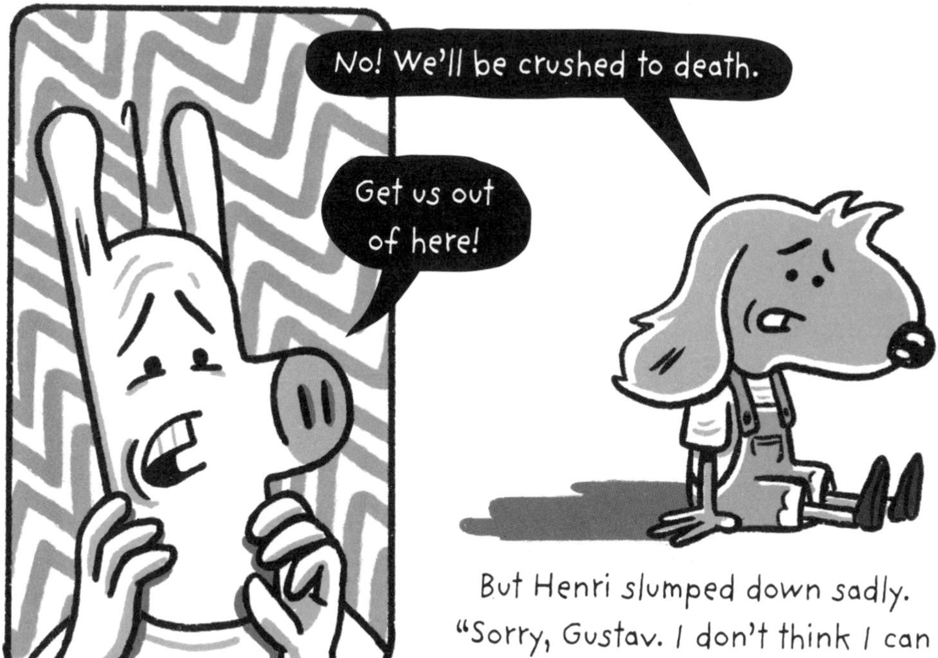
No! We'll be crushed to death.
Get us out of here!

But Henri slumped down sadly. "Sorry, Gustav. I don't think I can get us out of this one," she sighed.

The curator led a gawking crowd past their cage.

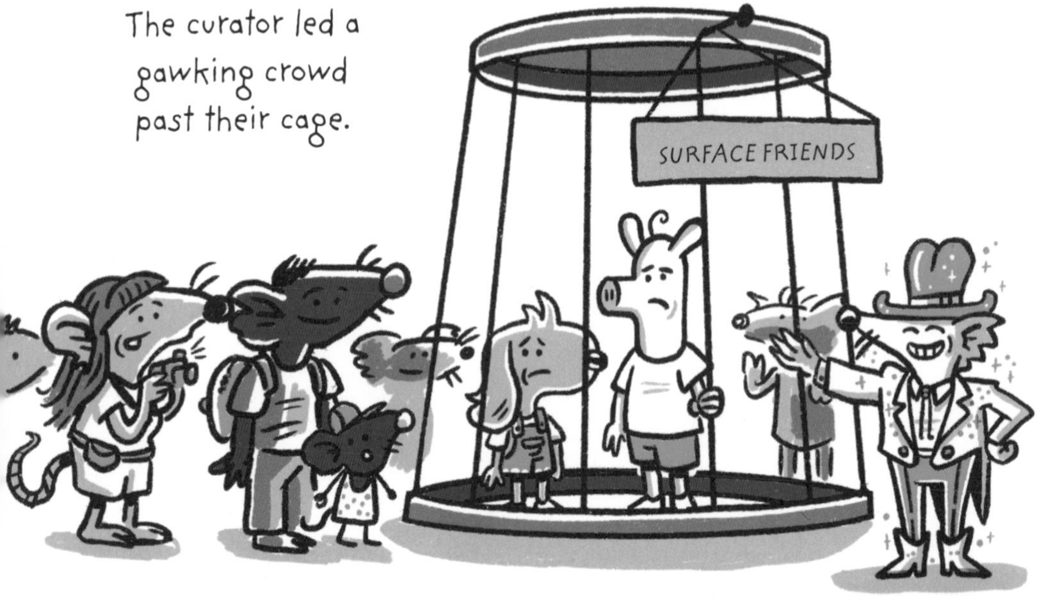
SURFACE FRIENDS

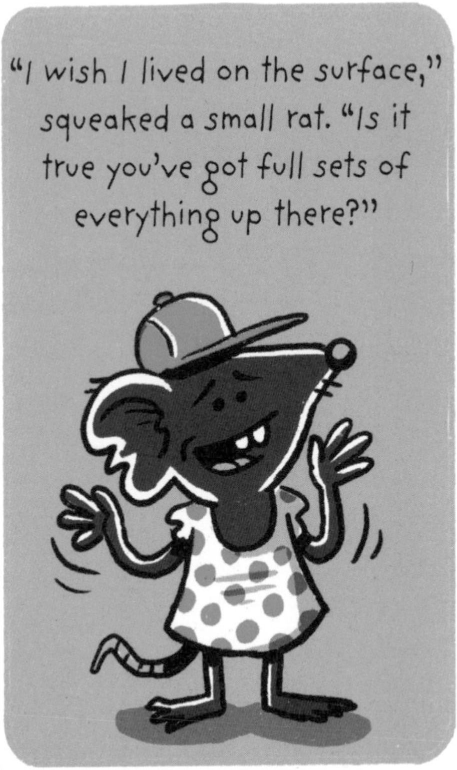
"I wish I lived on the surface," squeaked a small rat. "Is it true you've got full sets of everything up there?"

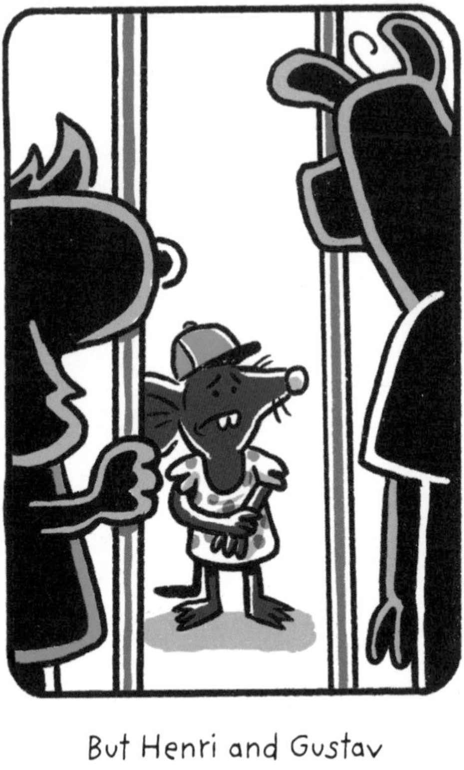

But Henri and Gustav were too glum to reply.

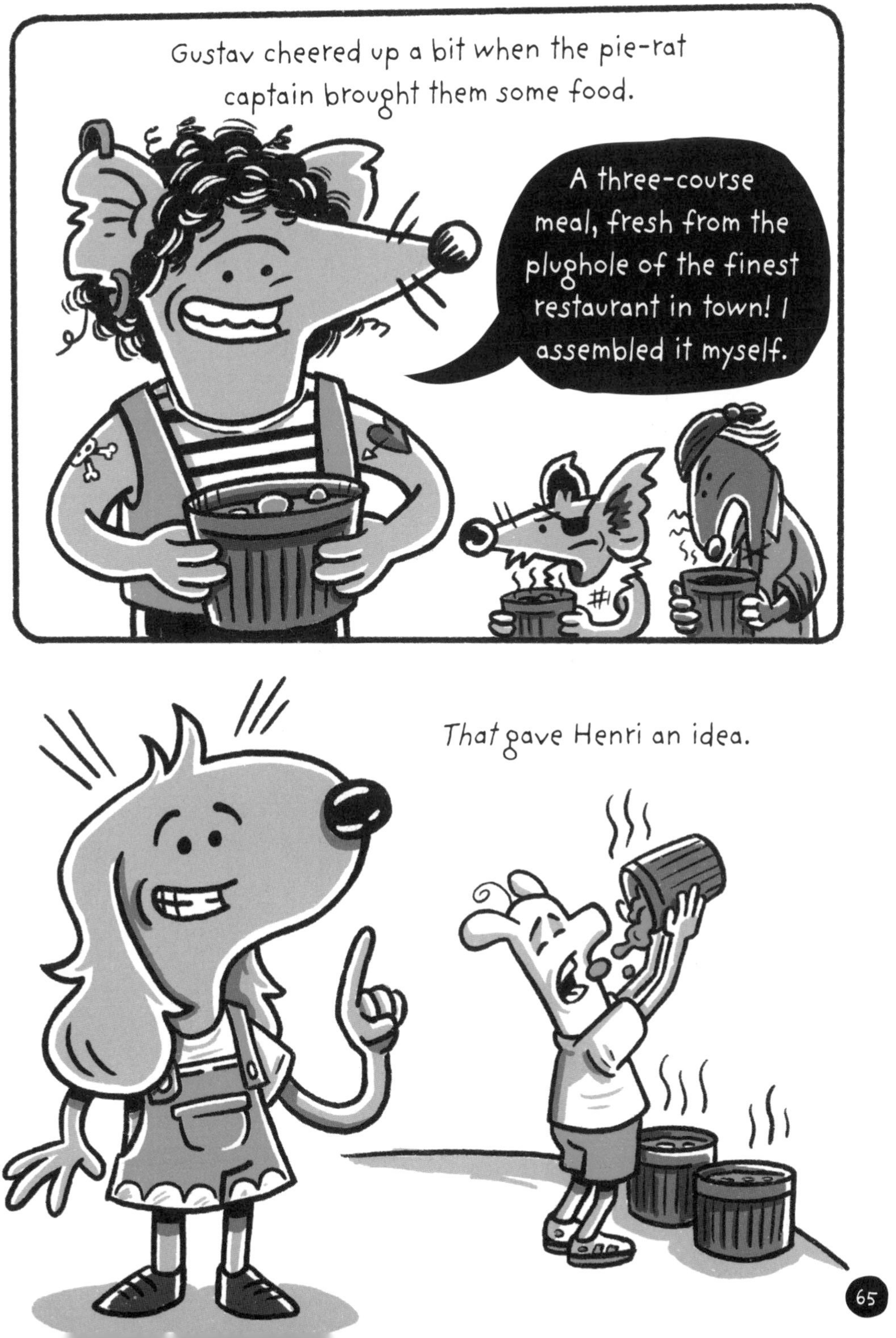
Gustav cheered up a bit when the pie-rat captain brought them some food.
A three-course meal, fresh from the plughole of the finest restaurant in town! I assembled it myself.
That gave Henri an idea.

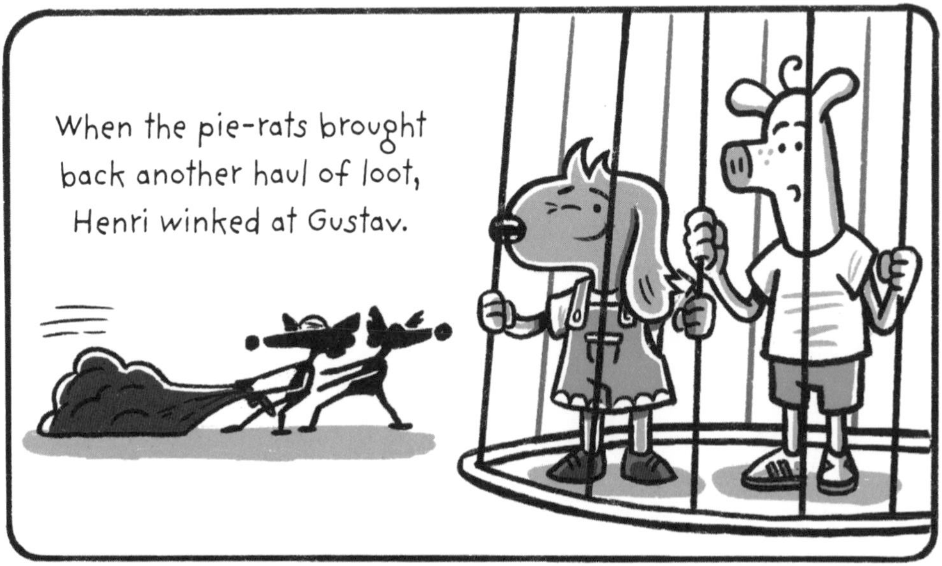
When the pie-rats brought back another haul of loot, Henri winked at Gustav.

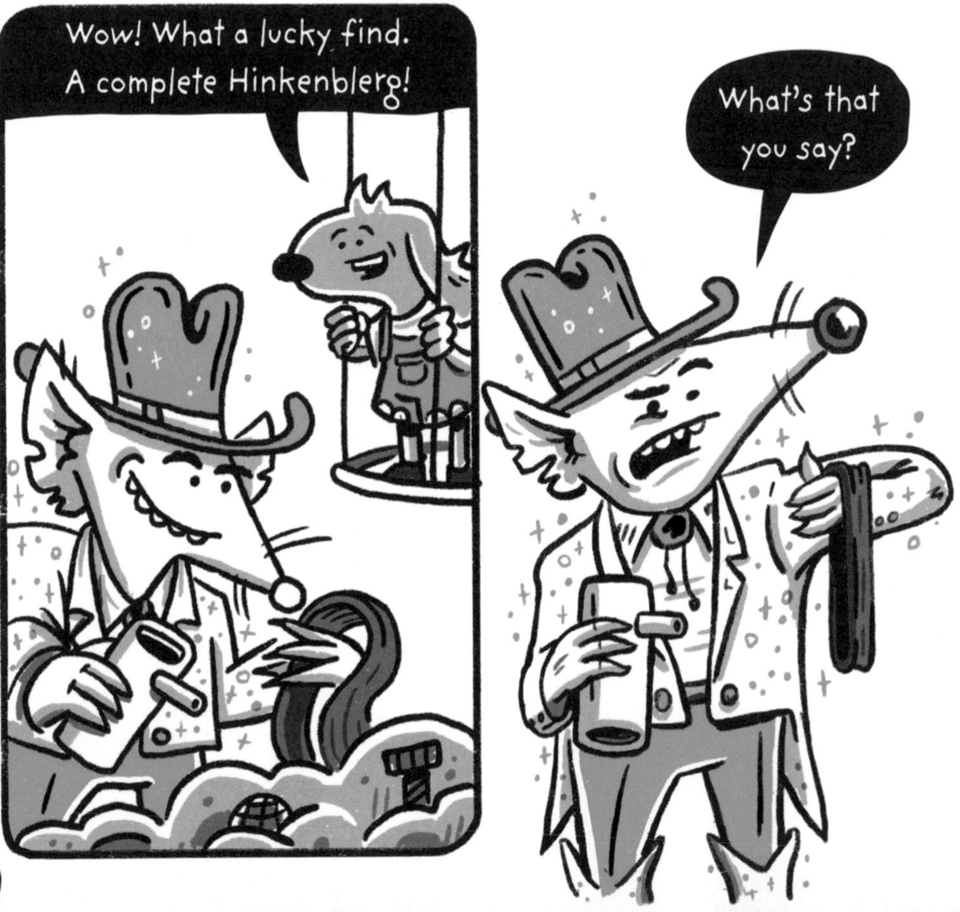
Wow! What a lucky find. A complete Hinkenblerg!
What's that you say?

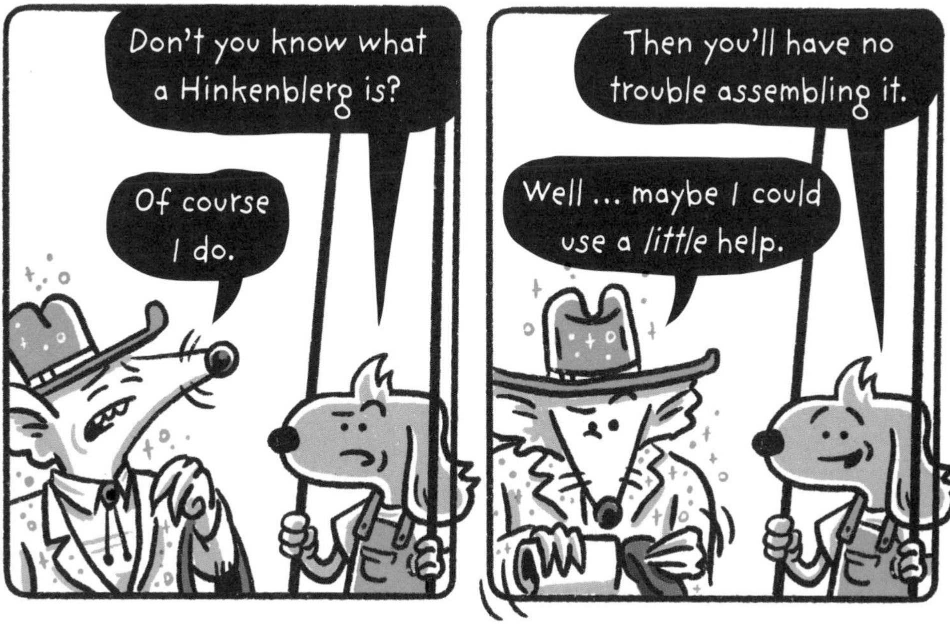
Don't you know what a Hinkenblerg is?
Of course I do.
Then you'll have no trouble assembling it.
Well ... maybe I could use a *little* help.

The curator let Henri out, and she got to work sorting through the pile of loot.

Soon, the Hinkenblerg began to take shape.

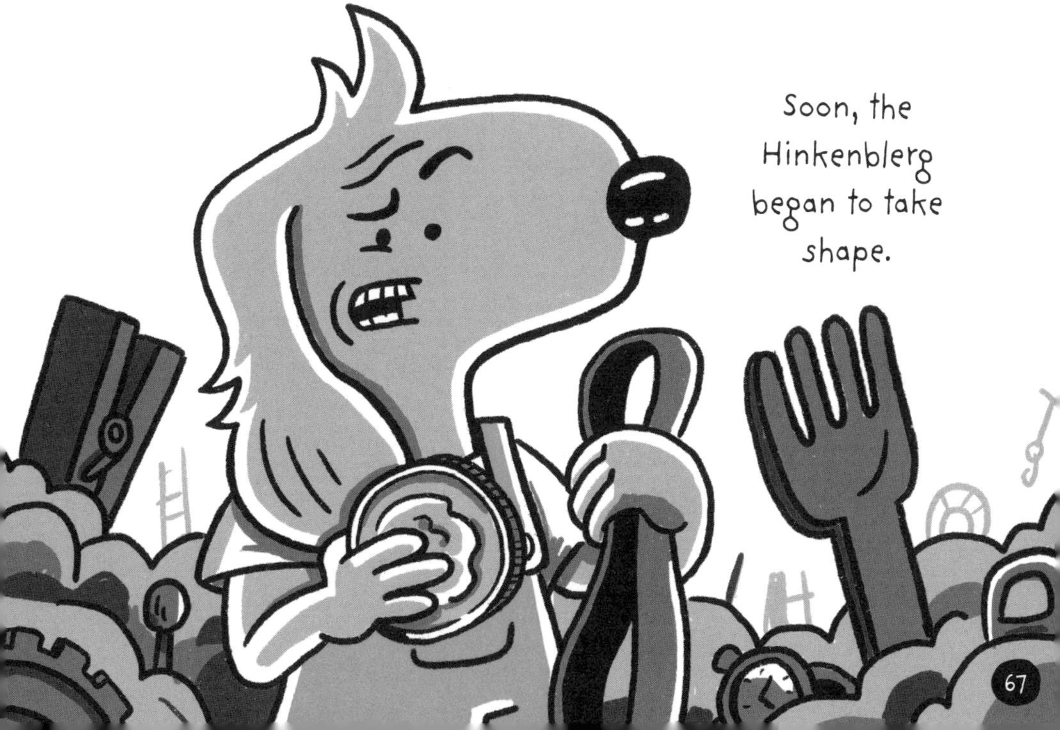

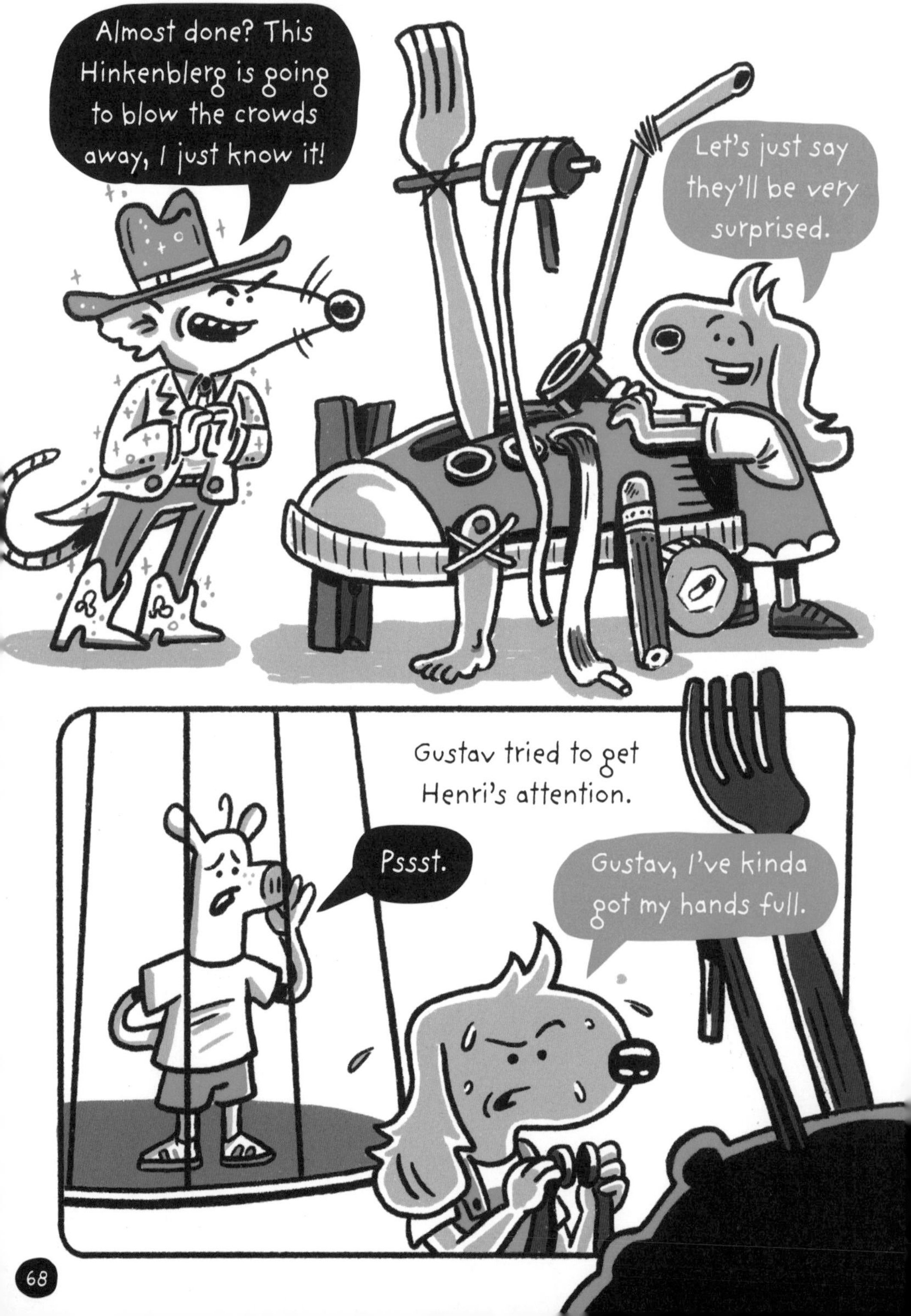
Almost done? This Hinkenblerg is going to blow the crowds away, I just know it!
Let's just say they'll be very surprised.
Gustav tried to get Henri's attention.
Pssst.
Gustav, I've kinda got my hands full.

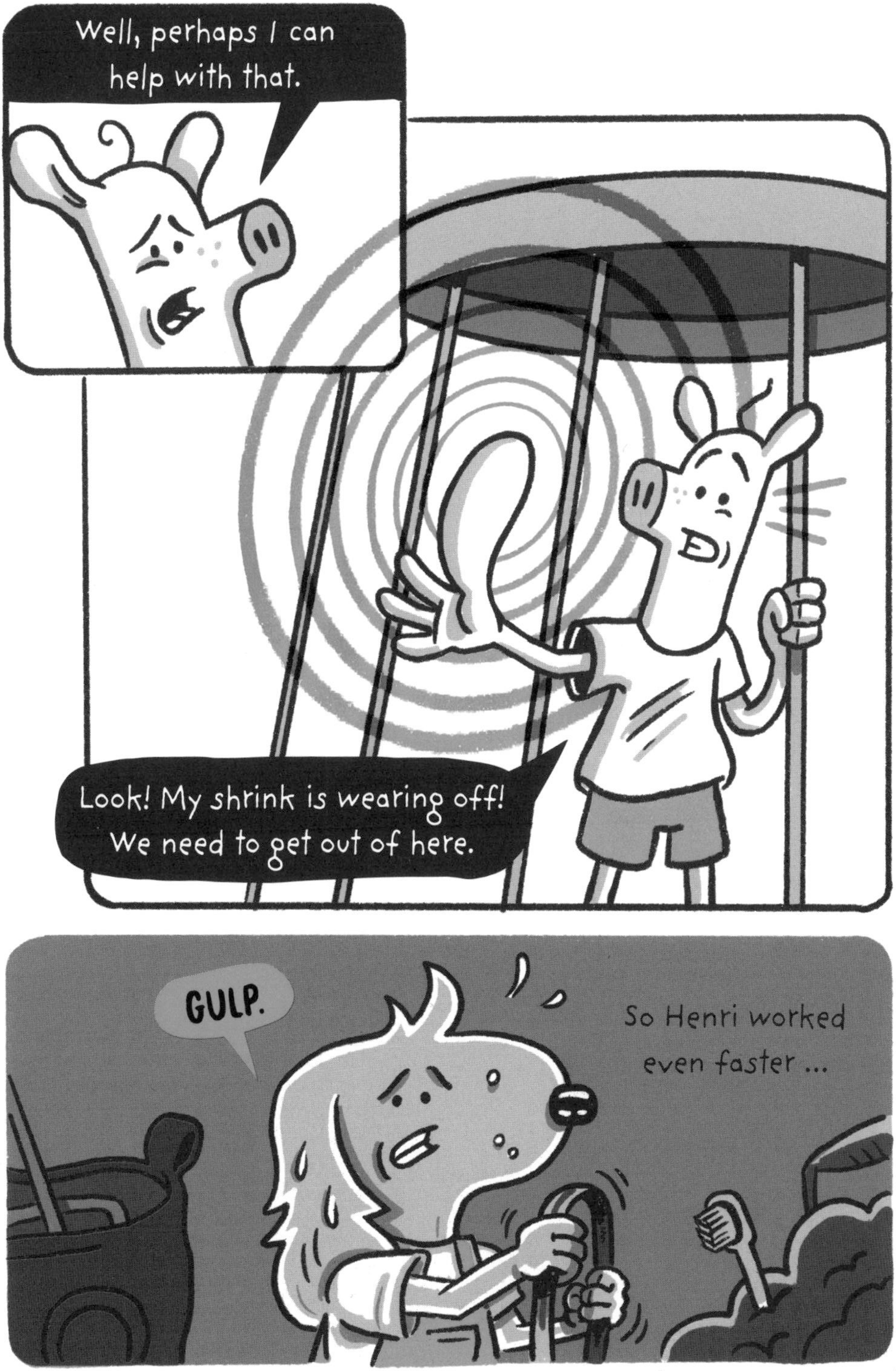
Well, perhaps I can help with that.
Look! My shrink is wearing off! We need to get out of here.
GULP.
So Henri worked even faster ...

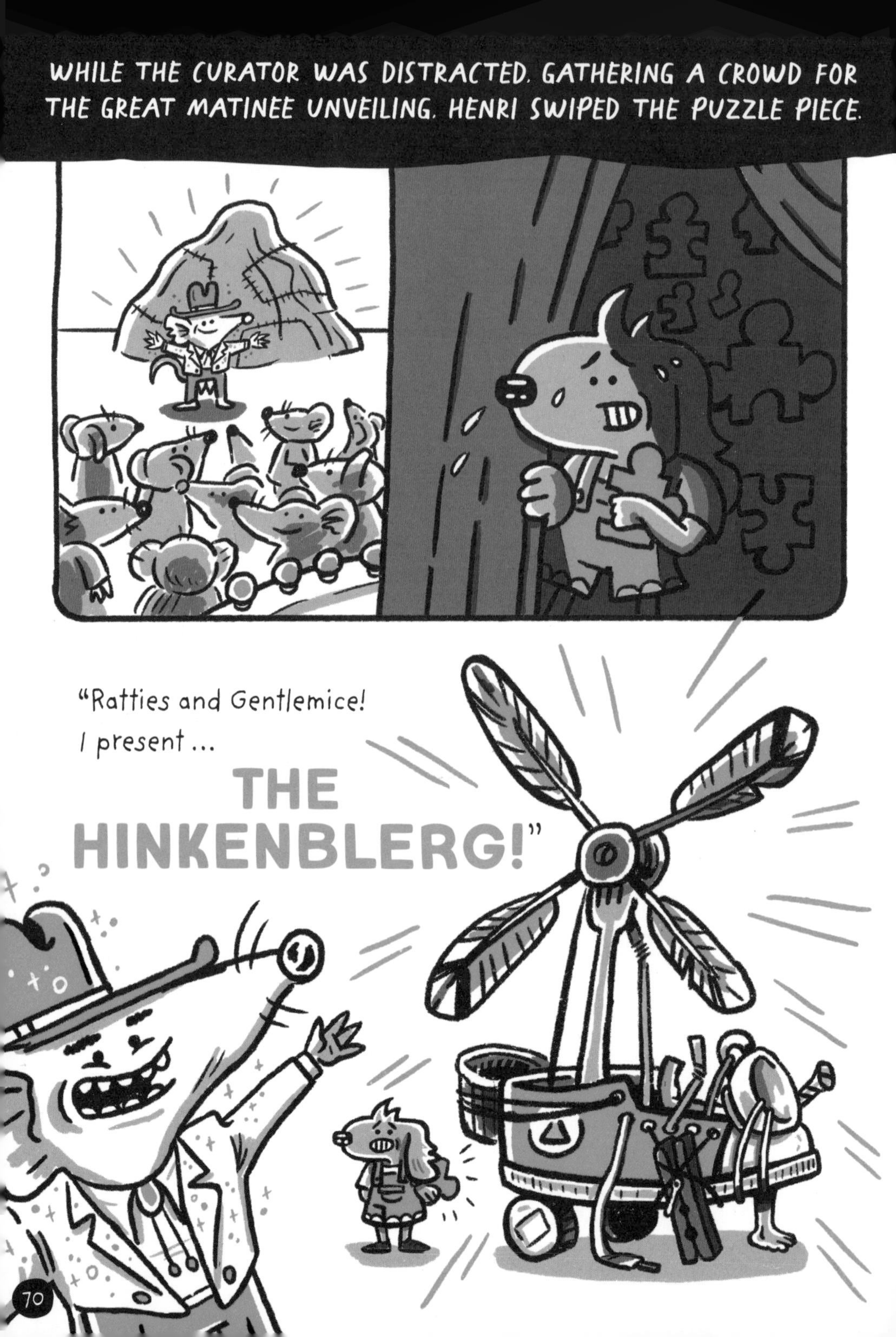
WHILE THE CURATOR WAS DISTRACTED, GATHERING A CROWD FOR THE GREAT MATINEE UNVEILING, HENRI SWIPED THE PUZZLE PIECE.
"Ratties and Gentlemice!
I present ...
THE HINKENBLERG!"

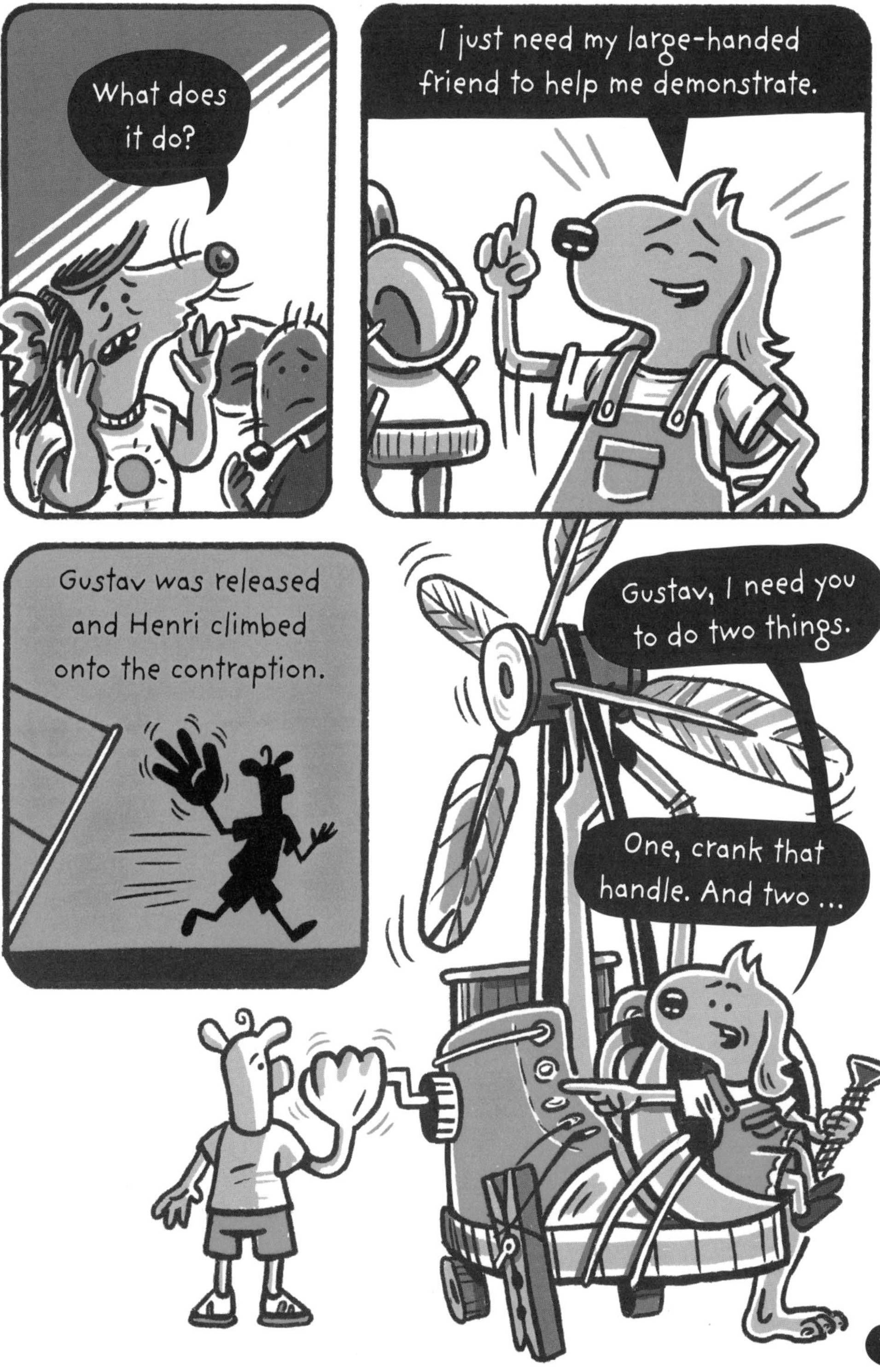
What does it do?
I just need my large-handed friend to help me demonstrate.
Gustav was released and Henri climbed onto the contraption.
Gustav, I need you to do two things.
One, crank that handle. And two ...

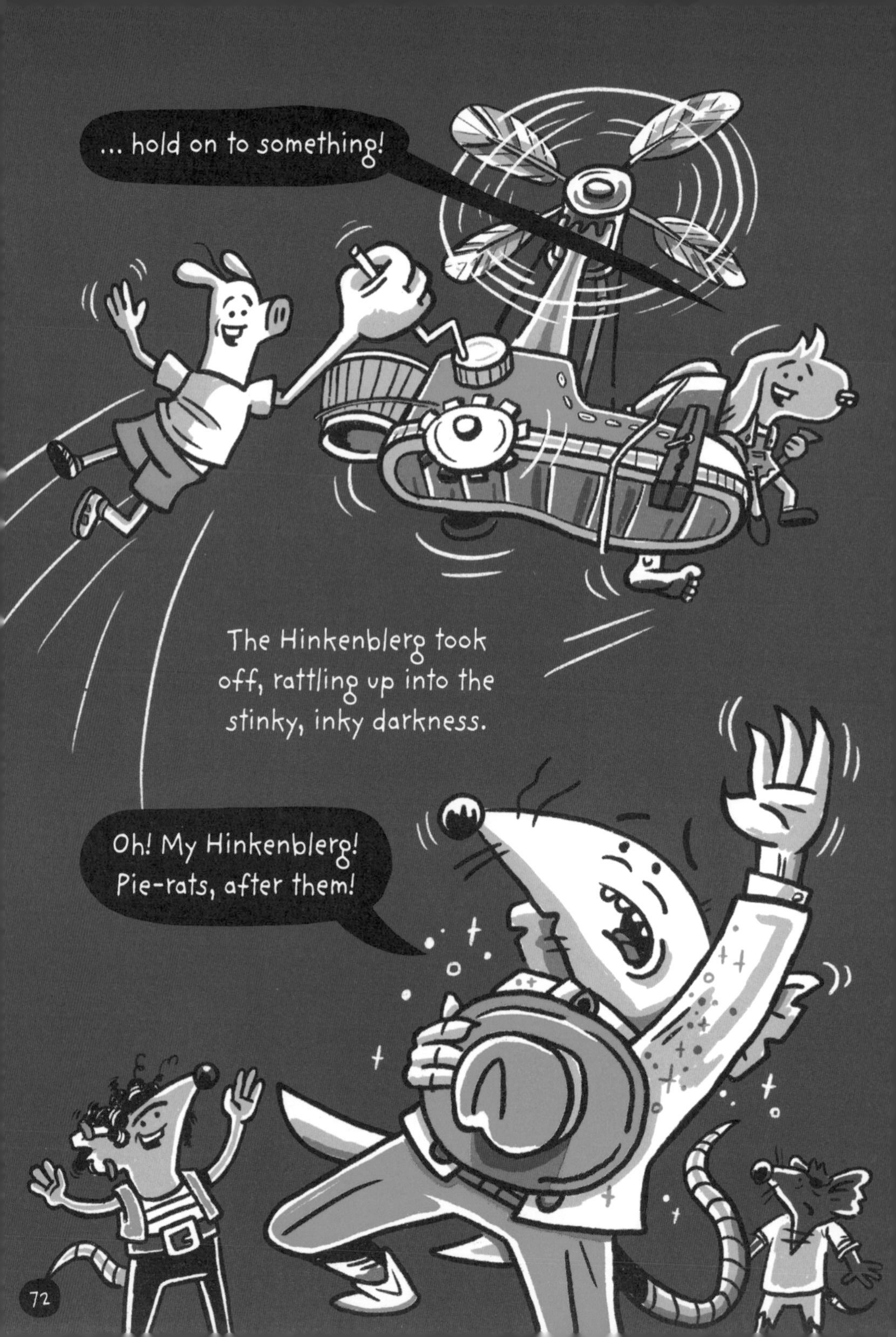
... hold on to something!
The Hinkenblerg took off, rattling up into the stinky, inky darkness.
Oh! My Hinkenblerg! Pie-rats, after them!

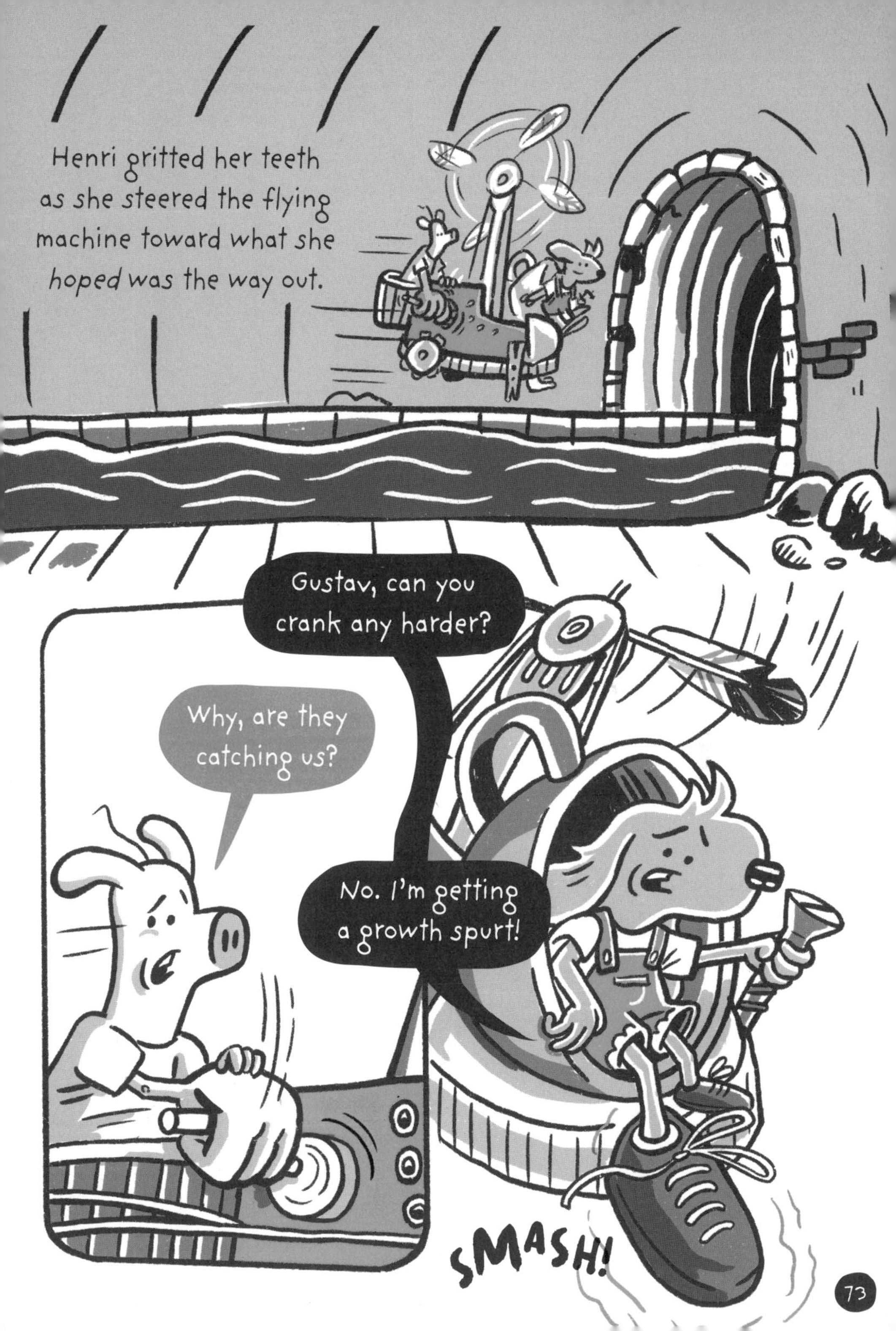
Henri gritted her teeth as she steered the flying machine toward what she *hoped* was the way out.
Gustav, can you crank any harder?
Why, are they catching us?
No. I'm getting a growth spurt!
SMASH!

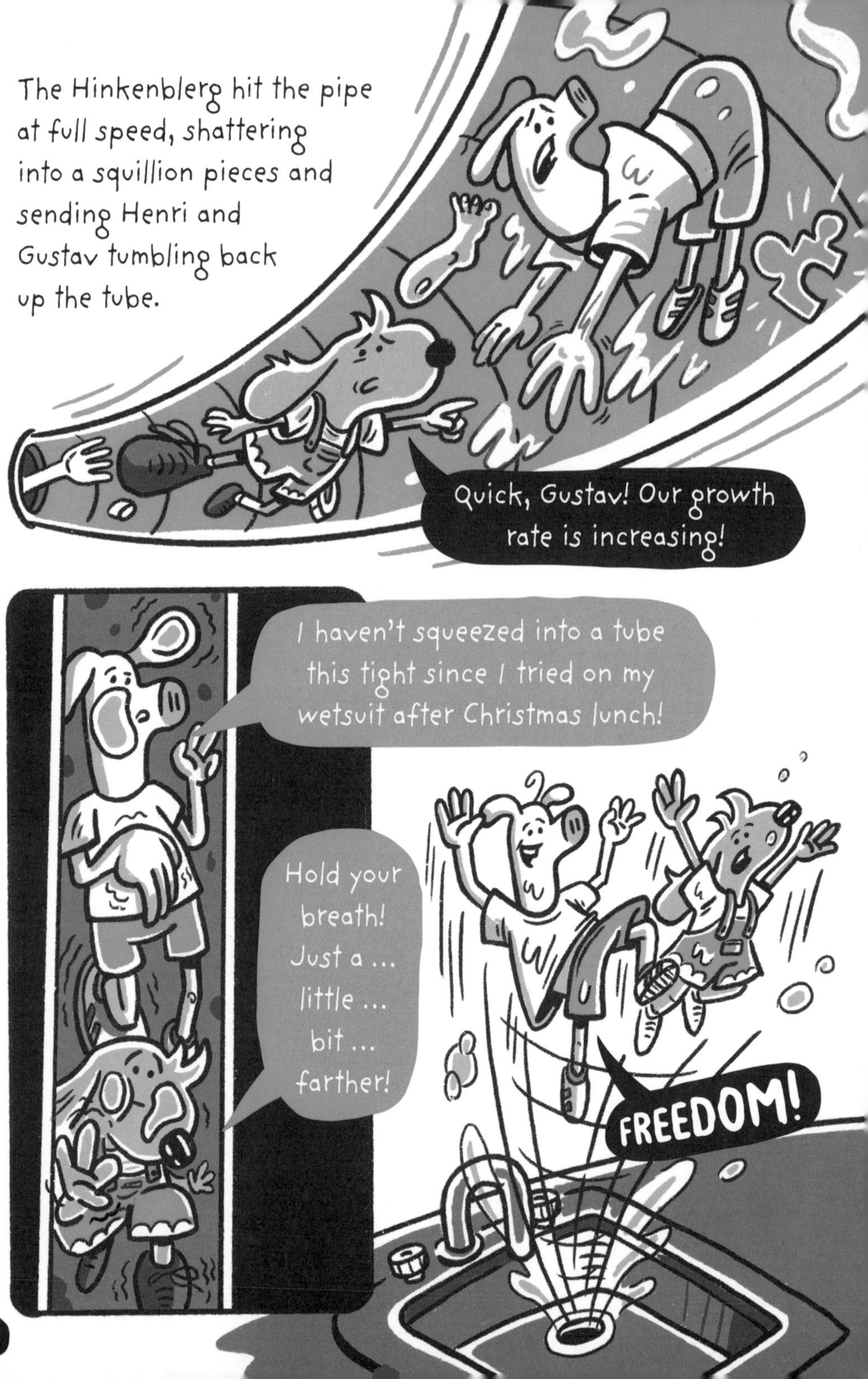
The Hinkenblerg hit the pipe at full speed, shattering into a squillion pieces and sending Henri and Gustav tumbling back up the tube.
Quick, Gustav! Our growth rate is increasing!
I haven't squeezed into a tube this tight since I tried on my wetsuit after Christmas lunch!
Hold your breath! Just a ... little ... bit ... farther!
FREEDOM!

Henri and Gustav sat panting on the kitchen floor.

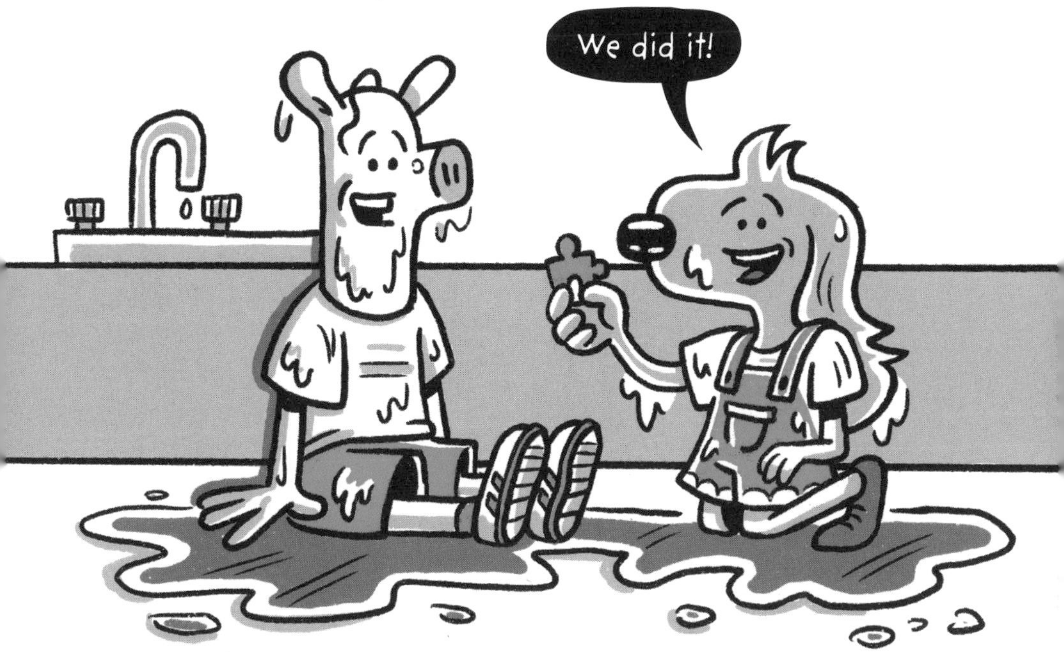
We did it!

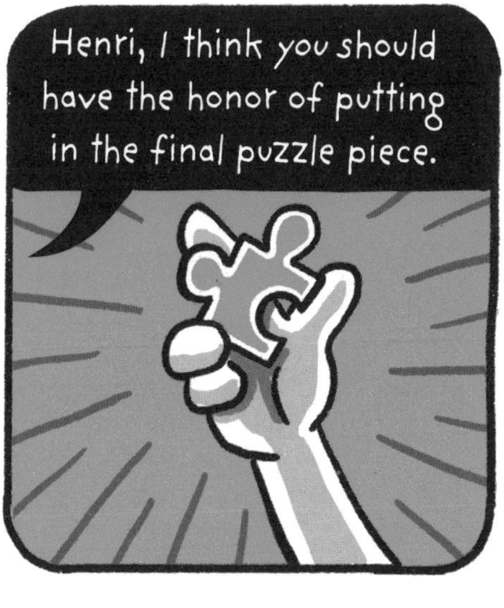
Henri, I think you should have the honor of putting in the final puzzle piece.

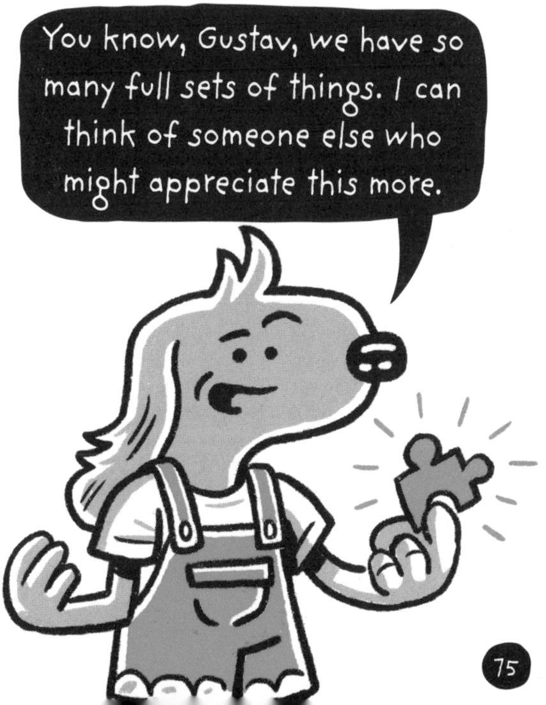
You know, Gustav, we have so many full sets of things. I can think of someone else who might appreciate this more.

But Henri had another idea.

It took a lot of flushing, but eventually the 10,000th puzzle piece disappeared down the drain.

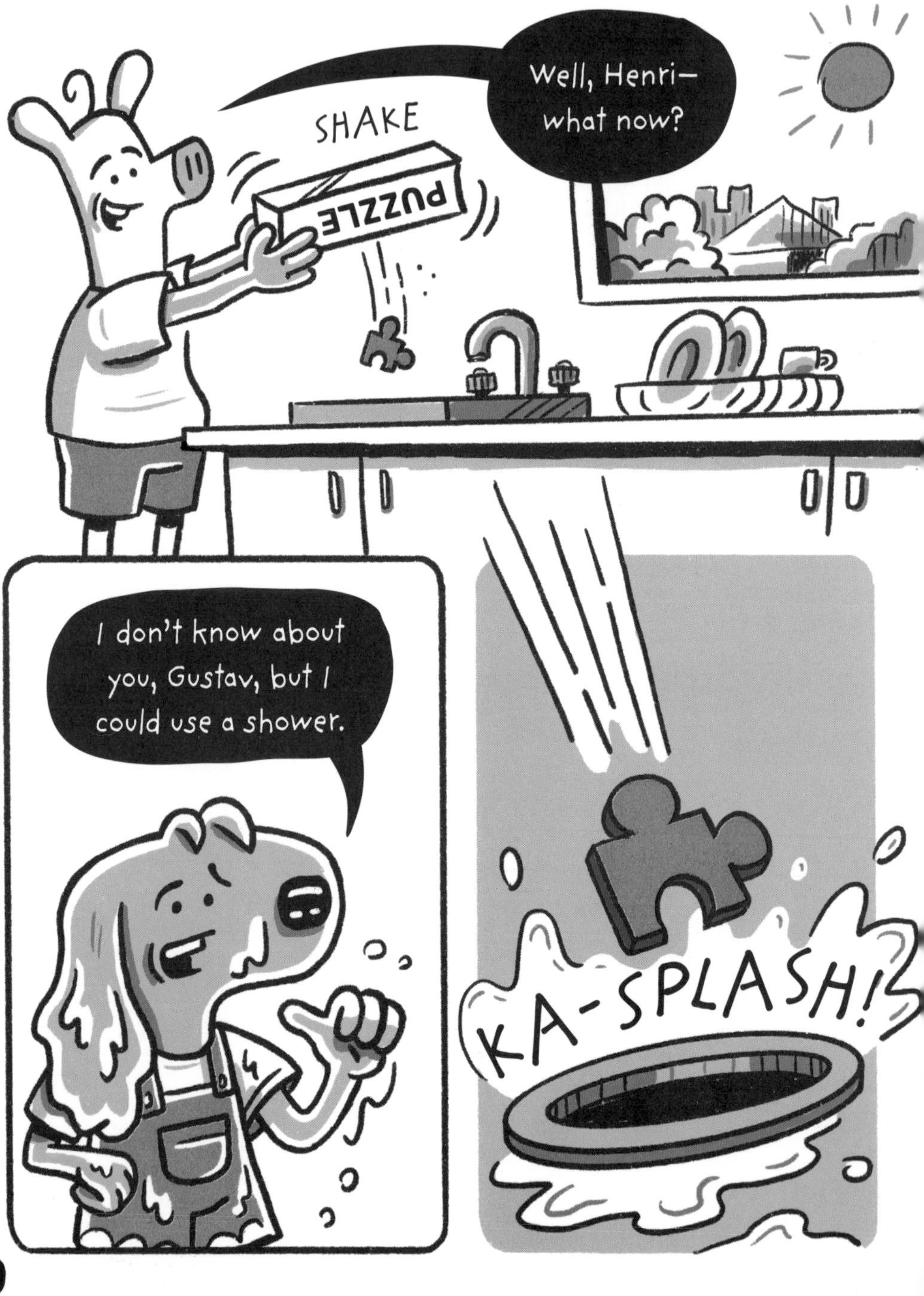
Well, Henri—what now?
SHAKE
PUZZLE
I don't know about you, Gustav, but I could use a shower.
KA-SPLASH!

SOME TIME LATER...

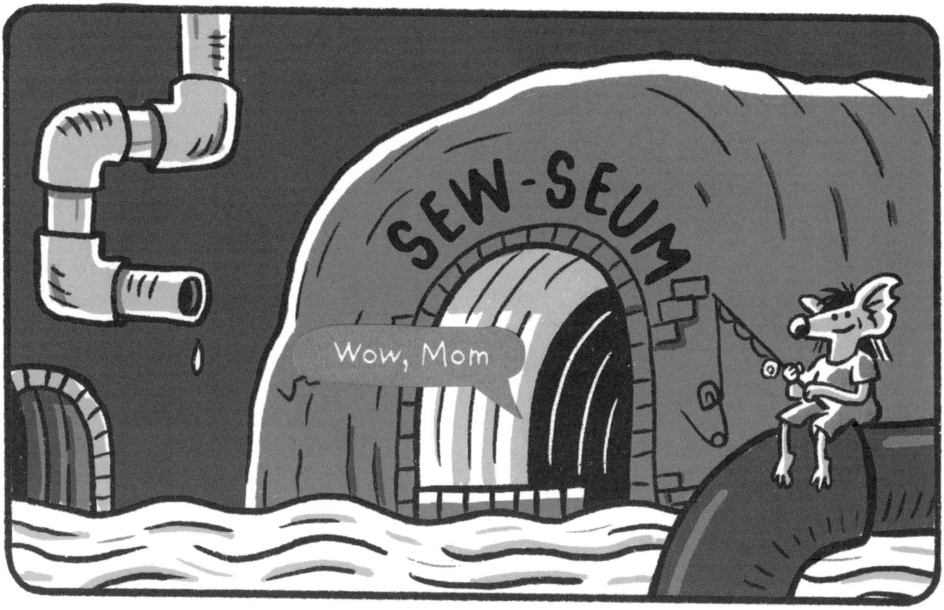
SEW-SEUM
Wow, Mom

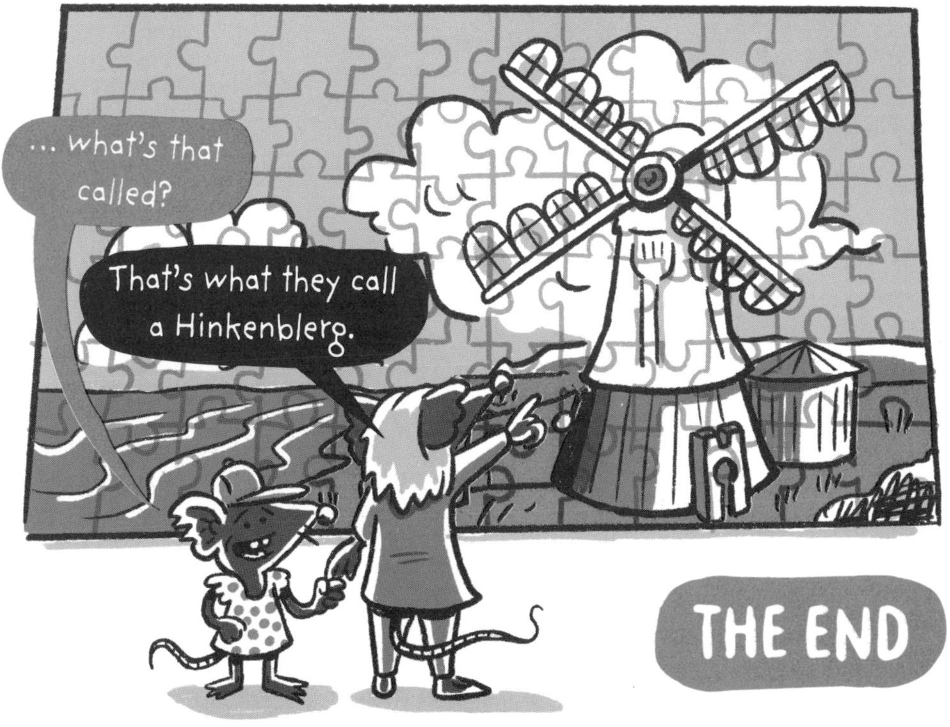
... what's that called?
That's what they call a Hinkenblerg.

THE END

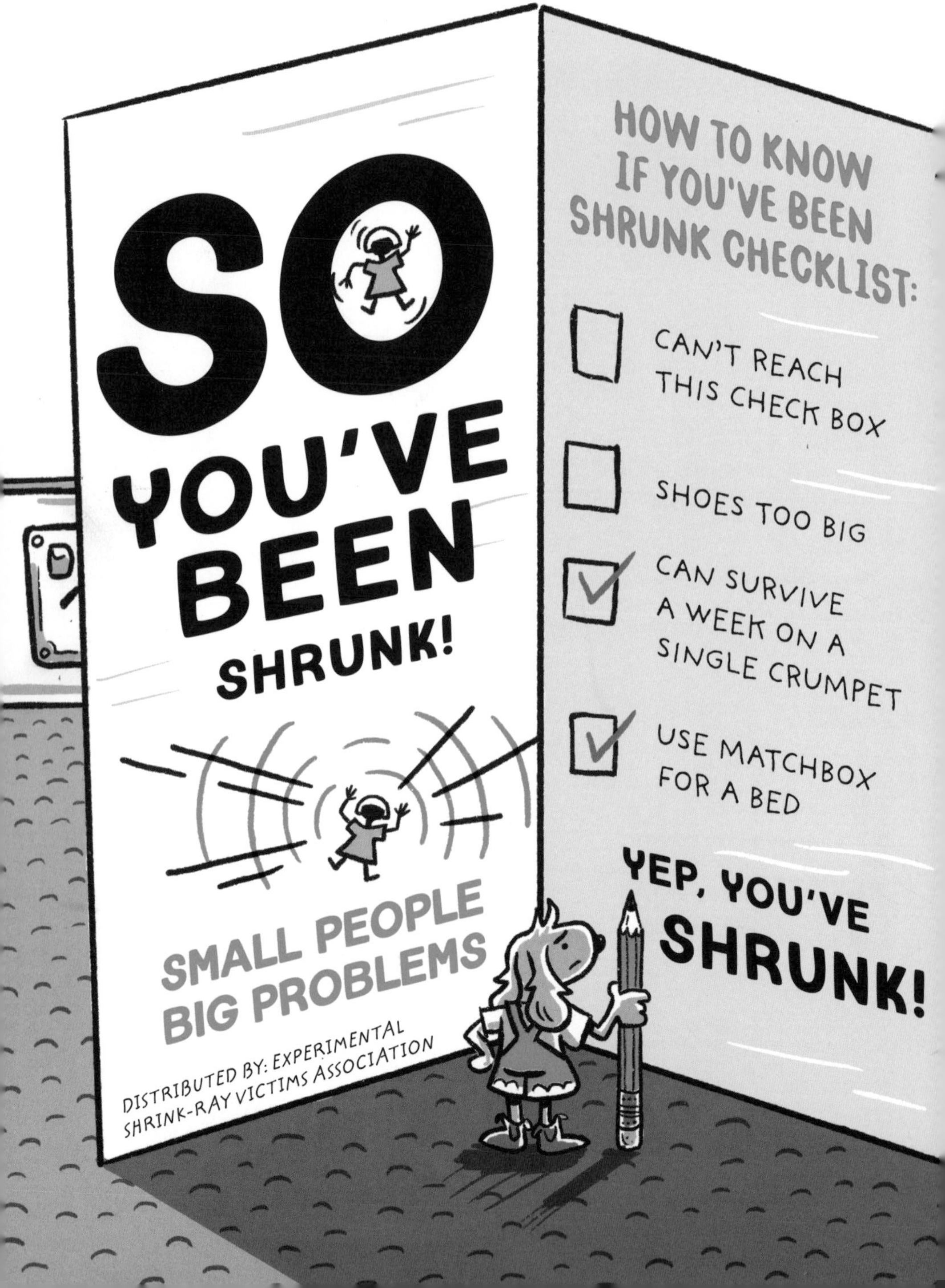
SO YOU'VE BEEN SHRUNK!
SMALL PEOPLE BIG PROBLEMS
DISTRIBUTED BY: EXPERIMENTAL SHRINK-RAY VICTIMS ASSOCIATION
HOW TO KNOW IF YOU'VE BEEN SHRUNK CHECKLIST:
CAN'T REACH THIS CHECK BOX
SHOES TOO BIG
CAN SURVIVE A WEEK ON A SINGLE CRUMPET
USE MATCHBOX FOR A BED
YEP, YOU'VE SHRUNK!

It's important to know what type of shrinking you have experienced.

CLOTHES AND ALL? YOU'RE IN LUCK!

This is one of the easiest forms of shrinkage to manage.

BODY ONLY?

If you find yourself tiny and nude, it's important to find some clothes that fit, and quick! We recommend doll's houses or the toy aisle of your local department store.

BIG TIP

In a pinch, a well-cooked ravioli can make a comfy pillow!

RISK OF ACCIDENTALLY BEING EATEN

AMOUNT SHRUNK

WARNING: under no circumstances give in to the temptation to go swimming in a bowl of cereal. The risk of accidentally being eaten is huge!

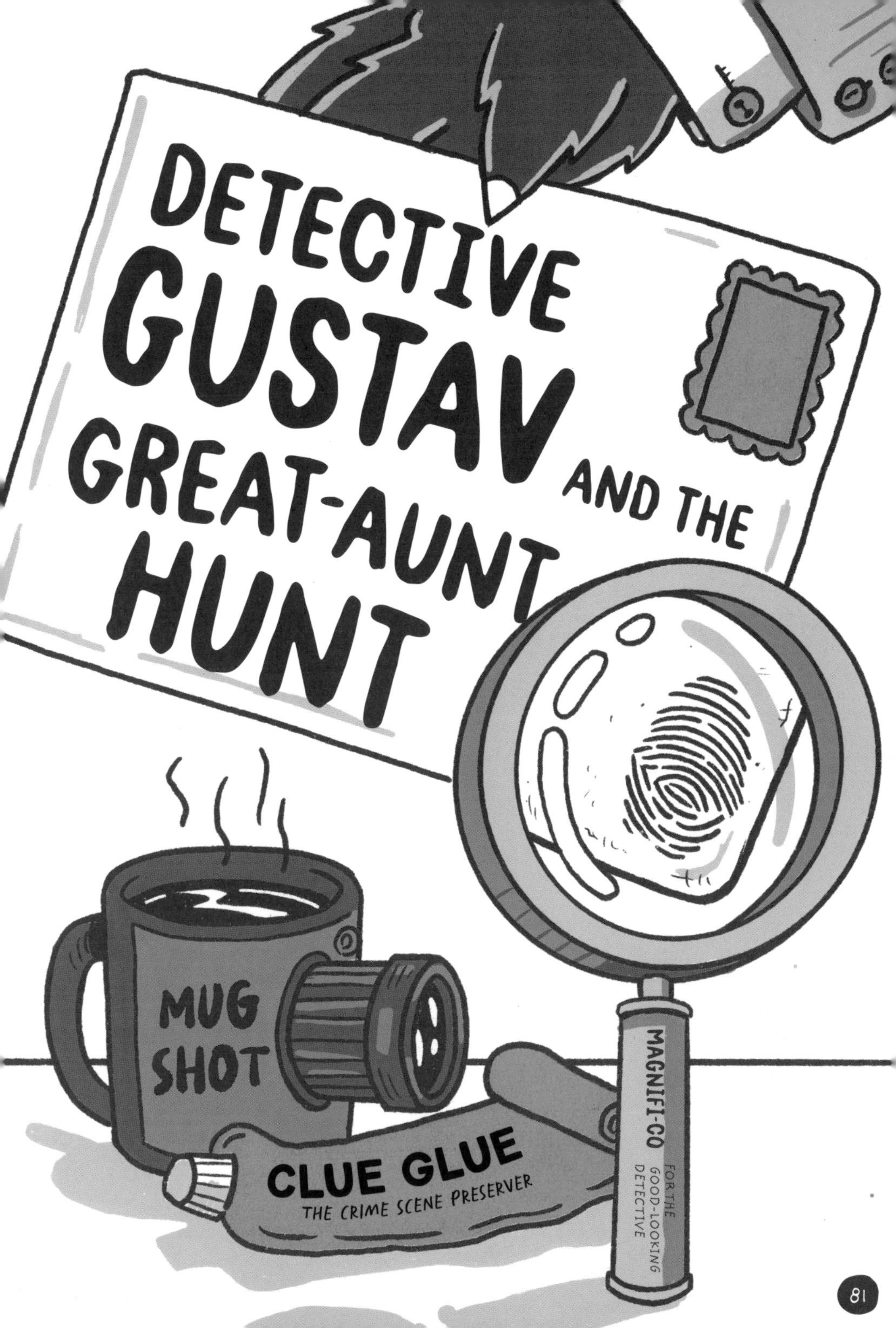
DETECTIVE GUSTAV AND THE GREAT-AUNT HUNT
MUG SHOT
CLUE GLUE
THE CRIME SCENE PRESERVER
MAGNIFI-CO
FOR THE GOOD-LOOKING DETECTIVE

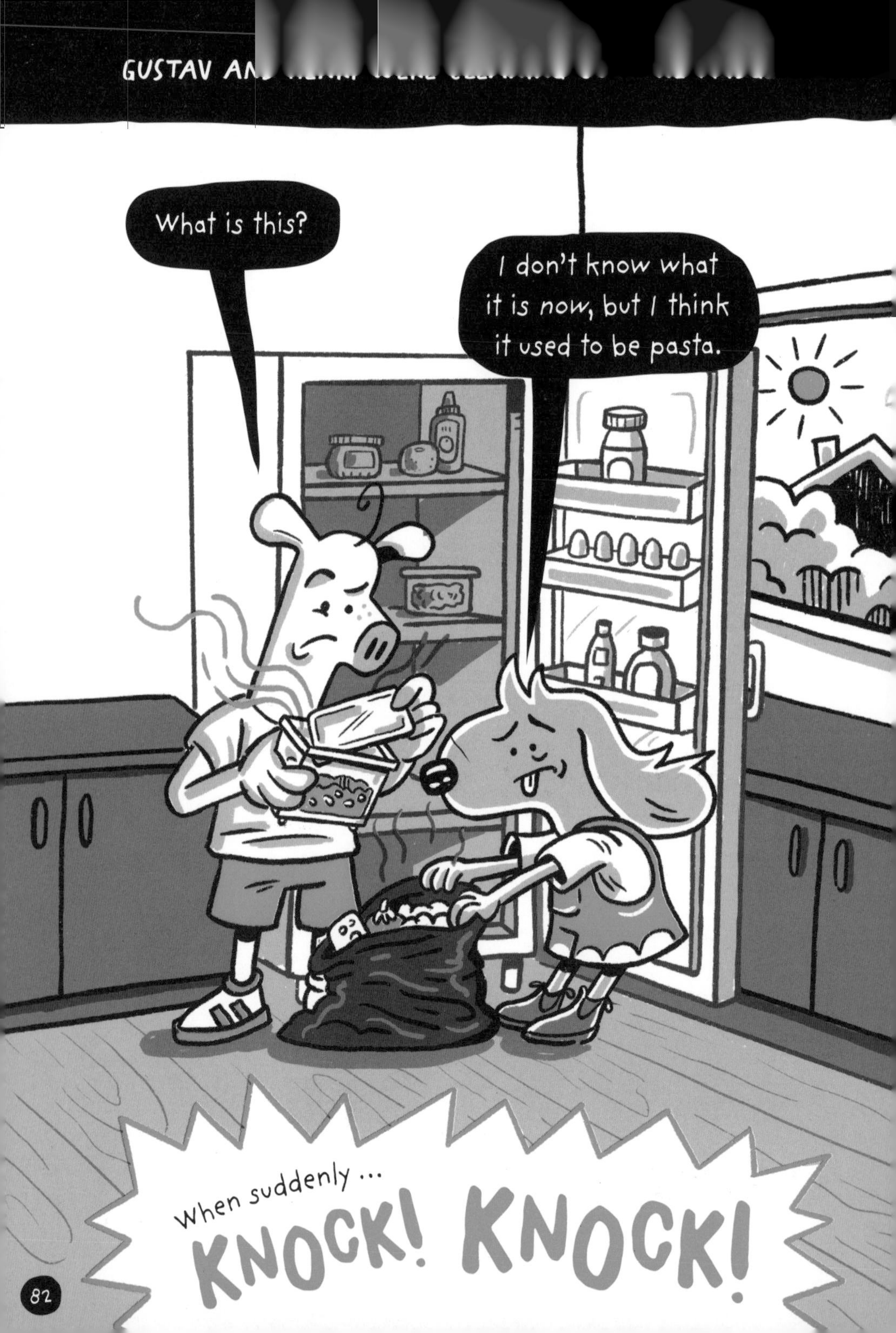
GUSTAV AN
What is this?
I don't know what it is *now*, but I think it used to be pasta.
When suddenly ...
KNOCK! KNOCK!

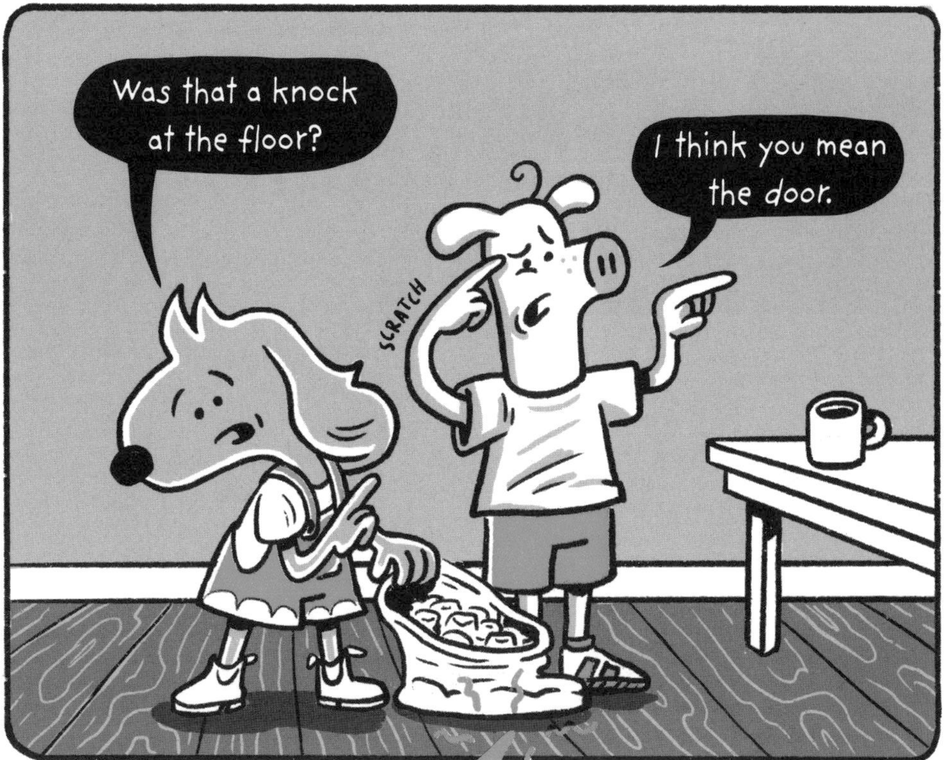
Was that a knock at the floor?
I think you mean the *door.*
SCRATCH

Mole Man! shouted a voice from below.

"You mean *mailman?*" replied Gustav.

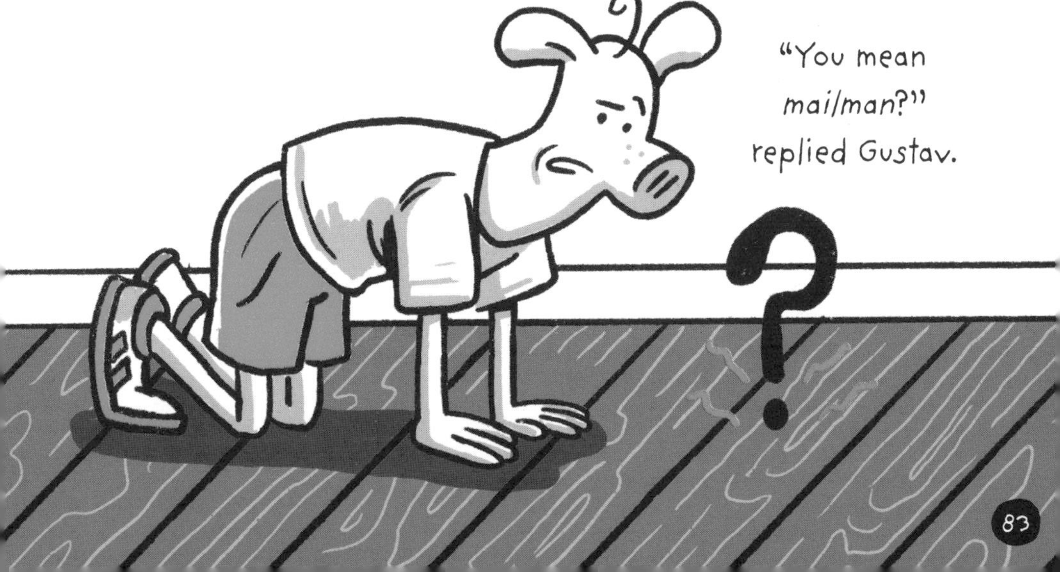
?

"No, it's a mole man all right,"
said Henri, prying up a floorboard.

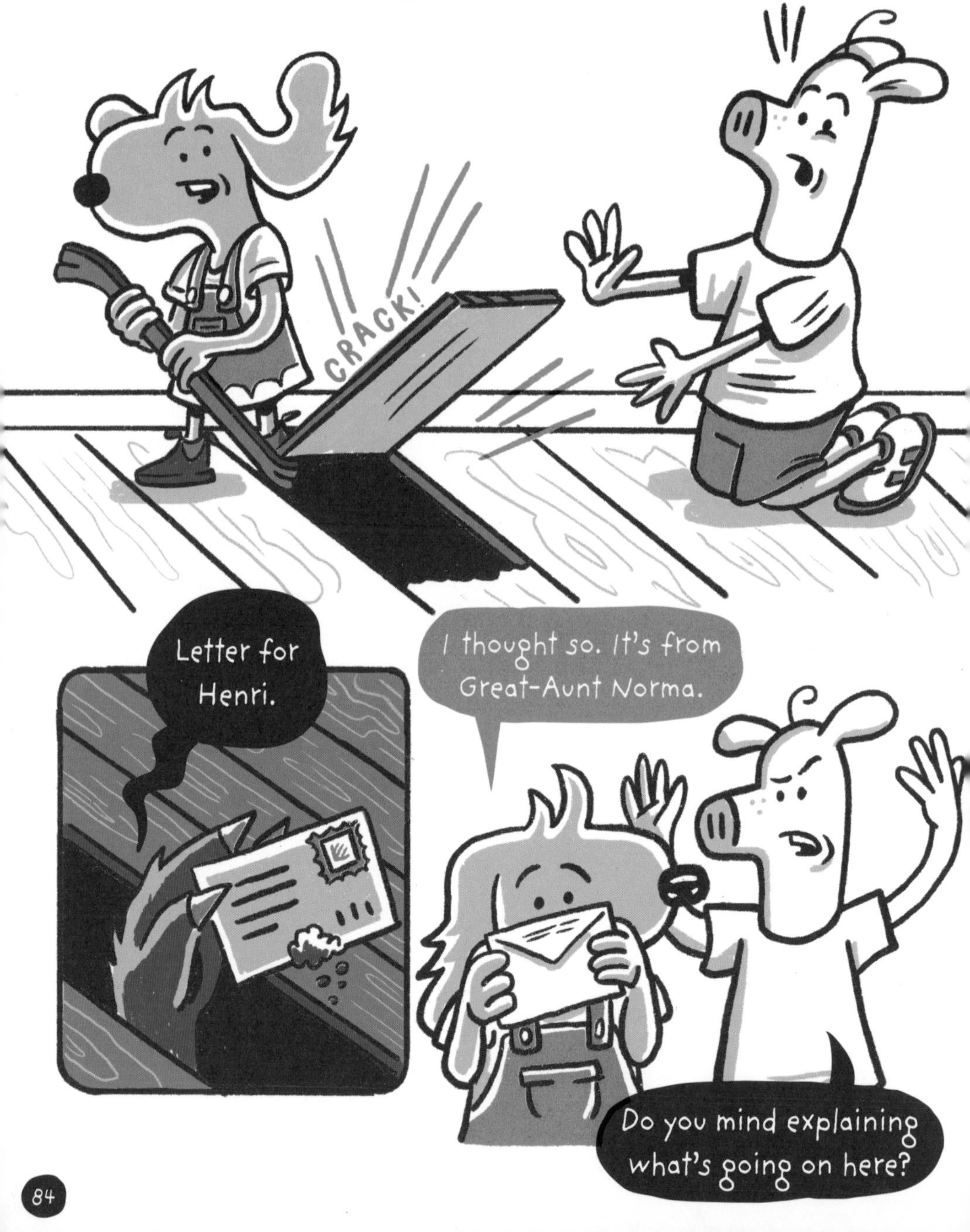
CRACK!
Letter for Henri.
I thought so. It's from Great-Aunt Norma.
Do you mind explaining what's going on here?

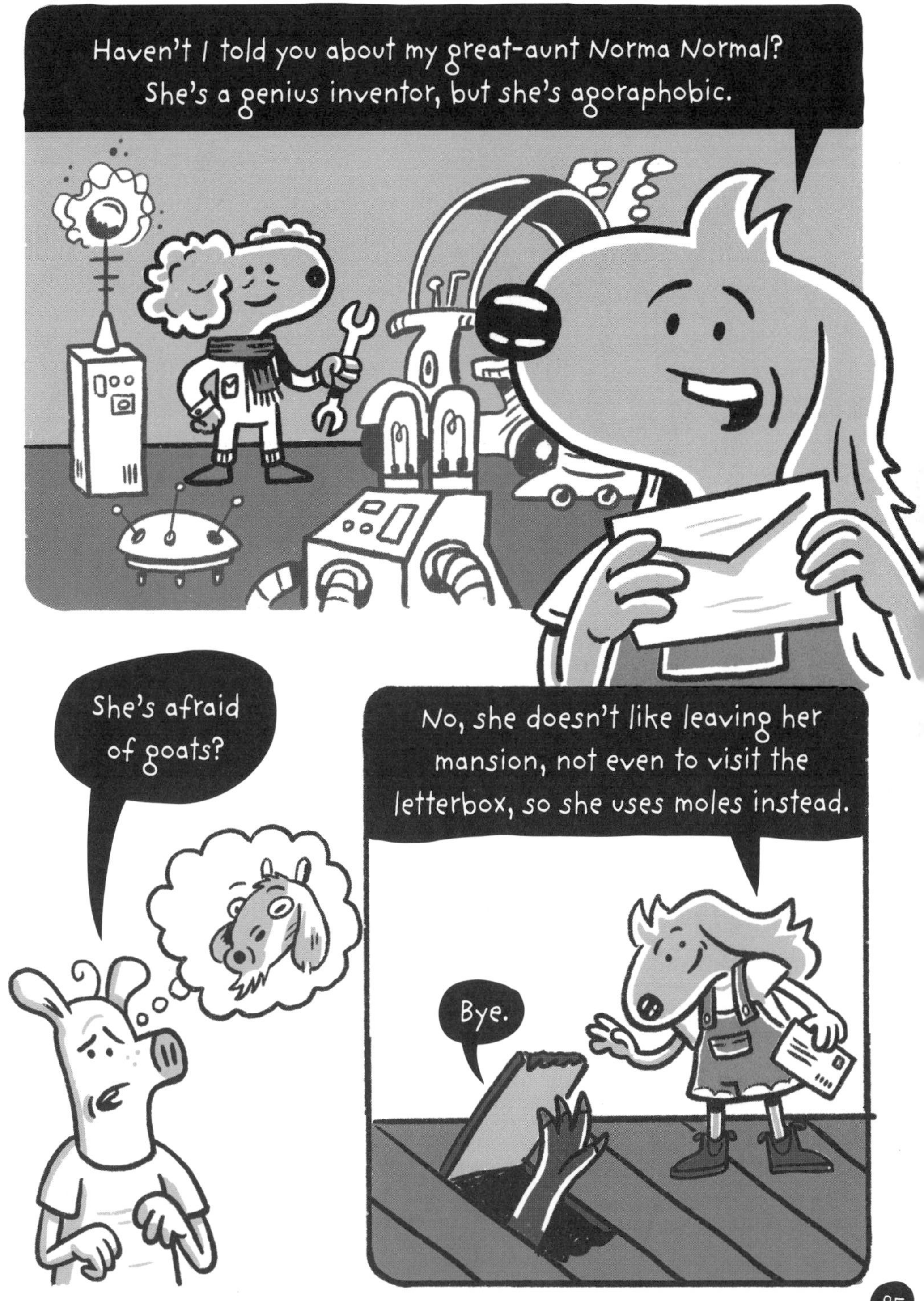
Haven't I told you about my great-aunt Norma Normal? She's a genius inventor, but she's agoraphobic.
She's afraid of goats?
No, she doesn't like leaving her mansion, not even to visit the letterbox, so she uses moles instead.
Bye.

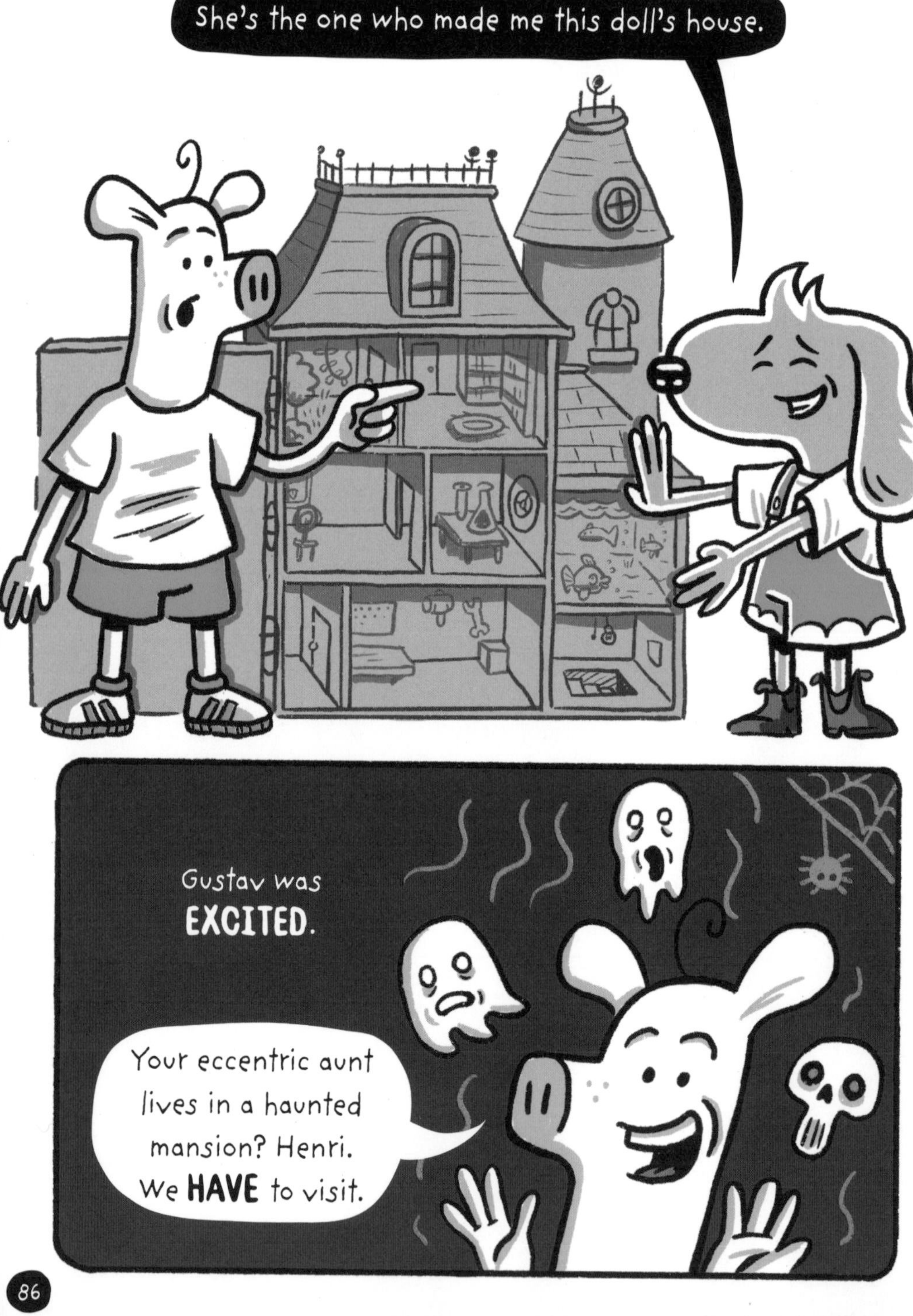
She's the one who made me this doll's house.
Gustav was
EXCITED.
Your eccentric aunt lives in a haunted mansion? Henri. We **HAVE** to visit.

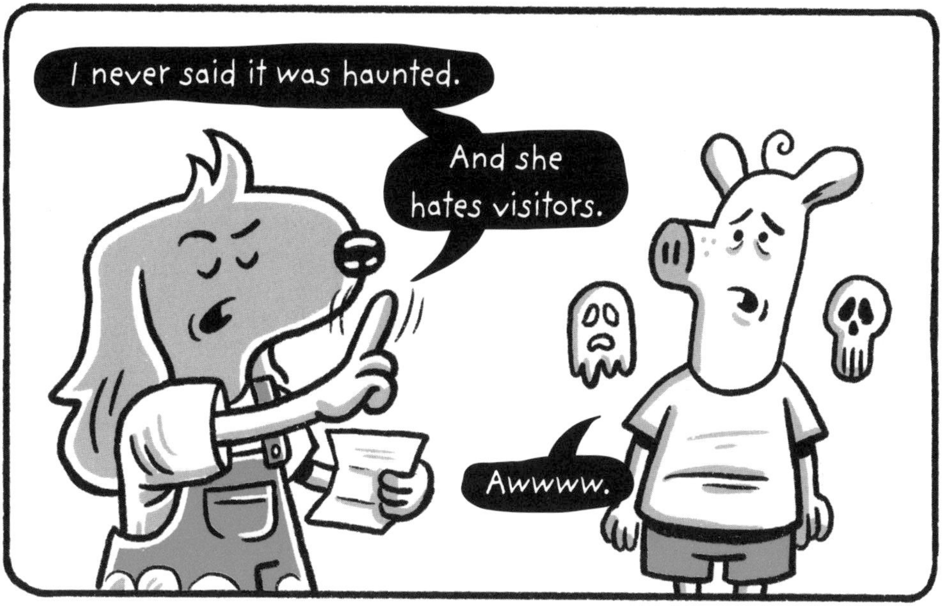
I never said it was haunted.
And she hates visitors.
Awwww.

But the letter disagreed.

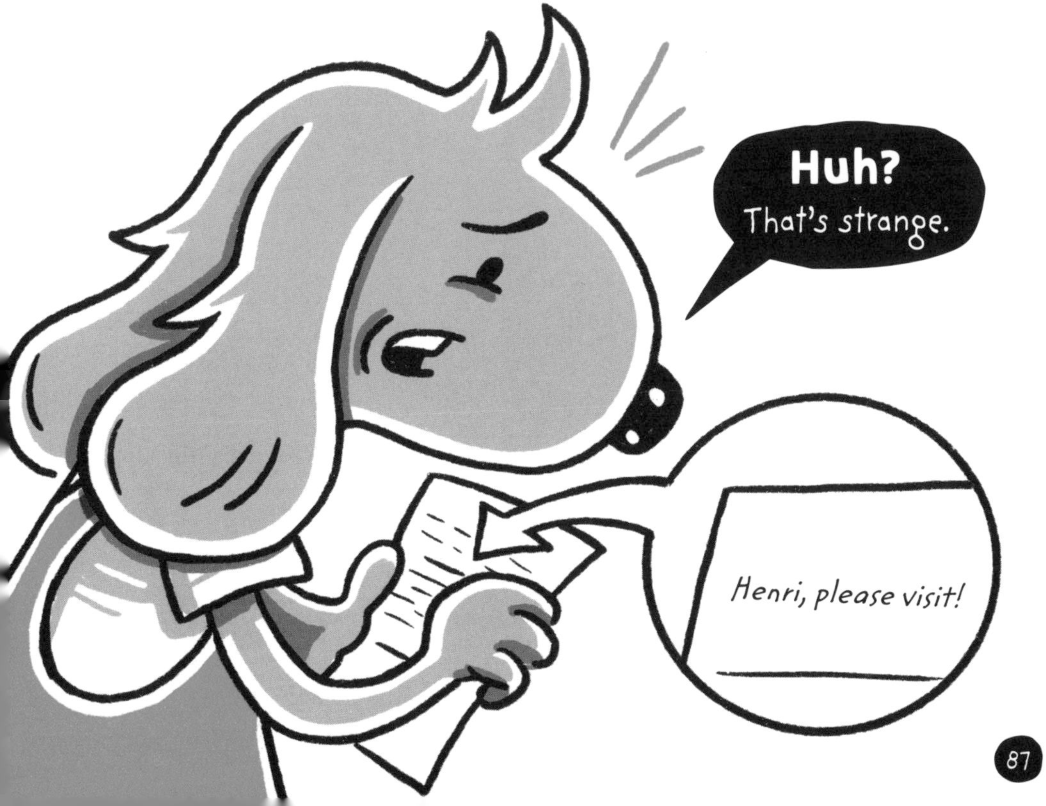
Huh?
That's strange.
Henri, please visit!

"Maybe I was wrong," frowned Henri, reading

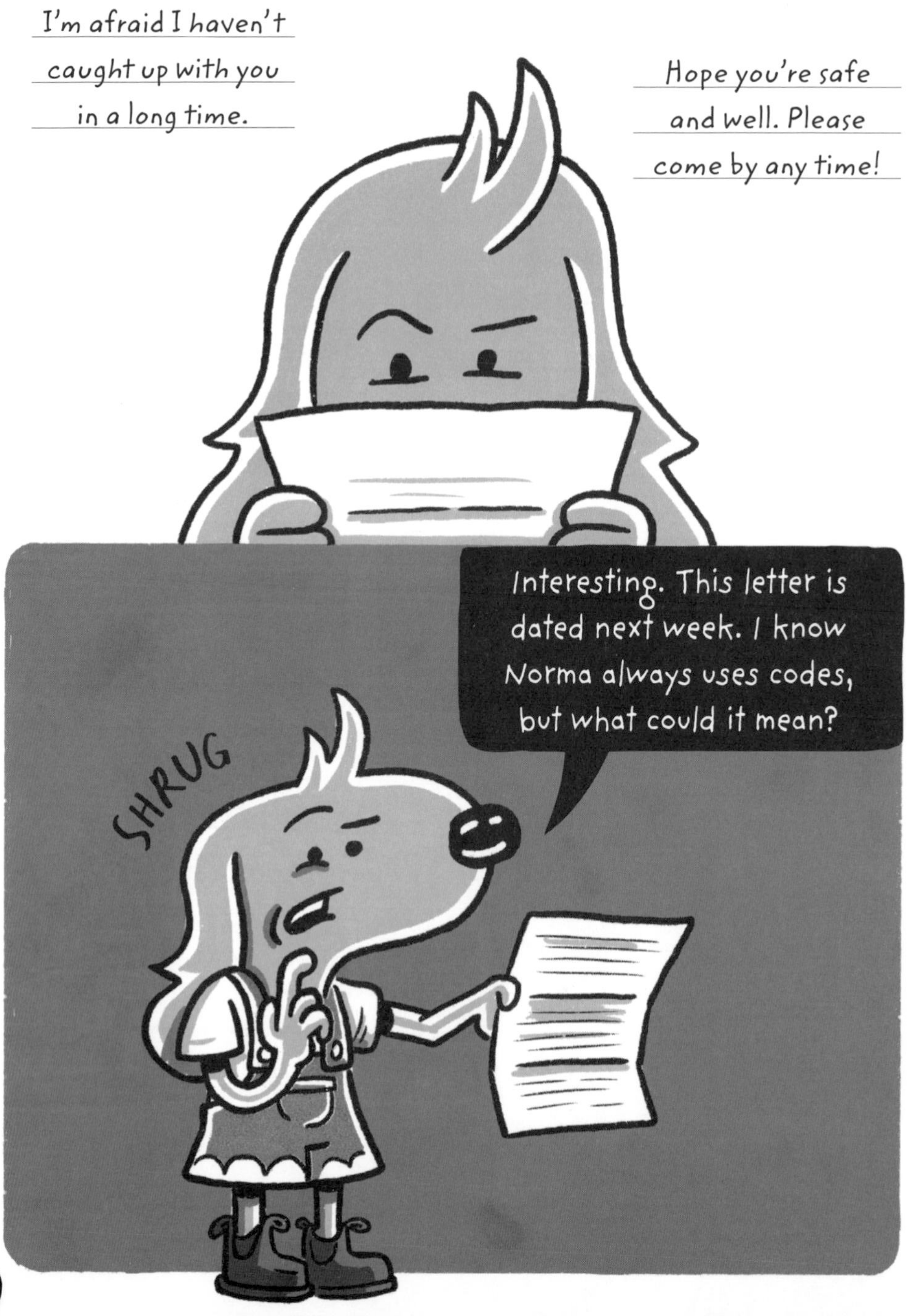
I'm afraid I haven't caught up with you in a long time.
Hope you're safe and well. Please come by any time!
Interesting. This letter is dated next week. I know Norma always uses codes, but what could it mean?
SHRUG

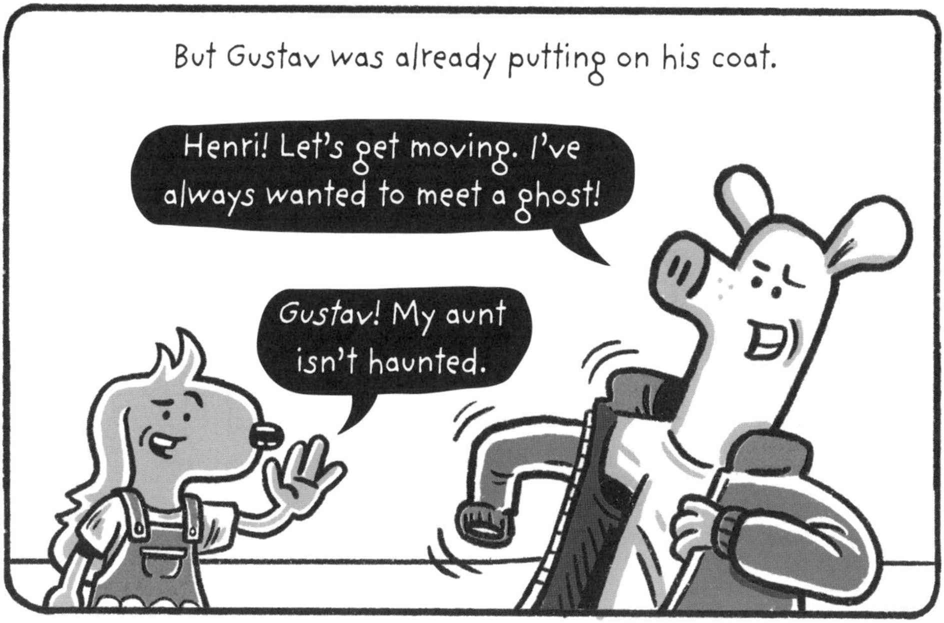
But Gustav was already putting on his coat.
Henri! Let's get moving. I've always wanted to meet a ghost!
Gustav! My aunt isn't haunted.

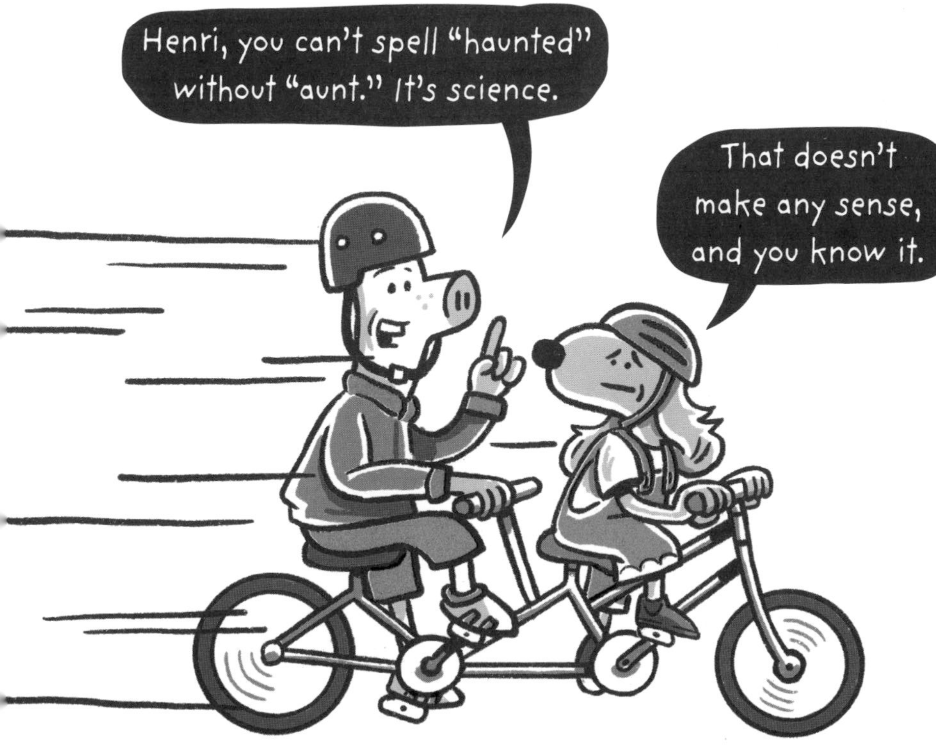
Henri, you can't spell "haunted" without "aunt." It's science.
That doesn't make any sense, and you know it.

When they arrived at
the mansion, Gustav was
amazed.

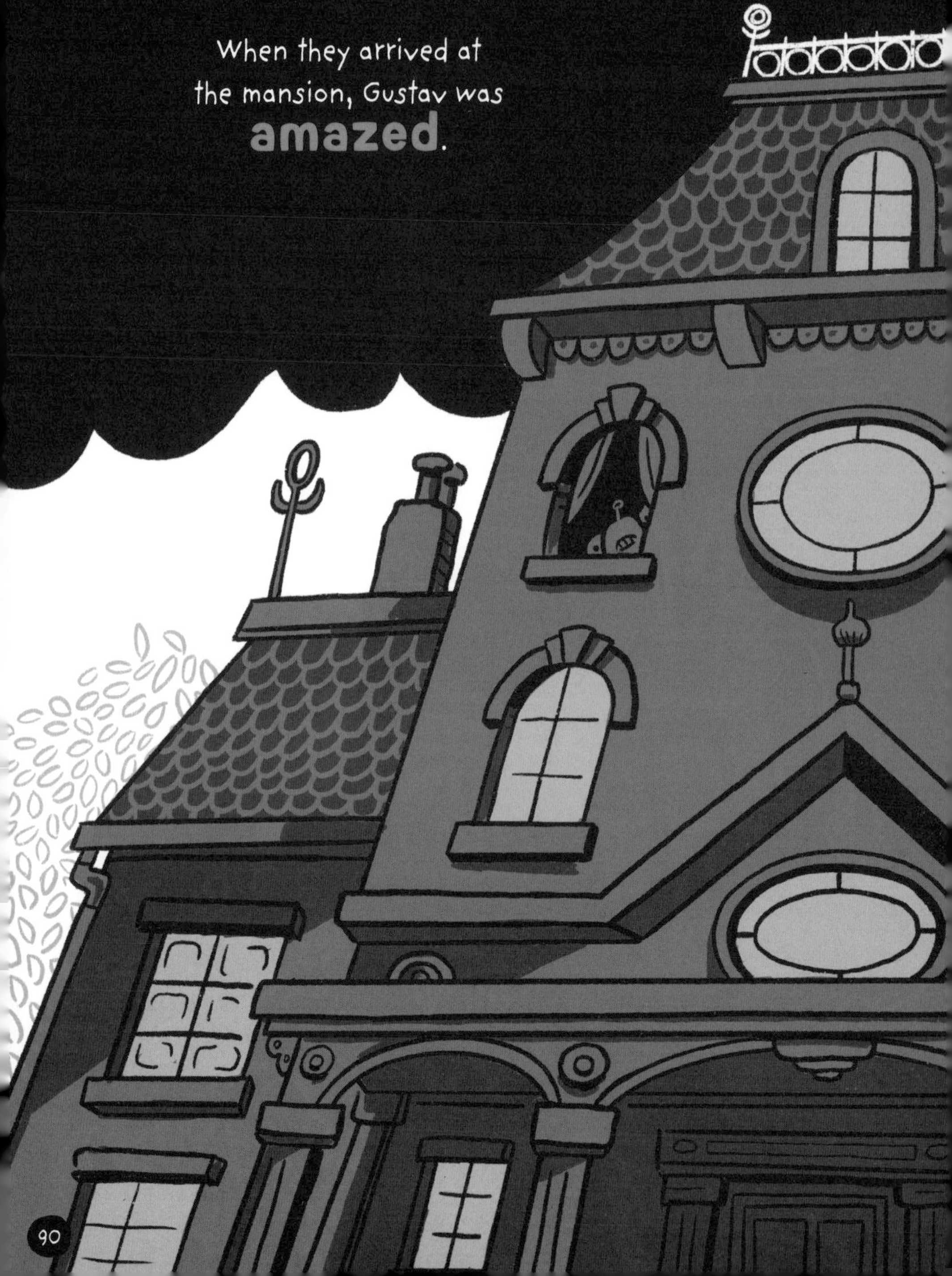

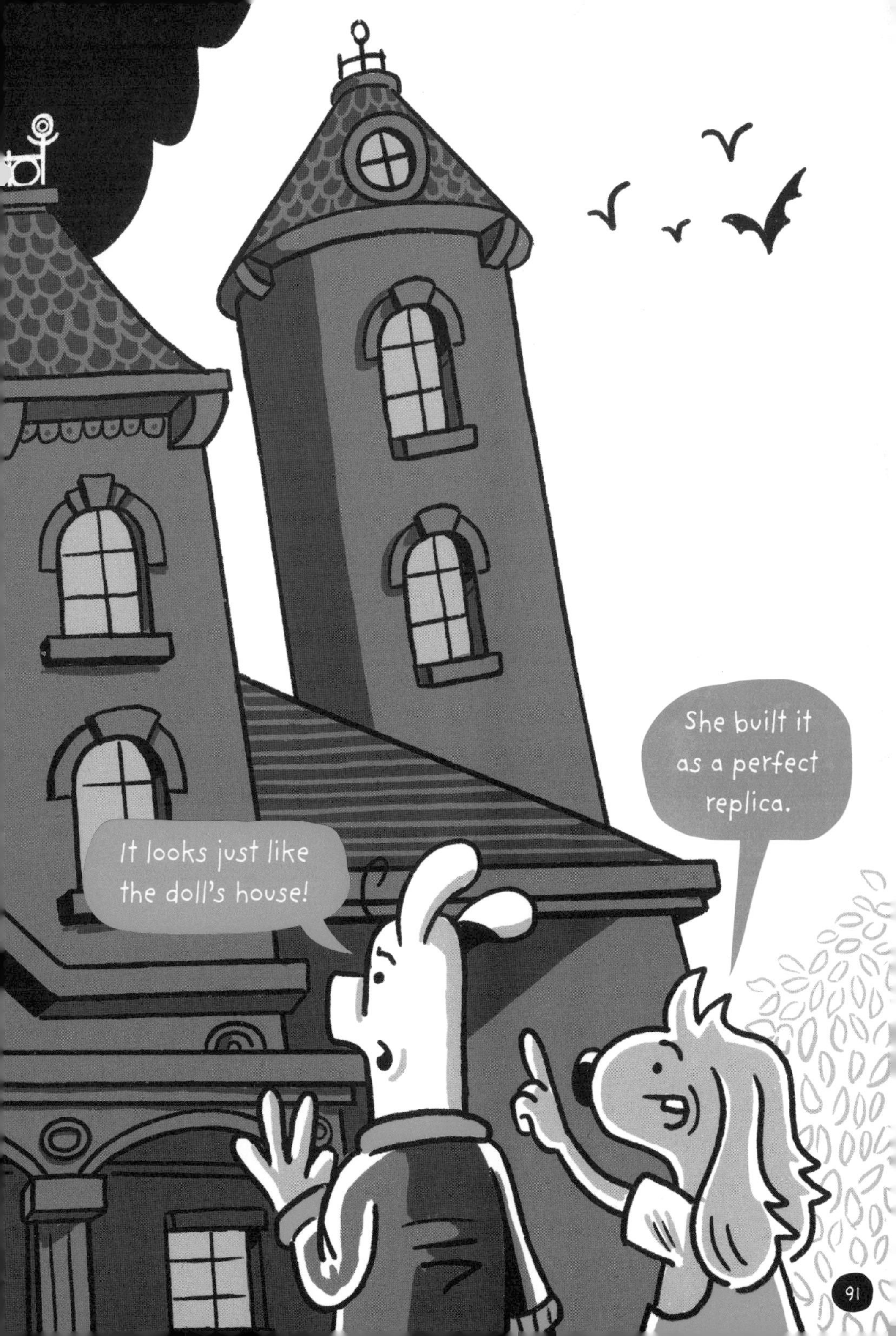
It looks just like the doll's house!
She built it as a perfect replica.

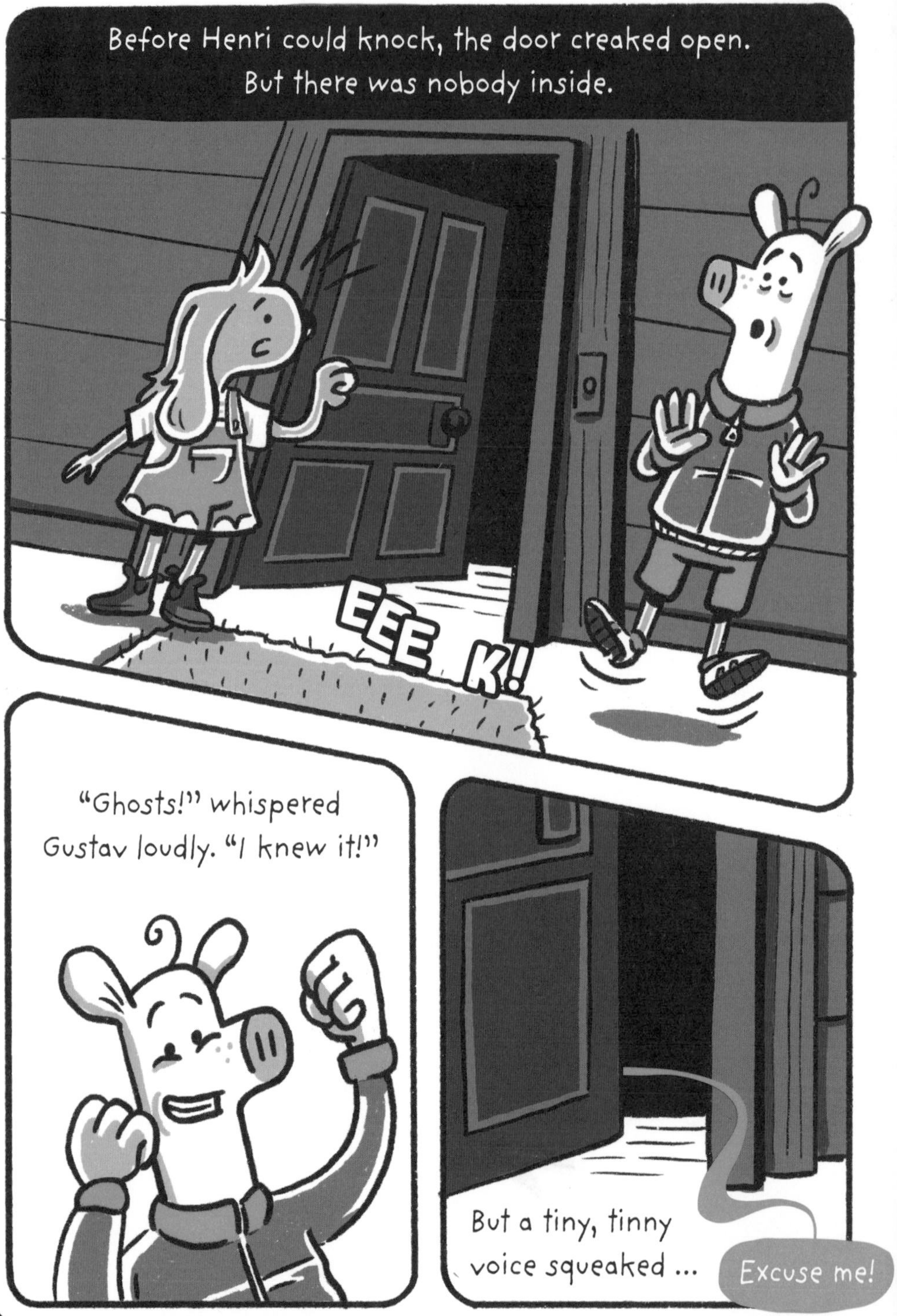
Before Henri could knock, the door creaked open.
But there was nobody inside.
EEEK!
"Ghosts!" whispered Gustav loudly. "I knew it!"
But a tiny, tinny voice squeaked ...
Excuse me!

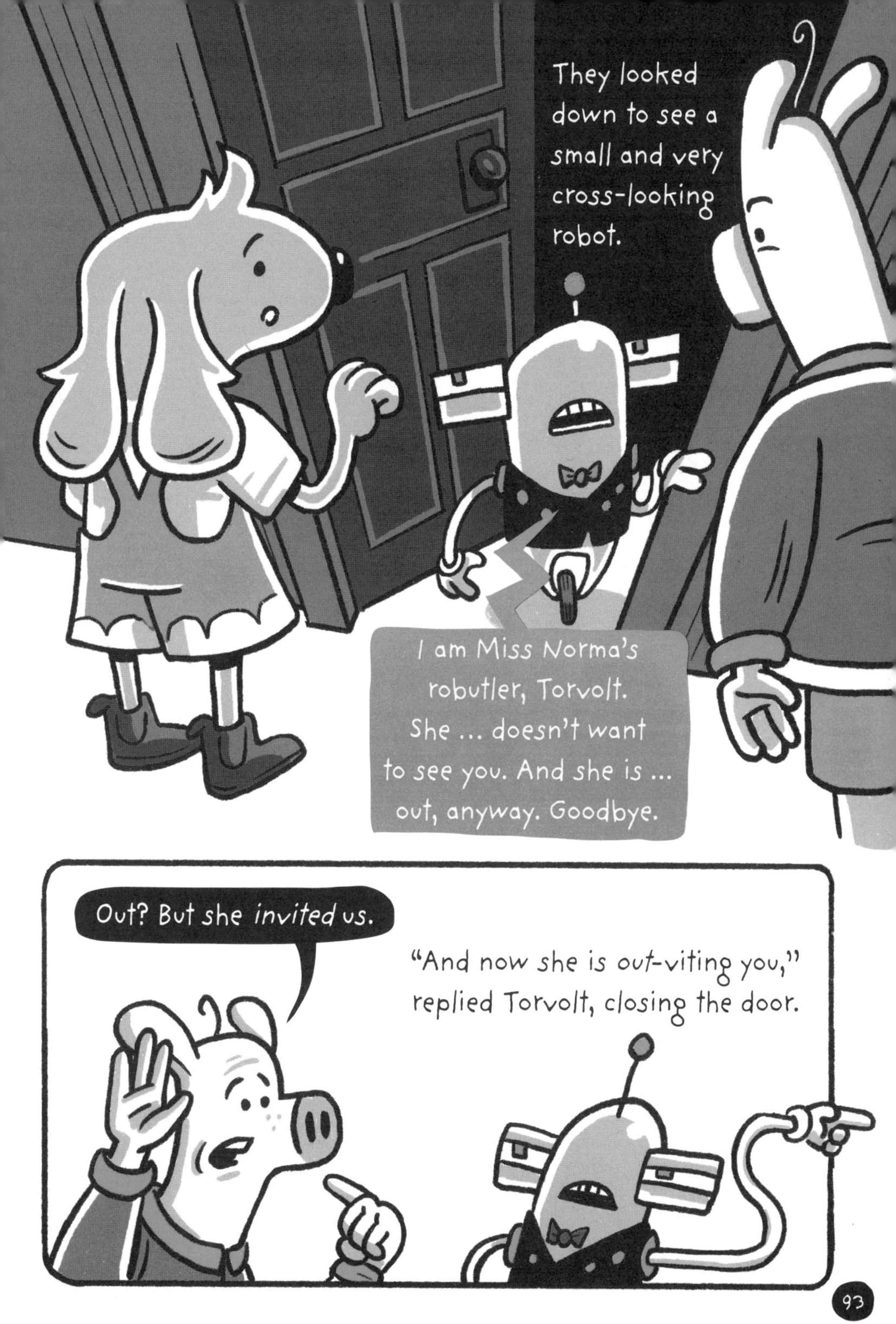
They looked down to see a small and very cross-looking robot.
I am Miss Norma's robutler, Torvolt. She ... doesn't want to see you. And she is ... out, anyway. Goodbye.
Out? But she *invited* us.
"And now she is *out*-viting you," replied Torvolt, closing the door.

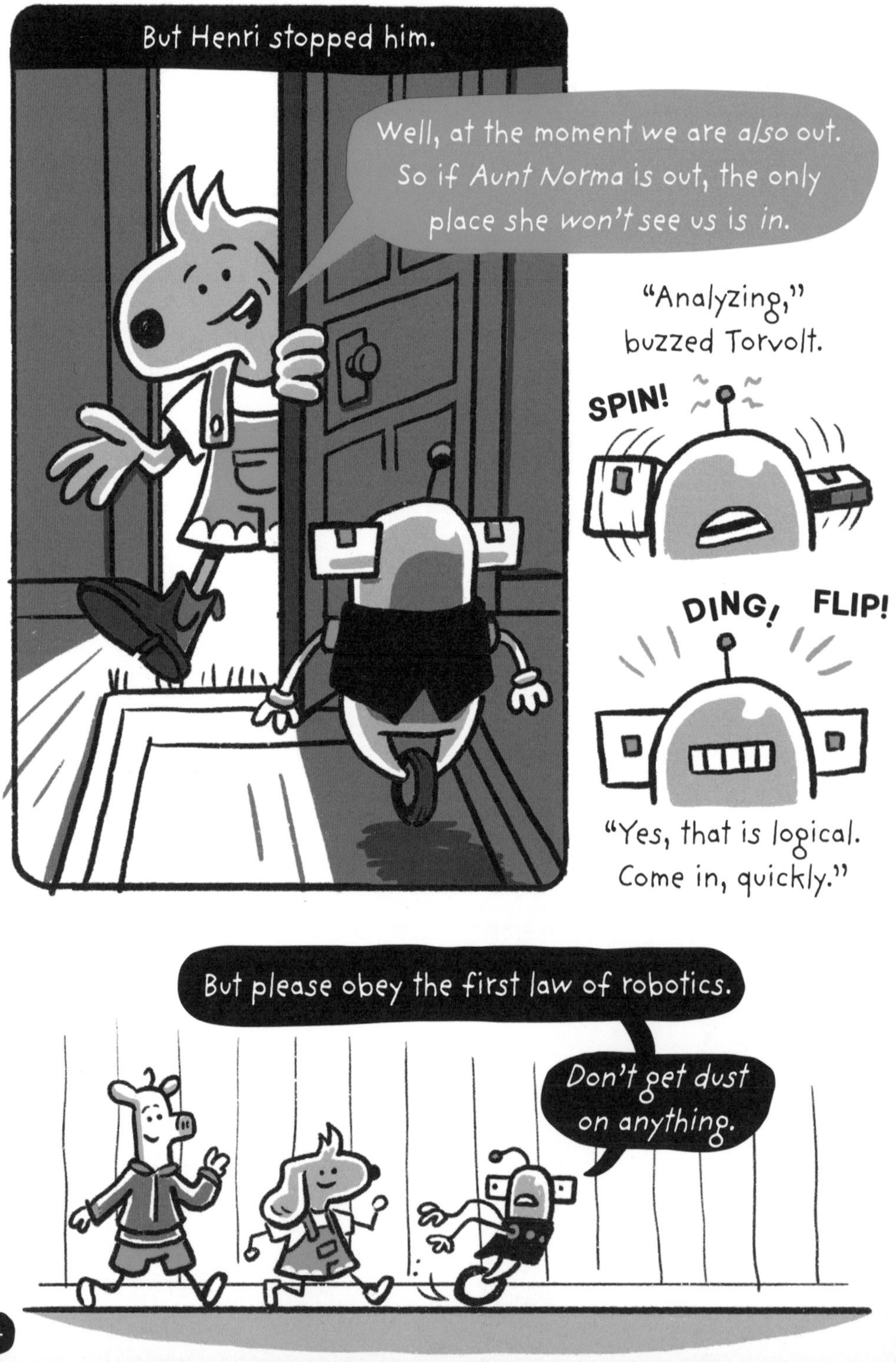
But Henri stopped him.
Well, at the moment we are *also* out. So if *Aunt Norma* is out, the only place she *won't* see us is *in*.
"Analyzing," buzzed Torvolt.
SPIN!
DING! FLIP!
"Yes, that is logical. Come in, quickly."
But please obey the first law of robotics.
Don't get dust on anything.

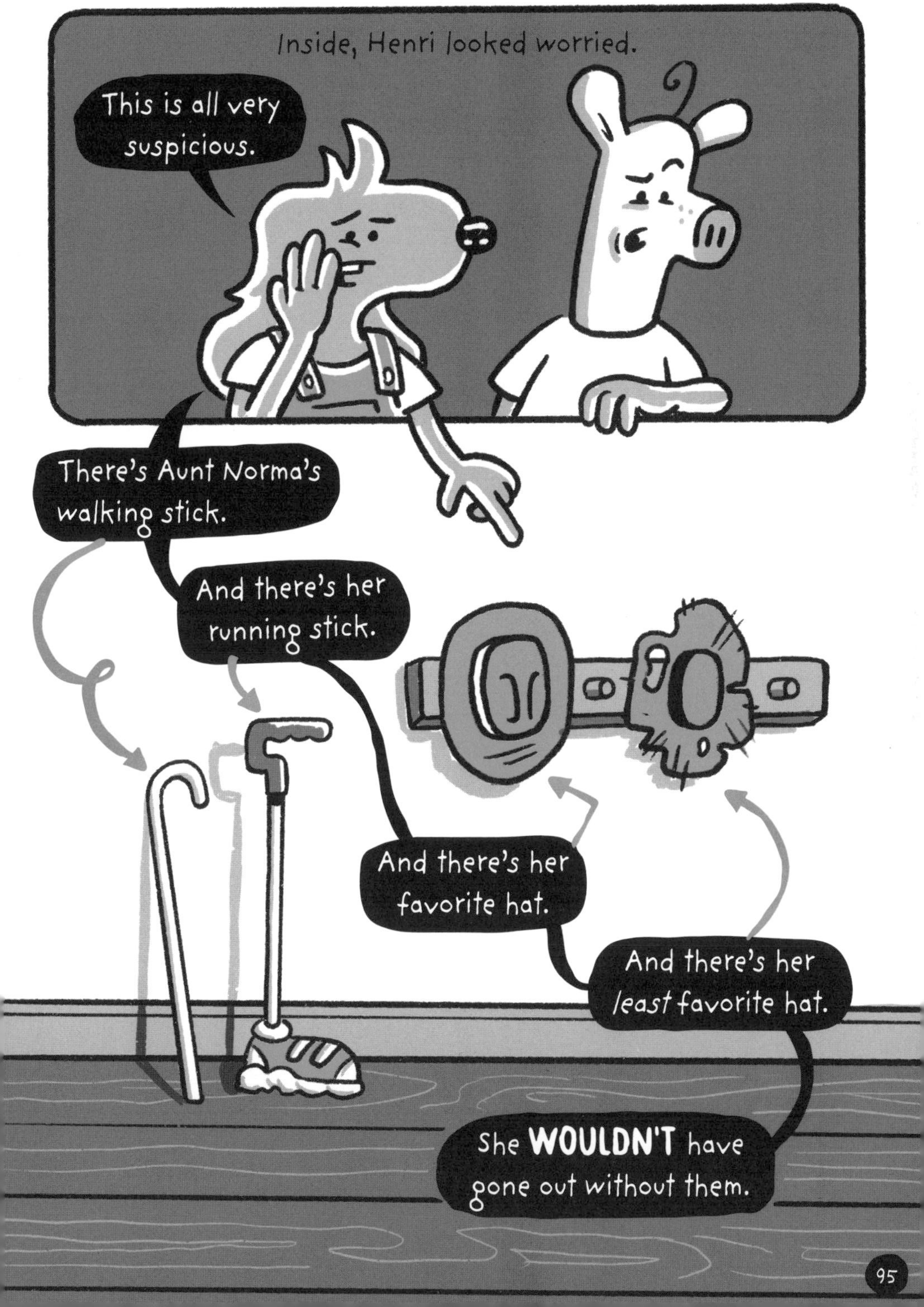
Inside, Henri looked worried.
This is all very suspicious.
There's Aunt Norma's walking stick.
And there's her running stick.
And there's her favorite hat.
And there's her *least* favorite hat.
She **WOULDN'T** have gone out without them.

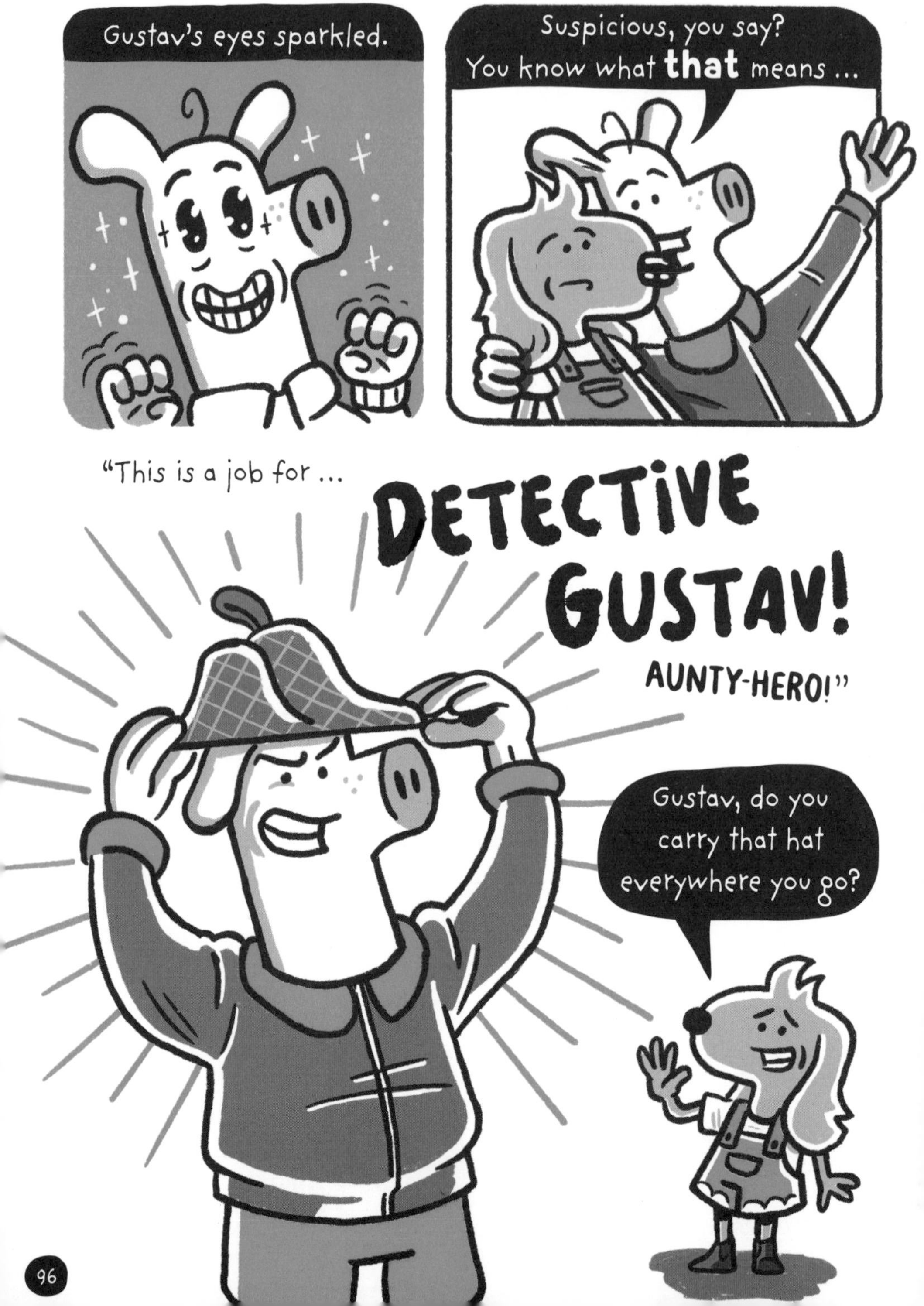

Gustav's eyes sparkled.
Suspicious, you say? You know what **that** means ...
"This is a job for ...
DETECTIVE GUSTAV!
AUNTY-HERO!"
Gustav, do you carry that hat everywhere you go?

With Torvolt dusting along behind them, they searched the house from top to bottom. And side to side. But there was no sign of Great-Aunt Norma.

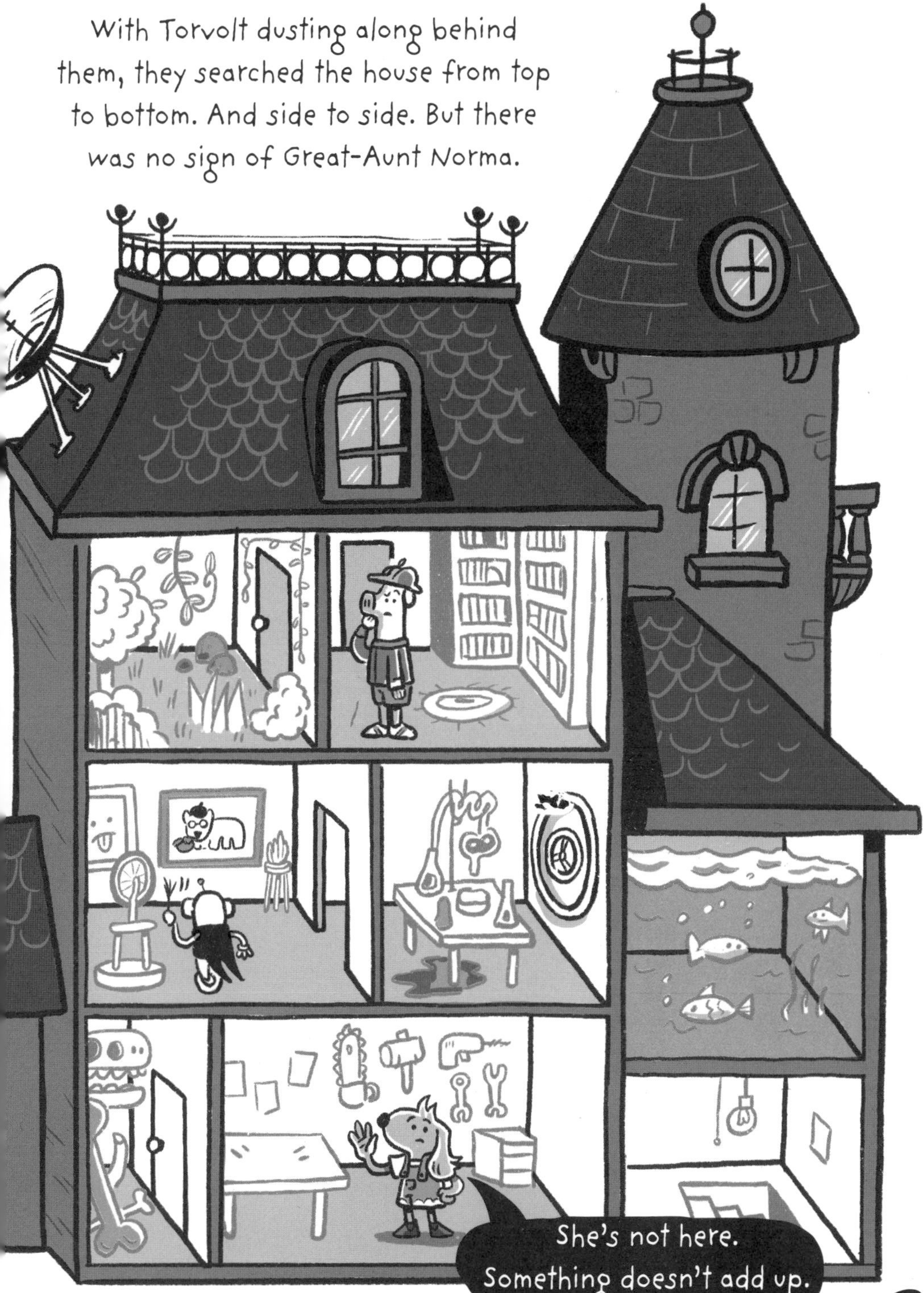
She's not here.
Something doesn't add up.

"Yes," said Detective Gustav, examining a large painting. "I can't tell how many legs this wombat has."

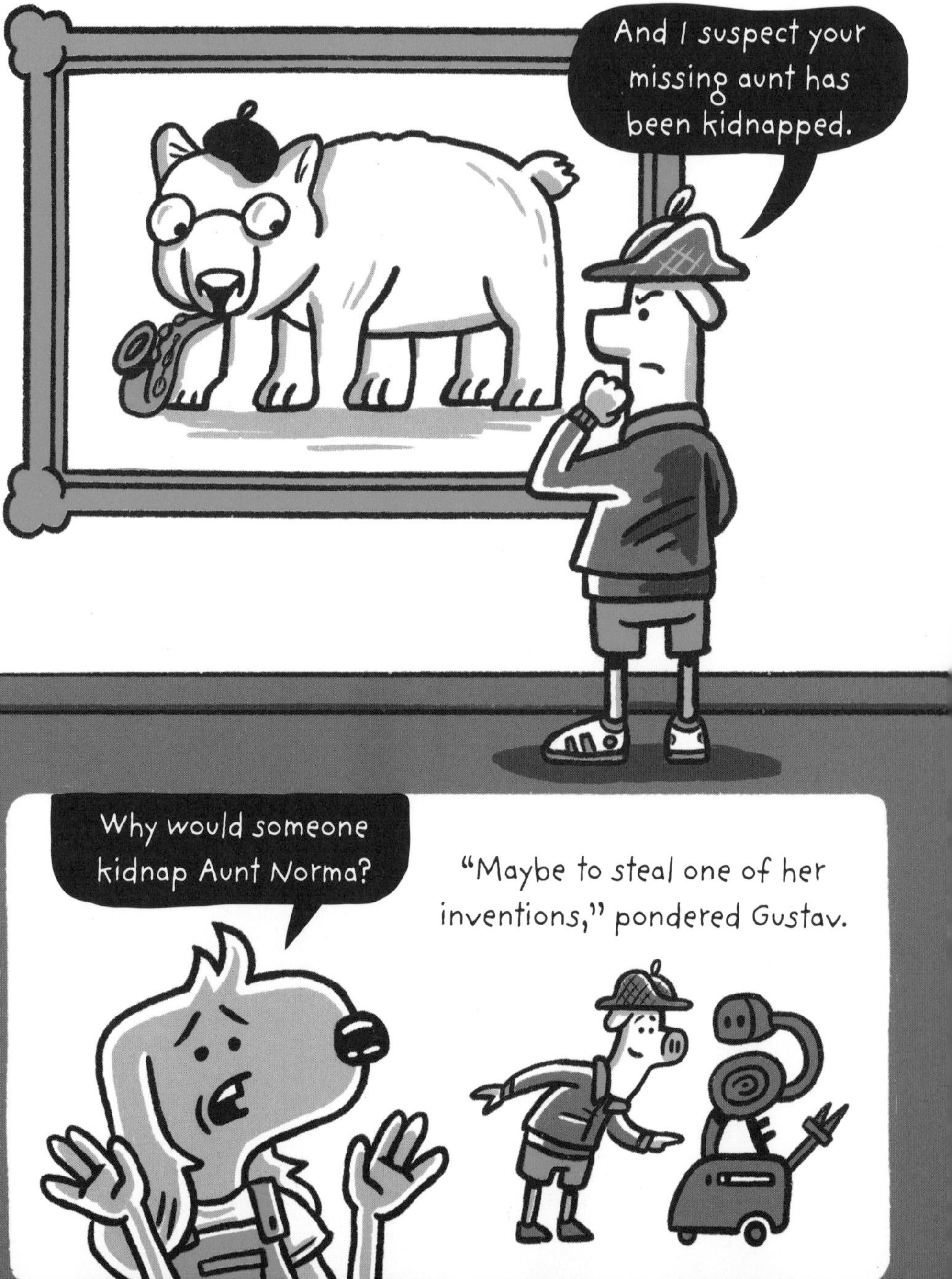
And I suspect your missing aunt has been kidnapped.
Why would someone kidnap Aunt Norma?
"Maybe to steal one of her inventions," pondered Gustav.

"Perhaps. She's definitely been building something,"
Henri nodded. "But whatever it was is gone."

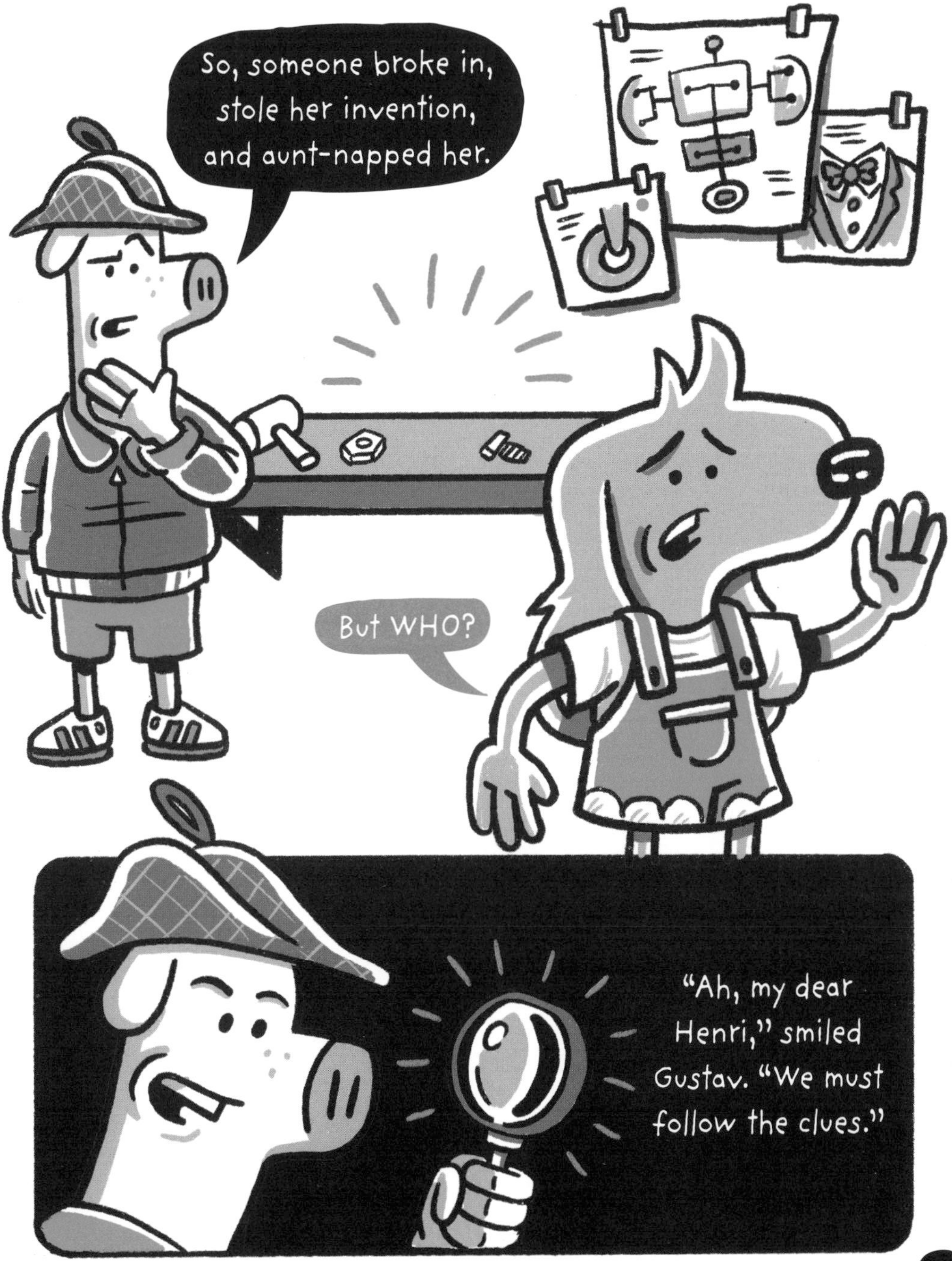
So, someone broke in, stole her invention, and aunt-napped her.
But WHO?
"Ah, my dear Henri," smiled Gustav. "We must follow the clues."

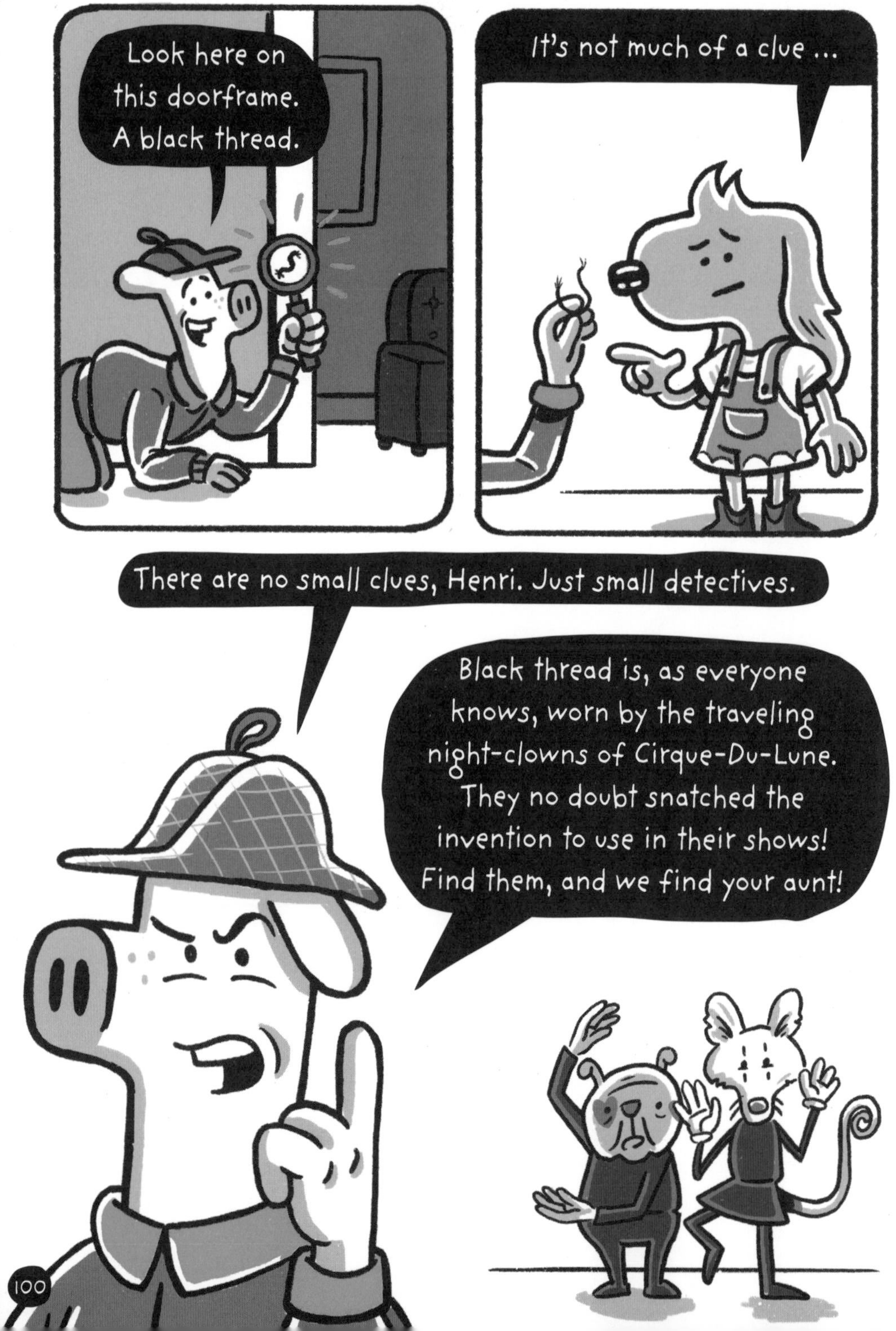
Look here on this doorframe. A black thread.
It's not much of a clue ...
There are no small clues, Henri. Just small detectives.
Black thread is, as everyone knows, worn by the traveling night-clowns of Cirque-Du-Lune. They no doubt snatched the invention to use in their shows! Find them, and we find your aunt!

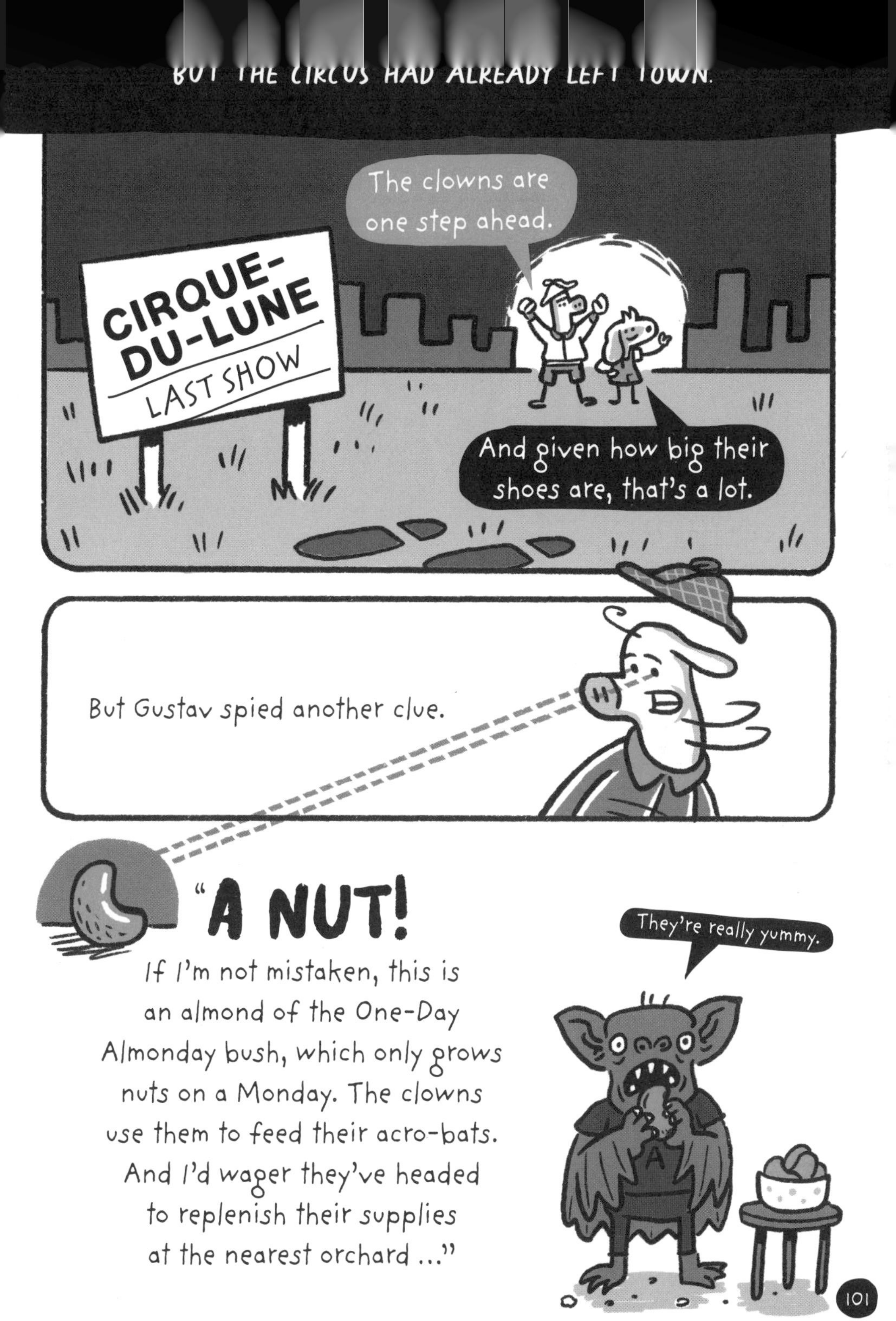
BUT THE CIRCUS HAD ALREADY LEFT TOWN.
CIRQUE-DU-LUNE
LAST SHOW
The clowns are one step ahead.
And given how big their shoes are, that's a lot.
But Gustav spied another clue.
"A NUT!
If I'm not mistaken, this is an almond of the One-Day Almonday bush, which only grows nuts on a Monday. The clowns use them to feed their acro-bats. And I'd wager they've headed to replenish their supplies at the nearest orchard ..."
They're really yummy.
A

SADLY, WHEN THEY ARRIVED IN THE ONE-DAY ALMONDAY GROVE...

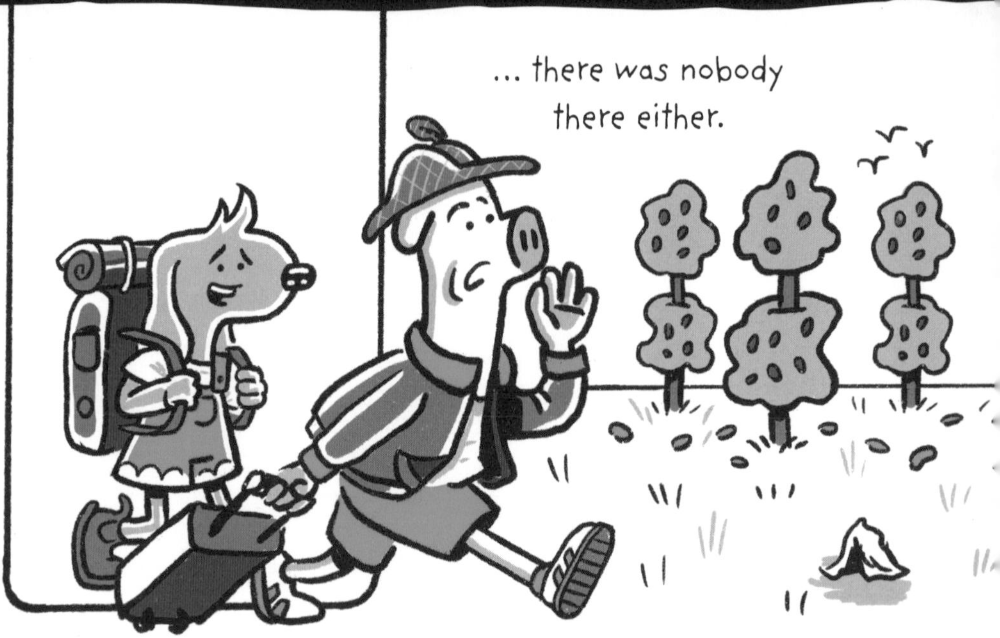
... there was nobody
there either.

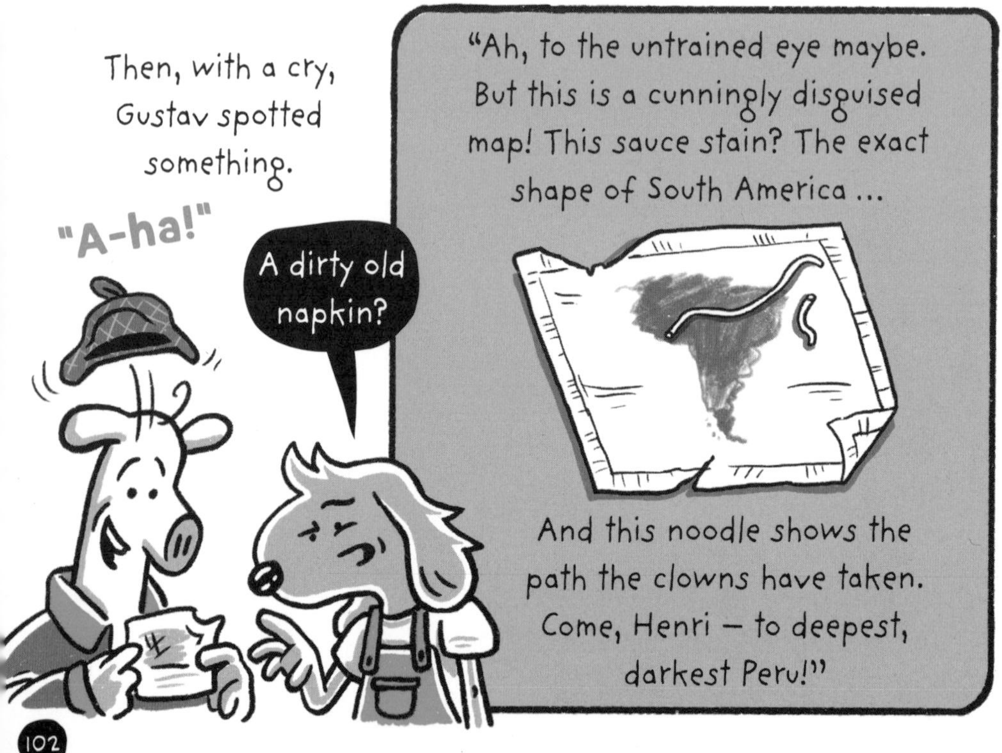
Then, with a cry,
Gustav spotted
something.
"A-ha!"
A dirty old
napkin?
"Ah, to the untrained eye maybe.
But this is a cunningly disguised
map! This sauce stain? The exact
shape of South America ...
And this noodle shows the
path the clowns have taken.
Come, Henri – to deepest,
darkest Peru!"

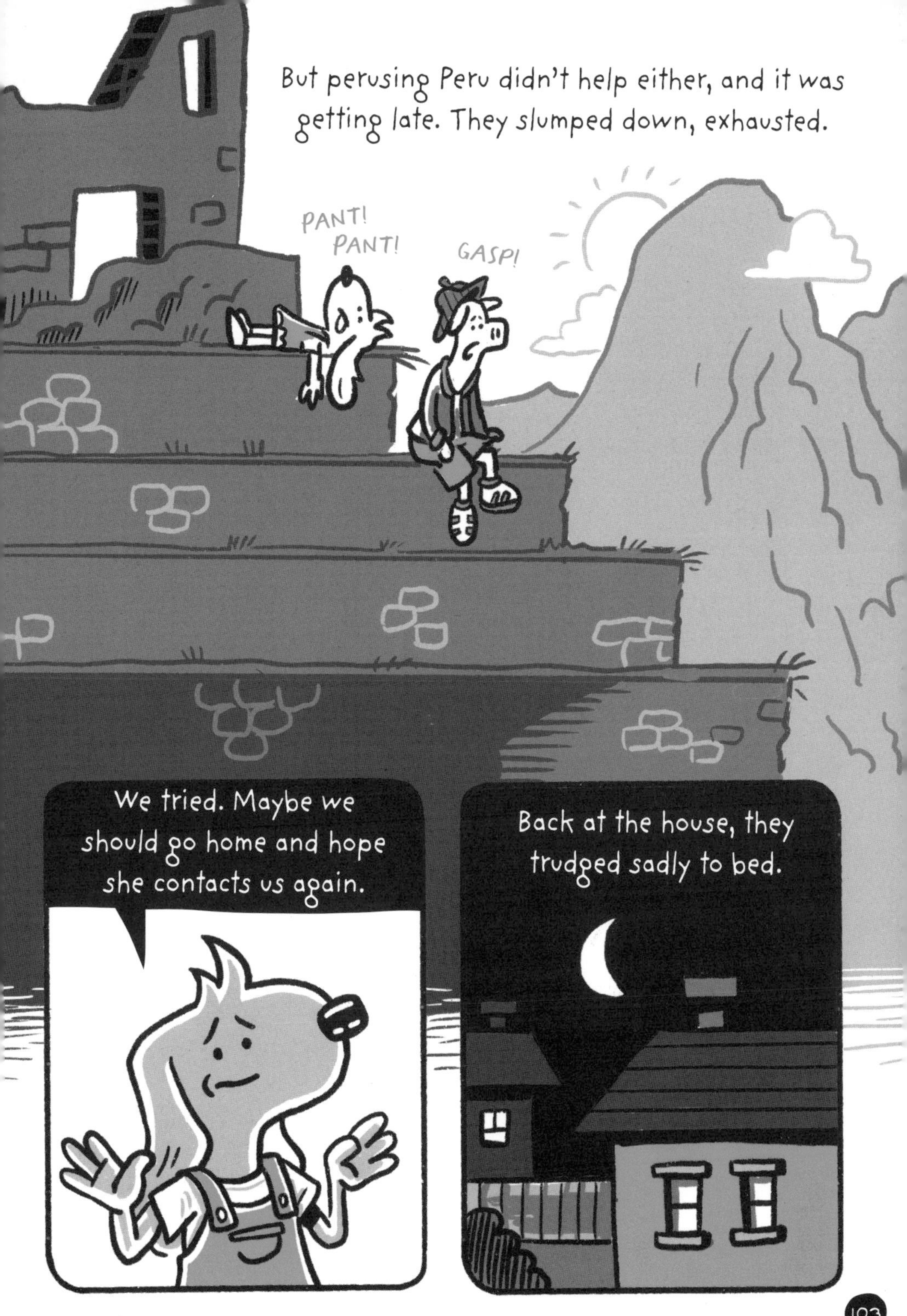
But perusing Peru didn't help either, and it was getting late. They slumped down, exhausted.
PANT! PANT!
GASP!
We tried. Maybe we should go home and hope she contacts us again.
Back at the house, they trudged sadly to bed.

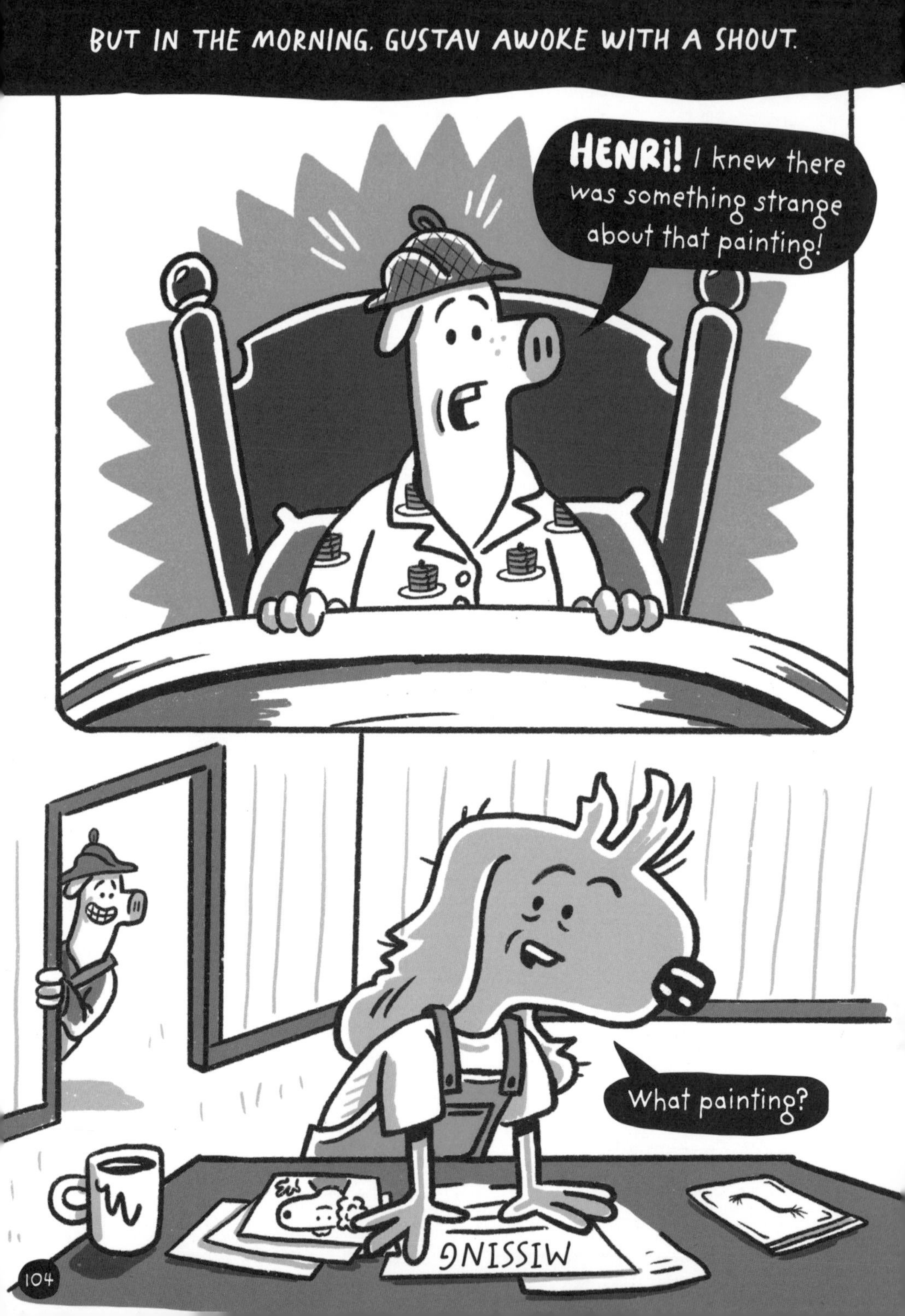
BUT IN THE MORNING, GUSTAV AWOKE WITH A SHOUT.
HENRI! I knew there was something strange about that painting!
What painting?

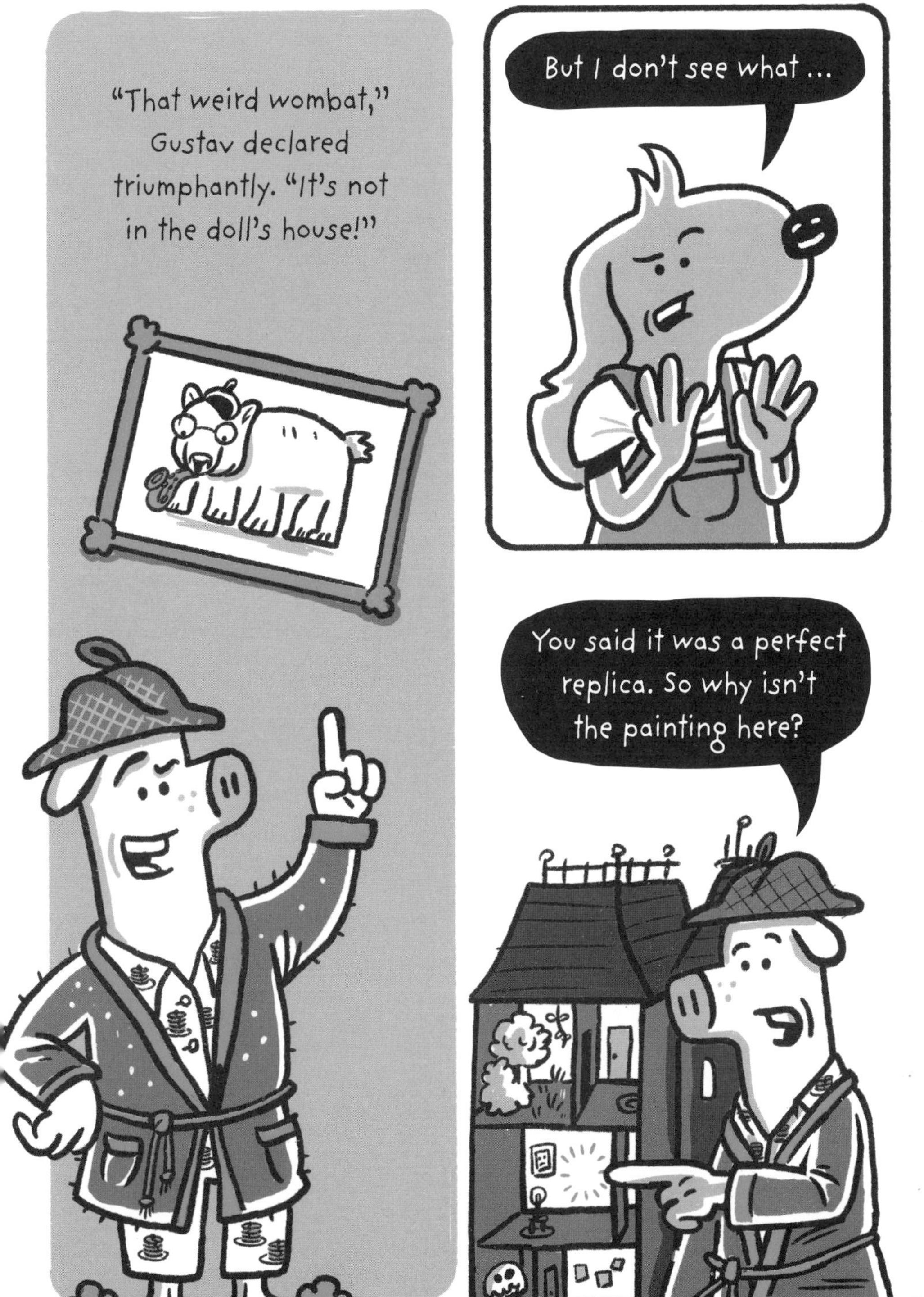
"That weird wombat," Gustav declared triumphantly. "It's not in the doll's house!"
But I don't see what ...
You said it was a perfect replica. So why isn't the painting here?

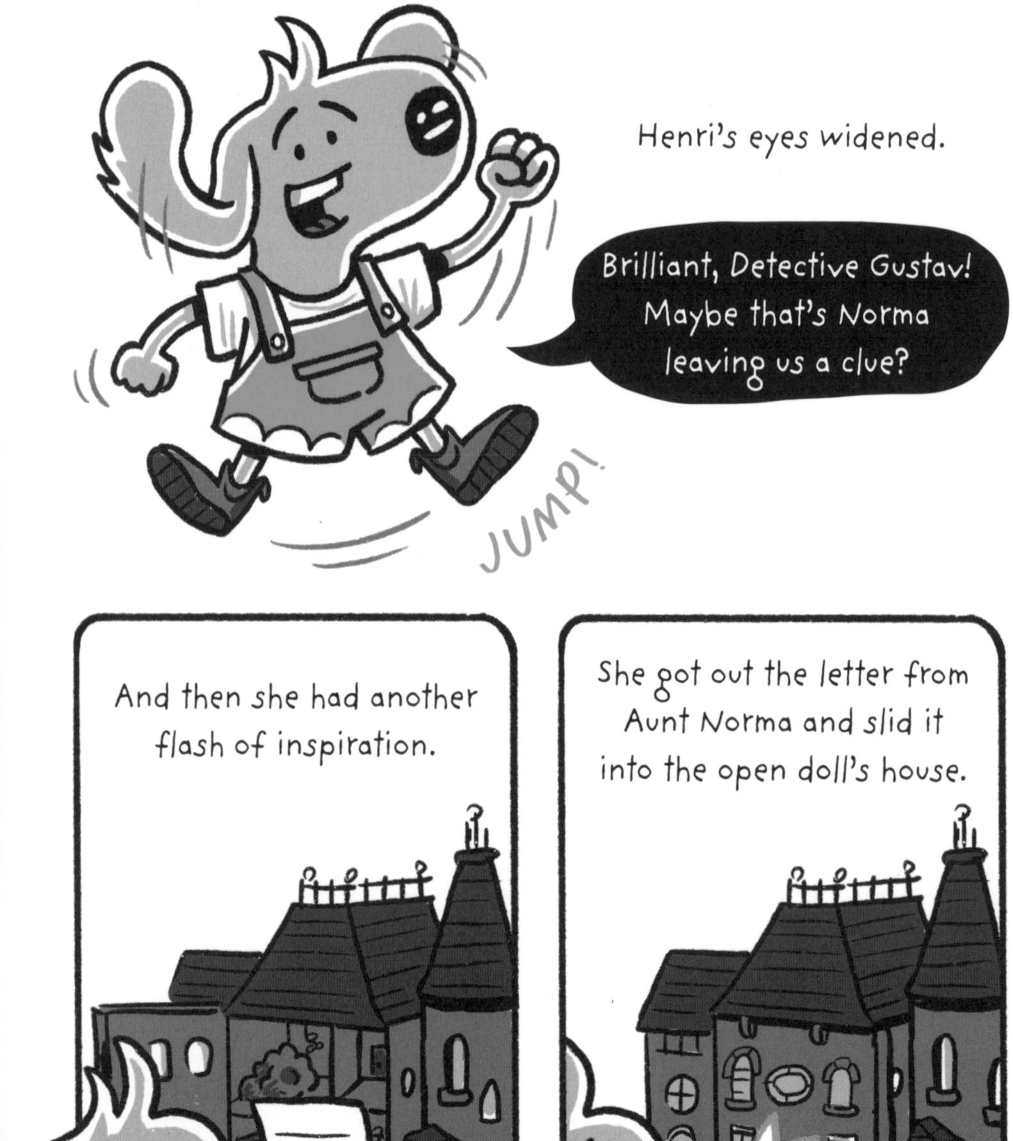
Henri's eyes widened.
Brilliant, Detective Gustav! Maybe that's Norma leaving us a clue?
JUMP!
And then she had another flash of inspiration.
She got out the letter from Aunt Norma and slid it into the open doll's house.
SHUT!

Then she read the words through the front window.

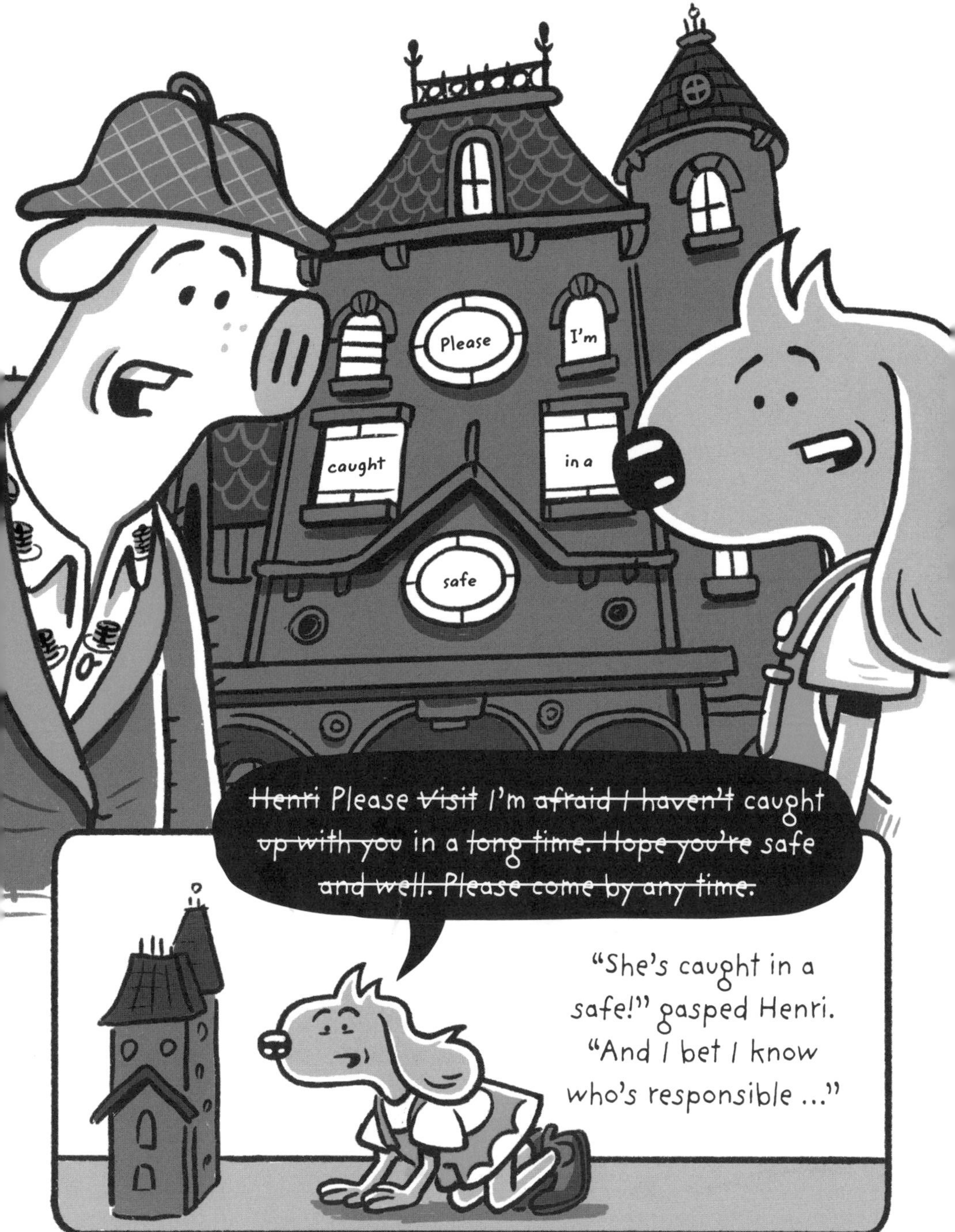
Please
I'm
caught
in a
safe
~~Henri~~ Please ~~Visit~~ I'm ~~afraid I haven't~~ caught ~~up with you~~ in a ~~long time. Hope you're~~ safe ~~and well. Please come by any time.~~
"She's caught in a safe!" gasped Henri. "And I bet I know who's responsible ..."

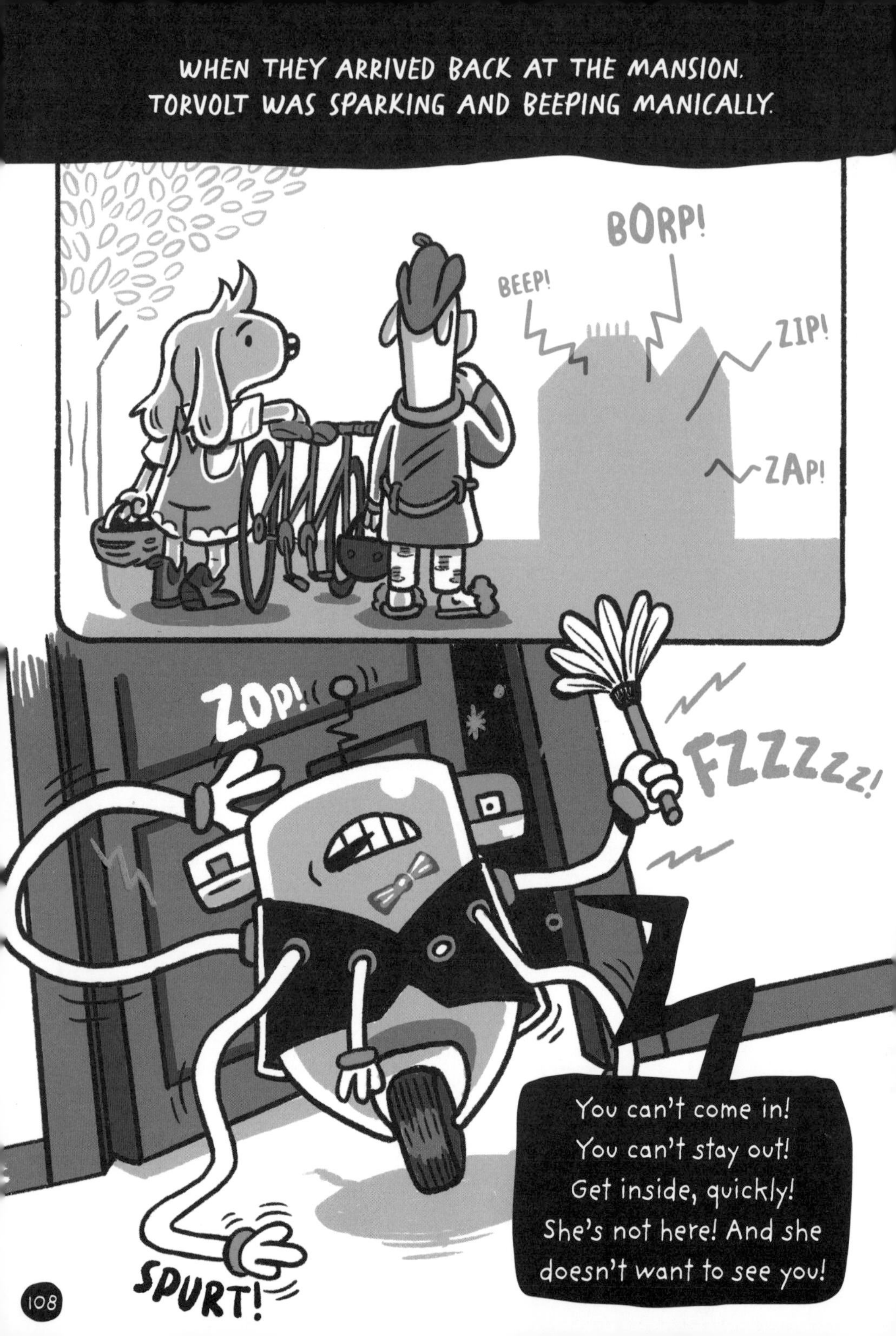
WHEN THEY ARRIVED BACK AT THE MANSION, TORVOLT WAS SPARKING AND BEEPING MANICALLY.
BEEP!
BORP!
ZIP!
ZAP!
ZOP!
FZZZzz!
You can't come in! You can't stay out! Get inside, quickly! She's not here! And she doesn't want to see you!
SPURT!

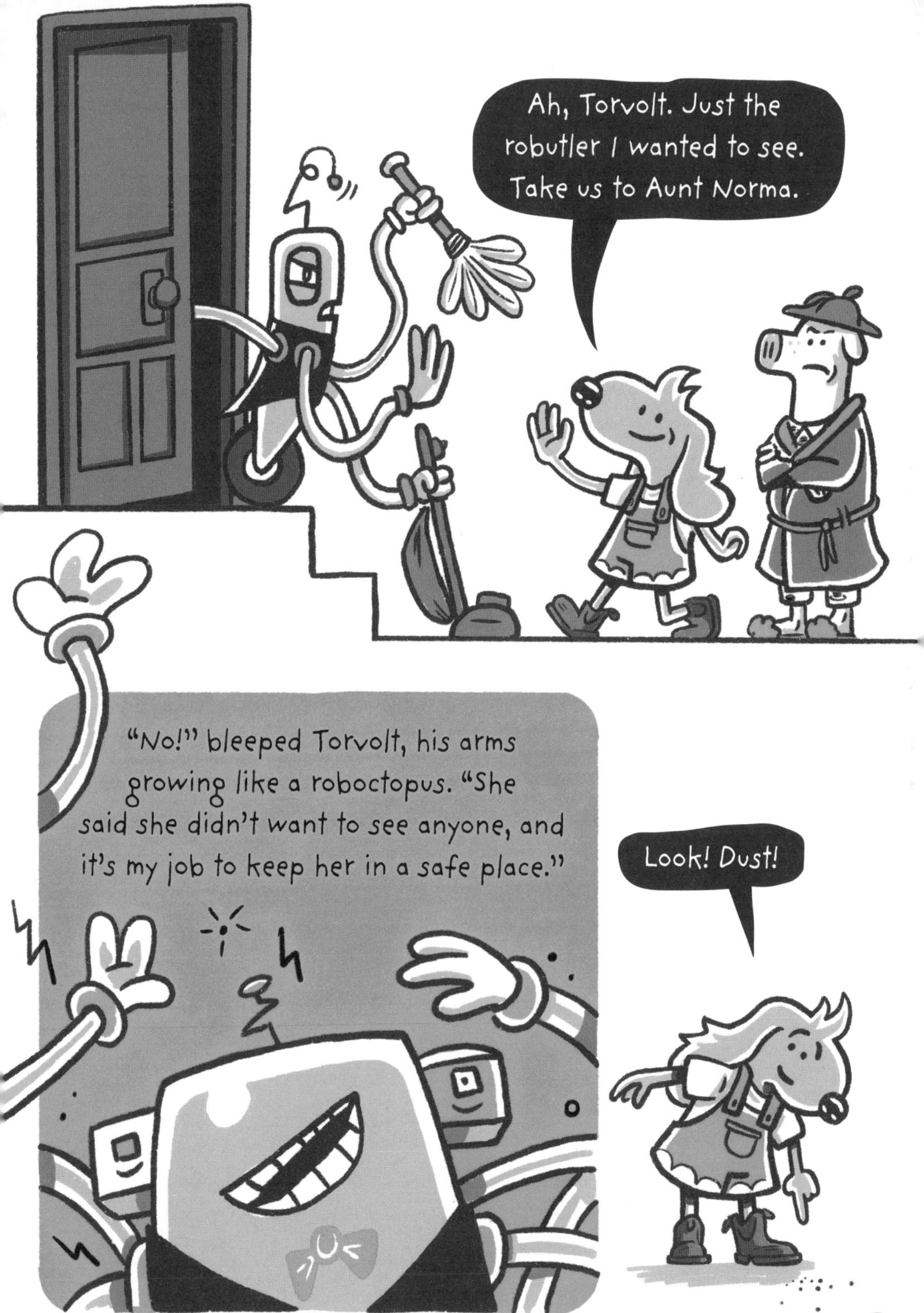
Ah, Torvolt. Just the robutler I wanted to see. Take us to Aunt Norma.
“No!” bleeped Torvolt, his arms growing like a roboctopus. “She said she didn’t want to see anyone, and it’s my job to keep her in a safe place.”
Look! Dust!

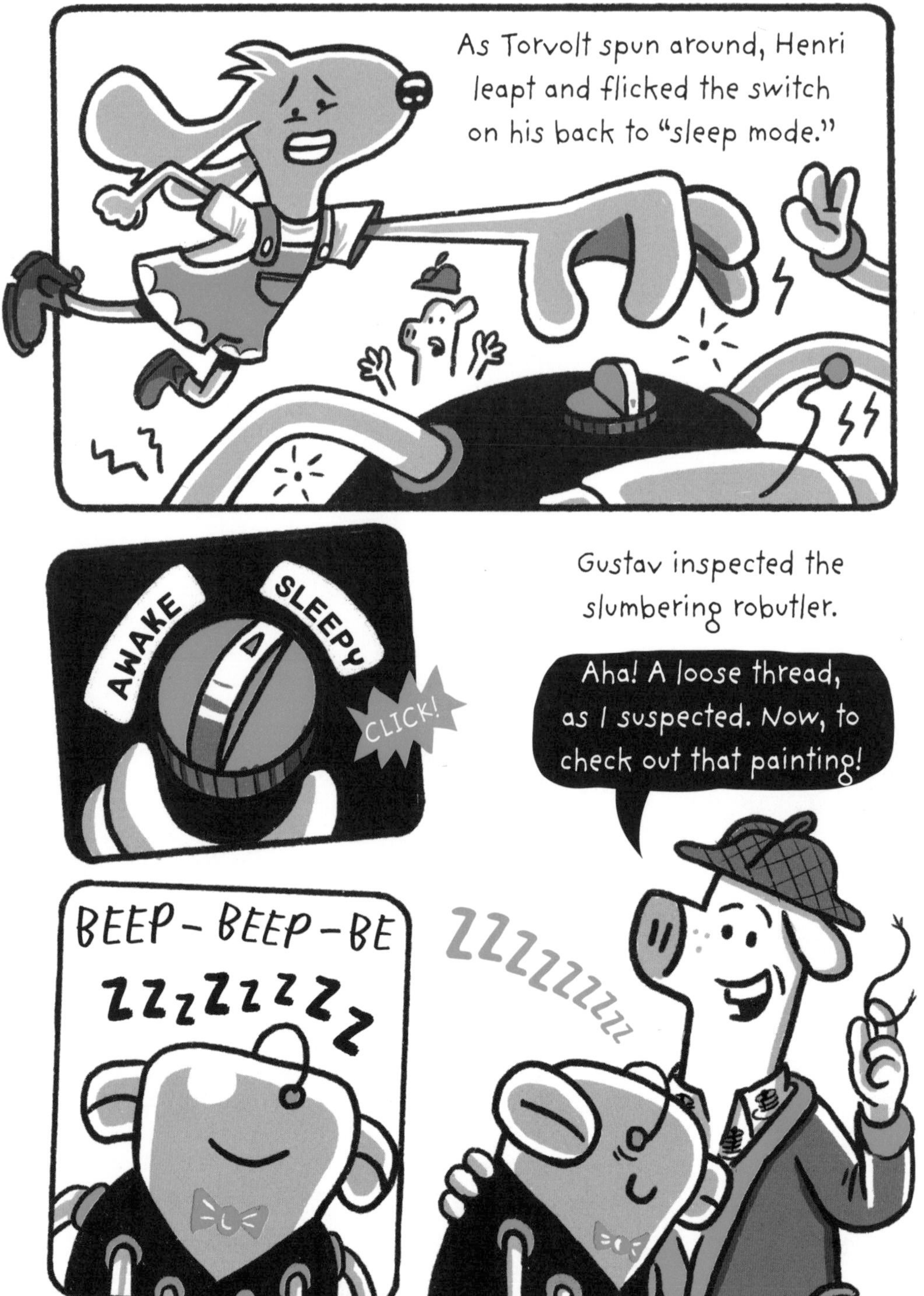
As Torvolt spun around, Henri leapt and flicked the switch on his back to "sleep mode."
AWAKE
SLEEPY
CLICK!
Gustav inspected the slumbering robutler.
Aha! A loose thread, as I suspected. Now, to check out that painting!
BEEP-BEEP-BE
ZZzZZZZZZ
ZZZZZZZZZZ

Sure enough, the painting swung open to reveal a large safe.

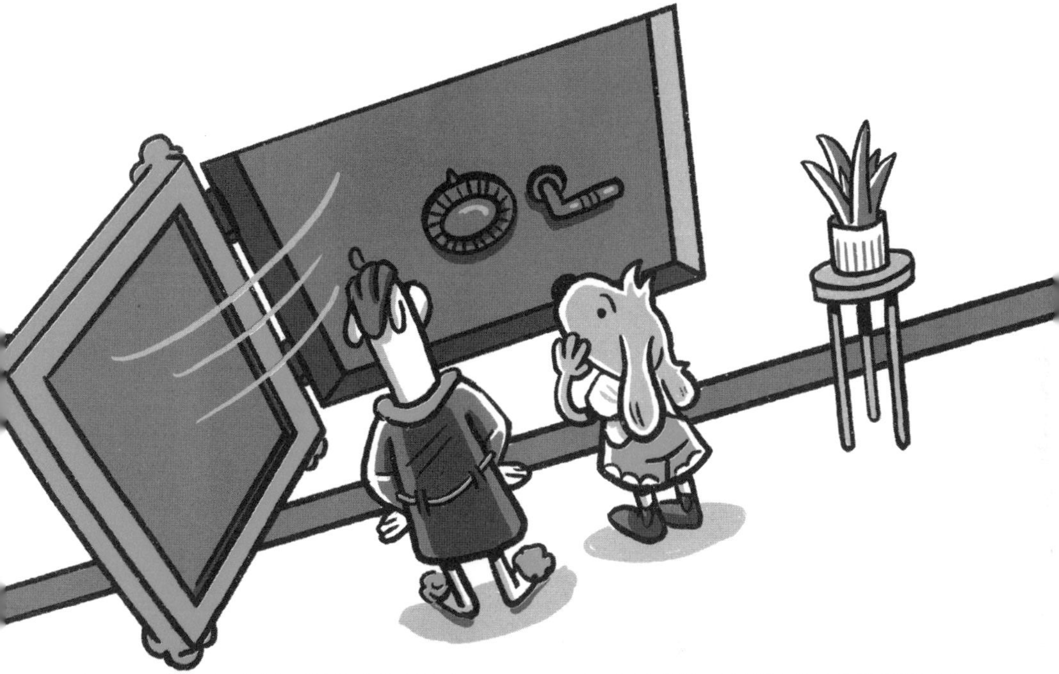

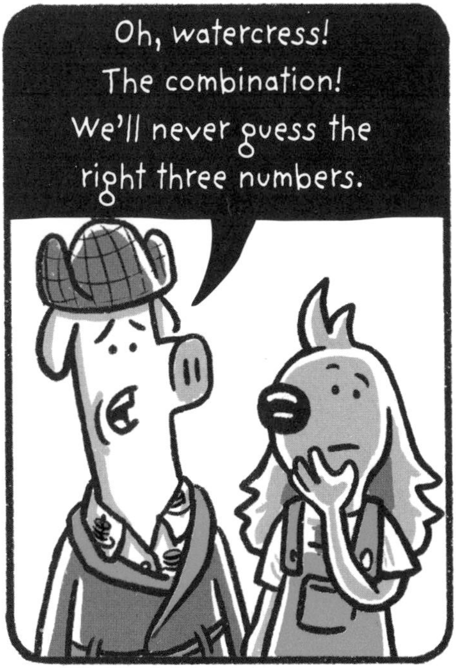
Oh, watercress! The combination! We'll never guess the right three numbers.

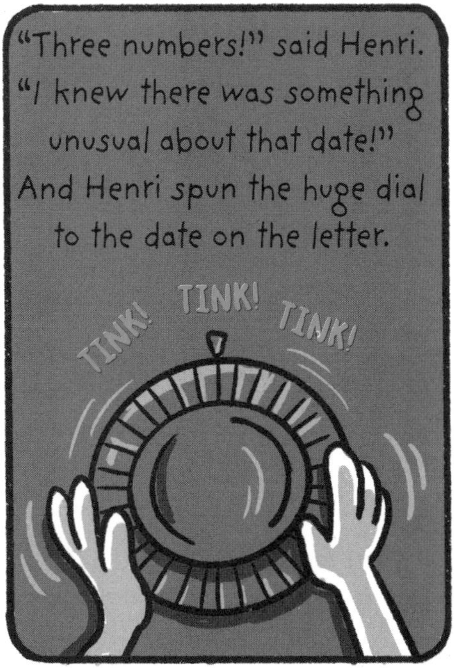
"Three numbers!" said Henri. "I knew there was something unusual about that date!" And Henri spun the huge dial to the date on the letter.
TINK!
TINK!
TINK!

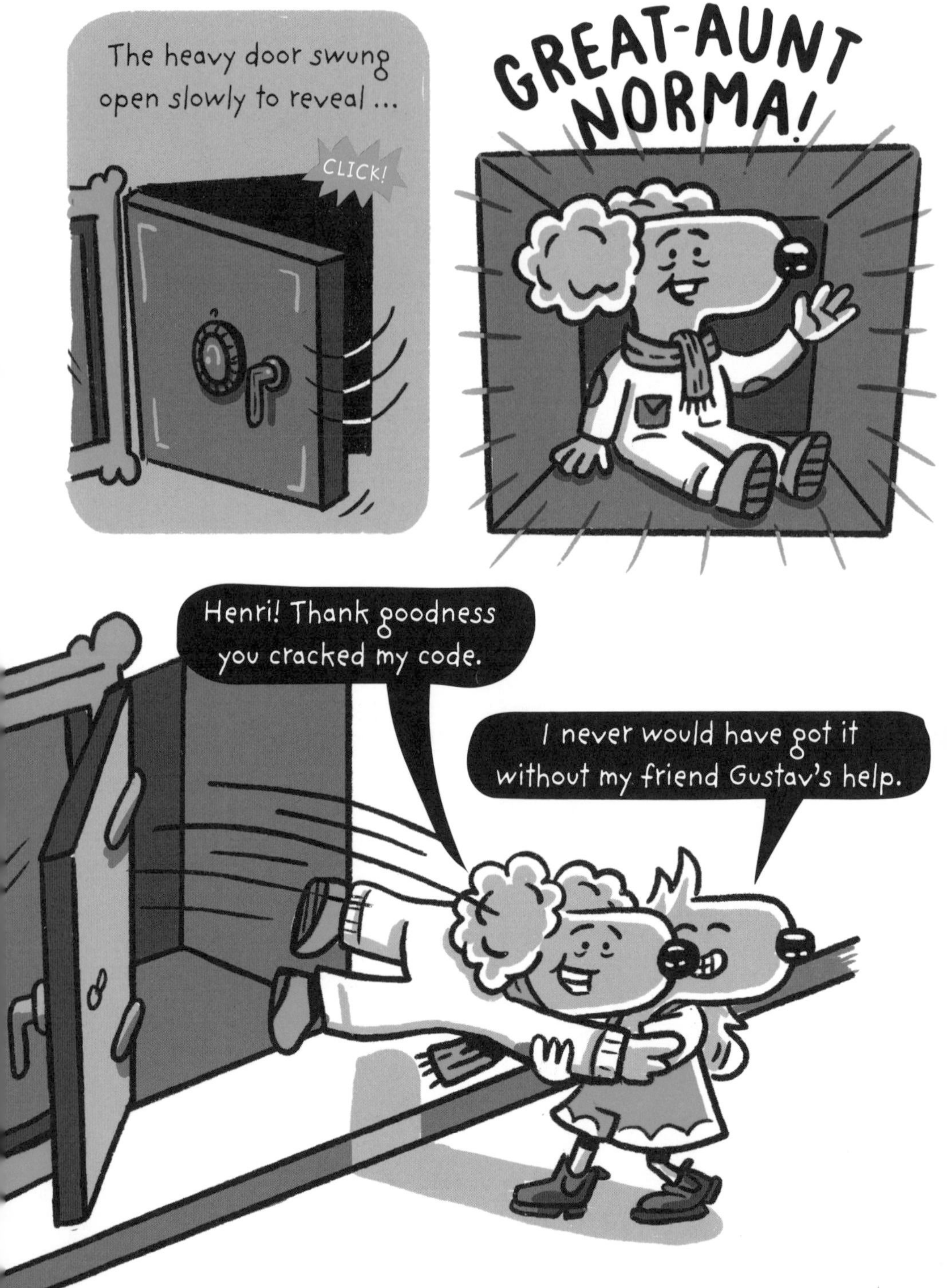
The heavy door swung open slowly to reveal ...
CLICK!
GREAT-AUNT NORMA!
Henri! Thank goodness you cracked my code.
I never would have got it without my friend Gustav's help.

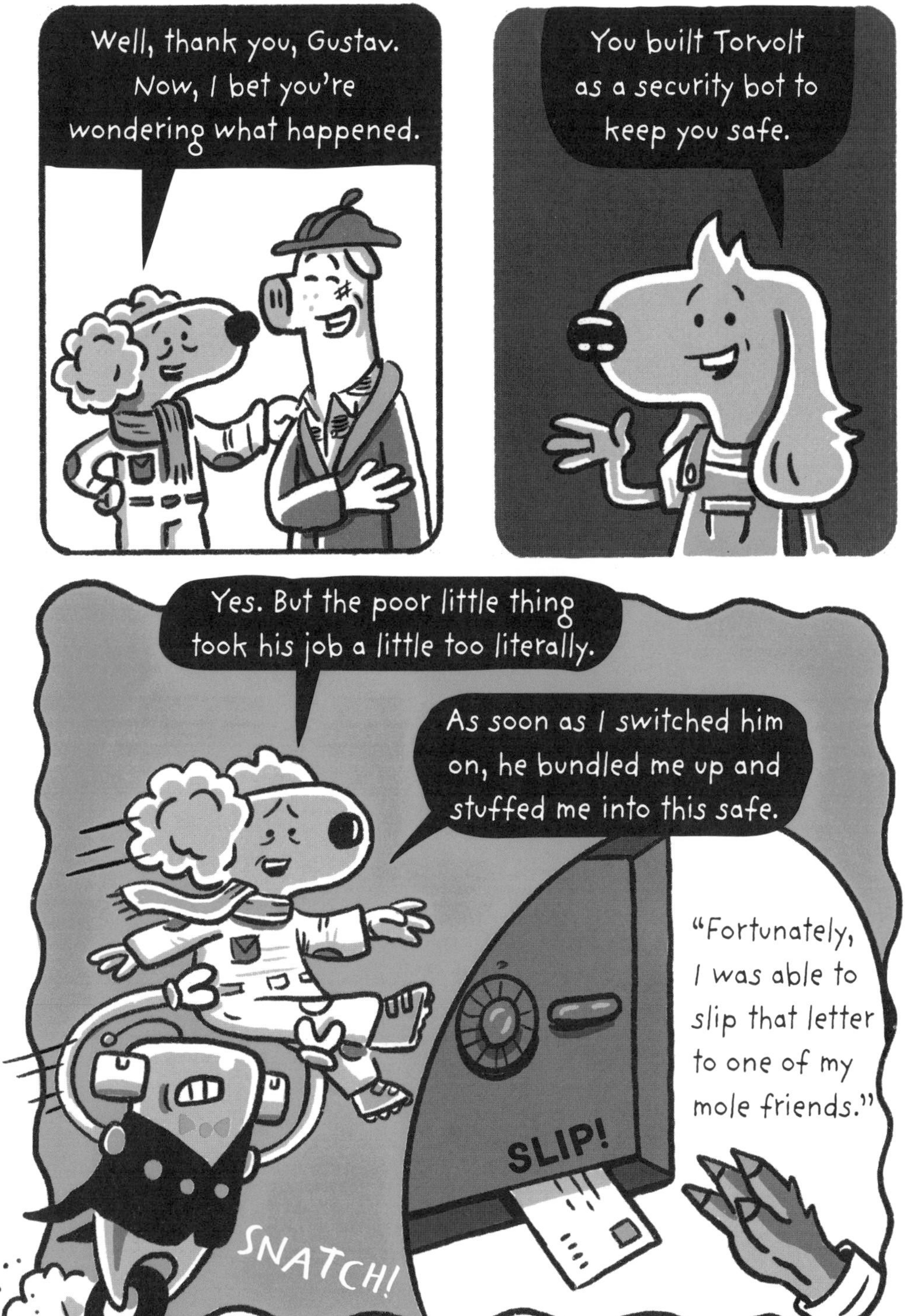
Well, thank you, Gustav. Now, I bet you're wondering what happened.
You built Torvolt as a security bot to keep you safe.
Yes. But the poor little thing took his job a little too literally.
As soon as I switched him on, he bundled me up and stuffed me into this safe.
"Fortunately, I was able to slip that letter to one of my mole friends."
SLIP!
SNATCH!

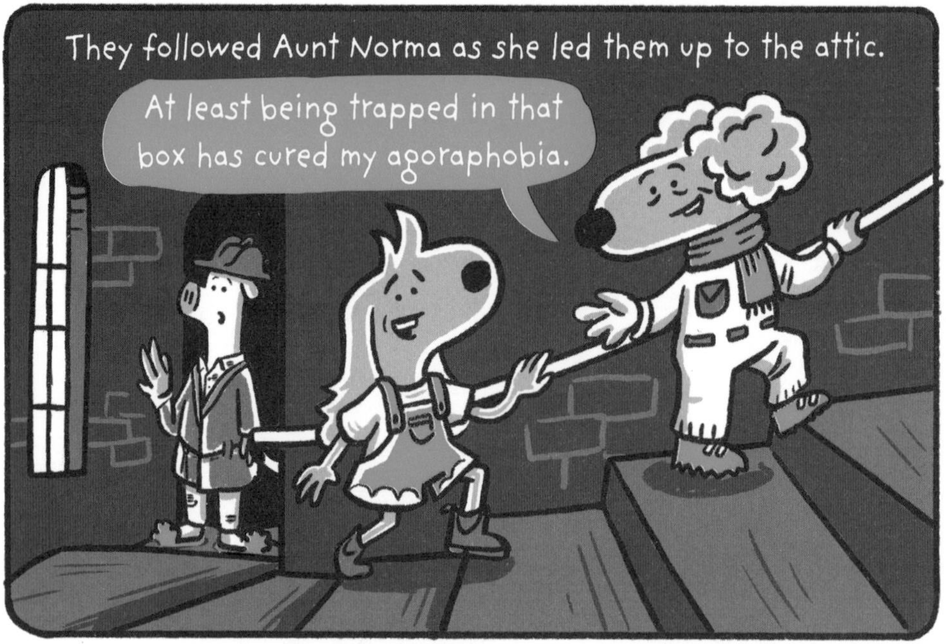
They followed Aunt Norma as she led them up to the attic.
At least being trapped in that box has cured my agoraphobia.

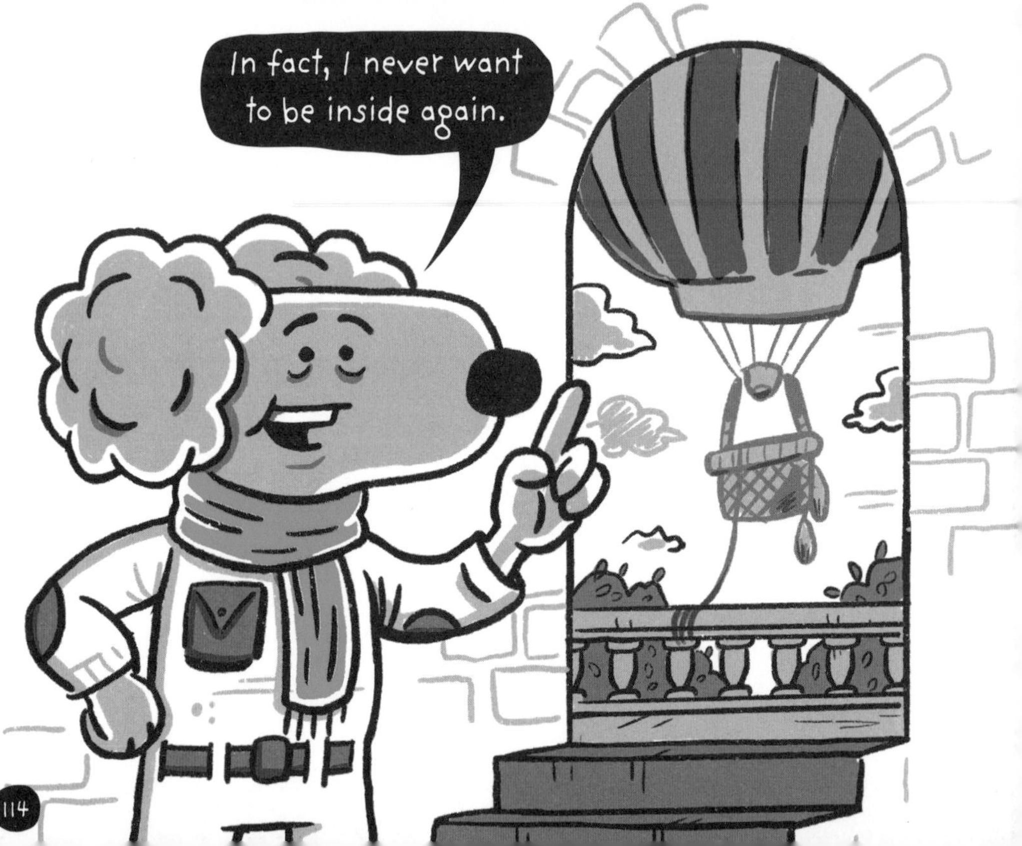
In fact, I never want to be inside again.

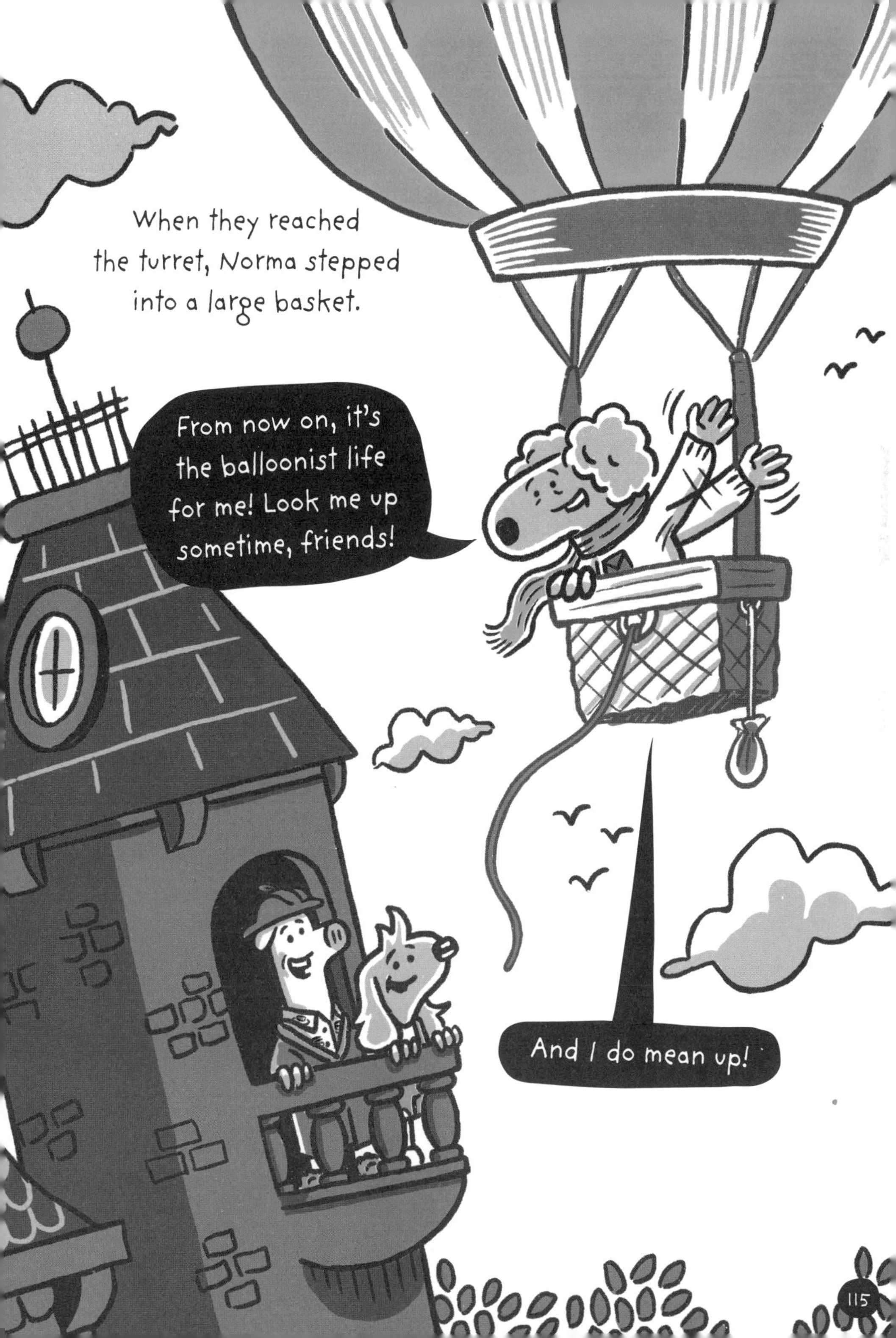
When they reached the turret, Norma stepped into a large basket.
From now on, it's the balloonist life for me! Look me up sometime, friends!
And I do mean up!

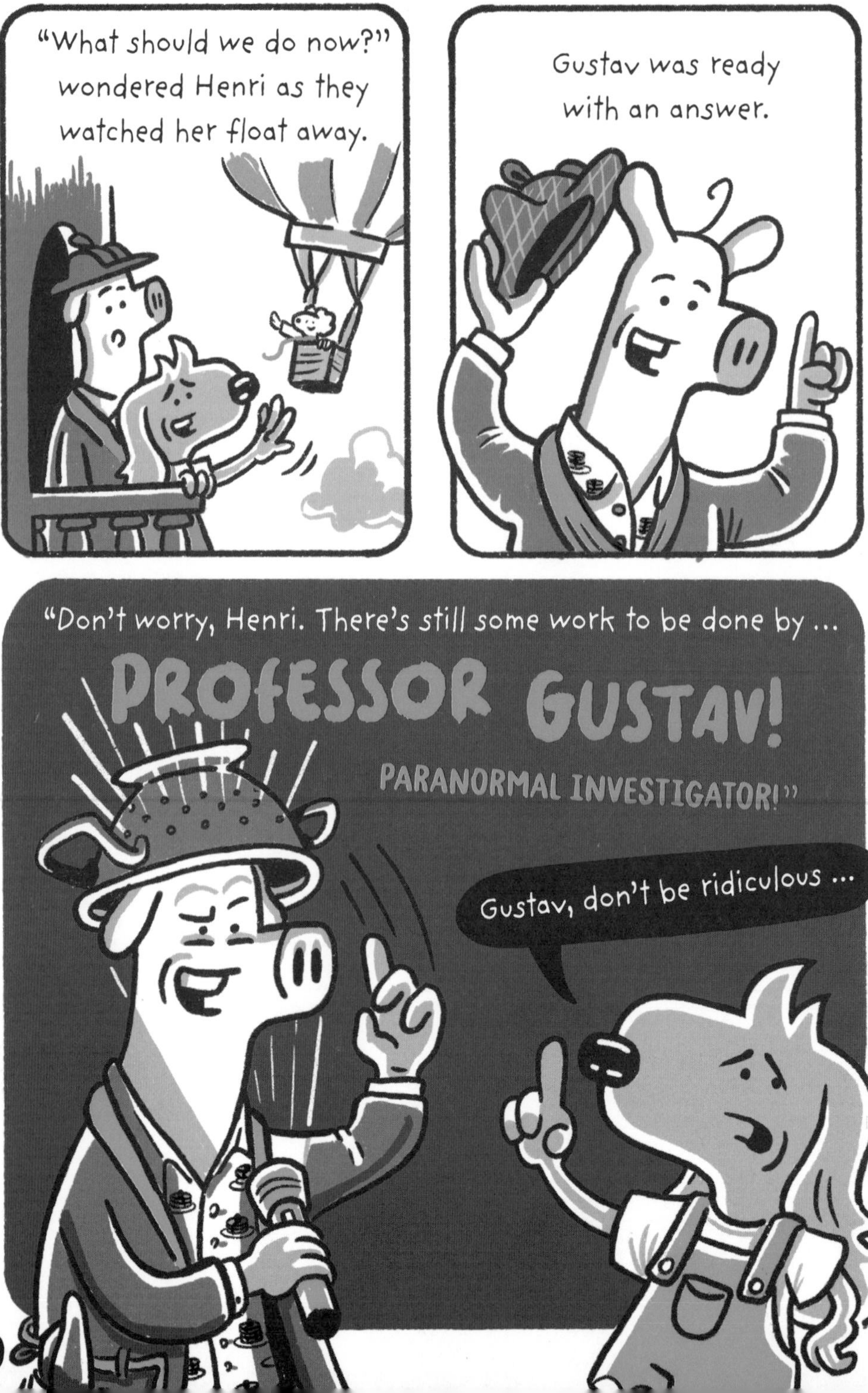
"What should we do now?" wondered Henri as they watched her float away.
Gustav was ready with an answer.
"Don't worry, Henri. There's still some work to be done by ...
PROFESSOR GUSTAV!
PARANORMAL INVESTIGATOR!"
Gustav, don't be ridiculous ...

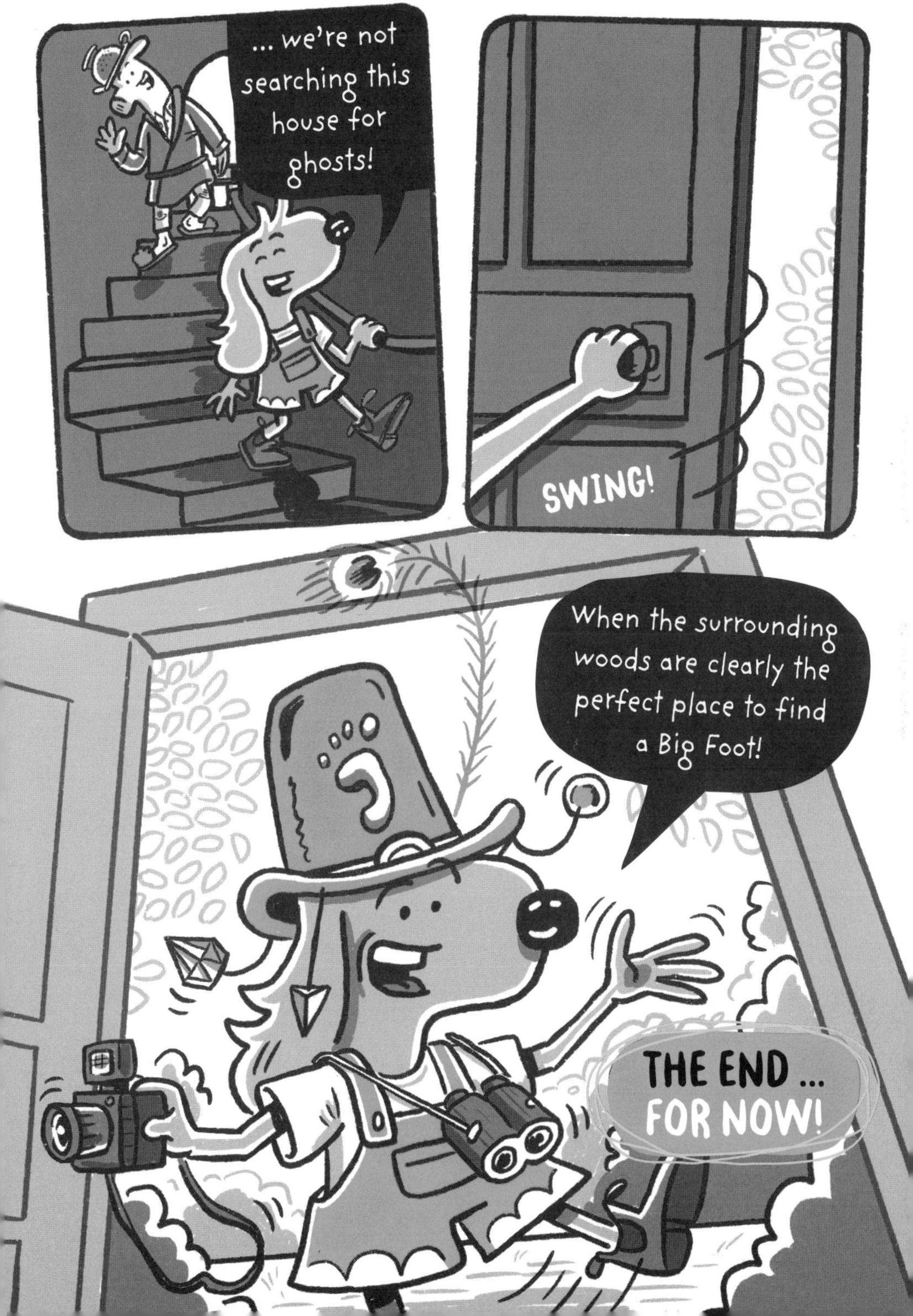
... we're not searching this house for ghosts!
SWING!
When the surrounding woods are clearly the perfect place to find a Big Foot!
THE END ... FOR NOW!

Detective Gustav's

CLUENIVERSITY

DETECTING 101

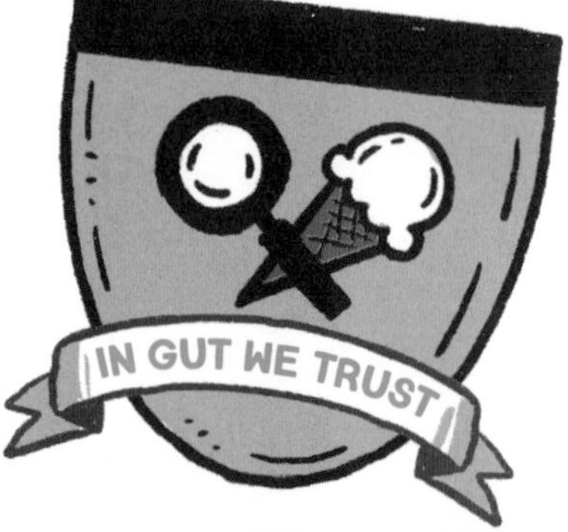
IN GUT WE TRUST

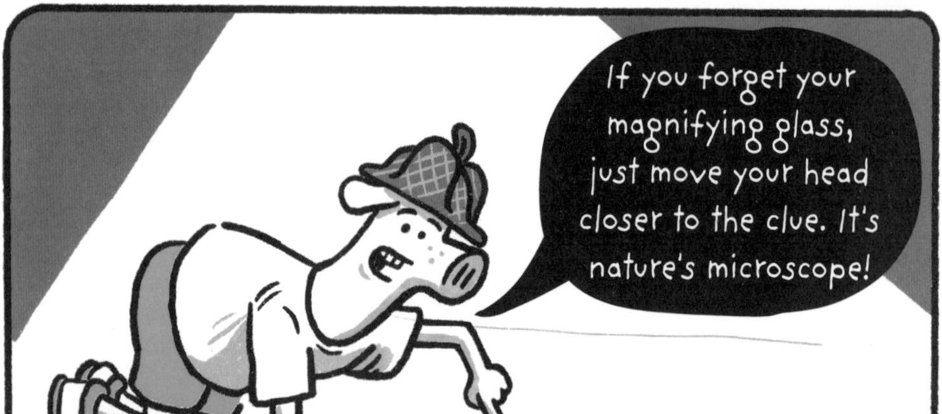
If you forget your magnifying glass, just move your head closer to the clue. It's nature's microscope!

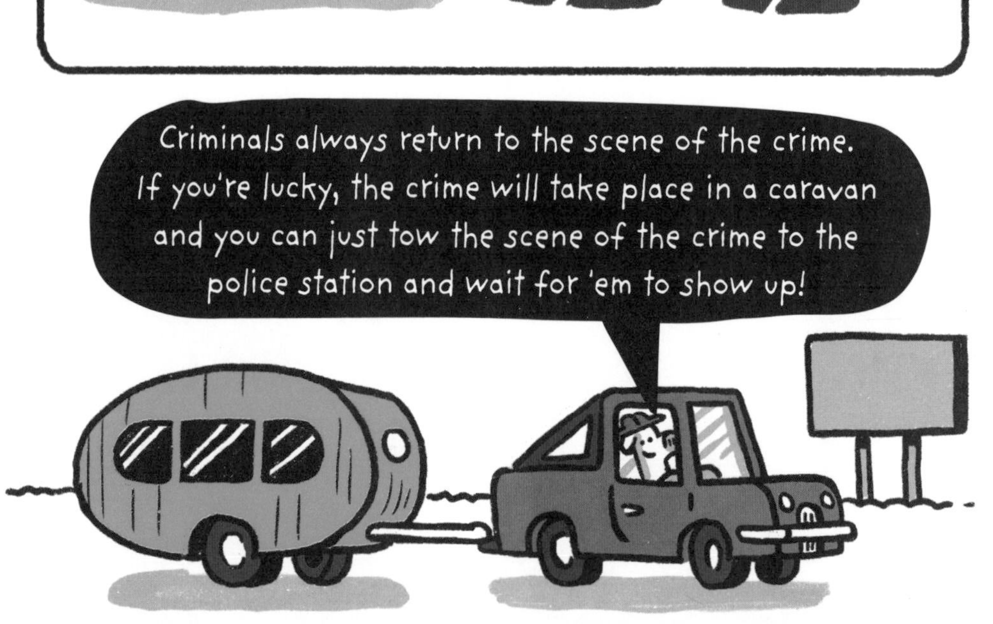
Criminals always return to the scene of the crime. If you're lucky, the crime will take place in a caravan and you can just tow the scene of the crime to the police station and wait for 'em to show up!

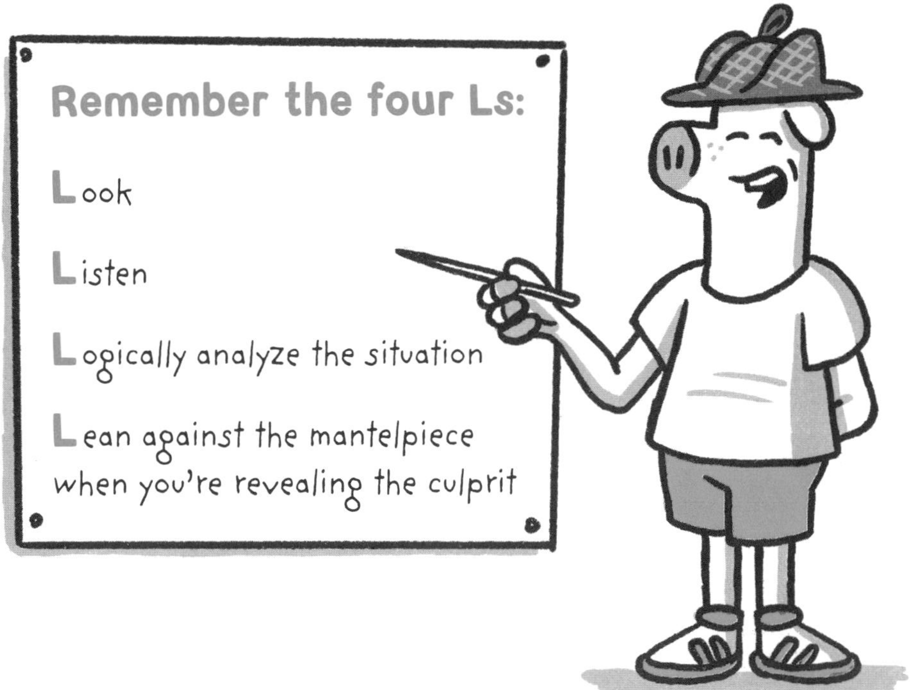
Remember the four Ls:
Look
Listen
Logically analyze the situation
Lean against the mantelpiece when you're revealing the culprit

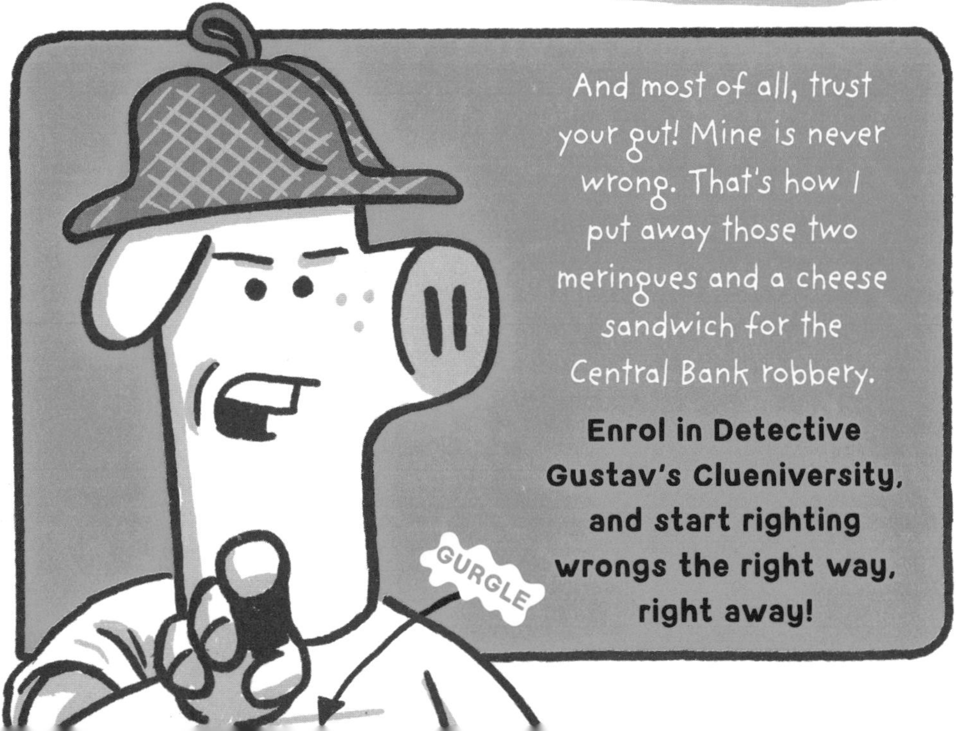
And most of all, trust your gut! Mine is never wrong. That's how I put away those two meringues and a cheese sandwich for the Central Bank robbery.
Enrol in Detective Gustav's Clueniversity, and start righting wrongs the right way, right away!
GURGLE

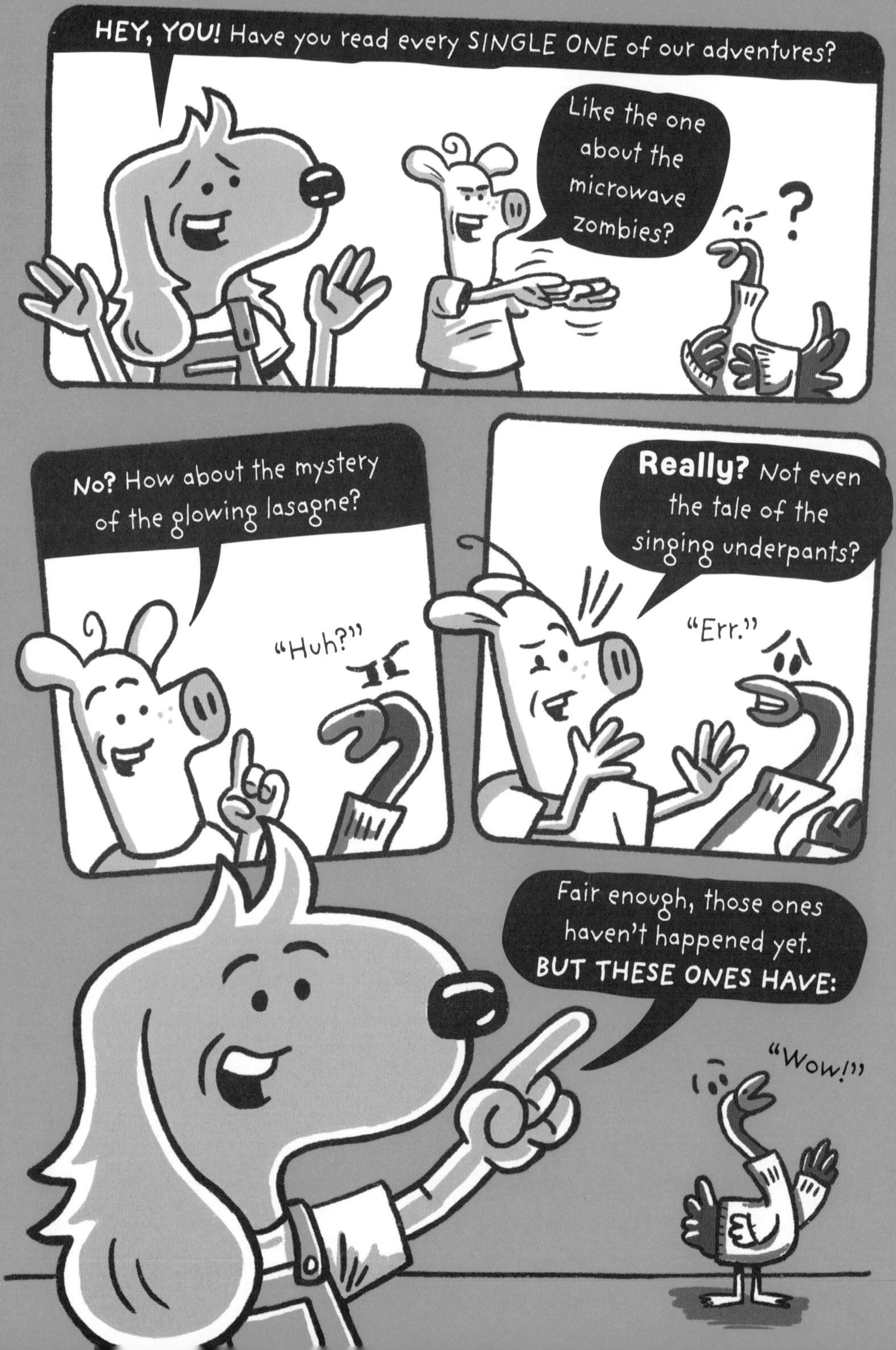
HEY, YOU! Have you read every SINGLE ONE of our adventures?
Like the one about the microwave zombies?
?
No? How about the mystery of the glowing lasagne?
"Huh?"
Really? Not even the tale of the singing underpants?
"Err."
Fair enough, those ones haven't happened yet. BUT THESE ONES HAVE:
"Wow!"

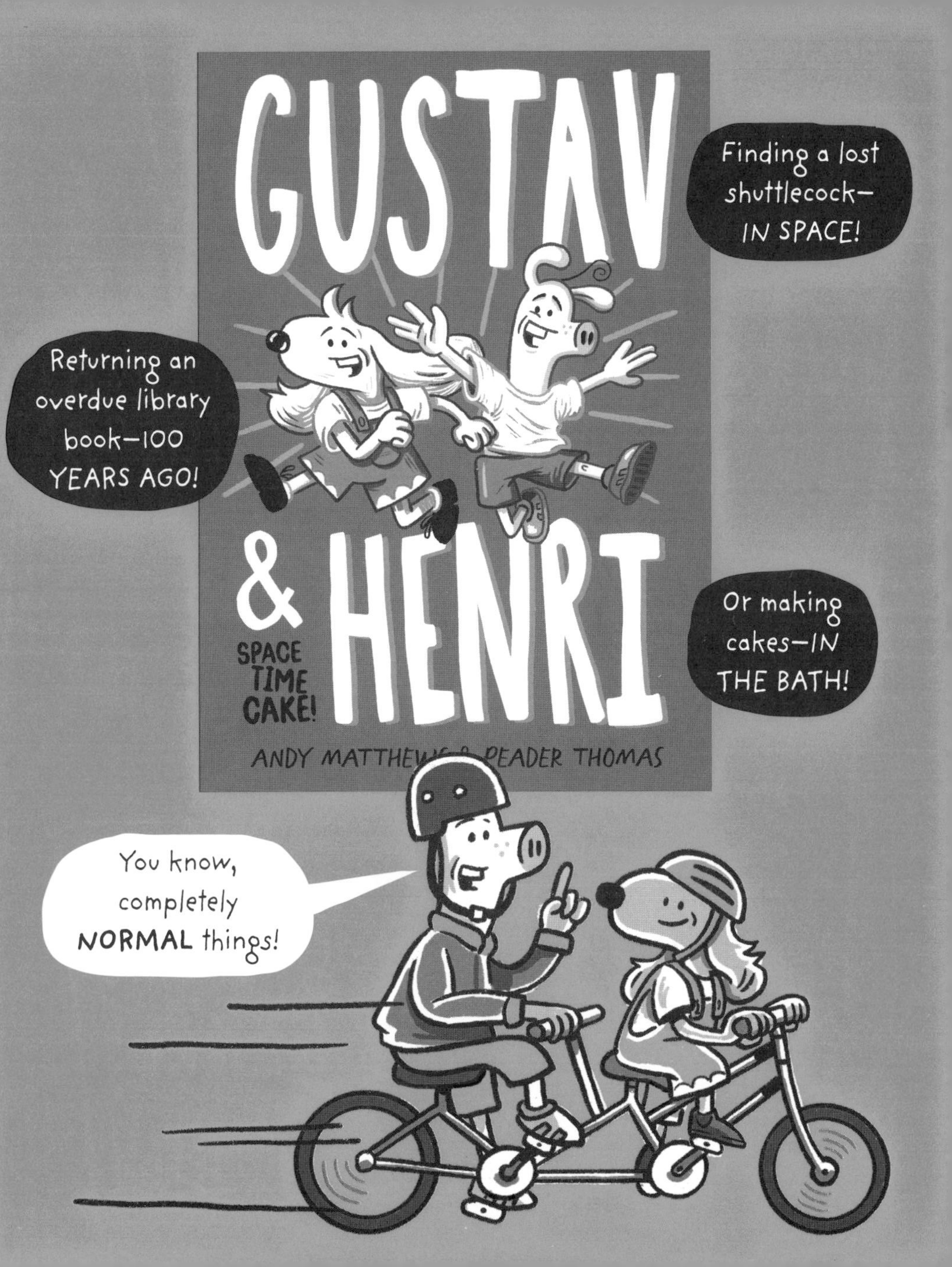
GUSTAV
&
HENRI
SPACE TIME CAKE!
ANDY MATTHEW EADER THOMAS
Returning an overdue library book—100 YEARS AGO!
Finding a lost shuttlecock—IN SPACE!
Or making cakes—IN THE BATH!
You know, completely NORMAL things!

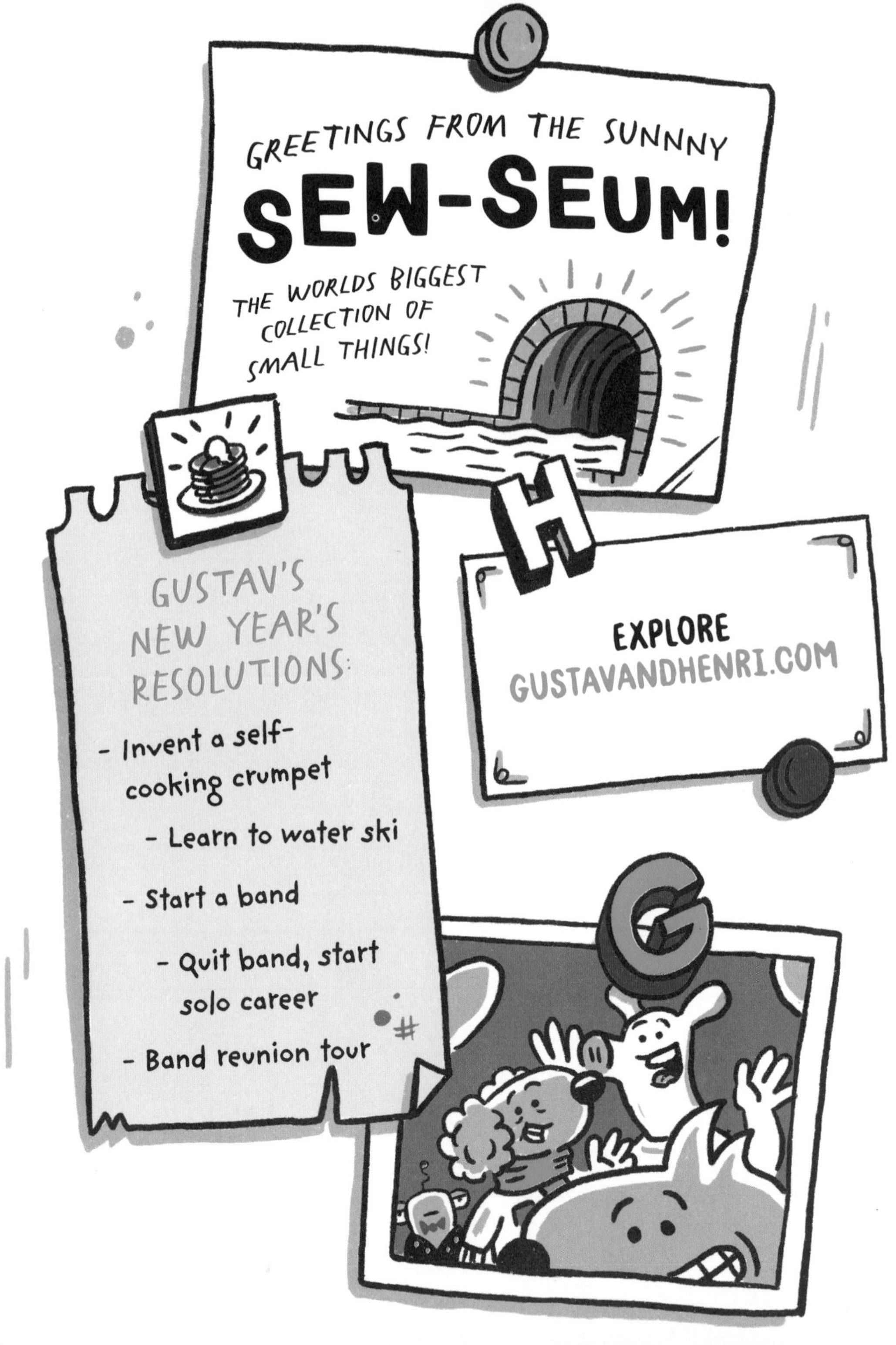

GREETINGS FROM THE SUNNNY
SEW-SEUM!
THE WORLDS BIGGEST COLLECTION OF SMALL THINGS!
H
EXPLORE
GUSTAVANDHENRI.COM
GUSTAV'S NEW YEAR'S RESOLUTIONS:
- Invent a self-cooking crumpet
- Learn to water ski
- Start a band
- Quit band, start solo career
- Band reunion tour
G

ANDY MATTHEWS
(who drew the words)

Andy is a comedian who likes eating cheese and digging big holes for no reason. He created *Gustav & Henri* with

PEADER THOMAS
(who wrote the pictures)

Peader is an illustrator who likes weird comic books and dislikes falling into the holes Andy digs in his garden. He created *Gustav & Henri* with

FOR CARLY, WHO LOVES ADVENTURES!
-A.M

FOR VIOLET, I LOVE YOU.
THANK YOU FOR SLEEPING.
-P.T

Gustav & Henri Volume 2: Tiny Aunt Island
This edition published in 2023 by Red Comet Press LLC, Brooklyn, NY
First published in 2022 by Hardie Grant Children's Publishing, Australia

Text copyright © 2022 Andy Matthews
Illustration copyright © 2022 Peader Thomas
Design by Pooja Desai

Library of Congress Control Number:
2022938967

ISBN (HB): 978-1-63655-048-0
ISBN (EBOOK): 978-1-63655-049-7
22 23 24 25 TLF 10 9 8 7 6 5 4 3 2 1

First Edition
Printed in China

RedCometPress.com